IN THE
FOREST AT
MIDNIGHT

IN THE
FOREST AT
MIDNIGHT

A NOVEL BY

RITA PRATT SMITH

DONALD I. FINE, INC.
NEW YORK

Library of Congress Cataloging in Publication Data
Smith, Rita Pratt.
In the forest at midnight.
I. Title.
PS3569.M537925I5 1989   813'.54   88-45859
ISBN 1-55611-131-2
Manufactured in the United States of America
10 9 8 7 6 5 4 3 2 1

Designed by Irving Perkins Associates

To Ray, with love and gratitude

*I was not aware of the moment when I
first crossed the threshold of this life.*

*What was the power that made me open
out into this vast mystery like a bud
in the forest at midnight!*

—Rabindranath Tagore, Gitanjali

CHAPTER ONE

I had often heard it said that Aunt Letty broke her father's heart when she married a heathen she'd met at the All India Medical Arts Institute. I was eight then and played with images of Grandpa's heart parting neatly into two lobes like a hot bun, or perhaps shattering like a teacup into sharp fragments—in which case, were these fragments safely contained by his surrounding flesh, or had they spread through his body, lodging here and there? Was this why he was so often irritable? When that happened, Aunt Margaret, his only sister, who had always lived with us, usually said, "Now then, John, have your bowels moved today? I can always tell when you have not swallowed your oil." Following his stroke, she had sole care of him.

Which brings me back to Letty. For that was when Grandpa fell to the floor like a stone, after Letty walked away. Sounds of their quarrel carried to the storeroom behind the house where I often played among the bags of grain.

My memory of that afternoon is very clear. Grandpa's

1

voice, peculiarly high and shaking, said something about her everlasting soul. ". . . Marry him then if you must," I heard him say, "but I implore you not to become a Hindu."

Although she spoke in softer tones than he did, the words, "I cannot marry him otherwise, Pa," reached me with a clarity and finality I remember to this day. That was all she said.

It became obvious that the partial paralysis of Grandpa's left side would remain. Each evening, when the Angelus rang from the steeple of St. Mary's Church, we assembled in his room to say the rosary—all but Papa, who wasn't much for prayers. Grandpa was unable to kneel; instead, he sat on the edge of a chair in a sort of half-crouch behind a table covered with sacred pictures, piles of *St. Anthony's Messengers,* vials of holy water and holy oil and small statues under glass domes. His faded striped pajamas hung loosely from his gaunt frame. Aunt Margaret, who had a bad knee, sat in an armchair responding absently, "Holy Mary, Mother of God . . . ," her thoughts straying perhaps to the latest of the penny romances to which she was addicted. Her white hair was pulled back into a severe little knot so that the bones of her face stood out shiny and yellow. As if to make up for Papa's laxity, Mama knelt on the stone floor, back straight, eyes welded shut above clasped hands from which her mother-of-pearl rosary dangled. I strove for Mama's fervor, but the pressure on my knees would force me to sit back on my heels.

Thus we prayed every evening in the thin grey dusk. We always said an extra decade of the rosary for "those poor souls in need of our prayers." Letty's name was never mentioned in Grandpa's presence, in prayer or any other circumstance, although once at breakfast, when I was nine, as he was about to break his egg yolk with a spoon, a ritual he cherished, I asked, "Who does Aunty Letty pray to now, Grandpa?" His spoon dropped with a clatter. He gazed dully around the table before he pushed back his chair and shuffled back to bed, leaving the egg intact.

In the ensuing silence, my mother became oddly solicitous of me. She patted my hand and cut my toast into fingers while Aunt Margaret poured a little coffee into my glass of milk, saying, "A little taste won't hurt you, Megan child." My father just cleared his throat loudly behind his napkin.

We lived on a dusty street in a colony of other English and Anglo-Indian sub-officials. My father worked for the railways as District Accounts Officer and traveled to various small towns and villages in Madras province. His frequent extended absences seemed not to upset my mother. She always slept alone on her narrow bed, hands across her middle, toes pointing skyward like an effigy on a tomb.

Unlike some of our neighbors who struggled to grow English country flowers in the parched inhospitable earth, the only thing that flourished in our grassless front yard was a large aloe. From time to time, scraps of our daily lives seemed to collect on the venemous green spikes: Papa's cigarette papers, coils of Mama's hair, leftover bits from dresses the little brown tailor sewed for us in cross-legged silence, and sometimes even a shred or two of Grandpa's queries regarding prayers and penances for parents of lapsed Catholics.

On the parlor wall, above the wireless shaped like a cathedral window, hung a picture of the Sacred Heart. "See how His eyes follow you?" Mama once told me before my First Communion. "No matter where in the room you stand. Just so, He sees everything you do." It was quite true. Whenever I glanced up from my homework or whirled suddenly while dusting furniture, I would encounter those tragic treacle-colored eyes, and I would then gaze back mesmerized. In the middle of His chest was a large red exposed heart with spokes of light radiating from it ". . . to show you how much

He loves you, Mama had explained. If that were the case, then it struck me as a rather painful affliction, something like a throbbing whitlow or an aching tooth.

My bedroom overlooked the backyard, which contained a well, now dry, and a casuarina tree that grew so close to my window I could actually touch the feathery branches that stretched coolly, elegantly upwards to the heat-washed sky. Its shape and foliage made me think of pines and firs that I had never seen except in dreams or in picture books, but which Aunt Margaret and Mama told me did so well in the gentle grey wetness of England.

My room was next to Mama's and across the landing from Grandpa's and Aunt Margaret's. Papa slept downstairs in the small room behind the parlor. I'd always wanted a dressing table of my own with a matching bench, but Mama said that would only make me vain. Instead I had a chest of drawers with a small round metal-framed mirror that tilted downward on its stand, unless it was wedged in place with a folded matchbox, or a piece of cardboard. Above my bed hung a picture of Saint Theresa, the Little Flower of Jesus, who Mama said had died rather than surrender her virtue. I pictured virtue, in those days, as spotless white cotton knickers with strings, the kind that looked like a laundry bag.

Mama had written to Letty, telling her of Grandpa's stroke, but it was many months—perhaps even as long as a year—before Letty responded by sending us a trunk filled with medicinal samples, vitamin pills, laxatives, bandages, two saris (a pink one with orange leaves for Mama and a gold one shot through with tinsel threads for Aunt Margaret), a large box of toffee and dangly earrings for me (I couldn't wear the earrings because my lobes were not pierced), and a pair of native slippers with curled toes for Papa. There was nothing for Grandpa.

Papa said that at least the trunk was useful.

After that the letters from Letty, who lived in Nerbudapur, a distant northern city, came often, and were answered by Mama, and somewhat later by Aunt Margaret. Sometimes the letters contained pictures of the large rambling bungalow, and of the clinic Letty shared with her husband, the two of them always pictured in the foreground. He was a smiling man, overweight, with an arm around her waist. She did not smile.

Although I had been eight when Letty left, I found that I was unable to recall her face. I could remember her small hands with the short square-tipped fingers dressing my cut knee and the way they darted across the piano keys like fluttering white moths, while Papa, Mama and I sang "Nelly Bly" and "There'll always be an England." I can still see how she sang then—her head thrown back, her strong vibrato trembling in her throat as if some small creature were there and trying to escape—but I was never able to see her face.

On Mama's dressing table there was a picture of Letty and herself when they were young girls on holiday in Darjeeling. Mama's elaborately puffed hair looked like an overblown blossom too heavy for the slender stem of her neck to support. It was always Letty though, to whom my eyes were drawn each time I brushed my hair. As I grew older, I often wondered what she might have been thinking then, as I gazed at the curve of her smile and the slant of her eyes half-closed against the sun. Her hair swung long and free. As I write this, I see again in my memory those two young faces framed behind glass, and realize that now, at nineteen, I am older than Mama and Letty were at the time of the picture.

Back then though it was this picture, so different from the more recent ones that came with her letters, imbued with vitality and movement, that became locked in my imagination. How clearly in my mind's eye I saw the tilt of her chin, the sparkle of her eyes between the lowered lashes, the flash of teeth behind the parted lips of the faint small smile. She alone remained constant while Mama and Aunt Margaret grew older.

There they sat each evening, Mama and Aunt Margaret, in shapeless cotton dresses with picture-frame necklines. Aunt Margaret was thin and gnarled as a root from a banyan tree. Mama's hair no longer resembled an overblown blossom but was now, some twenty years later, streaked with grey and cropped short as a man's. Each day she began to look more like Grandpa. Mama and Aunt Margaret would sit in faded chintz-covered chairs and listen to the wireless while knitting sweaters for the war effort and spinning stories of unbelievable mystery and romance about Letty. I loved to hear them tell how she rode to her wedding on the back of an elephant in a special *howdah* of marigolds and tinsel. I think it was mentioned in passing that her husband rode in grander fashion, but he was not essential to the stories, only a prop, a dusky paper doll. Letty was flesh and blood, their flesh and blood: our Letty, the doctor.

Of course, neither Mama nor Aunt Margaret had attended Letty's wedding. Yet, details of the gold kid sandals, the blood red sari of Benarsi silk with the four-inch gold border, the pearls in her hair, were argued and bandied about with vicarious pleasure made all the more intense since points of telling could be changed at whim.

The year I turned eleven Japan attacked Pearl Habor. Whenever I saw newsreels of bomb-torn London, I was reminded of giant decaying teeth: here a slice of house with its crest of intact chimney pots, there a gothic church door upright amidst rubble. In India, Indians were demanding home rule, peaceably for the most part, although there were some acts of sabotage, some factions that claimed the thing to do would be to side with Japan against Britain. Around the city, "QUIT INDIA!" was scrawled on municipal buildings and public toilets. It took Papa five coats of whitewash to cover the *"JAI HIND!"* on our garden wall—only to have it reappear the very next day.

But, for the most part, at our house it was the larger more distant war that occupied our attention as we sat around the wireless listening to Churchill's speeches ("By Jove! What an orator!" my father would exclaim), and Vera Lynn singing "There'll be blue birds over the white cliffs of Dover/ Tomorrow when the world is free."

Food was rationed. The unmilled rice we were issued in limited quantity, when cooked, became pink and spongy. Polished rice was available only to the military. Lorries filled with Tommies, their solemn young faces sunburned radish red, rumbled and lurched down dusty rutted streets.

In school during needle hour on hot sticky afternoons, while sweat trickled down our spines and yarn grew damp and then stiff in our hands, we knitted stringy woolen mufflers for "our boys" fighting in Europe. Sister Celestine warned us about wartime romances and filled our ears with stories of dark-skinned Eurasian girls being seduced by soldiers, only to be deserted—pregnant—when the troops moved on again. "It's our white skin that attracts these girls to our soldiers," Sister said, in her soft Irish brogue. Her pale fingers, with their puffy pink tips, deftly wielded long shiny needles from which flowed a river of knitted wool, the color of fresh dung.

To me, however, our skin seemed not white as milk is white, but a variety of subtle shades that ranged from palest cream to mottled pink to the color of potted beef.

I often saw the soldiers in the streets and in cinemas, hugging their dark-skinned girls who were like butterflies in their bright tissue-thin dresses. I often thought surely it must be the other way round, that it was white people who were attracted by dark skin.

And that is why I was not surprised when Letty married an Indian.

7

CHAPTER TWO

Grandpa had not always been this way. I remember our evening walks—before his stroke, before Letty went away—always after the sun had gone down. Then Grandpa would place his brown felt hat firmly upon his head, take up his walking stick and, under a darkening cobalt sky streaked with rose, we would set out, my hand in his. We walked by St. Joseph's convent school where I was enrolled in the first standard. In the compound, empty swings dangled from tall tamarind trees while mynas and crows, making soft sleepy noises, roosted in branches above. All the while, Grandpa told me stories I never tired of, especially of the time he'd almost been struck by lightning.

"I was coming home from work," he always began. "I'd forgotten my umbrella that day; only four in the afternoon and already dark. Grey clouds fat as the milkman's buffalo rolled across the sky, and I smack in the middle of Patterson field. The nearest house still more than a mile away. I made straight for the largest, closest tree and reached it just as the first drops hit my head, my shoulders, Splat! Splat!" He paused here for effect. "Suddenly," he stabbed his cane into the dirt at our feet. "Lightning and thunder *together*, like I'd never seen nor heard before. I prayed for the rain to stop—not on my account, understand, but only because I didn't want all of you to worry about me. What lightning! Not the ordinary sheet lightning we get in India, but like this," he said, scratching the letter *Z* in the dirt with his cane.

"Like in the picture of God speaking to Moses?"

"Exactly. And do you know what I found when I passed by the next day?"

"What Grandpa?" I clung to his large warm hand.

"Another tree, no more than three yards from the one I'd stood under, had been struck by that bolt. It stood there stripped of its bark, bare, shiny as bone. And each day it lost more and more leaves, more and more bark. If I'd sheltered under it, I'd be a goner today. But God, in His infinite mercy protected me, you see, because I was wearing my scapular." He looked down at me, eyes stern under bushy greying brows, "That's why you should always wear one too."

Sometimes we walked to church and knelt there wrapped in camphor-scented dimness and old Latin prayers. Less often we went to the club, where Grandpa drank a single whiskey and soda and I a lemonade, as we sat on the verandah in white wicker chairs with yellow cushions watching a tennis or cricket match. On rare occasions we walked to the bazaar, where I was dazzled by mounds of magenta and saffron *kumkum,* iridescent saris, fluttering ribbons and long luminous rows of glass bangles all the shades of the sunset; where noise and music pulsed like blood, and the smell of curries cooked on slow wood fires made my jaws ache and my mouth water. We walked past vegetable and fruit stalls, tea stands, the locksmith; beyond the tinker and the brass vendor, where women with henna-stained palms lounged in doorways and stared at us with kohl-rimmed eyes while others behind barred windows made soft fluting noises like caged tropical birds. At the sweet shop, Grandpa left me with Pushpa, the proprietress, and said I could buy whatever I wished up to a rupee.

Dizzy with excitement and impatient at my own indecisiveness, I surveyed the pyramid stacks of orange *mysore pak* and silver-foiled *barfi,* the smooth globules of *jamun, rasgulla* glistening with syrup, the delicate pastel-tinted halva.

"Take the *jamun,* missy baba," Pushpa urged, "it is fresh today." Sweat beaded her smooth brown forehead. She smelled of warm damp sandalwood.

Later, discontented with whatever it was I'd chosen, I chewed on something cloyingly sweet and asked, "Where did my grandfather go, Pushpa?"

She shrugged, answered vaguely, "To see the fortune teller, perhaps." She waved a piece of rope over her sweets to disperse the flies.

"Pushpa! That would be a mortal sin!"

She flung her hands in the air. "Then who knows? Maybe he went to the money lender, maybe the pundit. Here, taste the *jellabi.*"

Walking home, Grandpa was often grumpy, sometimes euphoric, always evasive. At dinner, I had no appetite for doughy shepherd's pie and creamed carrots.

Aunt Margaret would always blame Grandpa. "John, what have you been feeding her?"

Depending on his mood, Grandpa would perhaps call his sister a meddlesome old hen and stamp off to bed, or stick out his chest to say expansively, "Ah Maggie, what you need is a spot of port to settle your liver."

While Mama muttered something about asking for typhoid, the dining room clock often would chime the wrong hour if Papa were away. He was the only one who wound it.

All this changed, of course, after Letty left.

Once, as I sniffled in church, Letty slipped me her hand-kerchief, and in the years since she left, I held it to my nose from time to time trying to recapture her scent of lavender, which grew ever fainter as the handkerchief itself yellowed with age.

Then something happened inside me. The more I pined for Letty, the more I began to shrink from my grandfather. When was it I first became aware of the change? Had it come before my Confirmation? Before my twelfth birthday? Certainly it had not taken place overnight, but was, instead, a gradual swell of resentment, a white-hot cinder that flared into rage, sometimes at the mere sight of him—the way his shoulder drooped, the way he walked dragging one slippered foot, the stale moldy odor that followed him—and, at such times, I would think: God may have protected you from lightning, but He's punishing you now for sending your daughter away.

Like an apple left too long in the sun, Grandpa withered and decayed. He was bedridden and incontinent. Now fourteen, and stronger by far than either Aunt Margaret or Mama, I lifted and turned and cleaned and bathed him. Each morning I entered his room with loathing. He lay undisturbed in a puddle of damp sheets, his eyes blank as marbles, staring into space. Each day he grew more frail. I remembered occasions in the past when he had laughed uproariously, his chest lifting and expanding and his belly shaking. Now there was no chest, no belly, only bones protruding sharply from under folds of papery skin.

As I sponged the back of his hand one morning—it lay on my palm, each bone articulated like an ancient and intricate ivory sculpture—he grunted, and his hand tightened suddenly on mine.

11

I dropped the sponge and tried to pry his bony fingers loose. He held fast.

Then I looked at his face. His eyes were fixed on mine, his mouth working as if he wanted to shape it around one last desperate word. I fell to my knees.

"Grandpa!" I cried out. "Oh Grandpa!"

Then Mama and Aunt Margaret were in the room, weeping and arguing about which suit Grandpa should be laid out in, and whether the coffin should be bought at Williamsons', an English establishment, or ordered from a carpenter in the bazaar.

"It's the least we can do for him now," Mama said, as she opened a dresser drawer to take out one of Grandpa's large white handkerchiefs. She blew her nose and wiped her eyes. "A bazaar coffin simply won't do."

"A coffin is a coffin," Aunt Margaret replied, and tightened her trembling lips. Then she went to turn over all the pictures, which hung on cords from the moldings so that they faced the wall.

Dazed, I stared at Grandpa lying so still, his pajama top rucked up on one side. His face seemed to collapse before my eyes: cheeks and chin covered with grey stubble slipping into the folds of skin at his neck. Aunt Margaret had closed his eyes and mouth, and folded his hands. "How peaceful he looks," she had said, as she smoothed his drift of silver hair with her palm. Mama had agreed. I thought my grandfather looked worn out, and very sad.

All day Grandpa's rigid, flattened body lay in the parlor. Candles flickered at the head of his bier under which a large tub of melting ice was placed. Wads of cotton wool were inserted in his nostrils and when one of these slipped out Aunt Margaret tucked it back in with the tip of her little finger. There was a sickening stench of flowers and cologne, which did not mask the other smell.

People filled the room, walked around the imitation-teak coffin, then spilled onto the front verandah and into the yard, where they moved about, solemn as crows. Papa stood at the front door and shook everyone's hand, while women embraced Mama and Aunt Margaret, telling them to be brave. The neighbor boy, who was my age but soft in the head, went around asking people to spell the word "phlegm," until Aunt Margaret made him sit down and gave him a piece of seed cake and a picture book. But what I remember most clearly of Grandpa's funeral is this: everyone staring, in silence, at the two old Indian gentlemen dressed in crisp white muslin, who appeared at the open front door.

Mama, intercepting them, said, "This is not a peep show."

The taller of the men brought his palms together in traditional greeting. "It is only," he said softly, "that we wish to pay our respects to Mr. Curtis sahib whom we worked under many years ago. That is why."

The other man tried to give Mama three mangoes.

Their patient dignity as they turned to leave filled me with shame and an unfocused anger. I wanted to run after them, to thank them for coming, to accept their mangoes. Instead I just stood there and kept the flies from settling on Grandpa's face.

Letty was unable to attend the funeral. She lived too far away. Grandpa's body had to be buried within twenty-four hours or it would putrify.

Days later, walking home from school, I came upon the neighbor's dog, Marmaduke, lying dead in a ditch amidst soggy newsprint and skeletal parchment leaves. A continuous moving thread of ants was looping through one nostril and eye. I ran home weeping hysterically. The strange thing was I hated Marmaduke, a fat yellow dog with a pointed snout and a curled-up tail. He had never failed to chase me, snapping and barking. Once he tore the skin on my ankle.

Mama met me at the front door. When she realized the

source of my distress, she was furious. "Not one blessed tear for your grandfather," she said, bitterly. "Now, look at you. Inconsolable over a disagreeable pye-dog that even bit you."

"Hush Lavinia," Aunt Margaret said, "Don't you see?" She led me, still sobbing, into the parlor where she made me lie on the chintz sofa.

I must have slept poorly that night. Twice I woke to see Mama sitting on my bed in her white muslin nightgown. I'd cried out in my sleep, she said.

By now the Japanese had reached Burma. Our daily paper, *The Madras Mail,* was full of horror and carnage. Headlines— "RANGOON BOMBED!" and "RANGOON TODAY, MADRAS TOMORROW?"—were regular fare. Only the Bay of Bengal separated Rangoon from Madras. The harbor, with its troopships and freighters, made us all vulnerable. On the night that the single Japanese bomb was dropped on the harbor, I slept through it all. Mama and Aunt Margaret said it was the most fearful sound in the world. Yet it did not wake me.

One day a new girl appeared at our school. She was Anglo-Burmese and had nervous button eyes and pale yellow skin. Her parents had had enough money to flee their home, she told us, but had to leave everything behind. Others were less fortunate, she said. "They are raping women left and right, you know. Just ripping off their clothes and doing you know what in the street."

We listened and shivered.

Letty wrote: "You mustn't stay. The Japanese are practically at your doorstep! With Arthur traveling about, he is reasonably safe. But three women alone in wartime is utter folly. For Megan's sake, at least, you must leave. My husband

14

and I open our home to you. Come, we have plenty of room. Please come!"

But we went to Bellary instead, where Papa's office was evacuated. There we lived in a large old house with a leaky roof set in a vast compound, upon which nothing grew but thorny scrub. Despite our efforts to keep them out, wild donkeys grazed on these thorn bushes and brayed loudly in the blazing afternoons. From pain? I wondered. Or hunger? Our nearest neighbors were miles and miles away.

Looming over everything was an enormous rock. It sprang straight up from scorched earth. At the very top was an ancient fort where long ago a Maratta king had resisted, then been defeated by, the British.

I was a day student at an orphanage for Indian and Eurasian girls. There was no other school. Papa said we should be grateful for what we had. Mama said if she survived the war at all, she'd head for England like a shot, that she was sick of frying her brains in this incredible heat.

I enjoyed that brief time in Bellary because Papa did not travel as much. He and I spent weekends hiking, exploring the rock and the fort, Papa in khaki shorts and shirt, with his handkerchief on his head knotted at the corners.

"Papa," I asked, pinching my wet shirt away from my shoulder blades, my tennis shoes grey with dust, my twill shorts no longer white, "do you think India will get home rule?"

We were resting in the shadow of a crenellated battlement and sipping lukewarm water from our canteens. On the wall opposite, someone had painted in drippy white letters, "QUIT INDIA!"

Papa slapped a mosquito on the side of his neck, sunburned red as a pillar-box. A lock of his fair hair escaped from under the handkerchief to lie damply across his flushed, sweating forehead. "Hard to say," he said slowly, drawing on a

15

cigarette and blowing the smoke out. "It's their land, all right. But we've done it a lot of good. Unified it, for one thing. Then, railways, roads. This country would be in a sorry state without railways. Don't worry, it won't happen. Not in my lifetime, anyway."

"But if," I persisted. "Say if, they are granted home rule, will we go home to England?" Home! This was the way we spoke of England, a country my parents had left voluntarily, a country I had never even seen.

"Certainly. There'll be nothing here for us, then. It will be hard to leave—but I don't think it'll come to that."

I nodded. It *would* be hard to leave. I wanted to see England, of course, but I didn't want to live there even if it was home.

But Papa was wrong. Less than two years after Japan was defeated, on August 14, 1947, at the stroke of midnight, India achieved independence.

It was impossible not to feel the joy that blazed on every Indian face, a feeling that manifested itself by rows of tiny flickering oil lamps placed along rooftops and windowsills, and exploded in fireworks spangling the sky. Public buildings outlined in colored lights at night were like fairytale ships moored on a still, velvet sea. How can I describe the feeling? It was something like a bird in flight—playful, wheeling and banking on breeze, throat wide, wide open. Singing. Singing.

There was a new Indian flag to replace the Union Jack, and a new national anthem instead of "God Save the King." There were gentle loving speeches by the Mahatma and impassioned ones by Nehru: that India was home to all—Hindus, Moslems, Sikhs and Christians—there was room for everyone. But with the Indianization of the industries, the tea and coffee plantations, the railways, it was only a matter of time before the English left.

16

The sun, our sun, had finally set on this dominion of the empire.

The song became a lament after Partition. One afternoon a trainload of Hindus fleeing their homes in what was now called Pakistan, steamed into the station with only corpses on board—almost every man, woman and child had been hacked to death before the train crossed the border into India. There were only two survivors: an old man and his small grandson who had hidden under a seat in a third class compartment. Another death train, similarly occupied, but this time by Moslems, was dispatched to Pakistan.

In the bazaar pigs' blood was splashed on mosques. Moslem shops were burned and looted. Azad Ali, from whose shop we bought the glowing *dhurrie* rug in the parlor, was found among his smoldering carpets, his head in a corner of the room separated by some three feet from his charred body. On the wireless Nehru pleaded for an end to the bloodshed. Gandhi vowed to fast unto death unless the mindless violence came to an end.

"The man's a saint," Mama said, as she sat in a wicker chair on the front verandah darning a navy blue sock of Papa's. Her needle-basket stood on the wicker table beside her.

"The man's a fraud," Papa snapped, flipping open *The Madras Mail* and lying back in his easy chair, his legs elevated on the fold-out extensions. "He has hoodwinked everyone in this country, and England, as well." There was a worn spot on the sole of his left shoe.

Startled by the tone of his voice, I looked up from where I sat, on a wicker hassock, working on a crossword puzzle. Pencil poised, I waited for him to go on, but he said nothing more. And so I was to remember my father, for it was a long time before I saw him again: grey argyle socks wrinkled at the

17

ankles, heels planed smooth at their outer edges, the dull gleam of his gold signet ring, on which his initials were barely legible any longer, the neatly trimmed fingernails, the fine hairs on the backs of his hands and the way those hands looked against the smudgy grey newsprint. In months to come I would struggle to recall some additional image, strain for some small detail, of the way my father looked then.

Saint or fraud, by Gandhi's fasting there came an end to the bloodshed and riots, and order was restored in the cities. And in the bazaar, Azad Ali's widow and eldest son opened another shop next door to the chemist.

CHAPTER THREE

Oh, Megan," Mama said, as she fanned herself with a folded newspaper. She sat at the desk in the parlor staring at her accounts book open on the blotter, but she didn't pick up the pen. "Do be sensible. A great thumping girl of seventeen. Anyone would think we were sending you off to China instead of on a short train ride—"

"It's not short," I interrupted. I stood beside the desk, leaning on my hands. "Two days and a night is not a short train ride. And besides I have to change trains at Itarsi Junction with only fifteen minutes to spare. What if my train's late and I miss the connection? What will I do there all by myself?"

"You won't *be* by yourself," Mama said crossly. Tension drew a white line around her mouth. Her brown cotton dress was shiny with starch. "You know perfectly well Letty is sending her nephew to Itarsi to help you. For all we know, now that her husband's part of the new government, she might even arrange for the train to be held up indefinitely until you board. Indians control everything, now."

19

From the parlor window we could see the standpipe across the street. It stood in a muddy puddle, surrounded by servants from various houses up and down the road who collected each day's water supply in assorted pots and pails. As the day progressed, the puddle grew steadily wider while servants gossiped and laughed, shouting friendly obscenities at each other. Nearby a piece of road machinery folded and unfolded its long hinged arm. Dust hung in the air like a transparent ochre curtain.

"I simply don't understand you," Mama continued. Her nose, a delicate curve in the old picture with Letty, now overpowered her face with the sharp angled curve of an axe. "All these years you've been mooning about Letty. Don't you want to see her?"

"Of course I do," I said, crumpling my cotton skirt in my fist. "But . . . why can't you go with me? She's your sister. Don't you want to see her?"

"Someone has to stay here. Aunt Margaret's knee—"

"Leave me out of this," Aunt Margaret said tersely, raising her voice but not her head. She sat reading in a chintz chair, her bad leg raised on a small stool.

"—makes it hard for her to travel," Mama finished as if Aunt Margaret had not spoken. "It's no use. You'll just have to go alone." She turned her head away, but not before I caught the glimmer of tears in her eyes.

Across the street, the road machinery groaned and clanged while I stood there awkwardly, unable to bring myself to ask my mother why she was sad.

That night on my way to bed, I overheard Aunt Margaret and Mama speak in hushed voices on the darkened front verandah. I stood very still behind the door not wanting to listen, but quite unable to move. A gust of wind caught the curtain and it fluttered wraith-like against my bare arm. Aunt Margaret said, "You are very wrong, you know. Sending her to Letty."

"Oh, for heaven's sake," Mama said in a fierce whisper. "What else can I do? Go on, tell me."

"You can tell her the truth."

Mama began to cry, softly. "I can't. Oh God, I simply can't." There was a pause, then she said, "I don't want her here when he leaves . . ."

My heart slammed slowly, painfully in my chest. I wanted to leap at them, shouting, "Talk to me! Not about me! I deserve to know!" But another part of me shrank from knowing and wanted to hide, anywhere, in the storeroom, under the bed. I was terrified they would only confirm that what I'd always known would someday happen had happened; that my parents no longer loved each other and were going to separate.

". . . Oh Lavinia," Aunt Margaret was saying, "you can't deprive her of that."

Mama made a muffled sound.

In bed, I lay awake for a long time listening to night sounds of crickets and frogs and the casuarina tree scratching my windowpane. In the distance a jackal howled, and a faraway drum throbbed like a heart. A bullock cart rumbled by, the cartman's song a frail lonely sound fading away into silence.

The next morning I found Mama sitting on her bed sorting laundry. It was Tuesday, laundry day. Soiled clothes and linens lay in clumps on the floor at her feet. On the bed were stacks of freshly laundered shirts, sheets and serviettes. The *dhobi* stood nearby, clasping his shiny dark sinewy hands with the air of one ready to defend himself against the weekly tirade over missing buttons and garments cleverly folded to conceal rips.

My mouth was dry. "Is Papa going alone to England?" I

asked as casually as I could, gazing at the picture of Pan and the Minotaur that had always hung in Mama's room. I tensed for her answer, even as I idly wondered how she'd come by something so frivolous.

"What makes you say that?" Mama replied; her grey cropped head was bent over her long, black-covered ledger.

Unsure of what to say next, I just stood there hoping she'd scold me as she'd done countless times before about my unruly hair, my constant scratching of prickly heat and mosquito bites, my fanciful, wild imaginings. Especially my imaginings. Finally, I whispered, "Why?"

"Why what?" Mama answered, listlessly. Sweat ran down her face.

"Why is he going without us?"

"He's going for treatment."

Treatment! Surely she could've come up with a better story! Why my father was strong as a dray horse. Once he lifted Mama and me together, one in each arm, and spun us both around, Mama screaming in mock fear. And all the times in Bellary when we'd hiked and climbed that rock, he shirtless, his chest brown and wide as a barrel. I couldn't remember a single time he'd ever been sick. I turned from her, and ran. Ran down the front steps and down the street. I ran and ran, past the school and the church and the club, past the bus stop, Scott Shop, Patterson field. After a while, I found I was running at a steady, paced rhythm, and further, that I was going by all the places where Grandpa and I had walked so many years before. I rushed down the main street of the bazaar, dodging cows and pedestrians, and collapsed panting and heaving at Pushpa's sweet shop. My chest was on fire, sweat stung my eyes and mosquito bites, my drenched blouse clung like skin, but I felt a strange exhilaration, as if I'd reached a different, more rarified plane.

Perspiration glistened on Pushpa's face and formed dark

map-like areas under the arms of her blouse. "Missy, please!"
she scolded, as she pointed at me with an extended palm.
"Why to rush? You will spoil your female parts. Then who
will want you?"

Choking and giggling, I tried to wipe my face on a dripping
forearm. "Why, then," I said, as I gasped for breath, "I shall
just join them." I waved a shaky arm in the direction of the
prostitutes across the street.

"*Chee!* For you to say like that. You, granddaughter of fine
Englishman sahib."

I stood feet apart, hands on hips, and stared at the women
across the street. They stared back, mouths sulky and full of
betel. I turned away and, flinging myself down beside Pushpa,
said defiantly, "I know where my grandfather went those
times he left me with you. I've known for a long time now."

"What if?" She shrugged.

"I'm not a child. I can understand things."

"Mens are like that only, missy. They cannot help." She
sighed and mopped her face with a corner of her red cotton
sari. "You are having regular menses?"

"Mens? Or menses?" I asked giddily, tossing my head.

"I am telling you for your own good," she said, all in a
huff. "I am seeing you from little *batcha*," she showed,
holding her hand a foot above the floor, "then growing,
growing," she raised it progressively higher. "Now you are
beautiful young memsahib—Ah, *hai bebe!* Not to cry. *Hai,
hai.*" She gathered me in a humid sandalwoody embrace and
rocked me, crooning softly in Hindi, "Still your tears, my
lovely/Your day will dawn/You will serve a warrior, with
gladness in your heart . . ."

I walked home slowly through the bazaar. I saw cows, skin
tight over bones, nose thoughtfully in gutters among rotting
rinds and soggy newsprint, naked potbellied children with
matchstick arms and sun-bleached hair shrieking with laugh-

23

ter, women in bright saris who strung fragrant ropes of jasmine, or gathered cow dung to dry for fuel, monkeys scampering on rooftops, hugging their babies in long encircling arms, and the absolute trust of those babies. My father was leaving; my mother was sending me away. Would I ever trust my parents again?

I looked about me as if for the last time and without knowing why, knew that I would always remember this precise moment, of this particular day.

CHAPTER FOUR

The word, NIRVANA, was carved into massive stone posts that stood like sentinels on either side of tall wrought-iron gates. From there the drive curved between an avenue of flame-of-the-forest trees and around lawns that were being rolled smooth by a middle-aged man and a boy who strained against a bulky contraption. There were scarlet swords of cannas and yellow roses swaying gently in the late afternoon sun.

A chauffeur-driven car had been sent to meet the train. Now as it approached the house, I wished I were alone. Not that I was ungrateful to Munnar, Letty's nephew, who had escorted me from Itarsi. He was a friendly lanky young man with large long-fingered hands that pushed the curly black hair away from his forehead as he spoke, from where it sprang back down instantly. He was a student at a local engineering college, he told me. Yet, seeing the house for the first time—mullioned widows gleaming like wedges of inset gold in the molten light, magenta bougainvillea splashed against yellow walls, trellised porches laced with fern, fountains leaping, splashing—a strange excitement, which bordered on dread, took hold of me and I thought it must surely show on my face.

If Munnar noticed, he only said, "You will not tell Aunty I smoked, will you?"

"What? No. No, of course not." The small hairs on the back of my neck were erect.

"She says smoking is damaging to health." He laughed. "My health only. Not hers; for she also smokes. She does not—how do you say it?—practice like what she preaches."

"She didn't smoke before," I said absently. "My grandfather was very strict about that. He was a bit of a Tartar, really . . ." I leaned forward suddenly, my awareness focused entirely on the thin woman who walked down the steps as the car came to a stop under a columned porch. She was wearing a peacock blue sari.

"Megan, dearest," she said, opening her arms. "How positively marvelous to see you again. After all these years. Oh, Munnar, thank you for taking care of her." She embraced me and drew back a little, "I must have a good look at you. Was the journey too awful? Oh, my dear, dear Meg." She hugged me again, then led me by the hand into the house. "Come along, Munnar," she called.

Her voice had changed, or perhaps I'd forgotten its slight nasal quality. And forgotten, too, the red mole at the base of her throat that looked like a drop of blood, pulsing.

I could hardly bear to look at her.

Inside, I glanced at the deep couches and polished woods, at the silver bowls filled with yellow roses, at the painting of Letty herself—looking pale and distant—that hung over a cabinet, on the front of which was carved a single gigantic flower with a long curving stamen.

"Munnar, dear," she said. "Will you ask Maharaj to serve tea?"

"Yes, Aunty, but unfortunately I cannot take tea with you. I have an exam in Mechanics tomorrow." He added jovially, "Ten A.M. sharp, Professor Dutta will come, stopwatch in hand. So, I must prepare." He bowed slightly to me, then bent to touch Letty's feet ceremoniously.

Absurdly, his departure filled me with dismay. I wanted to beg him not to leave, to wait at least until after tea, to yell, "Please don't abandon me—" But, I suddenly reminded myself, I was not alone. I was with my beloved Letty, and he was someone I had known for less than four hours. Yet, at that moment, she was the stranger. My heart raced. I managed to say to him, "Thank you very much for your help. I can't think what I would have done without you."

He bowed again, and said, "It was nothing. I will see you again, then."

After he'd left, Letty said, "You look a little flushed. Would you prefer something cold? A shandy, perhaps. It's quite mild, really, just lemonade and a little beer." She went to the cabinet and opened the doors, splitting the flower in half. She poured herself a drink and lit a cigarette.

"No, thank you. I know what a shandy is. I've had it before. Often." I wondered why I'd said that, for I'd never tasted liquor of any kind. "I'd like to wash my hands, if I may."

"By all means. You poor tired little thing. Although," she glanced at me sideways, "you aren't so little anymore. Eh?"

I followed her across the spacious room and out into a hallway that held a massive, ornately framed photograph of a young Indian couple: the bride no more than fourteen, her eyes wide with bewilderment; the groom older, his face stern and moustached under the turban.

"My husband's parents," Letty said with a wave of her hand. "They'll be here later in the month." She talked incessantly about how she'd intended to meet me at the station, but her idiotic cook had bought the wrong lentils for the kedgeree her husband enjoyed. Twice she called me Lavinia. We entered a small bedroom where I saw on the triple-mirrored dressing table the same picture of Letty and Mama that had always fascinated me.

Following my glance, she said, "Lavinia has a copy too, I think." She picked up the picture and I noticed that the glass was cracked. "I've been meaning to have this repaired," she said, almost to herself, and added, "I thought you'd like to have it in your room." She turned to leave. "I hope you'll be comfortable. Let me know if you need anything, anything at all." At the door she paused, and I wondered if she would stay after all, but she only gave me a swift, shy smile. Her lipstick was on crooked.

I heard her cough once in the hall.

Confused, I sat on the bed. I missed Aunt Margaret and Mama and everything familiar and comforting about the home I had just left. Letty's house, despite its elegance, reminded me of the convent school's front parlor with its stiff furniture and brooding life-size statues, which chilled me even on the hottest days. But there was more, I knew, much more than just the strangeness of my surroundings that upset me. I leaned against the headboard of the bed, inlaid with different woods in the shape of a spread lotus.

On the wall facing me hung a picture of some bizarre pagan god with multiple arms. I turned from it with distaste and resolved to move it very soon to a less conspicuous spot, perhaps facedown on top of the wardrobe. A white wicker rocking chair stood beside the wardrobe, and seeing it, I was instantly transported to the club where Grandpa and I had sat on the wicker chairs with yellow cushions. I shut my eyes to shut out the crowding images, and when I opened them again they lit, at once, upon the picture on the dressing table of Mama and Letty.

Then I knew: the image of Letty I had carried around in my mind like a fading picture all those years, was gone forever. I felt its loss, keen and painful.

By now the light in the room had changed to a raw sienna, like the wash on an old tintype. I was struck by the quiet. I heard the muted cries of birds, the dim rumble of traffic in the distance, but that was all; not a single vendor's cry reached me, no raucous discussions around a muddy standpipe. The house was still as a tomb.

I left the bed and picked up the photograph. I examined the faces, Letty's and Mama's, young forever under the cracked glass like perfect moths in a display case, and thought that they were roughly my age at the time: seventeen.

Putting it down again, I went into the bathroom that adjoined my room. I washed my hands, working up a thick lather. Tiny rainbow-hued bubbles swelled and burst on my hands, lifted and sailed from my fingertips. I continued to scrub. When I was finished I dried my hands carefully. The tips of my fingers were as pale and ridged as blanched almonds. I trimmed my nails; then I went to rejoin this new Letty whose personality seemed oddly flattened by the sari she wore—its glowing folds stiff and artificial as if the garment held itself away from her body—and whose once long, free-swinging hair was now cut and clung to her scalp in stiff, pinched waves.

I wandered into the dining room. Cabinets of some dark wood with beveled glass doors were filled with glassware and crockery. An elderly woman servant in a white cotton sari was polishing silver platters and bowls and pitchers at the large oval table, which was covered with newspaper. When she caught sight of me, she smiled broadly, exposing betel-stained teeth, and spread her arms, a bowl in one hand, a

29

blackened rag in the other. "I am Gopi," she said, patting her chest with the rag. "Memsahib there," she pointed her chin at a closed door. "You go. I bringing tea."

I knocked and, receiving no answer, opened the door. The room was empty. Pink silk covered the walls and chairs and hung at windows. A chandelier slid light patterns across the ceiling. It was like the inside of a gigantic, silk-lined jewel box.

"Aunt Letty?" I called.

"In here, Megan dear," she answered from an adjoining room.

I stood in the open doorway blinking in disbelief. She was lying in the bathtub up to her armpits in water. I saw her small pale breasts, the patch of dark hair at the fork of her legs.

"Come and talk to me," Letty said, an empty glass in her hand. An ashtray with a lighted cigarette rested on the edge of the tub—a real porcelain bathtub, not like the round galvanized one we used at home. "You can sit there on the pot." She waved the glass at the flush toilet. "I'll ring for Gopi to bring your tea."

"She said she was bringing it."

"Oh good. All nicely settled in, then?"

"Yes."

"Everything *tik hai?*" she asked, sticking her thumbs in the air.

I nodded.

"Oh, come. Where's the old salute?"

"Tik hai." I lifted my thumbs, but took no heart in the familiar Hindi expression that signified all was well.

Sister Celestine had instilled in us that modesty is a woman's chief attribute: respect for one's body begets respect, she'd repeated over and over.

I'd never seen Mama naked. She always changed her clothes behind the open door of the wardrobe that she used as a screen, emerging fully dressed with, perhaps, a feathered hat tilted over one eye, or in a crochet-trimmed cotton nightie that reeked of starch.

Gopi entered with a cup of tea for me; the silver toe rings on her bare feet rang softly against the marble floor. Without a word exchanged, Letty handed her empty glass to the servant who took it away and returned it refilled.

I had the odd sense that this was not actually happening. Could this really be me sitting here on a flush toilet in all this scented steamy warmth, sipping tea, as I watched Letty take a bath?

All the while, Letty held her glass beneath her chin and spoke dreamily bout Mama and herself and their black cat, Cleo. She told me that Cleo had lived to a ripe old age, until one day as the cat dozed in the sun on the top step of the front porch, the neighbor's dog—it was an Alsatian, Letty thought, or perhaps, an English Bull—caught Cleo by the small of her back and pranced and strutted and tossed its head, with Cleo in its jaws, causing blood to splatter the porch in wide arcs. Grandpa had rushed at the dog with a cricket bat, screaming, "Fiend, demon . . ." Letty paused.

"What happened then?" I asked. "Did Cleo die?"

Letty's eyes had a faraway stare.

"Did Cleo die?" I repeated, more loudly.

"What? Of course. Dead as a doornail. I did a postmortem on her behind the servants' latrine. Crushed spinal cord, ruptured spleen, punctured lung filled with blood . . ."

I suddenly felt sick in that room with its heavy scent, colored soaps and bath oils, and towels thick as carpets.

"Hand me a towel, please, Megan dear." Letty stood shaking on the bathmat. How could she possibly be cold? I wondered. It was suffocating.

The only light came from a small window set high in one wall. In the dim, steam-filled room, Letty's body seemed

31

elongated, with brittle thighs and flat belly, like the strange, twisted, human-shaped ginseng root that hung from a nail in the back of Pushpa's sweetshop. I thought of all those times when Grandpa and I had gone to see Pushpa, and how Pushpa would break off an "arm" or "leg" of the root that she would then crush and steep in hot water. Grandpa would gulp down this strange drink like it was medicine. He would then square his hat on his head and, without even a glance in my direction, turn on his heel and leave me there.

"Aunt Letty," I said, my voice sounding thin and desperate. "May I . . . go to my room?"

"Dear me, yes. How unforgivable of me. You must be exhausted." She wrapped herself in the towel. "Dinner will be eightish," she called after me. I heard the sound of ice swirling around in her glass.

Much later that night Letty's husband came home. He was a large man in a shantung suit, with thinning hair through which his scalp was visible, and a double chin that shook when he laughed. He laughed often, the chins in motion, and Letty always laughed when he did, her eyes seldom straying from his face. She moved around him as a pale astral body, having no light of its own, orbits the sun. She waved away imaginary insects, wiped perspiration from his face and neck, and screamed at the servants to bring more rice, more curry, more lentils, more water.

He patted her arm or her shoulder, a hip perhaps, whatever part happened to be within easy reach, as she ministered to his comfort. It was the type of caress one would bestow on a child, or a faithful old pet.

He ate Indian-style, with his fingers, smiling amiably at me. Letty and I had eaten earlier. "This is how food is meant to be enjoyed," he said, his plump hand moving swiftly across the

plate with surprising delicacy, mixing small portions of rice
with different sauces and transferring the compact mass to his
mouth. "I read somewhere that eating with a fork is like
making love through an interpreter. Very funny, is it not?"
He stretched his mouth in a soundless laugh and pinched Letty
affectionately on her sparse bottom.

When he had finished eating he held his hand over the plate
until Letty rinsed it in a finger bowl and dried it on a small
towel. As she cleared away his dishes, her husband belched
loudly and to my horror I began to giggle, and was soon
laughing hysterically, uncontrollably. Helpless tears ran down
my face.

Letty whirled, still holding the finger bowl and towel, her
face white, her nostrils pinched. "How dare you," she said,
very softly. "How bloody well dare you."

"Nah, nah, Letty, my dear," her husband said, gently.
"Perhaps she does not know our Indian custom. To belch
means to show approval for good food." To me he said, "It is
just the opposite, I know, in your English society."

The effect of Letty's words was instantaneous, as if I'd been
slapped. I stopped laughing and rose uncertainly. "I'm sorry,"
I mumbled. "Please excuse me." Then I fled.

Back in my room I began to brush my hair angrily, but not
before I had snatched up the picture of Letty and Mama and
placed it facedown on the table.

Before long, Letty knocked and entered. She stood behind
me and looked straight into my mirrored eyes. She held a
lighted cigarette between two nicotine-stained fingers.

"Did you know I once had the same color hair as you?" she
said, lifting a strand of my hair. "Chestnut. That's when my
husband fell in love with me."

"Aunt Margaret says yours was much darker," I said,
staring back at her reflection.

She dropped her eyes.

33

"What else does Aunt Margaret say about me?" She spoke wistfully, her eyes still averted. "Please tell me. Tell me everything." She looked at me then, resting a hand on my shoulder. With a shock of almost disbelief I recognized the square-tipped fingers. Her face was flushed. At that moment, she came closest to the Letty of my imagination. But in the very next instant the resemblance faded.

I continued to stare at her reflection and said calmly, "There's nothing to tell."

Her hand trembled as she raised the cigarette to her lips. "Oh Megan, but surely there must be. Something?" She smiled that quick shy smile.

I shook my head.

Letty sighed. Her shoulders were hunched as she turned away and picked a flake of tobacco off her tongue.

"All right, then. Goodnight, dearest Megan. Sleep tight."

CHAPTER FIVE

I tried to make it up to Letty the next day, asking her to tell me about herself and Mama when they were young. She required little urging. Her eyes shone with pleasure as she spoke. "Lavinia was the pretty one. She had the serenity of a Botticelli angel. But . . . *simple,* and so terribly . . . *predictable*." She laughed heartily.

We were walking to the servants' quarters at the far end the compound. It was Letty's habit, she told me, to visit the servants' families each morning. I carried a basket filled with medicinal supplies, leftover food I recognized from the previous night's dinner, a pair of khaki jodhpurs with a hole in one knee and a bag of lollipops.

Until now I'd thought the dark wood fence that backed the kitchen garden was the extent of the compound, but I found as we passed through a gate in the fence that we faced an expanse of land at least as extensive as Patterson field at home. It was dotted with clumps of coarse grass, outcroppings of red rock and towering red ant hills. A grazing cow seemed

35

oblivious to the crow perched on its back. The crow, in turn, was feeding on vermin off the animal's hide.

"One day," Letty continued, "Lavinia was not to be found anywhere. I told Aunt Margaret, 'I know where she is. She's at the Murphy's taking care of the baby.' And sure enough there she was. She loved babies, you know. These Murphys— oh, the mother had run off with the Muslem chauffeur, or something—anyway, the children, there were six of them, I think, sat around Lavinia who was telling them a story while she fed the baby from a bottle. You know," Letty said, thoughtfully, "I wondered at the time if she might not have married Bill Murphy, kids and all." She paused. "He was so splendidly handsome and, oh, how he loved her. Yet . . . she married someone else—"

"I'm glad she married my father," I said loudly. I thought it perfectly natural and unselfish of Mama to want to help a motherless family. I couldn't help thinking that at least she didn't do what you did, and was startled when she said, almost as if I'd spoken aloud, "Yes, the things we do."

As we approached, parakeets streaked from a thicket of mango trees in a flash of green so brilliant I was astonished the trees were not leached of their color. I gasped.

"Magnificent, aren't they," Letty said. "But a nuisance. They eat the fruit and their droppings poison the grass, the gardeners tell me." She waved her arm. "You see these trees? Would you believe they are only ten years old? Just look. A forest. Actually, we had to plant them as a buffer against the servants' quarters. All that noise. And the music."

I heard a thin reed-like song, along with the hollow slap, slap of wet clothes against stone.

"What a sad song," I said. "It sounds almost like weeping."

"Yes, their music is awfully sentimental. Have you ever seen a Hindi motion picture? All the action comes to an abrupt halt for a twenty-minute love song. This predilection of theirs for melodrama, pathos and tears is . . . a little wearing. Ah, Megan," she reached over and hugged me around the shoulders, "it's so good having you to talk to. I can't believe you're really here."

The servants' quarters was a row of attached godowns under a common corrugated metal roof. There was a well in front surrounded by a low concrete platform. Two women washed clothes, beating them against the concrete; the one who was singing, a toothless woman with a shaved head, fell silent. Barefoot half-clad children, their legs covered with red dust, chased two elderly goats and a small, dark, furiously squealing pig. Women came to cluster around Letty who was wearing a crisply starched cotton sari. They looked like bright ragged butterflies hovering around a pale odorless hothouse flower. She passed among them distributing the contents of the basket. Some of the women carried babies on their hips: naked babies with huge, dark, kohl-rimmed eyes and runny noses.

"Is he eating better now?" Letty asked a mother as she prodded the baby's swollen belly. "I will send you some more oranges and medicine." In an aside to me, she said, "Scurvy."

A little boy hurled himself at Letty, wrapping skinny chocolate arms about her legs and burying his face against her thigh. "Ravi," she said, rubbing her knuckles in his glossy black curls. "Are you being a good boy?" He nodded vigorously. "Because, if you are naughty, this bird will come and sit on your head and sit, and sit, and sit. A big black bird, with claws. It will watch you every time you pinch your little sister, and it won't leave until you promise never to hurt her again."

The women murmured and smiled and nodded.

As we turned to leave, they extended their hands palms down in Letty's direction, but did not touch her, then lifted their hands to their foreheads, their closed eyes. I was

37

reminded, somehow, of a saint's day at church when we knelt at the altar rail to kiss a sacred relic—a sliver of bone from Saint Jude's thigh, say, or a scrap of Saint Thomas's robe, sealed in glass and set in gold—that the priest moved from mouth to mouth.

"They are so grateful for the slightest attention," Letty said, swinging the empty basket as we walked back. "It's a responsibility I don't take lightly."

I wondered with dismay if Letty felt the same of me. That I, too, was grateful for the slightest attention, that I, too, was a responsibility not to be taken lightly.

"Coo-eee, Lett-eee. Over here." A woman's voice clear and high floated on the sunlit morning air. Letty increased her pace as if she'd not heard. Reflexively, I turned my head in the direction of the voice and then stood still. Advancing toward us from the adjoining compound was the most beautiful woman I'd ever seen. She seemed to float across the patchy brown grass, perhaps because her feet were not visible beneath the soft folds of her lemon chiffon sari. As she moved, the sari clung to her waist and outlined her hips and the languid perfection of each of her thighs.

Beside me Letty muttered, "What did you stop for? Now we're in for it." She turned towards the woman with a tight smile. "Good morning, Nila. Lovely day."

"Heavenly. I see your niece has arrived." She said to me, "Welcome to Nerbudapur. I hope you had a pleasant journey." Her eyes were the color of limes in the sun.

"This is Megan," Letty said. "And this is Major—beg pardon, Nila—Lieutenant-Colonel Bhatt's wife. Nila is from Kashmir. She writes poetry, in the best Urdu tradition. Yes, Nila?"

Kashmiri. That explained the fair skin, the green eyes.

"Oh my goodness," the other murmured. "How you exaggerate." She turned to me, but spoke to Letty, her eyes

on my face, "You must let me borrow this lovely child. I wish
to show her off. That russet hair, that lambent skin. She does
not—. She must take after her father's family."

Uneasy, I glanced at Letty, who only shrugged.

"She must go with us to the parade on Saturday. Oh, and
you and Doctor sahib, also. It will give Prem and myself very
much pleasure."

"Megan might enjoy that," Letty said, edging away. "We'll
see. After she gets settled."

After we'd left Nila, Letty began to walk swiftly and in
silence towards the house. Presently she said, "That woman
has nothing whatsoever to do with her time. Women like that
are leeches—"

"You said she wrote poetry."

Letty looked sideways at me, and away. "And what earthly
good is poetry to anyone?" She was full of scorn. "Can you
eat a poem? Will it cure a headache?"

"But, Rabindranath Tagore, Shakespeare," I protested
weakly.

"In any case, she writes pure piffle. 'That rusty hair, that
lambent skin,'" she mimicked. "Lambent! Where in God's
name did she find that word?"

"She said russet, not rusty hair." I hurried to keep up with
her.

Letty slowed her headlong dash. "Poor creature, I suppose
one should feel pity for her."

"Why? She's so beautiful," I exclaimed.

"Hmmph! A lot of good it does her. Everyone knows her
husband prefers men."

"Then it's lucky he's in the army. It would be worse if he
didn't like them."

Again the sideways look. "You don't know what I'm
talking about, do you?"

Sensing a trap, I was silent.

"Have you heard the word homosexual? It means a man whose sexual preference is other men."

I could feel the blood come to my skin. As calmly as I could, I said, "Oh, I see," although I really didn't. I felt sorry for Nila in a vague dutiful sort of way, but only because I thought someone so lovely deserved to be cherished. A fleeting thought.

After our walk to the servants' quarters, we toured the rose garden where Letty inspected foliage for aphids and blackspot. Her hands swift and sure, she snipped off faded blooms that she placed in the empty basket she'd carried back from the servants' quarters.

"What was your favorite subject in school?" Letty asked, as she fingered a leaf with a cluster of minute white specks on its glossy dark underside.

"English."

She scraped the specks off with her thumbnail, muttering, "Blasted aphids, I shall have to spray these again. English? Not mathematics? Science?"

"You said, favorite. English was my favorite subject, especially Composition, although I enjoyed English Text, too. We read Shakespeare, and Dickens, and Jane Austen. Most of all, I admire—"

"There's nothing wrong with English, Megan. But there's a crying need in this country for women doctors, and in qualifying for medical college all the King's English is useless without science and mathematics."

"But I don't want to go to medical college."

"What do you want then?" she said, pinching off a dead blossom.

"I'm not quite sure . . . yet."

She straightened. "Listen to me, Megan," she said, briskly.

"Choose law or medicine. Today, in India, women lawyers are still only a novelty. In any case, something tells me you'd be no good at it. Too passive, I think. But just think of the prestige that a career in medicine brings to a woman. The respect. The trust. Look around you." She waved the clippers to take in the landscaped grounds that stretched in every direction as far as the eye could see. "I have never regretted my choice. Not for one instant. My husband and I had a thundering practice, until my accident, which made it impossible for me to work."

She turned back to her task. I wanted to slap her.

Straightening suddenly, Letty caught my gaze and stepped back, her eyes on mine. "My God," she said slowly, "your eyes are exactly like Pa's."

She turned and walked away from me towards a small shed; the basket bouncing against her hip scattered a trail of dead petals behind her.

At the end of the fourth day—a night so dark, so dense, it seemed that if I extended my arms into it they would rest in soft dark fur—I sat alone on the back steps as I had done each morning since my arrival, listening to the Brahmin priest pray before the sacred *tulsi* plant in the center courtyard. I loved to sit in the pale early sunshine, the only one in the house awake, and listen to the soothing Sanskrit chants that seemed not so different, after all, from the Latin ones I was used to.

Now faint music from the servants' quarters floated on the night air—despite Letty's barrier of mango trees, I thought spitefully—along with the scent of jasmine and oleander and the acrid odor from fires fueled with dried cow dung.

I thought of Mama, not the mother who was often impatient—and so irritable before I left, I was almost glad to leave—but the one who touched my hair at rare moments

41

under pretext of brushing it behind my ear or straightening a hair pin, the one who had once fought savagely with Mother Superior about a class mark she felt was unjustly assigned me, the one who had made me a white mull dress she knew we couldn't afford when I passed high school with distinctions in English. That Mama. And I wept for her.

It was not just that I missed Mama, but Letty was so . . . impossible, so utterly different than I'd remembered, so determined to change me. What did it matter if I was unable to arrange flowers in a silver bowl? Or forgot to pour milk first into the cup before the tea? And the business of having me read the newspaper aloud to her about all the boring squabbles that went on in the Houses of Parliament among men with unpronounceable names. What did I care about dams, or the failures of crops, or whether the English name of a government office should be changed to an Indian one. "You've had a very frivolous education," she told me. "You know nothing about our new India." Yet she, herself, referred to Indians as "they" and "them."

Earlier, at lunch, Letty's husband had asked me, "And how is your father's health?"

I intercepted the look Letty flashed him. A look I absorbed immediately and struggled to interpret. "I think my father is very well, thank you." I spoke clearly, with just the faintest hint of swagger. "And how is your health?"

He chuckled richly. "It is quite well, my dear young lady."

"I think it's time you addressed my husband as Uncle," Letty said, between sips of water. She dabbed at the corners of her pale wet mouth—the color of her nipples, I suddenly thought—with a crisply starched serviette. "I am your aunt, he is your uncle. It's disrespectful to not address him in some fashion."

I recall her tone of frosty detachment, as if she were deliberately overlooking my impertinence, no more than the rudeness of a child. It was an attitude she used whenever she lectured me in his presence. Outright anger, even Mama's carping, but . . . I wiped my nose on my sleeve. Letty's husband was a kind man, a gentle man, who always seemed mildly startled at seeing me, as if in between times he'd forgotten all about my presence in the house. He was away for most of the day. I saw him at breakfast, lunch, and then much later at dinner. We always waited for him until he returned at eight, or even nine o'clock, so that we all could have dinner together. Letty offered no explanation for his absences, so I simply assumed he was busy.

But, what of my parents? What was that swift look of warning that had passed between Letty and her husband? Where was my father? Would I ever see him again? Was he as lonely and unhappy as I? Or had he already forgotten us? Maybe by now he was in love with someone else. Maybe he'd had her on the quiet all these years. Someone young and smiling with smooth skin and small soft hands like temple flowers. They would plead with me to live with them, beg me to come and stay, even a few days. But I would have to decline out of loyalty to Mama, cranky as she was.

With the soft tinkle of ice against glass, the sigh of clothing, Letty settled herself beside me. She did not touch me, or speak; just sat there sipping her drink. After some time, she said, "Leaving home was the hardest thing I've ever done."

I did not answer.

"The mechanics were ridiculous," Letty said, with a small tight laugh. "Absurd, really. I got on the wrong train and rode till Avadi, until I was told I had to go back the way I'd come. I'd hardly been able to see for tears when I got on the first train at Madras, but when I had to pass through it again, on the right train this time, I locked myself in the lavatory and stayed there listening to the tea and fruit vendors and all the other commotion outside on the platform, until the train left the station."

"Weren't you tempted to just"—I snorted disgustingly—

"open the bathroom door and go home?" I could not help asking.

"Oh, I was. I certainly was. But, you see, all of a sudden I had a terrible attack of diarrhea and couldn't get off the pot. The irony." She lifted a hand, palm up. "I had nothing with me but my purse and very little money. Such terrible cramping pains." She tipped her head back and a laugh burst from her throat.

After a while, I said, "I sometimes get diarrhea when I'm frightened. When I sat for my music exam in the convent front parlor and played the first Bach study, my stomach cramped so badly I was afraid I would mess the piano bench."

"Goodness! Not the piano bench. In the convent front parlor? In plain sight of Saint Joseph, and Our Lady of Fatima, and the Little Flower?"

"And," I lifted an index finger in the air, "the Music Examiner from Cambridge!"

"Oh, thank God," Letty cried, raising her face to the sky and pressing her glass to her chest, "the child has a sense of humor, after all." She turned to me and placed a hand on my head. "Honestly, Megan. You're serious as an owl at times."

Fireflies made pinpricks of light. I thought of the time when I was six and I'd put two fireflies in the sewing box lined with blue silk that Grandpa had brought me all the way from Bombay. I thought it was the only container lovely enough to be a firefly house. Days later all that was left of the insects was an ugly brown stain on the blue silk.

I said, "How frightened you must have been."

She did not answer immediately, then said, "Not nearly as frightened as when I was expecting you."

Astounded, I wanted to say something. I sensed she expected me to respond. I struggled to think of something appropriate, but nothing came to mind. Then the silence enlarged, grew into a wall.

"You need friends," she said, at last. "I'll ring Munnar. He can take you to the club for a game of tennis, or something. Did you bring your tennis costume?"

"No. That is . . . I don't have one."

"Oh. But do you play?"

"No," I mumbled. "I'm not good at games."

"Nonsense, you can learn. Anyone can learn anything. Munnar will teach you. Just what you need, fresh air and exercise. You mope around too much. When I was your age I had loads of friends."

Then, quite by accident one morning, I discovered Letty's library.

While waiting for the others to wake, I decided to help Maharaj weed the haphazard kitchen garden where onions jostled parsley and coriander, and carrot-tops straggled in feathery wisps between pale fat cabbages.

"Oh missy, look look. You have pulled out a radish," Maharaj complained. "You go now, thank you very much."

"But the leaves look just like this," I protested. "See," I picked up a limp weed from a pile of others and held it out, "the leaves are exactly the same."

"Not at all same. You go to work in rose garden."

"I hate the rose garden. I detest flowers." I sat back on my heels and brushed the hair from my eyes with a damp wrist.

"*Arre* missy! Now you are squashing capsicum plant."

"Where?"

"There only," he said, and pointed with a muddy accusing forefinger. "Underneath underneath."

I lifted up on my knees and turned to look behind me. Sure enough, a small bell pepper plant was all bent over and its tender new fruit, no larger than my big toe, flattened.

"I'm sorry," I said, and carefully rose to my feet. "But

Maharaj, if I only knew where things are planted . . ." I didn't finish the sentence, for it was then that I saw, off in the distance, sun splintering on beveled glass. Dazzled, I shaded my eyes and thought I could make out a brick structure.

"What is that over there, Maharaj? There by that old banyan tree?"

He glanced over his shoulder in the direction I pointed. "Is memsahib's library," he answered. "She no using now. You go see. Many many books."

"Are you sure you can manage without me?"

"Yes, yes. My pleasure only. You go."

"I'll come again tomorrow."

"Not necessary."

"But I want to."

I left him muttering over the plant I'd accidentally squashed.

Letty had not mentioned the library to me, although she knew I loved books. It was part of a wing of the house that Letty had said was now used only for storage. Its outer walls were nearly hidden behind the foliage of surrounding trees and the heavy tangle of undergrowth. It was the only area of the compound that was left untended and wild, as if by intention.

Drawing nearer, I found that the room was actually a separate structure that stood apart from the rest of the house by about five feet. Leaded glass panes in a graceful bay caught long slanting sunrays that seeped through the dense greenery. The library seemed to nestle in the undergrowth like some dusty mislaid jewel one discovers by chance in a clump of grass.

The door was unlocked. Inside, there were deep cushioned window seats along the bay window and floor-to-ceiling book-cases that lined the remaining three walls. In one corner, like an interrupted spiral staircase, was a set of library steps. A heavily stained oriental carpet and an overstuffed chair, also badly stained, were the only other furnishings. Dust covered everything; cobwebs festooned the ceiling and hung in shreds in corners. A lizard clung to the ceiling, throat pumping, feet spread like tiny human hands.

I was struck by the quality of light in the room, a pale shifting green, and was reminded of the time Papa had taken me to the Harbor House Aquarium where we peered into each murky tank inspecting blowfish and angelfish, sharks and eels. Only now it seemed that I was inside one of those tanks, looking out. It was oddly pleasant, almost dreamlike. I sat in the chair and leaned my head back, inhaling the aroma of old leather, book paste, age and dust, and was lulled by a contentment so deep I could have dozed, curled on my side. But I rose, instead, and walked around slowly, touching all the books, running my fingers along their spines. Occasionally I took one down and parted the pages to sniff deeply its wonderful dusty scent. Colette, Tolstoy, Eliot, Austen, Twain, Tagore, Naidu, Nehru, Churchill.

Every day after that I spent my early mornings in the library. My decision not to tell Letty about my discovery was instinctive at first. I was afraid she might object. Then I began to see the room as my own, my special retreat, my refuge, and not hers at all. After all, I told myself, just look how the books were uncared for, the room neglected. From time to time, I would read from portions of books, "Bangle-Sellers" from Sarojini Naidu's *The Sceptred Flute,* or Jane Austen's *Mansfield Park,* but my joy in my discovery was still too keen to absorb anything more than the room itself. I was a miser content only to count my fortune.

It was there that I read and reread my first letters from home. Mama wrote: ". . . You must be grateful to Letty for her generosity, her hospitality, but don't lose sight of the one true faith . . ." She ended it, "All my love, Mama," All her love: doled out for the past seventeen years, now heaped upon me and all at once, at the end of a letter.

In Aunt Margaret's letter I learned that Sister Celestine had gone mad and had to be sent home to Ireland. Poor old soul, Aunt Margaret wrote, she couldn't cope any longer.

I carried them in the back of my missal. I attended Mass occasionally. I found it comforting and wonderfully familiar.

Curled in the chair one morning, writing letters, my pen slipped from my hand and into the crevice between the cushion and chair arm. Fishing for it, I pulled out a few coins, a button, a pencil, some linty peanuts, and a letter. It was from Mama to Letty informing her of Grandpa's death. The ink was smeared and the paper waffled as if something wet had dripped on it. In one corner was a brown stain. I stared at Mama's slanted pointy handwriting ". . . skin and bone. It was his time . . . the funeral . . ." I quickly refolded the letter and slipped it back where it had lain all those years.

In the next batch of letters from home there was even one from Papa in the same envelope with the others. It was very short, one brief paragraph. He hoped I was well. He was sorry he had not said goodbye, but Mama and he had decided that the course they had chosen was for the best, and that goodbyes were never satisfactory, anyway. He wanted me to know he loved me very much. He signed it, "Your loving Papa." There was no return address, no request for letters, nothing at all.

It was obvious he'd sent the letter to Mama to send to me. Mama had seen the letter first. My letter. *They* decided the best course for me without even consulting me, not once. I crumpled the letter in both hands and flung it from me. It landed in a far corner of the room.

Later I retrieved it and smoothed it out as best I could.

CHAPTER SIX

It is a pity your aunt and uncle will not be joining us," Nila
said. "I admire them. They used to be the backbone of
Nerbudapur society." She gave a small laugh and added,
"Such as it is. Although your aunt never leaves her house
anymore. Why, I do not know." She shrugged and turned a
hand in the air. "I suppose you are familiar with a much
higher level of society. What was your father's position?" She
stretched out on the flowered chintz cushions of a wicker
settee and bent an arm behind her head. I saw the pearly sheen
of her inner wrist and the arch of her throat.

"He was District Accounts Officer in the railway."

"Gazetted?"

"I don't know."

"Gazetted is best, of course. Your father's position was not
so important, but one cannot control such things no matter
how ambitious. Take my Prem; he could not rise above major
until your people left. But that is another story." She said all
this without rancor, or even resignation, but rather with great

indolence. I took no offense at her comment about Papa's position, and upon reflection decided that what she said must be true for, since we were not rich, Papa's position must not have been important.

We were in the front room of Nila's house with its simple wicker furniture and whitewashed walls, its profusion of daisies and phlox casually arranged in baskets placed on the broad windowsills and glass-topped tables. Nila's eyes were shut; her lashes made small dark fans against her flawless skin with its faint amber gloss. I felt relaxed and quite lazy myself, sunk deep in a chair, my legs stretched out before me.

Suddenly Nila sat bolt upright. "I have a wonderful idea," she said. "I have been watching you— Yes, yes. Do not look so surprised. I was only pretending to have my eyes closed. It is my trick. I can study people like that. There is something about you that reminds me of my youngest sister. Why do you not wear a sari to the parade and we will tell everyone we are sisters." She clapped her hands. "For a lark. What do you say?"

"Well . . . all right," I said, unsure, but reluctant to dampen her enthusiasm.

"In that white cotton dress you look like Alice in Wonderland. I will dress you like a queen. Come." She rose and took my hand. "What fun! Let's see, I think blue or lavender, something soft to—what is the word?—enhance your coloring, not fade it out. Lambent skin."

"What does lambent mean?"

"I am not too sure, but I think it means flickering, like fire. The way red comes and goes in your face. I like to say new words, taste them like *gur* on my tongue, before I use them in a poem."

In a large bright room lined with mirrors, our bodies and movements were reflected and repeated, over and over, till it seemed we swam in silvered light.

"May I read some of your poetry?"

"Of course. But now we are too busy."

She pressed the edge of a mirror and it swung open to reveal rows of shallow drawers. She tugged on them, one after another, releasing a cascade of shimmering rainbow-colored saris onto the carpeted floor. She selected a pale blue one, with a narrow woven border of silver, which she held against my shoulder, eyeing me critically. Discarding it, she picked up a coral georgette with birds of paradise embroidered on it in gold and silver. "Bah! Makes you look jaundiced," she muttered, and tossed it aside as well. She pulled open some more drawers. "Where is that mauve . . . Ah, this one. Oh look! Just see how it makes your eyes like violets." Her mood was infectious.

Obediently, I slipped on and fastened the brief, snug *choli*-blouse, and stood silently as Nila circled me pleating, draping, and tucking the six-yard length of chiffon sari into a long skirt tied at my waist. She made me promise to keep my eyes shut until she was finished. I thought it all a waste of time for it was my impression that European women looked awkward in saris, something to do with bone structure, or coloring, or both. Letty was a case in point. But I couldn't say any of this to Nila. And as I felt the fleeting touch of her fingers at my bare waist, my collarbone, my spine, I thought of how Letty, unable to reach Munnar by phone, suggested, reluctantly at first, then insisted, that I accompany the Bhatts to the parade. She said my loneliness was dreary and becoming pathological.

And now I was very grateful.

With a cry of pleasure, Nila said, "You can open your eyes. You are . . . transformed."

And transformed I was. Not that I was suddenly made beautiful, but my body now had a certain dignity that it hadn't before. There was a flow of line from breasts to waist to hips to thigh, sculpted by the sari's soft folds, that I'd observed in other women and in art, but had always steadfastly denied in myself. My hips and breasts that I'd once dismissed as lumpy useless things that made my frocks fit badly, now seemed not so . . . useless, but had form; their function I would discover later. This I knew. I felt a woman. I was a woman.

"You should be proud of your body. Show it off. Do not hide it." Nila stood behind me, her hands resting lightly at my waist. "You are pleased? Yes?"

"Yes."

"Good. I will dress now. Then we will be sisters." She picked a nile green sari from the pile on the floor and deftly draped it around herself without even a glance in a mirror. "Have you ever worn a sari before?" she asked.

"No, never," I answered. "I didn't think it suited white women—" I broke off in confusion and looked away. "My mother says it's a very graceful dress. In fact, she wore one to a fancy dress ball and won third prize. The Governor was there." I was babbling.

I thought I felt her intent gaze, but when I looked back she was seated at the dressing table applying mascara to her lashes with a tiny black brush: swift delicate little strokes, a procedure that seemed to absorb her completely. When she finally spoke her tone was light, even idle. "You are thinking of your aunt, maybe?"

I did not answer.

"Your aunt is a very fine lady who looks very terrible in a sari. She does not tie it properly, not because she does not know how, but because she insists on doing it the way her husband taught her."

"How do you know?"

"He told me. He told me that when they were first married none of the women of the house went near her. So he did it for her."

"Why didn't they go near her?"

"Because they are Brahmin and to them she was un-touchable—"

Shocked, I whispered, "Like the beggars in the street, and the sweeper?"

Now she was arranging tendrils of hair around her face. "Like that, yes." She put down the tortoiseshell comb and said to me over her shoulder, for I was standing some distance behind her, "But now everything is all right, I am told. So you need not upset yourself."

I was about to ask Nila the circumstances under which my uncle had revealed all this to her, when the door was flung open and a stocky, khaki-uniformed man entered. He carried a swagger stick in one hand and a clutch of papers in the other.

"Chits, Nila," he extended the hand with the papers. "More chits."

She whirled to face him. "Ah, Prem. You have come at last. Please hurry and change—"

"You promised, no more—"

"This is Dr. Letty's niece from Madras," Nila said quickly, waving an arm in my direction. "Her name is Megan Man-ning, and she is wearing a sari for the first time. Does she not look lovely?"

He turned and saw me then. His face was expressionless. Tucking the stick under his arm, he swept the visored cap from his head. His forehead was damp and the cap had left a red crease along it. He bowed.

"You honor us, Miss Manning." A moustache like a heavy stroke of ink crossed his upper lip. "And you complement the garment."

I was conscious of a slight breeze from the open window, felt it stir the folds of my sari and graze the hollow of my waist.

Acutely uncomfortable, I managed to smile and murmur,

"Thank you," but all the while my eyes darted from one face to the other. Had my presence in the room prevented some kind of discussion, confrontation? Nila calmly swung back to face the dressing table mirror and busied herself fastening on jade and pearl earrings, revealing nothing. Her husband smiled at me politely. His teeth were very white and protruded slightly.

"I'll excuse myself, then. Must try to make myself presentable," he said, paused, and added as an afterthought, "I shall be the envy of every blighter in the stadium." His speech was meticulous and lacked the singsong inflection characteristic of the typical Indian accent—my uncle's, for instance, and Nila's. He bowed and then appeared to notice the slips of paper he still held in his hand. Frowning slightly, he shoved them into his trouser pocket.

At the door he paused, his hand on the knob. He stood there, tapping his swagger stick against a khaki-clad knee, and said, "I'll meet you at the car in fifteen minutes." Then he left, shutting the door carefully behind him.

"But, of course, she is my sister. Do we not look like sisters?" Nila fluttered and twirled like some bright bird in a mating dance. We were surrounded by a host of young officers. A handsome Sikh, with melting dark eyes and an impressive turban, hovered closet. To Nila.

"*Arre* Nila. She has blue eyes and pink cheeks," he said. "You are brown, like us."

"I'm not brown, you naughty boy." She pouted, and drew a line with the tip of her finger from the edge of his turban to the end of his nose. "You are."

His face turned dark red.

There was no sign of Colonel Bhatt. He'd left us at the canopied dais, and disappeared.

The afternoon was warm and smelled of dust and freshly

scythed grass. I held a glass of lukewarm lemonade. I looked around me with interest. On the dais English and Indians were fairly evenly represented. Although many of the Indians smiled at me, none of the English so much as glanced in my direction. Perhaps they were too well-bred to evince even the slightest curiosity about an English girl in a sari.

"May I bring you a fresh drink, Miss Manning?" said Colonel Bhatt, who suddenly appeared at my elbow. "The ice in your glass seems to be gone."

He returned with a frosty glass.

"What is the parade for?" I asked.

"It's a send-off for the British troops who will sail from Bombay next month." We stood slightly apart from Nila and the young officers. He wore dark glasses. In the brilliant sunshine his face was deeply shadowed by his visored cap. Only his white teeth and moustache stood out clearly. "I am not at all sorry to see them go, yet one has to admit their efficiency will be missed." He paused. "I'm sorry, I was thoughtless. They are your people."

"It's all right."

"Where will all this leave you?"

"I'm not sure I understand."

"What will your family do now? Will you be returning to England, too?"

I choked on lemonade. Tears sprang to my eyes. As if from respect for my unguarded state he removed his glasses. It was a simple gesture, unconscious even, but suddenly I was telling him all about Papa. He raised a hand and I thought he was going to pat my back, but he only turned me round and led me to the rear edge of the dais where below, under the trees, waiters in fanned turbans and red sashes were busy setting up long, white-clothed tea tables, rattling cutlery, rolling napkins into tall snowy crowns to place them on each crested regimental plate.

"I am quite sure your father has gone to England to find a

job, look for a place for all of you to live, and prepare for your arrival. I know your mother mentioned treatment, which is also possible, but one does not preclude the other."

I felt the stone in my chest dissolve. I laughed out loud. Of course. Why hadn't I thought of that? It was so logical and real. Papa had gone to England to prepare for us, and also to have treatment. "Thank you, thank you," I said.

He waited while I took a few calming sips from my second lukewarm lemonade, which tasted wonderful, and said, "Come. We must join the others."

The parade began: a dazzling procession of gaily caparisoned prancing horses, slow-footed swaying elephants, kettle drums, bagpipes, uniformed men marching in precision rows, heads turned stiffly in our direction, sun glinting off polished buttons. Brown men and white men marching side by side, saluting officers of both colors.

Afterwards we had tea. I sat between Nila and an elderly Indian captain who complained of dyspepsia. As I chewed the dry cucumber sandwiches with their stiff curling edges, he told me, "Cucumbers are very worst for digestion. Seeds collecting here and there in nooks and valleys in intestines . . ."

I nodded absently, as I recalled Mama and Aunt Margaret talking on the darkened front verandah that night in Madras when I first heard that Papa was leaving. "You can tell her the truth," Aunt Margaret had said. And Mama had cried, "I can't. Oh God, I simply can't." It all came back. The way I ran all the way down to the bazaar the next day to collapse at Pushpa's sweet shop. It all came back.

It was not at all the way that Colonel Bhatt had suggested. Nonetheless, I was grateful to him. I thought it couldn't possibly be true that he only liked men. Or, how could he be so kind to women?

In the car Nila suggested a drink at the club and her husband agreed. He said he had something to discuss with the steward and I wondered if it had to do with the chits he'd brought earlier to Nila's dressing room.

The Nerbudapur Club was an imposing, white stuccoed building with tall pillars, much grander than the Railway Officers' Club that Papa had belonged to in Madras.

"Come with me to the Ladies'," Nila said to me.

I waited while she entered a cubicle. Over the sound of her urination, she called, "You were quite a hit. People were telling how nice you look in a sari. It suits you."

I blushed with pleasure.

I heard the rush of water as she flushed the toilet. She came out straightening the folds of her sari. "Don't you need to use the loo?"

"Well, perhaps I should," I answered.

"I'll wait for you outside."

But the verandah was empty when I left the restroom. Off to the side of the building a tennis match was in progress. I heard the pock-pock, back-and-forth volley of the ball. A man's voice called, "Five love." Outside on the lawn, under soaring rain trees, people sat at small round tables sipping drinks.

I turned down a hallway. High on the whitewashed walls ancient heads of game animals were mounted on plaques: a black buck with lopsided antlers, a leopard with only one glass eye, a moth-eaten black panther. Below the heads hung a curious collection of hats: solar topees, straw boaters, bowlers, trilbys, even a silk top hat. Dusty things. To whom did they all belong? At the end of the hall I saw Nila speaking to a heavyset man in a grey suit. Something about that broad grey back looked familiar, and I suddenly realized that it was my uncle. Was he confiding more details of Letty?

As I approached he reached out and stroked her wrist with a fingertip. A swift little movement, intimate as a kiss. I stood quite still.

Nila saw me first.

"Just see," she exclaimed, "who is here. Doesn't your niece look beautiful?" I was certain that the high color on her cheekbones and forehead was not rouge.

He stared at me blankly, then his eyes lit with recognition and he smiled. "My dear young lady, how very fine you are looking. In a sari. You look like my Letty did long ago."

"Megan takes after her father," Nila said coldly.

Why did I have the impression that he was making a conscious effort not to look at her? "But what are you doing here?" he asked me, still wearing his amiable smile.

Nila answered. "She went with us to the parade. We stopped for a drink. Will you join us?"

"Thank you very much, but I must get back to my game. Bridge." He sidled away.

By now Colonel Bhatt had joined us. I was becoming used to his popping in and out of sight like the Cheshire cat. "Shall we have that drink now?"

"Actually, I have rather a headache." The color in Nila's face had faded and all at once she did look tired. "The glare, and those awful bagpipes. Do you mind, Megan?"

"No. Not at all." I stared at her smooth golden wrist and saw again a plump brown finger—a disembodied one this time—caressing it.

CHAPTER SEVEN

While Letty was always eager to talk about the days when she and Mama were growing up, I found she was markedly reticent about discussing the period following her marriage. I was haunted by what Nila had told me the day before about the way my uncle's female relatives had treated Letty.

Letty and I were having a mid-morning cup of tea on the front verandah among the arching fronds of large potted palms and trailing lacy ferns placed on stone pedestals. Small clay plots filled with flame-colored crotons lined the edges of the plinth. They had been freshly watered and the scent of damp earth was soothing after our morning visit to the servants' quarters and the usual fiddling about in the rose garden.

"Where did you live after you were married?" I asked, as I stirred sugar into my tea.

"With my husband's family."

"In this house?"

"No. We built this years later. The family house is in Nagpur."

Outside, deep within the broad thick-leafed foliage of an old teakwood tree with its bridal-bouquet plumes of white blossoms, a bird called: five notes in ascending scale, repeated over and over again.

"The brain-fever bird," Letty said, "announcing summer. The hot weather may come early. Last year it stayed cool well into March."

"What was it like living with them? Were they good to you?" I thought her lime green sari sallowed her skin. Why didn't she try to make herself more attractive? I wondered. Like Nila.

Letty took a sip of tea, replaced the cup in its saucer. "Of course. What a silly question! Now, you tell me about yesterday. Did you enjoy the parade?"

"Yes. I liked the elephants, though everyone that followed had to watch where they stepped."

"Did you meet people?"

"Lots."

"Good. Now maybe you'll go out and do things and not mope about so."

I fished out a tea leaf with the tip of my spoon. "Nila asked me to go to a moonlight picnic at Marble Rocks next Saturday."

"Did you accept?"

"Should I?"

Letty gave an exasperated sigh. "Oh Megan, for heaven's sake, do what you want. The rocks are beautiful by moonlight." She took another sip of tea, then looked at me quizzically. "Are you shy or something?"

"It's not that. It's . . ." An image flashed through my mind of a brown finger on a golden wrist. "Well, it's because I think you don't like her," I finished lamely.

"I don't *dis*like her. I find her bothersome. Fluttery as an insect. And with a brain to match."

"She says I look like Alice in Wonderland in my cotton frocks."

Letty snorted. "Well, for once, I agree with her. Your clothes are quite dreadful. What can Lavinia be thinking of? Dressing you as if you were ten."

"It's not Mama's fault," I said sharply. "I like these frocks. They are comfortable."

"But they don't fit. That one," she said, and pointed with an extended palm, "is tight across your chest and pulls at the shoulders. I'll send for the *derzi* this afternoon. He can make you some that fit at least."

I leaned forward to place my empty cup and saucer on the wicker table. Impulsively, I said, "Why don't we just go to his shop? It will be fun to walk in the bazaar."

A look of terror crossed her face. "Where's the need?" she said breathlessly. "He'll be happy enough to come here and sew for us on the back verandah."

I sank back in my chair. I didn't tell her about my seeing her husband at the club. I wondered if *he* had. Nor did I say anything about the sari I'd worn. Just as she'd not told me about the library, and I'd not mentioned having discovered the library. Deceptions. But why? Why did we not speak of these things? And the biggest deception of all: Mama not telling me the truth about Papa.

To my intense disappointment, and all because the schedule of the household had undergone a radical change, I was kept from my early mornings at the library. Instead of their usual habit of sleeping till almost ten, Letty and her husband now rose, bathed, performed the ritual *puja* to the gods in the god room and were at breakfast before the sun sailed free of the mango grove.

The change had been wrought by the presence of Letty's

mother-in-law, who let it be known that only fools and drunkards slept till all hours. She had arrived two days earlier along with her grandson, his sister and the girl's husband.

On the morning of their arrival I woke to an uproar outside my door.

"But this is the room I always occupy. I wish to stay in this room."

"I'm sorry, Mummyji, my niece is in there."

"She will understand. I will talk to her."

"The green wing is being prepared. The rooms are exactly the same. You see, we were not expecting you for another fortnight."

"Green is an inauspicious color. At our house every wall is white . . ."

I stumbled from the bed, opened the door, and stood there gaping at Letty in a magenta floor-length robe, her hair sticking up around her head, her eyes red-ringed and puffy with sleep. Beside her stood a small hunchbacked woman whose orange sari was tied to form pantaloons around her bony yellow shins. I stared at the woman's bare feet, almost square, with silver toe rings on each second toe. But it was to the bright eyes gleaming with malice that my own were eventually drawn.

"Your niece?" she asked. So this was Letty's mother-in-law. I thought of the bewildered young bride in the wedding portrait at the end of the hall, and saw neither a glimmer nor a shadow of her in this old lady. The transformation was awesome.

"Yes. My niece, Megan—"

"Niece Megan, I wish to stay in this room. It is all right?"

"Of course."

"Megan, please," Letty made an impatient sideways gesture at me, her eyes fixed on the old woman, "you are not moving from this room. Mummyji, tell me how can green be an

inauspicious color when it's one of the colors of the new flag?
Let us talk to the priest when he comes—"

"No need," the other cut in crisply. "He will tell only what
you want, since it is you who pay him. Oh yes, I am knowing
all about priests. No, simply it is when I am having indigestion," one tiny claw-like hand traced urgent little circles in the
air near her abdomen, "then green upsets me. Sometimes,
blue also upsets me. Like now," she squinted up into Letty's
face and turned away with a small moan, pressing a fist to her
middle, "even your blue eyes hurt me just here."

Letty tightened her mouth.

Then I remembered that the library was located just off the
green wing that Letty had once said was now only used for
storage. "Aunt Letty," I pleaded. "I don't mind. Please let
me."

Letty turned on me, her face shiny and fierce, "Who asked
you? Put your clothes on."

I shut the door and slid to the floor behind it, tears of rage
stinging my eyes.

But I couldn't shut out the discussion.

"We have medicines for indigestion—"

"Oh no! Please do not concern yourself. I will go quietly to
the green room if that is your wish. I can cover my eyes with
a piece of cloth. Somehow I will manage." A pause. "Ah, and
what about Prethima and Vijay? Prethima must have a feather
mattress for abdominal trouble."

"A feather mattress?"

"Yes. She must turn on her belly after . . . afterwards . . .
on the feather mattress and speak Shiva's name, so she may
conceive. It is six months now."

"She needs a thorough examination, not a feather
mattress."

"Yes. That is what I am saying, too, and why we have
come."

Their voices grew fainter as they left the hall.

"And what about Ashok . . . ?"

I heard the rattle of pots and pans and Maharaj shouting to his helpers with a zeal I'd not heard before, to fetch this, that, and the other, and I wondered with a sinking heart how long it would be before I could seek refuge, again, in Letty's library.

At breakfast I met Prethima and Vijay, who were married, and Ashok. They were Veena's children, Veena being the youngest sister of Letty's husband. All three sat across the table from me and ate *puri,* the fried puffed bread I would have preferred to the dreary boiled eggs on toast we ate each morning. After the initial introductions, no one spoke.

Letty and her husband, stupid with sleep, sat at their usual places at either end of the table, he breaking the silence now and then with gargantuan roaring yawns that seemed to trigger a similar, though more genteel, response in Letty, who smothered hers in her serviette. The mother-in-law was absent, and I wondered briefly if she were lying down fighting nausea, her eyes bandaged against the green walls of her room.

I tried not to stare at Prethima. She sat almost without movement, her right hand with its henna-stained nails and palm resting on the edge of her plate. Occasionally, she pinched off a piece of *puri* and lifted it furtively to her lips. Her sari of the palest pink gossamer was draped over her head, its narrow gold border just brushing the arched brows, imparting a rosy glow to her mouth and small pointed chin, on the side of which was a tiny black mole. But what struck me more than the delicacy of her features, was that here, sitting before me, was the embodiment of the young bride—or, rather, her grandmother as a young bride—in the picture that hung in the hall outside my room. I was certain that her eyes, when she lifted the straight black lashes, would be wide with bewilderment.

I guessed at her age; three or four years older than the bride in the picture, which would make her about seventeen, maybe eighteen. Inexplicably, my hand began to tremble and I dropped my fork. It bounced on my plate, then slid to the floor. Everyone stared—Letty's eyes were expressionless—everyone, that is, but Prethima. Her doll-like composure was eerie.

To cover my confusion, I said, too loudly, "Uncle, isn't your mother having any breakfast?"

He gave another agonized yawn before he answered, "Young lady, she will take her meals in her room."

"But why?" Surely it was carrying things a bit too far to expect her to eat blindfolded, as well.

Letty said with a rush, "Prethima, dear. Mummyji tells me you're trying to conceive—"

There was a resounding thump at the other end of the table. Then another as Letty's husband slapped the table again. China and silver danced. "Silence," he bellowed. "How dare you speak to her of such things in the presence of men?"

After the initial shock at such uncharacteristic behavior, I wanted to leap to Letty's defense, to shriek: How dare you speak to my aunt that way in the presence of nieces and nephews. I turned to Letty and reached out a hand to her. She didn't take it. Maybe she didn't see it. She sat head bowed, hands in her lap, demure as Prethima.

"Megan," Letty said, later that afternoon, "If you have any questions, ask me. Privately. That entire incident at breakfast could have been avoided, but for your questions."

Furious, I said, "Oh? How?" It was so like her to blame me.

I glared at her in her horrid sari of red and green shot silk; each crimped hair of her head seemed glued in place.

We were sitting on my carelessly made bed. Earlier, seething after Letty had said I could not move to the green wing, I had simply yanked the counterpane over the rumpled sheets. From outside came the squeak and rattle of the lawn being rolled. The brain-fever bird called relentlessly.

"I'm sorry. It was not your fault." Letty took my hand in both of hers. "The reason Mummyji doesn't eat with us is because it's against her beliefs. It's something like eating meat on Fridays being a mortal sin for Catholics."

I resented the comparison.

"Do you see?"

"No."

"Well, let me put it this way. She is very high caste, and the reason she doesn't eat at the table is because you are not caste. She would become unclean and have to go through all kinds of complicated purifying rituals—"

"You mean, I'm untouchable, don't you?" I said, pulling my hand free. "Like the beggars on the street."

"Oh now, let's not be melodramatic. You are obviously not a beggar on the street. She can speak with you, she just can't eat with you." Letty sighed and reached for my hand again, but I withheld it. She clasped hers; one hand kneading the other's fingers till the knuckles whitened. "It was far worse when I came into the family. Then, no one ate with me. I ate alone on the verandah, attended by a servant girl. Now Uncle eats with you, his nephews and niece share the table with you." Her blue eyes dreamy, she looked into the distance. "I am hopeful that in the new India all this caste rot will fall by the wayside.

"Try to understand," she went on. "I thought you would keep on asking questions about why she ate in her room, and I was so afraid you might get an answer that would hurt your feelings. So I made a stupid blunder."

"He was rude to you," I raged, leaping up to pace the stone slab floor. "And in front of everyone. Couldn't he have talked to you in private, at least? Later?"

"No. It had to be done in front of them to stress his authority in the family. He is the oldest son. Oh, Megan. You have to look at it their way, too. He was supposed to marry a Brahmin girl and have children, especially a son to carry on the line and to pray for his soul to cross the river into the next life."

To cross the river into the next life. How beautiful, I thought. So unlike heaven and hell and purgatory. Just . . . crossing a river.

"As it turned out, we couldn't have children. Ha." The sound burst from her. "Perhaps I should have flopped about on a feather mattress. Christ! Megan, can you find the whiskey and bring it here without anyone catching you? It's naughty of me to ask you to do this."

"It's all right. I think I can manage it."

"Look at my hands shake." She held them out. Small square hands, with lightly ruched skin on their backs, the right trembling more than the left. "It always happens. It always happens when she comes. The old barracuda. All that stuff and nonsense about green rooms and blue eyes."

I encountered no one on the way to the liquor cabinet in the front room, but as a precaution for my return I stuffed the bottle under my frock. It was true, as Letty had said, my clothes were too tight. The bottle's shape was unmistakable, straining against the thin cotton fabric. Picking up a cushion, I held it against me.

Her bare feet making no sound, Letty's mother-in-law came up behind me and said, "Ah, it is you, niece Megan."

I sat heavily in the nearest chair.

"You are having a stomach ache?" she asked, staring at me

67

as I hugged the cushion encrusted with mirrored embroidery.

"Just a little one." Then, remembering, "Is your indigestion better?"

In her orange sari, her white hair drawn back into a tight bun, she sat cross-legged opposite me on an armchair upholstered in raw silk. At first she seemed puzzled at my question. Then her eyes sparkled with mischief. "Yes yes." She wagged her head sideways in the Indian way. "Now I am quite all right. Where is your aunt? She is not in her room. I looked."

"Well, I'm afraid I don't know." How long would she continue to sit here? I wondered. I hoped Letty was not in too much of a stew.

"You should lie down."

"Actually, it feels better if I sit and press a cushion to me. That's what my mother always told me to do." I was grateful that, at least, the last part was true.

"Is she also a doctor?"

"No. She was a teacher. A Montessori teacher. She taught me the alphabet and to count when I was four."

"What good is learning to a woman?" She lifted her hands shoulder high, palms upward. "I myself cannot read. A man, yes, but a woman needs only to know how to be a good wife and to teach her children to honor the gods. Nothing more."

She continued to peer at me intently, so intently that I began to worry lest she suspect the real reason for the cushion. Was the bottle neck poking up over the top edge of the cushion? I was afraid to look.

"Is it your time of month?" she said at last.

"Yes," I said, frantically clutching at the excuse she'd provided.

"I knew!" she said like a triumphant little buddha. "That look I can always tell." She became chatty. "Prethima also suffers the same way. Once you bear a child it will become better. When I was a girl, I would roll about the floor crying from the pain. Terrible." She sighed and shook her head. "Has anyone come for your hand?"

"My hand?"

"That is what you people say, is it not? Hand in marriage, like that?"

I thought of someone asking for my hand. Which one? I'd ask in return. Right or left? Speak up or forever hold your peace. I smiled.

She smiled, too, her face crimping like a drawn curtain. The effect was startling, almost uplifting.

"Yes. There is an expression like that," I replied. "A funny one, come to think of it. No one has asked to marry me yet."

"But you are seventeen already." Again the upraised palms. "Or so your aunt tells me. In three years you will be too old. Then it will be very difficult to find a good husband. I myself was married at fifteen. There were so many that came to ask my father. Some said, 'No need for dowry. We want only your daughter.' In the end I married my own cousin. A good man, but dull. See how I am telling you all this."

"So, there you are. Both of you," Letty said, entering the room. I could tell, after she'd flicked a glance at the cushion, that she'd taken in my predicament. She looked distraught.

"Why have you not given this poor girl some medicine," her mother-in-law demanded. "She is having severe menstrual pain."

"I'll get her something now," Letty said quickly. "Mummyji, come with me to the dining room for a cup of tea."

"How can you say take tea? You know very well tea gives me indigestion."

Days had passed, and I had put off removing the picture of the many-armed god facing my bed. At first, I had not wanted to offend Letty. After all, it was her house and her picture; I was only a guest. Once I had taken it down, but the wall seemed so cold and bare that I hung it back up again.

Now, in bed, I thought of the phrase Letty had used earlier: *To cross the river into the next life*. It lingered like a persistent song. Unable to sleep, I turned on the light and sat up, hugging my knees. I gazed at Shiva's picture on the opposite wall: the precision of the body balanced on one leg, the hair flying in a fan behind the head, the face with its long eyes and thin smile, the fluid grace of the arms—all four of them—and I decided it was no stranger, really, than the Sacred Heart at home.

CHAPTER EIGHT

The young people grew friendlier. Munnar came by frequently to see his cousins. Soon the house was full of joking
and teasing laughter. Everyone was relaxed—everyone, that
is, except Letty. This did not mean that she was not unfailingly
charming and witty with her guests, but by mid-afternoon I
would notice the almost imperceptible tremor in her hands
that I might have missed had she not herself pointed it out to
me that afternoon in my room on the day her in-laws arrived.
And knowing this, I sensed other signs of strain: the way she
held her head, the tension of mouth and jaw, the deepening of
the furrow between the brows. Then she would excuse herself
and withdraw to her room for about fifteen minutes. When
she emerged she would be smiling again, her hands perfectly
steady.

No longer demure, Prethima was gay and talkative. She
covered her head only in my uncle's presence. Full of admiration for Letty, she gushed, "Aunty is so brave to marry
outside her community, and so modern. Not like my mother,

who doesn't speak English; she understands it all right, but is afraid to speak it."

"Your grandmother speaks it very well."

She gave a short laugh. "My grandmother can do anything. She is a very determined lady. Nobody goes against my grandmother, not even my grandfather. Is your mother like Aunty?"

"No. I suppose she's not very modern either."

We sat on a stone bench in the rose garden in the dappled shade of a *gul mohur* tree. The morning was warm with a slight breeze that cooled the skin and carried with it the scent of roses. In a floral chiffon sari, Prethima was sketching on a large pad, head bent to her task. Her black hair was drawn smoothly behind her ears and fastened in a bun at her nape.

She turned to me, her expression arch. "Ashok thinks you are pretty."

Astonished, I felt my cheeks flare.

She put down her pencil and gazed into my face. "How do you do that?"

"What?"

"Make your face go red like that?"

"I don't know. It just happens."

"I think you have a pretty face, only you are a little too tall." She gestured upward with the pencil held vertical.

At first I thought she was working on a border design of roses, but it turned out to be an intricate frieze of men and women tangled together, with dreamy rapturous smiles and long slitted eyes.

"Who are they?" I asked, peering over her shoulder.

"Some godlings and their consorts," she replied. "There is a border like this in the Konarak temple."

"Are they making love?"

"Oh yes. But in a holy way."

"Why are they standing up?"

"These are some positions from the *Kama Sutra.*"

"It looks uncomfortable."

Prethima smiled mysteriously. "When you are married you will learn about such things." She touched the marriage chain of black and gold beads around her neck.

Will I? I wondered. Had my parents done such things? Letty and my uncle? *Nila* and my uncle? I doubted that he could maintain his balance on one leg, though I could see Nila's lissome legs twined around his bulk like bineweeds around the banyan tree outside my library.

"Had you met your husband before you were married?" I asked. Now, with swift little strokes of her pencil, she was shading a cushiony rump.

"I saw him, but we did not speak." She sketched a rounded thigh, then smudged the outline with a henna-stained fingertip.

"Weren't you . . . wasn't it awkward for you on your wedding night?"

She looked at me with her wide dark eyes. "Oh my, I was so very frightened, but . . . Vijay was . . . very kind." She smiled again, smug in her happiness. Then she sighed and bit on the end of her pencil. "If only I could give him a son."

"What did the doctors say, Prethima?" To me the idea of marriage, coupling in strange positions, wanting a child, was like grappling with the concept of eternity.

"That my womb is tipped. They said a lot of big words that I could not understand. Vijay and I wish to make a pilgrimage to the temple in Mahabalipuram, which is near your home in Madras, to pray before the Shiva *lingam.*"

I laced my hands around my knees. "I don't think I could do things with a boy I didn't know. With us the tradition is for the boy and girl to meet, fall in love, then marry."

"But not with us," she said firmly, closing her sketch pad. "We fall in love only after marriage. It is the best way. Our parents arrange the match after the astrologers and the priests have been consulted. What do I know about picking a husband? Of course, people do fall in love before, like Uncle and Aunty, and there was a girl in my school who fell in love with a Moslem. But they drowned themselves in a river, tied together with her sari."

The *derzi* arrived, bearing bolts of cloth and an old sewing machine, and was installed on a mat on the back verandah. By now, feeling set apart and conspicuous in my cotton frocks, I allowed Letty and Prethima to coax me into adopting Punjabi dress, which consisted of long loose trousers gathered at the ankles, a knee-length tunic, and a long filmy scarf that draped across the shoulders and breasts and floated down the back. It was graceful and comfortable and, unlike the sari, I found it easy to move in. Over Letty's objections I turned away from the peacock blues and magentas and chose, instead, aqua and lilac and grey. "Such dull colors," she complained. But I stood firm. Nila will approve, I thought.

And she did. "You look like a Kashmiri girl," she exclaimed, when I saw her again at the picnic to which Prethima and the others were invited as well. I was helping her to set out, on the pillared verandah of the guest house, platters of fragrant *pulao* and steaming cauldrons of curry. Candles sputtered on the table that had been placed against one wall. Apologizing for the lack of electricity, the watchman lit several kerosene lanterns that then cast swaying pointed shadows across the walls and ceiling.

"Did you tell your aunt about the parade?" Nila asked, as she arranged silver-foiled sweets on a tray. I watched light flicker across her lovely face.

"Oh yes," I said as I unwrapped cheese sandwiches. "I told her about the elephants and horses. I enjoyed it all very much. Thank you for inviting me."

"Our pleasure." She turned from me and stretched across the table to move a plate of sliced tomatoes an inch or so to the right, then moved the plate back again. I saw a wide expanse of bare midriff. "And," she said in a tight voice, "did you also tell her about going to the club?"

"Actually," I said, after a fractional pause, "I forgot to mention that." It was true I hadn't mentioned it, but not because I'd forgotten.

She nodded. "That day your uncle was telling me about his recent trip to Delhi where they are setting up the new government. He is representing our district. He is an important man—No, Rupa," she said to one of the other women, "put the *chappatis* here. They should be next to the potato *bhaji*."

Colonel Bhatt, it seemed, was away in Kashmir where the border disputes with Pakistan still continued.

Prethima and Vijay sat primly off by themselves on a bench under a large tamarind tree; her sari and his shirt glimmered in the darkness. I went to sit beside Prethima. "Isn't Nila beautiful?" I said to her.

"Yes, but she is too free with the men," Prethima replied, and covered her head with the edge of her sari.

There was the usual group of young officers paying court to Nila, the handsome Sikh very much in evidence. She kept them busy running errands: fetch this and carry that. Most of the women were shy and huddled together like roosting birds. One of the young officers attached himself to me. Someone had brought along a gramophone; we jitterbugged to "In the Mood," my grey chiffon scarf fluttering like a flag. He was a fine dancer and I enjoyed it.

Ashok and Munnar watched us awhile, then Munnar said something to Ashok and they turned away laughing. Later they told me that my partner had terrible halitosis and they wondered how I was able to tolerate being so close.

After dinner we walked to the river under an oval, waning

75

moon and then rode barges down to the rocks that rose immediately ahead—lofty and luminous in the moonlight—on both sides of the water. As if by tacit consent, no one spoke, the silence being broken only by the splash of oars. I had the sense that the glistening cliffs were gliding by silently like time and that it was the boat that was still. One of the boatmen began to sing; the others joined in. It was a chant more than a song, in a minor key, plaintive. It broke the spell.

Across from me, Nila sat beside the young Sikh, her body angled to his, her back brushing his sleeve. He yearned above her although he sat very stiffly; only the tense angle of his head tilted above hers betrayed his longing. She lifted her hair with both hands; her rounded arms and softly curved throat gleamed alabaster in the moonlight. As she let her hair fall back on her shoulders, one strand drifted across his mouth. He closed his eyes; I averted mine. Beside me the young officer I'd danced with cleared his throat. "Why don't you come with Nila to the tea dances?" he said. I sniffed the air for lingering traces of bad breath, found none, and, irrationally, was furious at Ashok and Munnar for suggesting the poor man had halitosis. My answer was brief.

It was close to midnight when we boarded the army lorries for the trip back. We sang "As Time Goes By" and "Amapola," Girl Guide rounds. Nila's young Sikh sang a soulful Hindi film song. I was thankful for the darkness; I didn't want to see his face.

I was surprised to find Letty in my room, sitting on the bed, head bent, rocking back and forth. A rosary was twisted around her clasped hands. I thought at first she was in a kind of religious trance like some wandering, ash-smeared *sadhu*. When she raised her eyes to mine I saw they were glassy; then I caught the woody odor of whiskey and realized she was drunk.

"Oh Megan, she says it's my fault our baby was born dead, that it's retribution for sins I committed in a previous life . . . You didn't know that we'd had a baby, did you? He was born dead at seven months. His penis was so tiny, so delicate. Like a new bud. Tell Pa. Please tell Pa."

I made her lie down and covered her with the counterpane. She clung to my hand. I looked down at the small square hand in mine, at the closed eyes, at the slightly parted lips through which she breathed noisily.

"It's not your fault, Aunt Letty, no matter what she says."

"I know. It's not just that. I'm used to her attacks." She drew a deep shuddering breath and released it. "Megan, what am I going to do? He rang to say he won't be home tonight." Tears slid into her hair and ears. Sobbing, she said, "I keep thinking of the time we first met. I wish I could tell you what it was like. His smile. Have you noticed it, Megan? That enchanting little space between his teeth?"

"Yes Aunty Letty," I whispered, stroking her hand. She grew calmer.

"The first time I saw that smile, it was like stepping into a patch of sunshine . . . He loved me. *He loved me.*"

I was terrified of her, for her. What if she died? Did drunk people ever die? I tried to rise to get a flannel from the bathroom to wipe her face, but she wouldn't release my hand. Our joined palms grew clammy. I thought suddenly of Grandpa. He'd clung to my hand too, as he died. Was Letty going to die? And I thought of her dead baby. I lay my head on her chest and heard the beat of her heart. Or was it my own heart pounding in my ears?

Her bracelets jangled as she flung an arm across her eyes. "Oh I'm so sick of this place," she said, and abruptly fell asleep.

Where was my uncle? Was he with Nila? Colonel Bhatt was away, she'd said. I watched my aunt sleep. Despite the tear tracks she smiled faintly, and I was reminded of the holy

77

pictures in my missal. Letty's face had the same eerie beauty of a martyred saint whose ecstasy derived from pain. I sat beside her for a long time until her grip on my hand relaxed, then I climbed into bed and curled up against her. In the morning she was gone.

Letty's husband was not present at breakfast the next day, nor at lunch, but at half past six in the evening his car skidded to a halt under the portico. Hearing the noise, I looked out my bedroom window and saw him alight and, gesticulating, order the chauffeur to shut the heavy wrought-iron gates at the end of the drive.

He hurried up the steps and disappeared into the front room. I could hear him shouting, "Letty, Letty," and I raced across the hallway. Letty came running, and so did the others. We converged in the dining room.

"Gandhiji is dead. He's been shot."

"Who did it?" his mother demanded. "A Muslim?"

He shook his head. "I do not know. The trunk call came through to the office only a few minutes ago. I have ordered the gates locked. We must stay in the house. There may be riots."

Letty's face was very pale. "A terrible thing," she said quietly.

I was not sure whether she referred to the day's tragedy, or to her ordeal of the previous night.

There was no violence. The assassin was a Hindu.

That night Nehru spoke on All India Radio: "The light has gone out of our lives and there is darkness everywhere . . . Our beloved leader, Bapu . . . is no more. The light has gone out, I said, and yet I was wrong. For the light that shone in this country was no ordinary light . . . In a thousand years that light will still be seen . . ."

All next day we sat and listened to the wireless. The commentator in Delhi described the crowds that came to pay their final respects to their Mahatma: throngs that jammed the route of the funeral procession, clinging to lampposts, tree-tops, rooftops, for a glimpse of the man who had defied the English and led their country to freedom.

We left the room only to eat and returned to it immediately after, huddling together, joined in grief, and joined too with the masses that mourned the slaying of such a man.

That day, for the first time in my life, as I listened to the crowds' wails coming from the wireless, I felt that I, too, was an Indian.

CHAPTER NINE

One evening as the three young people and I played cards at the oval dining table under the ornate chandelier of silver and cut glass, Munnar arrived with a friend. His name was Ajai Pande and he was slim and tall, though not as tall as Munnar, with wavy dark hair and olive skin. He had a narrow arched nose, high cheekbones, and he wore the traditional loose cotton *pyjama* and long-sleeved muslin *kurta*. He smiled, and I felt the strangest sensation, an inner lurch almost like fear. When he caught my eye I looked away in confusion, feeling again the flutter in my throat, my thighs.

"Ajai is General Secretary of the Students' Union," Munnar announced, as he slouched into the armchair my uncle always occupied at the head of the table. "He is studying law at Nerbudapur College, which is quite near to my college. We have been discussing the suspension of Supplementary Exams. Without them, how can we make up grade deficits?"

"Study harder," Ashok said, as he shuffled the cards in a showy way. "Then your problem will be solved."

Irate, Munnar shot a hand in the air. *"Yar!* What are you talking? You are studying only History. I have to learn about vibrations. All the maths and theories."

Ashok sniggered. "Vibrations? Like this?" He half-rose from his chair, wagging his narrow bottom. "Man, History is not only facts and dates. It shapes the future."

"It's not just a question of deficit grades," Ajai said. He sat opposite me, arms folded on the table. "But when a classmate missed the final exam because of illness, the professor refused to believe him even though he brought a letter from the doctor. They are making him repeat the course."

"How unfair!" My voice sounded shrill.

"Right, it's not fair, but we are still negotiating." His eyes were a clear brown, their lashes long and curved. He smiled at me, the smile widening as he studied my face.

I felt bathed in radiance, sparkling shots of light . . . Surely not! How could it happen so suddenly, so absurdly? One minute I was arguing with Ashok about a palmed card, the very next I was behaving like some languishing lunatic from one of Aunt Margaret's romance novels. Was this what Letty had felt when she first met my uncle? That night in my room she'd told me it was like stepping into a patch of sunshine. Dazed, I breathed in and out slowly, counting each breath.

Munnar shouted, "We should strike!"

"Strike what?" Letty entered the room dressed in a salmon pink sari; she seemed calm, fully in control. "Ajai! How nice to see you. Are your parents well?"

"Yes, Aunty, thank you. They are well." He waited till she was seated, then sat down again. I knew that he addressed her as Aunty only as a sign of respect, and not because they were related.

For Letty's benefit, Munnar launched into a tirade against the injustices of college administrations. She listened sympathetically enough, but offered no comment. Sunbeams slanting in the open french doors reflected off the glass cabinets and filled the room with splendor.

Ajai said, "Actually, we came to ask if anyone wanted to go to the temple festival."

"Oh, yes," Prethima said; bouncing in her chair, her small heart-shaped face glowing with excitement. Vijay smiled at her indulgently. He was a quiet man who spoke only when addressed, and he looked at Prethima the way Letty looked at my uncle.

"What a good idea," Letty said.

I glanced quickly at her. "Will you go too?"

She laughed. "You'll be cramped enough as it is with the six of you. I'd have to ride on the car roof or the bonnet."

"I won't leave you."

"Go."

"I'll stay with you, Aunty," Ashok offered grandly.

"What nonsense! Go, all of you, and have a jolly time."

Ajai's car, a black Austin, was rusted and had dented fenders crudely hammered out; the tailpipe rattled. Munnar rode in the bucket-seat next to Ajai. I sat in the back wedged between Ashok and Vijay, who held Prethima on his lap. Half-listening to the banter of the others, I pondered the business of physical attraction. *That's* what it was, I thought— not love, only physical attraction. It was an ailment like a sprained ankle, perhaps, or a stiff neck, something to be endured until it got better.

The evening was still. The setting sun trailed purple and mauve banners across the sky. We had to climb a hundred and fifty stone steps to reach the temple at the top. Crowds streamed past us, all moving upwards: women wearing bright saris and flowers in their hair, fathers carrying small children, old couples helping each other up the steep stairs worn smooth by countless bare feet and by the passage of time. Lamp smoke hung in the air, which was already dense with sandalwood, musk and sweat.

I stumbled and felt my arm grasped firmly, steadying me. "Take my hand," Ajai said, "or you'll be swept away in the crowd."

And so we made our ascent, stopping three times so I could catch my breath. We found the others waiting at the top by the stone *ruth* upon which the roly-poly figure of dancing Ganesh—the elephant-god sun of Shiva and Parvati—was all but buried under garlands of marigolds.

"I got here first," Ashok boasted.

"Only because you did not stop to help your sister," Munnar accused.

"She is strictly Vijay's responsibility now. Else why did we marry her off? And at such great cost."

Prethima was panting and holding her side. *"Abba!* Must surely be a thousand steps."

Ajai still held my hand. I felt secure and safe like the times in Bellary when Papa and I went hiking. But, more than that, I felt currents of pleasure, almost painful, from that quite ordinary contact of two joined hands.

It was cooler up here. People strolled about buying fruit and sweets and small clay figures of Ganesh from stalls lit with oil and gas lamps. In the main pavilion of the temple, bared-to-the-waist priests chanted, prayed and clinked small brass finger cymbals while feeding the sacred fire with grain and *ghee.* The dancing flames lent subtle movement to carvings that adorned pillars and shadowy walls: narrow-waisted stone goddesses moved sinuous hips, granite lips flickered with secret smiles. The thought struck me that these gods were human, our God was not. It was the first time I'd entered a place of worship that was not a Catholic church, and I wondered briefly if I were committing a mortal sin. We placed our offerings of fruit, flowers and money among all the other offerings, on the carpet that was spread before the fire.

Later, during our descent, Ashok said to me, "You should not hold the hand of a strange fellow."

"But he's no stranger. He's Munnar's friend and Aunt Letty knows his family."

"Indian girls do not hold hands with men in public."

"Really!"

On the way home, jammed against Ashok with Prethima's sandal scraping my ankle on the other side, I thought about romantic love and how it had brought only anguish to Letty. My parents too had failed in their pursuit of it, as had Nila and her husband. Aunt Margaret did not seem to have known it at all. As for Prethima and Vijay, who knew what the future held for them?

Then I looked at the back of Ajai's head, how the black hair curled just above the collarless neckline of his white *kurta*. I remembered the feel of his palm against mine, his fingers curled protectively around my hand, and I was awash again in sweet misery.

Three days later, Letty's mother-in-law announced it was time to go home. Prethima's eyes filled with tears as she hugged me. "Please come to see me in Nagpur," she begged. I said that I would try. Vijay stood awkwardly beside her. Ashok was glum. Only their grandmother was in fine form.

"Next time I come, please paint those rooms white," she told Letty who stood by stiffly. "Make sure my son does not eat any eggs, and no onions." She indicated that I could ceremoniously touch her feet, and I realized it was a tremendous concession on her part.

"You are a good girl, niece Megan," she said, and touched the top of my head as I bent down, blessing me.

I was sorry to see them go. I would miss them, although now I could return to my library.

*　　*　　*

For a while, burdened with her despair and my compassion, I was self-conscious with Letty, although I tried hard not to show it. It seemed to me that in some way she was unaware of what had taken place that night in my room, of the things she had told me. Yet waking in my bed the following morning must have caused her some wonder. If so, she said nothing, asked nothing.

Why did she stay with him? I asked myself. The answer came to me instantly: she loved him. She would bear anything to be near him. She was sustained by his presence. I thought of all this in my library. I thought of Ajai too, whom I had not seen again. For the moment the books, the room and the aqueous light filled me with peace.

One morning as I sat in the stained armchair writing a letter to Mama, the door opened and my uncle walked in. He was wearing a sleeveless undershirt and a *lungi* tied at his waist.

"Oh, it is you, young lady." He looked stunned, as I was.

I leaped to my feet scattering letter paper and fountain pen. "I am writing a letter to my mother," I said loudly, as though that explained my presence in the room.

He recovered first. "I thought you were my Letty," he said, rubbing his eyes with forefinger and thumb, "only . . . the Letty of long ago . . . Please do not disturb yourself. I am just looking for a book. A poetry book."

"By whom? Perhaps I can help you find it."

"Sarojini Naidu. *The Sceptre and the Flute,* or something like that."

"*The Sceptred Flute.* It's over here." I took the book from its shelf and handed it to him. "Do you like poetry?"

He laughed and shook his head. "No, no. A friend asked to borrow it. Thank you. You have saved me much time. I would not have known where it was." He looked at me, head cocked, the book tucked in an armpit. "Do you like to read?"

"Yes."

He sighed. "There was a time when my Letty did too. I built this for her." He glanced around the room. "She specified that it had to be separated from the house." Then he caught sight of the stained chair and stared at it, transfixed. "That was supposed to be thrown away," he muttered fiercely.

"It's a comfortable chair," I said, but I don't think he heard me.

I said more loudly, "Is it all right if I come here sometimes?"

It was as if I had dragged him back from some distant place. "Why not?" he said, stripped of his customary affability. "Someone may as well use it."

He left.

I retrieved my letter and fountain pen from the floor where they had fallen, but did not return to the chair. I sat on the window seat instead.

The next morning the chair was gone, as was the oriental carpet, and in their place were two wicker armchairs and a square of reed matting decorated with a border design of elephants. The room had been cleaned, obviously at my uncle's instructions; the windows gleamed. I did not miss the heavy chair and carpet. The simple new furnishings shimmered in fresh light.

I was touched.

Now the room was incontrovertibly mine. There was nothing of Letty's remaining in it except for the books, which she no longer cared about, and the library stairs. But what good were library stairs without a library?

Four days later, my uncle returned with the book. He was wearing a plaid dressing gown with *chappals* on his feet. He seemed pleased at the transformation of the room and pleased, too, at my obvious delight. I thanked him profusely.

"There is no need for thanks. The room has been vacant for too long," he said.

"Did your friend like the book?"

"Yes. She is a poet." He looked at me. "Are you happy here?"

"I'm getting used to it. I've never been away from home before."

"It must be dull for you, a young girl. Letty never goes anywhere."

"Why is that?" The question simply popped out.

He looked at me and away, ran his hands through his hair, cleared his throat. "Well . . . she is a depressed personality . . . How can I explain all this to you?" He cleared his throat again. "It has been terribly difficult for her. After our child was stillborn, she was very sad. We left my parents' house in Nagpur and came to live here. We built this house, our practices were flourishing, but she could not conceive again. She stopped working, stopped going out and began to drink too much. Too much." He darted a glance at me. "You may have noticed."

I didn't answer.

"Then her father died—your grandfather. First came the telegram. Then a letter from your mother—" He stopped suddenly and turned to look out the window, hands clasped behind his broad, plaid-covered back. Presently he added, "Ah, she tried so hard to be the perfect Hindu wife to show my mother and sisters, but one cannot be that without children, you see. Then—" He stopped again.

I waited, but he remained silent.

"I must be getting back," he said, at last. "Before she wakes up." He turned to face me. "I am happy you are pleased with the room." He glanced at where the old chair had stood and I caught the glint of something like fear in his eyes.

"By the way," he said, "if you get lonely, go and see Mrs. Bhatt. I saw her at the club recently and she said that she has not seen you for some time."

"Yes, I will," I promised before he left.

CHAPTER TEN

The brain-fever bird had predicted accurately, singing its monotonous song day after day from the teakwood tree: the hot weather arrived before February ended. Early in the morning, servants went around the house shutting windows to barricade against the intense heat of day. They would open them again only after sunset. Red dust seeped around the closed windows and collected in small rusty mounds on the sills. At night we slept outdoors in the courtyard, on cots strung with rope.

Although Madras had been just as hot, there was generally an ocean breeze at night. But here in the plains, far from either coast, the scorching heat of Nerbudapur was unrelieved. Letty and I now went to the servants' quarters only at dusk. This evening, the visit completed, we were walking back across the field when, from the mosque in the marketplace, the *muezzin's* call, faint and plaintive, floated over the pinkish heat-haze.

"Why haven't you gone to see Nila?" Letty demanded, as

she swung the empty basket in which we had carried the usual assortment of leftovers, fruit and clothing.

"I haven't felt like it."

"She's no great shakes, I know, but she's better than nothing. You're starting to mope again, aren't you?"

"I don't mope," I said irritably, and kicked at a pebble.

"You certainly do, with a face long as a foot rule, making everyone else miserable, too."

Who was there besides her?

"It was such fun for you when Prethima and the boys were here. Why don't you go to Nagpur for a visit? Prethima invited you."

"I don't *want* to go to Nagpur. I want to stay here. Don't worry about me."

"Well, I do worry," Letty said, taking a hanky from her sleeve to dab at her forehead and upper lip. "I wonder why Munnar hasn't stopped in. He promised me he would, and bring Ajai with him."

I wondered too—but not about Munnar. It was almost two weeks since the temple festival. I felt peevish most of the time. Must be the heat, I thought.

I said in a sour voice, "Maybe they're busy with their stupid strike."

They turned up the next day in time for tea, which we had in the front room. Letty and Munnar sat on the raw-silk sofa among the colorful, richly embroidered cushions. She was effusive.

"My dear boys," she said, "I'm so delighted to see you. Tell me all about your plotting and sedition."

"No sedition, Aunty," Ajai said. We sat beside each other in chairs that matched the sofa. "Only a march, a peaceful march of all the colleges to the Vice-Chancellor's building. If they see our numbers maybe they'll be willing to talk to us."

"Talk! Only talk," Munnar said, and bit into a crumbly bun. "We should strike!" Crumbs flew from his mouth.

"Munnar, what a hothead you are," Letty said.

"Aunty, you know who is behind all this business?" Munnar said. "The Vice-Chancellor's wife. She is a bossy Bengali lady. Her husband is like this. A grass in the breeze." He swayed a long forefinger in the air.

Ajai turned to me. "How are you?" he asked. His eyes were warm and startlingly bright.

"Quite well." I did not smile. Why had he stayed away so long? With him in the room the excitement leaped again inside me, but I also felt a completeness I'd never experienced before. He could not withhold that from me, I thought resentfully. Yet, I reminded myself, I had no claim on him.

"Megan, why so glum?" Letty called gaily from across the tea cart with its plump, flowered teacosy nesting over the pot.

Munnar stared at me then. "She is looking pale. Heat is very bad this year."

"I think she misses Prethima and the boys," Letty said, "but she refuses to go to Nagpur."

"She'll be hot in Nagpur, too. It is just like here. You should take her to the hills."

They were discussing me as if I were a cushion! I was about to say something rude when Letty said, "I think we should all go to the club. Right now, before I change my mind."

"*Wah,* Aunty! The Nerbudapur Club? But we are not wearing coat and tie."

"Doesn't matter. This is not British India. Native dress is quite appropriate." Her face was pink, her eyes shone as she looked at me. "Would you like that, Megan?" she asked softly.

I thought my heart would burst. She would do this for me? Leave the house for my sake? I could not speak. Perhaps some of this emotion showed in my face. She looked away as if embarrassed by what she saw, but I noticed the half-smile of pleasure.

At the club, we sat under the rain trees whose foliage joined in a smudgy tangle far above us against a deepening violet sky. A star appeared and hung there glittering among the branches. Other stars filled the sky. Soon flood lamps were switched on and shadows were washed away in harsh white light.

"Munnar," Letty said, "go and see if your uncle is playing cards in the bar . . . Oh, Lord, here come the Mumfords. The man talks incessantly. Empties without thought, like the human bladder."

The Mumfords were tall and stringy and looked alike in the way that flowers pressed in a book, in time, flatten and fade to the same general form and color.

"Dr. Dube, what a pleasant surprise," Mr. Mumford hailed out. "It's been years since we last saw you."

"Surely not that long," Letty said lightly. She introduced Ajai and me.

"Your niece?" He eyed my clothes. "Has she gone native too?"

There was a small awkward silence.

"We are pushing off next month," he said hastily. "Sailing for home. We shall be sorry to go, but there's nothing left here, is there? End of the era of the sahib and his mem. Gone. Sucked into the atmosphere as if it had never existed." He made a vague gesture with his head, and his Adam's apple bobbed above his tie and back out of sight again. "In two years there'll be none of us left in this country. Mark my words."

"Edgar," his wife plucked nervously at his sleeve. "We must get back to the MacKenzies. We'll say goodbye now, Doctor. I'm sure we won't run into you again."

They shook Letty's hand, nodded at me, ignored Ajai and walked away across the brightly illuminated parched grass.

I glanced at Letty, face silhouetted against the darkened bandstand, hands folded in her lap. It struck me like a blow: the isolation to which she'd been relegated both by her husband's people and her own—particularly her own—for defying the laws we observed, for denying the God we worshiped. She was paying the penalty. It would always be this way.

"Oh ho! Just see who is here." My portly uncle, preceding Munnar down the front steps, waved at us. "Letty, my dear," he said, grasping her hands. "This *is* an occasion. I'll go and get that rascal, Venki, to come and take our orders."

Ajai leaned toward me. "Would you like to walk a little?"

I rose at once.

"Where are you going?" Munnar asked.

Letty placed a restraining hand on his arm. "Keep me company till Uncle gets back."

We walked past the tennis courts, now empty because of the heat. He asked me what I liked to do best. I wanted to answer: walking here beside you. Instead I said that I liked to read. I told him Mama was fond of saying that with my nose in a book, I'd be oblivious to a gun at my head. He talked to me of politics.

"The Congress Party has become top-heavy and corrupt. We must provide strong opposition."

"'What will you do?"

"I have joined the Janata Socialist Party, although I find some of their positions, for instance on the Scheduled Castes, distasteful."

"Then why do you stay?" My answer was slightly skewed. I meant to ask, "Then why did you join?" I was responding as if I were only half-listening, when in truth, my whole being quickened to him.

"I have asked myself the same thing. The only other alternative is Communism."

I was not shocked. He said the words so softly, and only to me.

"Will you become a Communist?"

"I don't think so. Yet, sometimes I feel it is the only solution in a country so diverse, so poor. Although I am certain India will never go Communistic because it is so steeped in Hinduism."

We stopped under a neem tree. I leaned back against the trunk feeling the bark through my clothes. Its harsh texture filled me with a strange excitement.

Ajai stood in front of me, his palm braced against the tree and only a few inches from my shoulder. He bent his head to look into my face. "What about you? What are your plans?"

I was ashamed to admit I had none.

"You are very young."

"I'm not," I shot back. "I'll be eighteen in less than a month."

"As old as that?" he teased.

I wanted to touch him, but of course I didn't. I moved away from the tree, and from him. As we walked back to rejoin the others, he said, "My family has a small soapstone mine on the Nerbuda River."

"The one by Marble Rocks?"

"Yes. By the way, the Rocks are soapstone, not marble. Our mine is further down the river. May I show it to you sometime?"

"I'd like that very much," I said, hoping it was dark enough so that he wouldn't see the color rush to my face.

The next day Letty slept later than usual. When she awoke she seemed unstrung and edgy. We were sorting linens in her bedroom, weeding out worn sheets and pillowcases to be given away to the servants or torn up for cleaning rags. It was dim in the shuttered room, muggy. The ceiling fan provided little relief. Sweat trickled down our faces.

"I shouldn't have gone out last evening," she said, viciously tearing a sheet.

"Why not?" I asked, as I unfolded a linen tablecloth. "It was a wonderful evening. Didn't you enjoy yourself?"

"I was petrified."

"My goodness! Of what?" I looked at her, but she did not meet my gaze.

"I don't know." She gave a short laugh. "Just a sense of general impending doom, I suppose."

Mystified, I said, "It's not good for you to be cooped up in the house every day, just walking to the servants' quarters and back, the rose garden and back. It's not normal." I flung the word at her.

"Stop lecturing—"

"You lecture me," I interrupted. "All the time."

"That's different. I'm much older than you. It's my duty to guide you."

At lunch, over *chappatis* and vegetable curry, my uncle announced, "The Health Minister will come to Nerbudapur next week. We must have a reception here for him and the delegation, and also for prominent community people."

"No!" Letty said, wide-eyed, one hand working at the neck of her *choli*-blouse.

"But Lettoo," her husband pleaded, "what else can I do? They rang today from Delhi. It is part of my job, after all. I am the Representative."

"I cannot do it." She looked terror-stricken. "Please don't ask me to do it."

I touched her arm. "I'll help you, Aunt Letty."

My uncle looked at me gratefully. "Megan will help you," he said. It was the first time he'd used my name. "Letty, my dear, I was so happy to see you at the club yesterday, so proud. I knew how much courage it took for you to leave the house. No calamity befell us while we were there, or afterwards. You are still here, Megan is still here. I am here."

She sat staring down at her plate, elbows on table, chin in hands. At length she said in a low voice, "Why can't you entertain them at the club?"

"Because this is our home; we built this house. We used to have all kinds of dinners and receptions and teas. Now you want to live like a hermit." He looked intently at her, his eyes bewildered and unhappy. She continued to stare at her plate, her posture unchanged. "I am the Representative," he repeated with emphasis as though attempting to convince her of the fact.

She raised her head then and looked at him through half-closed eyes. "If you order me to, I'll do it. Like a dutiful Hindu wife."

"Damn it, then! I order you."

The days that followed were full of some obscure anxiety on Letty's part and total bafflement on mine. In the past, merchants were always summoned to the house, but for this occasion, there was no alternative but for us to go to the shops to select from a wider range; to order linens made, select special foods, condiments and spices, and to speak to a sitar master who refused to see us anywhere but in the smokey staleness of his single room.

"This is what it must be like preparing for battle," Letty said grimly in the car one morning.

I nodded. "Yes, there's so much to do."

She didn't answer.

The reception was a stiff affair. The Minister, a hefty man who had hairy brown calves under his muslin *dhoti* and was wearing a white Congress cap, didn't even touch the specially made, drawn-thread serviette beside his plate. We were served at long tables in the rose garden. After dinner my uncle, the

Minister and some of his aides went into the house for a discussion, leaving Letty and me to deal with the other guests.

Letty was magnificent. In a muted blue-green sari, a color more becoming to her than the stronger hues she generally favored, she moved among clumps of people smiling and nodding, stopping occasionally to speak. If she suffered any nervousness, it was not apparent—at least, not to me. I saw no tremor in her hands as when her mother-in-law had been here. At first I followed Letty about with some foggy notion that if any problem arose I would be there to help—in what way, I was not sure—but then it became clear to me that my nursemaid attitude was unnecessary and, further, that it was somehow degrading to Letty. I moved away to sit on one of the stone benches that dotted the garden.

Nila, radiant, in rose-colored georgette, approached me. "Why is it I have not seen you lately?" she asked. "It has been some time since the picnic at Marble Rocks."

"I've been busy. First there were my uncle's relatives, and then I had to help my aunt get ready for this."

She looked around. "It is all very grand. Lights in the trees and everything. Like fairyland. But the Muglai Chicken was a bit tough."

"Do you think so? The piece I had was delicious." A pause. "How is Colonel Bhatt?"

"He is here, somewhere," She gestured vaguely. "You are looking very smart. Is that new?" She reached out to finger the turquoise silk of my tunic.

"Yes. My aunt had it made."

"The color suits you. Come tomorrow afternoon, I'll be free then." She joined a passing group and moved away before I could respond.

As I sat there in the fragrant, golden evening watching the brilliant throng group and regroup like the shifting chips in a kaleidoscope, I tried to analyze how I felt about Nila. I still admired her in the way one's senses leap at the sight of a perfect rose, or a graceful animal, but . . . beyond that, I was not sure. It had nothing to do with Letty, I thought at the time, for although I ached for my aunt, I recognized the difficulty of living with her, and thus could not blame her husband. Besides Nila was probably irresistible . . . Then I saw again the intense face of the young Sikh, as he sat beside Nila in the boat that moonlit night at Marble Rocks. How could she be so unaware, so unheeding of such misery? Great beauty should carry with it responsibility, I thought. The two should fit together perfectly like the halves of a unit.

"Good evening, Miss Manning. A penny for your thoughts, as the saying goes." Colonel Bhatt stood before me, crisp in khaki twill, his peaked cap in the crook of an arm. "May I join you?"

"Yes, of course." I slid over to make room for him. "How are you, Colonel Bhatt? Was your trip successful?"

"It's still too early to tell. Can't talk about it, anyway. This is a very elegant gathering. Your aunt has been singing your praises for all the help you've given her."

"I just helped her shop for things, the servants did the rest."

"Have you heard from your family?"

"My mother writes regularly and so does my great-aunt. They are well. I've had no word from my father."

He looked at me a moment, his dark eyes gentle. "Come," he held out a hand to help me up. "Let us walk about in these grand surroundings."

"That would be lovely," I said, struck again by his sensitivity and kindness. On an impulse, I said, "In fact, I have a very special place I'd like to show you."

"Aha! Lead on!"

As we walked he entertained me with unkind remarks about the people we passed: the loping bent-kneed gait of a very tall man ("a walking telephone pole"), a ponderous woman with small mincing feet ("a dancing elephant in a red sari"). We laughed together and soon left the others behind.

"This is where I spend my mornings," I told him as we drew near my library. "Have you ever considered that there is a special spot in this world for each of us? I mean a real physical place where one can feel restored, that this is where one is *meant* to be. Sort of, well, like everyone is supposed to have a double . . . I'm sorry, I'm not making much sense."

"On the contrary, I understand you perfectly. But, we are not always fortunate in finding our special spots, Miss Manning. After all, how many of us ever run into our likenesses?"

"Well," I said gaily, tossing my turquoise scarf over my shoulder, "Colonel Bhatt, I'm happy to say that I have found my special place."

"Ah. Now you have piqued my curiosity and interest. Where is this halcyon spot?"

"Here." We stopped by the banyan tree. "It's my aunt's old library. I've no idea why she doesn't use it any more . . . Why, there's someone inside! But who would . . . ?"

My voice trailed. Framed in the bay window, in the unlit room, were two figures. Who could they be? The library was too remote, its setting too unkempt for straying guests. A sudden rage at the intruders filled me. Nosey parkers! Touching my books, mucking up my retreat! I started for the door, then felt my wrist grasped firmly.

"Please." Colonel Bhatt drew me back into the leafy shadows under the massive old tree. I glanced at him. In the gloom, his eyes glittered strangely in his otherwise impassive face. They were fixed on the window where the figures drew apart, came together, parted again like shadow puppets in a dance.

The door opened. I saw my uncle emerge, look around, then stride across the few paces that separated the library from the green wing of the house. Nila followed, but instead of disappearing into the house as my uncle had done, she turned and began to walk rapidly along the path. As she passed the banyan tree, I smelled her perfume, spicy and exotic. It lingered like an echo on the still, late-evening air. We watched until she turned by the rose garden, her sari fluttering palely in the waning light. I was conscious only of the shallow, rapid breathing of the man beside me, and my thudding heart.

We left the banyan tree and walked back in silence. I struggled to think of something to say, but he spoke first. "I'm sorry, my dear. You were going to show me your special place." He placed an arm briefly across my shoulders and I realized then we were both trembling.

Stupidly, I said, "I thought he was with the Minister." It was almost a wail. "Maybe . . . maybe he was only showing her the books."

"Ah, my dear. You and I both know that was not the case." Then, to my surprise, he said in a husky voice, "Poor woman."

I stopped to stare at him. He smoothed his moustache with a knuckle while with the other hand he touched each shining button on his bush shirt, his fingers tentative as a blind person's, perhaps to make sure the buttons were all there and properly fastened. I wanted to take his hand in mine, to cuddle it like a wet bird to my chest.

"You see, she cannot help herself." He spoke slowly, heavily, as if he himself were facing some bitter truth. "It is not the first time, nor will it be the last. He will pass like all the others." He gave a short mirthless laugh and tapped his knee with his swagger stick. "Nila is not in love with your uncle. Of that you can be quite sure. It is his position she finds attractive. His power."

He fell silent and we continued that way, our footsteps crunching on gravel. As we approached the rose garden, its scent assailed us. Did I imagine the faint overlay of another, stronger scent, spicy and exotic?

The sound of conversation and laughter grew louder.

Colonel Bhatt clasped my arm. "Continue to see Nila, please. As a special favor to me. I know this must seem inconsistent behavior on my part. Bizarre, even. I should be the properly outraged husband, not urging you to befriend my wandering wife. But . . . ah . . ." He ran a hand through his hair. "Things are not always the way they appear."

I didn't understand; I didn't want to understand. I felt a dull throbbing ache behind my eyes. Just then the long quivering notes of a sitar reached us, each note a sustained sadness.

The following afternoon as I lay on my bed reading—or, rather, trying to focus on words on a page—Letty came to my room. She was wearing a long loose cotton wrapper and had her glasses on. Perhaps she, too, had been reading. "Nila's servant brought this note." She handed it to me. "He's waiting for a reply."

I unfolded the slip of paper.

Nila had written in a large unformed hand: "You promised to come. I have been waiting since noon. Now it is 3:30. Please come at once—Nila." I tossed the note aside.

"Well?" Letty asked.

"She wants me to come over."

"Are you going?"

"No."

"May I see the note?"

She scanned it. "She's a bit of a nuisance, isn't she? But I think you should go. It says here that you promised."

"Not seriously," I said, sullenly. "There were no special plans. She just said come over and didn't even give me a chance to answer."

"Still, she seems to expect you. She's been waiting since noon, it says."

"I really don't want to," I said, turning back to my book. "I don't want to at all."

Letty came to sit on my bed. "But why, Megan?" She peered at me over her glasses, a gaze so keen I thought it would probe my very soul till it uncovered my awful secret. I rolled over onto my stomach. More than anything, I wanted to just lay my head in Letty's lap and weep loudly and long. Tears began to prickle my eyes. Desperate, I slammed my book down on the bed and rushed to the bathroom, yelling, "All right! All right! I'll go and see her."

Why can't Nila leave me alone? I thought savagely, as the tears spilled down my face. She's not a nuisance; she's a bloody *leech*. I flushed the toilet and ran water full blast in the basin. Bracing myself on the edge of the sink, I leaned forward to glare into the mirror above as though my anger were directed at the tearful red-eyed creature reflected there. And, perhaps it was.

"Megan?" Letty tapped on the door. "What shall I tell Nila's man?"

Nila's man? Nila's men! Hordes of Nila's men.

"Tell him I'll be there in half an hour."

The sun was a heated weight on my head as I ran across to the house next door. Nila's compound was not tended like Letty's. Lawns were brown and patchy, shrubbery ragged and weedy. Tall teakwood trees that flanked the path were losing their leaves: broad as dinner plates, the leaves floated down to collect on the ground in crisp brown layers, leaving behind naked branches that stretched upward as though pleading for moisture from a bone-white sky. But the monsoon was still months away.

Nila was resting on an orange paisley *rezai* spread on the cool stone floor of her front room, directly under the ceiling

101

fan. The wicker furniture had been moved aside. She wore only a brief cotton *choli*-blouse and an underskirt. Her hair was piled on her head: a profusion of glossy curls and tendrils that stirred in the drafts of air.

"I have been waiting for hours," she complained, moving a little to make room for me on the quilt. "Please sit."

I folded my arms and remained standing. "What did you want, Nila?"

She spread her hands. "Only to see you. Are we not friends? Sit, sit. Why are you standing there? You want to see my poems? I have them here." She handed me a loose-leaf file. I took it reluctantly, but I took it, my curiosity getting the better of me.

I sat on a corner of the quilt.

The poems were written in pencil on lined paper; the handwriting was uneven. They were easy to read: lilting and lyrical. But as I read I became puzzled; they were so familiar. When I came to one entitled, "Ribbon Vendors," I suddenly knew she had copied them from Sarojini Naidu's *The Sceptred Flute,* the book of poems my uncle had taken from the library that morning several weeks ago. She'd changed a word here, a phrase there, but the meter and flow were identical. Nila's "Ribbon Vendors" was contrived from Naidu's "Bangle-Sellers."

I stopped reading and looked at Nila. She lay on her back with one knee bent and an arm behind her head. Her eyes were closed. Outside, except for the rhythmic jingle of brass bells fixed to the horn-tips of oxen as they hauled cartloads of stone, or sand, or manure, it was perfectly silent. Heat smothered sound, it seemed.

"Well?" she said, finally.

"They are like Sarojini Naidu's."

She thought I was complimenting her! Smiling brilliantly, she raised herself on an elbow. "Yes, we both write about the same things. I have met her. She is a very fat lady, but she writes pretty poems. The Nightingale of India, she is called. A very fat nightingale." She gave her high clear laugh, head tilted back, throat arched, and I thought again: How lovely she is.

Taking the folder from me, she set it aside. "Next Friday is a tea dance. You know that fellow you were dancing with at the picnic? He likes you. I told him I would bring you."

"Is Colonel Bhatt going too?" I couldn't keep the edge from my voice.

She glanced quickly at me, and down at her hands, suddenly absorbed with peeling the polish from a long thumbnail, nudging it off with the other in tiny red ribbons. "You know that he does not like such things." She spoke with patience as though explaining something to a child. "He does not know how to dance, even. He does not like such things." Then she raised her lashes and looked at me, green eyes glowing as if lit from within by candles. She caught her lower lip in her teeth; her breath came quickly. I felt she was about to tell me something; the tension that precedes confidence crackled between us. Then, just as suddenly, the luminous excitement faded from her face and she lay back down. "So," she said in a flat voice, "what about the dance, then?"

"I'm sorry, but I have somewhere else to go."

"With your aunt?" Both arms behind her head, she stared at the ceiling.

"No. A friend."

"What friend?"

"No one you know. We are going to see a mine."

"It sounds very dull. If you want to go to the dance, ring me."

CHAPTER ELEVEN

Picks, shovels and lanterns hung from nails on the rough board walls of the frame shack that surrounded the mine shaft. Ajai took a lantern down and lit it. His face was suddenly illuminated in white light: thickly lashed eyes under straight black brows, arched nose, wide sensitive mouth. I was acutely aware of the dark hair on his chest that curled at the deep neckline of his *kurta*.

"The steps are very slippery," he warned, lantern held high. "You'd better remove your shoes."

Unshod—the way we walked up to the temple festival—we now walked down to a depth of about thirty feet using steep circular stairs carved out of the soapstone and holding onto a heavy iron rod that served as a sort of banister. Illuminated only by the lantern, it was like descending into an ice cave whose curving walls glowed with an inner radiance all their own.

The stone surface was slick. Cautiously I crept down pausing at each step. The smell of something like damp talcum powder reached my nostrils.

"We take only what we need to fill an order," Ajai told me, his voice echoing. "It's used mostly for mosaic work, also some temple sculpture. In this form it's soft and easy to carve. Exposed to the elements, it hardens. It's amazing what a skilled carver can do with soapstone. Such detailed filigree, even to carving a neck chain, each link separate."

I could have sworn there were tiny pink and yellow lamps trapped behind the walls, which were opaque as melted wax.

"It's so lovely here." My whispered voice swept around the shaft.

"I wanted to show you something beautiful, and I think this is the most beautiful place in the world." His face, brightly lit as he leaned forward to set the lantern upon a stair, sank into shadow as he turned away. "Look over there," he pointed at a dark, gaping place in the wall, his hand at my shoulder. "A tunnel. And another there. And there." He turned me to face each cavernous hole.

"Yes." His hand electrified my skin through my thin cotton tunic. "Yes."

"We employ very few workers and they have been with us for many years. Would you like to go into one of the tunnels?"

"I don't think so." Breathless, I drew away from his hand.

"Megan," he said in a low voice, and he pulled me back and turned me to face him. My heart was beating so hard I thought it would leap out and lie between us like some live thing. There was a strange sensation in the pit of my stomach. I shut my eyes. We stood that way, holding each other, my cheek against the desperate pulse in his neck.

"Son?" A man's deep, hesitant voice called out from above us. "Are you down there? Shall I come?"

We flew apart. "Yes Papa—I mean, no Papa, no need," Ajai called back urgently. He whispered to me, "I'll leave the light for you," then bounded up the stairs. My heart thumping, I picked up the lantern, and feeling somewhat foolish, followed more slowly. When I emerged into the shack, Ajai was standing there talking to a tall thin man with stooped shoulders that seemed molded into that shape from years of passing through low doors.

"Papa, this is Dr. Letty's niece, Megan. I have been showing her the mine," Ajai said. His voice was unsteady.

His father regarded me gravely with very dark, deep-set eyes. His face was like Ajai's, but age had roughened the skin, sharpened the bones, lengthened the nose, dulled the eyes. The thought struck me: Ajai will look like this when he grows old. Then the man smiled, a gentle, vaguely reproving smile.

"I am honored to meet you," he said, bringing his hands together in greeting. He was wearing the white hand-loomed cotton clothing made popular by the Mahatma. "Your aunt has been immensely kind to my family. We will always be indebted to her."

Since he did not volunteer the form of that indebtedness, I was reluctant to ask. I simply stood there, big and silent.

Ajai took the lantern from me and extinguished it. "Aunty took care of my mother when she was ill," he explained as he steered us outside. "She came and stayed with us and made all the arrangements for Mama to go to a sanitorium."

This time I asked. "What was the matter?"

"TB." He said it matter-of-factly.

"Why is it you are in Nerbudapur?" The older man fired the question at me.

"I am staying with my aunt."

"For how long?"

"I don't know."

"For what purpose are you here? Are you attending college?"

"No."

"You do not wish to attend college?"

"I don't know."

"Papa," Ajai said, hastily, "will you walk with us along the river? I want to show Megan the crocodiles."

"No, my son," he answered, coughing delicately into a folded white handkerchief, "I only wanted to find out if Balu Ram completed the Vizagapatam order?"

"The lorry left today. I came straight here from class to check up on it. Everything's shipshape."

His father nodded as though considering this information. "Then I will leave you to the crocodiles," he said, chortling at his joke. "Miss Megan, I will take my leave of you." He bowed over his joined hands, turned to leave, hesitated, turned back and said, apologetically, "Son, do not neglect your studies."

Then he left.

Ajai stooped to pick up a pebble, tossing it from hand to hand. "My father is a hopeless insomniac. Anytime of the night you wake up you will find him reading in one room or another. My mother tells me he was totally helpless when she fell ill. If it were not for Aunty, I don't know how they'd have managed. I was away at boarding school."

"Is your mother all right now?"

"Oh yes."

We walked along the river, beside rattling clumps of bamboo and foamy plumes of pampas grass, pink with sunset. Frogs croaked from rushes while cicadas clamored first from one side, then the other.

"I don't think your father approves of me," I said.

He glanced at me in surprise. "What on earth gave you that idea?"

"Because I am not of your caste."

He threw back his head and laughed aloud. "We do not believe in the caste system. My parents always said that it was the number one curse of this country, even worse than the British. My sister married a man of her choice."

"And you? Will you marry a woman of your choice?"

107

He did not answer straight away. I turned aside and looked at the water that ran coral with the last of the sun; it was crossed with fallen logs. Ajai tossed a stick into the river and one of the logs snapped its jaws open. Then another, and another.

I jumped.

He slid an arm across my shoulders. "I'm sorry. I didn't mean to startle you. They're quite harmless, actually, left alone. If the water gets much lower though, they'll have to move away. There are people who shouldn't marry, I think." This last was said so softly it was almost drowned by the cicadas.

"Are you one of those people?"

"I have always thought so, but . . . now I do not know." I could smell his skin through the muslin of his *kurta*. He smiled down at me, wrinkling a thin, crescent-shaped scar at the corner of an eye. His arm was firm; his fingers gripped my shoulder. I felt again the tightening in my belly, my thighs.

"There are bees here, also," he said. "Have you ever seen bees building a comb?" His voice was hypnotic.

"No, but I've read that they deposit pollen in different places," I murmured.

"Though not indiscriminately. Once Munnar lit a cigarette here and the bees attacked us." He laughed again and released me. "How we ran! He hates this place."

The absence of contact was physical loss. I felt a sudden chill although the evening was sultry, and I rubbed the gooseflesh from my arms. "Tell me about your march," I said, hugging my chest.

"It's set for Tuesday." He shook his head. "I'm not hopeful of the outcome, but maybe I'm being pessimistic . . . Look, here is a kingfisher's nest." It was made of mud, grass and twigs, shaped like a Christmas stocking, tucked away in a secret, hollow place between two rocks. The tiny neon bird, with its knitting-needle beak darted away in panic. We left quickly, quietly, so it could return. "They hide their nests," he said. "Not like other birds."

"You know so much about the birds and bees," I said, quite forgetting about the other meaning of that hackneyed phrase, mortified even as the words left my lips.

Perhaps he'd not heard the expression. In any case, there was no reaction from him other than to tell me that since he managed the mine for his family, he spent a lot of time here studying on the riverbank, watching the bees and birds, and also the crocodiles.

"Would you like to go for a cup of coffee?" he asked. "There's a stall nearby."

I shook my head, suddenly afraid, of what I didn't know. "I promised Aunt Letty I'd be back before dark. Thank you, just the same."

"Of course."

In the car I glumly considered the paradox of my condition: I constantly craved to see him, and yet, alone now in his company, this terror sprang inside me like a flame. But was it terror? I asked myself. I simply didn't know. I looked at his hands on the steering wheel, at the long, elegant fingers with their oval nails. I had the sudden impulse to take these fingers one by one into my mouth.

Later that night, in bed, I wondered if Ajai's father were prowling through the darkened rooms of their house, silent as a ghost, deep-set eyes afire from lack of sleep. Despite Ajai's words to the contrary, I sensed that his father looked upon me with suspicion.

All day I thought about Ajai—it was the day of the march. All day the wind blew; dry, hot as a furnace. It whistled in trees and whipped around the house, snatching unlatched windows, shattering panes, lifting the shards before it in swirling diamond eddies. The sky was the color of lead, the sun an orange blur.

By late afternoon, however, the wind left as suddenly as it had come. Letty and I went around the house taking stock of the damage. There were four broken windows, several missing roof tiles and layers of dust on every surface. The dust got in our hair and our ears and I tasted it, gritty, in my mouth. Plants on the verandah had fallen over, clay pots in pieces exposing damp dark tangled roots. The wicker furniture had blown off the porch into bushes outside, and lawns were strewn with tree limbs and rubble.

Letty was unperturbed. "It was much worse last year. Then, practically the entire roof was lifted off."

"Does it often blow like this?"

"Once or twice in the hot weather. One gets used to it."

We did what we could to restore order. Servants were dispatched to summon the glazier, the carpenter, the tiler. Gardeners began to repot the plants. By sundown, we took chairs into the garden, Letty with a drink, and I with the newspaper.

"Anything interesting?" Letty asked. I'd stopped reading aloud to her some time ago.

"There's a picture of the Mountbattens and Pundit Nehru laughing together. The caption reads, 'Enjoying a joke.' "

"Let me see."

She looked at it, handed the paper back. "I can't think what he sees in her. She's as plain as a mud wall, and has no neck."

"What who sees in her?"

"Nehru. I've heard there's more than friendship between him and Lady M. She's the one who started him wearing the rose in his buttonhole, you know, which is now his trademark."

I stared at her aghast. "Not Pundit Nehru!" I whispered.

"Why not?" She seemed amused at my consternation.

"He's only a man. His wife is dead. Someday you'll understand the love between a man and woman."

The founding father of our country! A philanderer like my uncle? I felt her eyes on me. The intensity of her gaze made me wonder if she were aware of my thoughts. In agitation, I began to read from the paper. "Work has commenced on the Bharat Dam despite all efforts to block it by the Janata Party representative, H. Sunder Das . . ."

Letty swirled the ice in her drink, said gently, "Maybe it's just gossip. Who knows?"

We sat beside a bed of cannas. A dragonfly hovered over a scarlet bloom, its transparent wings still as glass. Overhead small bats swung through dust-laden air. Letty was wearing the peacock-blue sari. She rested her drink lightly on the arm of her chair and the condensation made a damp spot on the rattan. She looked at me, and away. "Megan, there is something I must say . . . I simply don't know how to thank you."

"For what?"

"For all you've done. It's something that cannot be put into words." She swirled the ice in her drink and took another sip.

I was used to these extravagant announcements that followed the first drink.

"You give me strength."

"Strength?"

"And courage."

"Like 'Onward Christian Soldiers'?"

"Don't laugh. I'm trying to tell you something. Something important—"

"Aunty! Aunty!" Munnar was shouting as he raced across the lawn. His face streamed with sweat, his shirt clung to his body in damp brown patches.

"Munnar, dear." Letty leaped up. "What in the world has happened?"

"They have taken him to police station. That is what has happened." He stood panting, his arms limp at his sides. He shook his head hopelessly.

"Taken whom to the police station?"

"Ajai! They arrested him as leader of the march. That is what I am telling. Classes were cancelled and police called a curfew. College was out-of-bounds for the day, but how could we turn back? We had made so much preparation."

"Sit down," Letty urged him into a chair, her hands on his shoulders. "Megan, get some ice and a towel."

I raced to the house and back, ice cubes rattling in a bowl, towel flapping from my arm.

"Is he all right?" I yelled, blood pounding in my neck and ears.

Letty said, "He will be as soon as he calms down."

"I meant Ajai."

Letty and Munnar stared at me: Letty speculatively, Munnar as if I were mad. "Would you be all right if you were beaten with a *lathi?*" he demanded.

I thought I would faint. The bowl slid from my numb hands. Dazed and dizzy, I watched the ice cubes skitter across the lawn, suddenly absorbed in the way they collected dust and small stiff pieces of dry grass. I wanted to kneel down and examine in minute detail the marvel of an ice cube. It seemed carved from soapstone. From our mine. Our secret place.

"Megan! You're standing there like a piece of wood," Letty scolded. She scooped the cubes into the towel and held the compress behind Munnar's neck, under his collar.

"Aunty, there were *goondas,* worthless hooligans with nothing better to do, waiting for us at the Vice-Chancellor's building. They must have heard about our march." Munnar spoke in a monotone as one totally exhausted. "And when we arrived they joined us and started throwing stones and bricks and bottles, breaking windows, cursing and shouting. One

112

teacher was hit in the head with a stone and had to be taken to hospital. Another was cut from flying glass. The police came and shot in the air and charged us with *lathis*. None of us were defying, only the *goondas,* but many of us were taken to police station, though some ran away when the police came. Only it is Ajai now they are holding, everyone else has been released. Uncle must help. They are saying they will send him off to Nagpur jail since he organized the riot and violated curfew. But it was not supposed to be a riot, Aunty, only a march. A peaceful march. Uncle must help."

Sweat trickled between my breasts and shoulder blades. I had an ache in my side as if I'd run a great distance. I want to go to him, I thought. I must go to him.

Efforts to track down my uncle at the office and the club were useless. I thought of Nila, but could say nothing, not for Nila's, my uncle's, nor even Ajai's sake, but for Letty's. When he finally arrived, Letty said, "Where were you?"

"Playing cards. Where I am always."

"We rang the club. Munnar went looking for you. No one could find you."

"But," he said, his arms wide, palms upward, his chins aquiver above the spread-open collar of his cream silk shirt, the breast pocket of which held a folded red and grey tie, "I tell you I was there all the time."

"Never mind, try to get Ajai out of jail."

But Ajai was already on a police lorry bound for Nagpur. My uncle rang the Inspector of Police who, it turned out, was away at a niece's wedding. The Deputy-Inspector told my uncle, who, in turn, relayed the information to us, that he had no intention of interfering, that since Ajai was a known troublemaker and the instigator of the riot, an example had to be made or hoodlums would be running the country. My uncle shouted at the man and called him a bloody fool, but in the end, he replaced the phone. "I will ring Delhi in the morning. Maybe someone there can help." He looked tired as he stood there blinking at Letty, his hands still resting on the telephone.

"What about Ajai's parents?" I asked. "Has anyone talked to them?"

"I have," Munnar said, "I will call on them again and tell them I am going to Nagpur tomorrow, on the bus."

"I'm going with you," I said.

"Not to a jail!"

"I'm going with you," I repeated.

"A woman cannot go to a jail."

Letty glanced at my face and said, "Take her with you."

"But Aunty—"

"Take her with you, Munnar."

The bus to Nagpur was crowded and stifling, the smell of perspiration oppressive. The aisle was clogged with cardboard boxes tied with string and cloth bundles that smelled of tamarind or asafoetida or garlic. A goat had been tied to the roof amid the larger pieces of luggage; it bleated unceasingly. The seats were hard, the ride bumpy. Clouds of dust billowed alongside the lumbering bus and wafted in the windows, settling on everything, covering my damp skin with fine red powder.

I sat jammed against a window with the taciturn Munnar beside me, his arms crossed. Beyond him was a mother nursing a child of two or three and facing us sat an old woman with a basket of squawking chickens on her lap. Despite the discomfort, I felt almost lighthearted, although guilty and apologetic to Munnar for having bullied him into bringing me along. "It's not so bad," I said, trying to coax him into a better mood. "Now we'll get to see Prethima and the boys again."

He merely jerked his head. The nursing child began to bawl, opening wide its mouth filled with sharp little teeth. Did those teeth not hurt the mother? I wondered, and felt my own nipple distend.

"Prethima is like a—" Munnar pinched his fingers together repeatedly, searching for words. "Like a bud that will never open."

"I like her."

"Liking her is all right. But you should have been at her marriage. She had to be practically carried to the *pandal*—you know, the special marriage tent," he moved his large hand laterally to illustrate a flat roof, "they have for the bridegroom and bride."

"She was frightened."

"Of course. Everyone is frightened at such things, but one should maintain . . . dignity."

"How would you know? You haven't been married."

He refolded his arms.

"When my niece was married," the woman with the chickens said, running a palm over her sparse grey hair stretched back into a skimpy knot, "how she howled. The man was old, true, but the girl, poor thing, had elephantiasis. Such a fat leg!"

Munnar scowled.

"But one has to take marriage wherever it comes, especially for unworthy girls," the woman continued. She shook a hand in the air. "Who knows what my niece did in a previous life to bring this disease on her?" She looked from side to side, measuring her audience. The woman with the child was listlessly jiggling it to sleep. Other people had nodded off in various corners of the bus. Within earshot, only Munnar and I seemed alert. "One never understands, only accepts."

"Old mother," Munnar said in a dignified voice, "this is a private conversation between my cousin-sister and me."

"Oh ho, if she is your cousin-sister then the Viceroy is my uncle."

"The cheek of these peasants," Munnar muttered. "Ignore her."

Just then the bus encountered a herd of goats and came to a shuddering halt. The bus driver swore at the goatherd and honked the horn. Bleating animals scattered on dainty hooves into the ditches on either side of the road, and the bus started up again. I wondered briefly if the goat on the roof might not have got loose to join the others, until I heard again the faint, plaintive cries from above, constant as the dust and flies.

Rice paddies spun by. Standing ankle-deep in the emerald water, bent-over, brightly clad women were transplanting the delicate new shoots. Their bent-over bodies were mirrored on the water's surface.

"Munnar," I said, "have you ever been in love?"

"We fall in love only after our marriage."

"Yes, I know," I said. "Prethima told me about all that. But, what I want to know is, have you ever felt shaky and . . . sort of . . . out of breath when you see a certain girl?"

"Never! Well . . . sometimes, when I see an actress in the cinema. When she sings to the hero, I sometimes pretend she is singing to me. And now and then I see a girl and think how it would be if she and I were married. But I know that is only dream stuff. My parents will pick for me the best girl they know. They only want my happiness, and I trust them."

How simple it seemed to trust your parents.

"But what if you don't like the girl your parents choose?" I said. "What then?"

"That sometimes happens. But one has one's duty to fulfill, one's *dharma,* one cannot escape it."

"How boring." I turned to look out of the window. In the fields oxen were turning a waterwheel, plodding slowly. I had the impression that even without the yoke or the wheel they would still trudge the same path from habit, wearing it down smooth and hard as an old wedding ring.

"Megan," Munnar said shyly, "there is a girl who rides our school bus. She is in biology; her name is Vimila."

"And you like her?"

"She is very beautiful. She looks like Nargis."

"Who is Nargis?"

"What? You do not know Nargis? She is the best actress in the world."

"An Indian actress, you mean?"

"Yes, of course, Indian."

"Well, I didn't know, Munnar."

"But you live in this country and do not even know our actresses." He was disgusted.

"I don't go out very much."

"That is only proper for a young girl, but occasionally there is no harm to go to the pictures. Anyway, one day on the bus Vimila's fountain pen slipped down the front of her tunic where she had clipped it," he pointed at the collar of his own shirt to illustrate. "It fell on the floor of the bus and I picked it up. It was warm. I . . . wished I was that pen."

"Munnar! Then you do know what it is like to be in love."

"Not love," he turned away only to confront the bawling child, and turned back again. "I only admire this girl. I do not know even what caste she is."

"Did you give the pen back?"

"Of course."

"Did she thank you properly?"

"Oh yes. She smiled also. She has dimples."

" 'Dimples,' he says," the old woman muttered, perhaps to her chickens. "Caste only is what counts." Then she leaned across the holy man who was telling his beads beside her, and spat a stream of betel juice out of the window.

117

Munnar was irate. "Why must you keep butting into a private conversation?" he demanded of the woman.

"I was not speaking to you," she retorted spiritedly. "But if you want to wear the slipper, it must fit."

"She is not hurting us, Munnar," I said, trying to soothe him, "and we'll never see her again. What does it matter if she listens."

"No. Present conversation terminated."

I leaned my head against the window-frame, looking out at the clouds of red dust that rolled along beside the rackety bus. I thought of Papa that last night I'd seen him stretched out on his easy chair reading the newspaper. I savored each detail of that image: his ring, the shapes of his fingers, the fine hairs on the backs of his hands, before I realized with sudden panic that I couldn't remember if his socks were blue or grey. I scrambled desperately for the detail. What if bits of Papa were erased from my memory? Then he'd be lost to me forever.

But the detail remained elusive.

CHAPTER TWELVE

At the Nagpur bus station Munnar rang the family house, and before long Ashok and Prethima arrived in a dark green Vauxhall to pick us up. Ashok smiled at me, and playfully punched Munnar's arm. Prethima, in a pale blue voile sari, was radiant.

"What a lovely surprise!" she said, hugging me. She smelled of jasmine. "I had such a feeling today when I woke up. Something told me a good thing would happen."

We settled ourselves in the car: Munnar and Ashok in the front, Prethima and I in the back. Our part was completely screened with green-striped cretonne, shielding us from the glance of passersby, but also from the slightest breath of air.

Prethima turned to me in the greenish filtered light, a hand on my wrist, dark eyes glowing. "I have wonderful news."

"Oh Prethima!" I flung my arms around her. "Is it really true?"

"Yes," she said, lifting her small pointed chin. Sweat stood on her upper lip and forehead and collected around the black

119

and gold beads of her marriage chain. "It is true. Vijay and me, we went to Mahabalipuram temple and offered *puja* before the Shiva *lingam*. When I prayed, I thought of how goddess Parvati had prayed before the *lingam* of sand and Shiva came down and made the blessing on her. Only one thing was in my head when I prayed: Shiva should bless me too. And he did."

"I'm delighted." I hugged her again.

"We also are delighted. Now I can show his family there is nothing wrong with me. When I did not conceive, they sent me back to *my* family. I was a defective bride, they said, and it was *my* family's responsibility to get treatment for me. But Vijay said, 'I will go with her. She is my wife. My place is with her.' He is a good husband. I am so very lucky. Some husbands . . ." She cast her eyes heavenward, and sighed. "But now, I suppose, we will have to return to my in-laws' house. I prefer to stay with my own family, but it is my duty to live with my husband's people. They own me now."

She took my hand, leaning forward to look earnestly into my eyes. "I am going to give you advice. When you are married, and I hope that will happen very soon—you are becoming somewhat old—you must give yourself completely to your husband. Just do what he wants, never mind what, simply do. Then only will you be blessed with child. And without that—" she shook her head slowly. "One must have a son to pray for one's soul." She released my hand and settled the folds of her sari. Lifting that small chin somewhat smugly, she said, "This I have learned."

"Prethima!" My temples and ears suddenly pounded; sweat poured from me, "Can we have the curtains open a bit?"

"Of course, my dear." She yanked the curtains back from the windows. Dusty air that smelled of baked earth and scorched vegetation filled the car, brushing against my sticky skin. I breathed deeply. "It's the heat," she said, solicitous. "You are not used to the curtains. We do not need them."

Prethima had made no attempt to lower her voice through-
out this conversation, as if the partition that separated us from
Munnar and Ashok in the front seat were concrete instead of
cotton. What she had said must surely have been audible to
them—certainly, Munnar's spirited retelling of the march and
subsequent mass arrests came through clearly enough. It was
as if the strictures of propriety had been satisfied by the mere
presence of the curtain. How well I recalled that morning at
breakfast when my uncle had harshly reprimanded Letty for
speaking of conception to Prethima in the presence of men.
Yet here was Prethima herself loudly discussing sexual behavior as if it were as commonplace an activity as brushing one's
teeth.

The house was square, two-storied and painted dark yellow, austere-looking despite the blue, almost frivolous, fretwork trim that adorned the eaves. There were none of the
splashing fountains and rose bushes and small stone benches
under shady trees as at Letty's. The scant front yard was
grassless and bare, except for a plastered-brick shed with a
corrugated-metal roof where Munnar parked the car.

We left our shoes at the front door. The stone floor inside
felt deliciously cool underfoot. We were immediately surrounded by women and children. Munnar touched the older
women's feet. They stroked his arm, touched his hair, then
fell back to stare at me as if I were a specimen from another
planet that had suddenly descended in their midst. A child in
his mother's arms reached out and touched my hair, then
looked at his fingertip as though he expected to see the color
transferred there. As Prethima explained to them who I was,
I looked around at the dark faces, and darker eyes rimmed
with kohl that stared back at me, some impassive, some
suspicious, some alert with curiosity.

A small egg-shaped woman bustled in, bristling ownership.

It was obvious she was Munnar's mother; the other women stood aside. Munnar stooped to the ritual obeisance and she placed a plump proprietary hand on his head. A ruby ring countersunk in an index finger gleamed dully.

Catching sight of me, she jerked straight and asked in rapid-fire Hindi, "Who is this?"

One of the other women replied, also in Hindi, "She is niece of elder brother's wife." Another added, "They came together on the bus from Nerbudapur." A third offered, "She looks exactly like that one," meaning, of course, Letty.

Munnar's mother's eyes grew wide, the corners of her mouth turned down. "Why did you bring her?" she said to Munnar.

He lifted his large hands, palms up, "Aunty said, 'Take her to see Prethima. She is missing Prethima.'"

Letty had said no such thing.

Prethima spoke up. "I invited her when I was back in Nerbudapur," she said, taking my hand. "She and I became fast friends. Grandmother also invited her."

The older woman seemed somewhat mollified, but remained wary. I knew what the others were thinking: that Munnar and I were doing the same thing that Letty and my uncle had done. Expecting something like that to happen again, they were frightened, yet stimulated at the promise of excitement. Incensed, I wanted to proclaim my innocence to them all; instead, I followed Prethima through the dark sparsely furnished house. Trunks and rolled bedding were stored in the corners of rooms whose walls were decorated with calendars and pictures of deities strung with garlands of wilted jasmine and marigolds. Somewhere in the house a noisy argument was in progress. I heard the wailing of a small child. We emerged into the courtyard in the white heat of noon-day sun. Like the house in Nerbudapur, it too was centered with its sacred *tulsi* plant. Porches with blue-painted railings both upstairs and down overlooked the courtyard and were hung with washing; saris billowed like bright sails.

The source of the loud argument was two women. One held a whimpering child and leaned over the top-floor railing, between the flapping laundry, to yell at a stocky young woman below who stood feet apart, one hand on a plump hip, the other brandishing shards of a mirror. Some of the other women who had trailed behind us into the sunshine now shifted their attention to the quarreling pair, siding first with one and then the other. It occurred to me, as I watched them, that in this closed environment there was nothing to stave off boredom but children, gossip and petty spats. How had Letty coped?

"This was a present to me from my husband even before we were married," the woman below shouted.

"Then you should have kept it in your trunk and out of the reach of small children. He has cut his hand through your carelessness," the other woman yelled back.

"They are always fighting. They do not like each other," Prethima needlessly explained. She indicated the string cots in the courtyard. "This is where we sleep in the hot weather. Men this side, women that side."

"Everyone? Even you and Vijay?"

"Oh yes. But, later," she leaned towards me to whisper rapturously, her breath warm against my ear, "when everyone is asleep, he will get up like he is going to the bathroom, then I will get up too and go to him."

"Why don't you just sleep together somewhere else?"

"We do not do like that." She seemed shocked. "Only after the marriage for two or three days we stay together, then we go back to the joint family."

Such elaborate subterfuge, I thought; it's a wonder they have children at all, yet I couldn't help noticing that children abounded. I tried to imagine the adults all creeping through the empty house intent on assignations with their own spouses. Like playing hide and seek.

"Come, I will take you now to see my grandmother," Prethima said.

We reentered the house. My eyes adjusted to the dimness. I followed her into a large room that she told me was the communal dining hall. It was high-ceilinged, empty but for the large, white, clinical-looking fridge that hummed against a wall. We passed through a door on the left and thence through various small dark rooms, each one resembling the last in size and furnishings. I had to stoop to enter some of the doors, and tripped occasionally over high thresholds. We walked down a long dark hall at the end of which was an open door. There, framed in the doorway, was the old lady, cross-legged and stiff-backed. She sat on a low carpet-covered platform, like some idol in the inner sanctum of a temple one reaches after first passing through many antechambers. As we approached, I saw that she was knitting a small garment. She looked up as we entered and frowned slightly, then her face creased into a wide, welcoming smile.

"Ah, niece Megan. You have come at last."

I bent to touch her feet as Prethima had done before me. She patted my head.

"Please sit, sit," she urged. "Prethima, bring tea."

Prethima left. The old lady held up her knitting: a tiny yellow sweater.

"See," she said. "For Prethima's baby, my first great-grandchild. The gods have been good. May they see fit to bless us with a male child."

"I am so excited for Prethima. I know that my aunt and uncle will be pleased, too."

"How is my son?" she asked, thrusting her chin up. The soles of her bare feet were pale as butter.

"He is well. So is Aunt Letty." I went on to tell her about

124

the dinner for the Minister, our preparations for it, and my amazement that the Minister had not even touched the lovely, drawn-thread serviette beside his plate.

"It is not our Indian custom to wipe our soiled parts," she said sternly, as she peered at me over the top of her steel-framed spectacles and wagged a knitting needle at me. "To wash is much more cleanlier."

Prethima arrived with a single cup of tea, for me. I remembered then they were not permitted to eat or drink with me because of caste restrictions. Awkwardly, I sipped the hot sweet drink, which made me perspire profusely, or perhaps it was their steady gaze that brought on the sweat. Like the other rooms, this one was spartan in its furnishings: just the carpet-covered platform and a picture of Shiva tucked into a niche in the wall, with a lighted wick in a clay saucer burning before it.

When I finished the tea, Prethima stood. The visit was over.

I had decided that customs being what they were, I would eat wherever I was served. There was no use in being upset over what couldn't be changed, anymore than I could alter the fact that I was seventeen and Catholic. I told myself all this, the while dreading that first meal. Imagine my surprise, then, when at lunch as I hesitated at the door, the old lady loudly commanded me to sit beside her.

She held my wrist. "This is a very good girl," she announced generally. "Modest and respectful and must surely have been a Brahmin in a previous existence. Or else," she added pragmatically, "will become one in the next. Let us welcome her." She patted my knee where I sat cross-legged beside her on the floor of the dining hall.

We ate with our fingers from large round trays that held silver bowls containing various curries and sambals, all delicately spiced, delicious and, of course, meatless. Even Mun-

125

nar's mother unbent enough to offer me a second piece of halva.

After lunch Munnar said, "Ashok will take us now to the jail."

"Why must you go?" Prethima asked me, her dark eyes wide with concern. "A jail is no place for a woman. There are bad men there who will stare at you."

"She has to take notes," Munnar said tersely.

"*Accha!*" Prethima wagged her head, full of admiration. "Just like a proper secretary. I will get you paper and pencil." She hurried away.

Take notes! How clever of Munnar! Despite his grumpiness, I was filled with gratitude.

"Do you have a pass?" the guard at the gate asked. He had a pitted sweating nose.

"No," Munnar answered. "We did not know."

"Oh ho! You thought this was the Taj Hotel in Bombay. But you must have lost your way for Bombay is five hundred miles south. Here, guests cannot come and go as they please."

"Where do we get a pass?"

"At the police station. Where else?"

"We would like a pass to see Ajai Pande who is in Nagpur jail."

"Visitors permitted third Saturday every month."

"But that is two weeks away!"

"Correct."

Driving back, Munnar was in a black rage. "How can we stay for two weeks?" He hit his knee with his fist. "I cannot miss two weeks of classes."

"Missing classes is very bad," Ashok said. "In our college we lose points."

126

"Call Uncle," I suggested. "Maybe he can help."

Munnar made an impatient sound. "What can he do? That inspector fellow did not mind him last night."

"But he said he would ring Delhi. Let's try, Munnar. We have to try."

My uncle promised to call us back that night, but Munnar said he had not sounded encouraging. There was nothing to do but wait.

During the course of the afternoon, Prethima took me to see her grandfather, a patient man with long discolored teeth, and her mother, who had the bewildered air of someone on the wrong platform watching an express train go by. I met aunts and cousins and sisters-in-law. They made comments about me in Hindi that Prethima, kindly, took liberties with in translating, thus: "She is tall as a man and has skin the color of unbaked dough," became, "They are telling you have a good figure and nice complexion." I understood the language. I knew what they were saying. But as long as they were saying personal things about me, I decided not to enlighten them.

The call from my uncle came at exactly five thirty-five: we could pick up the pass at the gate itself the next day. We were to say we were relatives of Ajai. My bones were filled with air. I felt myself float with relief and happiness. I would see him tomorrow! I would see him again! In the meantime I was among these lovely people who ate with me despite all their beliefs.

If only Grandpa had been nearly as tolerant.

"Let us go to the market," Prethima announced. "I wish to buy Megan a present."

I protested.

"As a mark of our friendship," she insisted. It was obvious she had her heart set on the trip. We piled in the car. "Take us to the bangle shop, Ashok," Prethima ordered.

"Take us here, take us there," Ashok grumbled. "For the past two days I have done nothing but drive people about."

"Yes, you have," I said quickly. "We should buy you a present. A book, maybe?"

"I can buy my own book," he snapped.

"*Arre!*" Munnar exlcaimed. "If you are going to be so rude, you can stay behind. I will drive the girls."

Ashok's only response was to back the car screechingly into the street.

"Ashok is very bad tempered," Prethima announced to no one in particular. "He needs a wife."

Munnar sniggered. It didn't improve Ashok's mood.

The shops in the marketplace were just reopening after the long rest period during the heat of the afternoon. Vendors were arranging their fruit and vegetables in precise pyramids: rosy mangoes glistening with sap, glossy dark brinjals, lobed peppers, lace-topped carrots. The air, still and warm, was laden with the smells of jasmine and ripe oranges, urine and rotting vegetables. Cows meandered from one overflowing garbage container to the next, crossing the road with lazy indifference, impeding traffic and pedestrians alike. Ashok honked loudly at them, to no avail. Finally, we reached the bangle shop where the shopkeeper spread his sparkling wares before us.

Prethima carefully selected a dozen clear-glass blue bangles that she said exactly matched my eyes, six for each wrist. They looked so fragile and small I was afraid they would shatter, but the shopkeeper expertly massaged the bones of my hands as he carefully slid the bangles over them.

"They are lovely, Prethima," I said with delight, turning my wrist this way and that causing the delicate circles to jingle softly.

"No mention." She bought some for herself. I was amazed to see the shopkeeper break the ones she was wearing, just snap each apart, before he slipped on the new ones.

As we drove home I looked about me at the marketplace, now teeming with people, and thought of that evening when I had run to Pushpa's sweetshop. How long ago that seemed to me now. I had the strangest feeling that the girl I was then was someone apart, someone I'd known and almost forgotten: a very young, distant cousin, perhaps. I recalled the song Pushpa had crooned to that girl in her ill-fitting cotton frock, about serving a great warrior, recalled her smell of damp sandalwood, the aroma of her sweets, the cloying scent of musk that drifted over from the brothel across the street. What would Pushpa say if she saw me now? I wondered. Would she consider Ajai a great warrior?

After dinner we sat in the courtyard on the string cots under a magenta and orange sky, the children chasing each other around the sacred *tulsi* plant. The men played cards or discussed business as they flicked ash from their cigarettes onto the chipped flagstones, while the women sang sentimental songs at the pale silver of moon poised on a rooftop. The grandmother, sitting beside me on a cot, peeling an orange, called out admonitions from time to time, "No Sushi, do not hit him with the bat," or "Ratna, your child is making poo-poo there in the corner." She turned to me and said in her imperious way, "Niece Megan, sing an English song for us." Then she shut her eyes, waiting.

I sang "Londonderry Air," lifting my face like an offering to the evening, and felt the notes leave my throat, clean and pure. They rose above the heat mass and, for all I know, might even have floated thinly across to Papa, whom I longed to see again.

I sang from joy and love, and also from an immense sadness.

CHAPTER THIRTEEN

The sun was already a white blur at ten in the morning when we drove to the jail. We picked up the pass at the gate as my uncle had instructed. The guard with the pockmarked nose handed Munnar a small green card and waved us inside the compound, which was enclosed by a high wall with barbed wire strung along the top. I heard the gate clang shut behind us. Munnar parked the car in the shade of a spreading tamarind tree. I looked up at the tall red-brick building with its small, barred windows. There was a stillness about it as though nothing inside were alive, nothing inside could survive. If I had not been obsessed with seeing Ajai again, I would have turned tail and fled. Grimly, I mounted the steps beside Munnar. He pressed the buzzer beside the door. A guard in a khaki uniform appeared behind the mesh-reinforced door pane and spoke to us through a grill.

"We have a pass to see Ajai Pande," Munnar told him, and held the green card up to the glass. The door was opened, the pass examined; Munnar was examined. I was ushered into an adjoining room where I was checked over by a burly woman in a khaki sari who smelled of stale sweat and coconut oil, after which I returned to the anteroom. Munnar was standing before the desk at which the seated guard made notes on a pad. "I am his brother," Munnar said. I glanced at him and, indeed, he did look a little like Ajai: The same lanky grace and dark curly hair. Sweat beaded the guard's shiny scalp across which were stretched strands of black hair. He continued to write steadily. A ceiling fan squeaked lethargically overhead, the sound circling inside my head.

"And this one?" The guard pointed his chin at me. "You are telling she is his sister?"

Munnar's response was swift. "She is his wife. A mute." He darted a warning glance at me. I felt the blood rise to my face.

"*Ai yi*. Why would your brother marry one with such an affliction?" He looked at me as if I were a cockroach.

"It was an illness that came only after marriage. Disease of vocal chords."

The guard hoisted himself out of the chair and began to grumble about people like us who pulled strings in order to see a prisoner at whim instead of waiting for visiting day like everyone else. As he unlocked a heavy metal door and pulled it shut behind us, he continued to complain about people like us causing extra work for already overworked, underpaid attendants like himself. The door closed with a whoosh and a thump, sealing us in. We followed him down a corridor painted a murky green and lit by a single dangling light bulb. The odor of mildew and damp, and something else, indefinable, filled my nostrils. We reached another door at the far end that he unlocked, motioning with a stubby forefinger for us to enter. He then left, slamming the door upon Munnar and me.

We were in a room with high windows, barred on the inside, and deal-wood chairs and tables upon which were

131

carved initials and hearts. Signs were posted in English and Hindi: "DO NOT SMOKE." "DO NOT PASS OBJECTS." "WRITING STRICTLY PROHIBITED." Munnar sat on a table swinging a leg as he drummed his fingers on the tabletop. Feeling on edge, I moved around the room.

The door was unlocked. Ajai, in loose grey prison clothes, entered accompanied by a different guard, who relocked the door and sat stone-faced beside it. Ajai's eyes were red-rimmed as if he'd not slept; there was a bruise above his left eyebrow. He approached slowly, cautiously positioning each foot as though testing ground, but when he saw Munnar his face brightened. "Munnar," he called out, his voice strong, almost daredevil. "How good of you to come."

"*Arre,* brother! Your misfortunes are mine. We are one and the same. Megan, she also came."

"Megan?" He turned his head then and saw me; his face grew blank, sullen. He glanced away. "Why did you bring her?" It was the second time in twenty-four hours that the question had been asked of Munnar, about me.

"I wanted to see you," I said quickly, and could think of nothing else to say. I gazed at the way his hair curved around his ear, at the ear itself so neatly sculpted, at the chiseled angle of his jaw, and felt again the familiar restless longing and also, for the first time since we'd left Nerbudapur, a sinking sense of having done the wrong thing. He turned to look at me again, his eyes shifting from my forehead, to my eyes, to my mouth, back to my eyes, while I struggled to fathom what he was thinking. He said, at last, to Munnar, "You should have known better."

"Oh, don't blame him." The words burst out. "I forced him to bring me."

Munnar glanced at me anxiously. "Ajai, she was very worried about you," he said, with gentle reproof. "We came by bus. You know what that is like, yet she never complained."

"There's no need for anyone to concern themselves on my

account." I spoke in the frostiest of voices as I stalked away and stood reading the words, "DO NOT SMOKE," over and over, concentrating on how the black letters tapered at the ends and thickened in the middle. As I examined them, a feeling of absolute isolation came over me. I felt set apart, not just from Ajai and Munnar and for the moment only, but from everyone else as well: Papa, Mama, Aunt Margaret, Letty. It was as if I existed alone in a windowless world, suspended, stalled between my previous existence—a safe world of cotton dresses and evening walks—and the one that loomed ahead shimmering with mystery like a mirage on a fiercely hot day.

Behind me, I heard Ajai speak to Munnar in a low unhappy voice about the march. He asked about their fellow arrestees and requested that Munnar post him his thesis since it looked as if he would be detained indefinitely.

I thought of how he'd led me up the steps to the temple festival with my hand clasped warmly and safely in his. I recalled our walk together at the club when he'd confided to me his political views. Above all, I remembered the evening at the mine where we'd embraced briefly, sweetly; each instant of that evening was as bright and vivid in my mind as an illuminated picture one views through a special instrument. Down in the mine shaft, I'd been sure he felt as I did. Now he was so cold, so denying; it was almost as if he hated me. I thought desperately: maybe I shouldn't have been so hesitant with him then; maybe I should have gone for coffee when he'd asked me; if only I'd entered one of those tunnels in the mine. Had Letty ever felt this agitated helplessness? Perhaps it was a mutant gene we shared, one that bypassed Mama and Aunt Margaret. And this too, I thought, was a mystery.

Behind me the guard cleared his throat loudly. I sensed the visit was about to end and turned to meet Ajai's eyes, dark and distant. He clasped Munnar's hand, and without another glance at me, followed the guard from the room.

I felt bereft. Munnar touched my shoulder briefly, but said nothing. Soon the first guard came and unlocked the series of doors. We stepped into the blazing sunshine. I took several gulping breaths of hot dry air. At least it was fresh.

"What happened? Did you take notes? Can I see them?" Prethima asked.

"Sorry. Confidential," Munnar answered.

Awestruck, she said, "Just like detective business. Did you manage all right?" she asked me. "Was the pencil sharp enough? Plenty of paper?"

"Plenty."

"Come. Rest. I will bring you tea."

"Let us go to the pictures," Ashok said to Munnar. "There is a new one at the Roxy."

"Munnar," I called after them. "When does the bus leave?"

"Five P.M."

It was two in the morning when we finally returned to Nerbudapur. The bus station was deserted except for the homeless with no other shelter and sleeping passengers swaddled in sheets waiting for early buses. The bodies that lay huddled outside under the eaves and on the floor of the waiting room looked like so many corpses.

We took a tonga at the station. Munnar rode in front with the driver; I sat in the back. The bells around the horse's neck seemed the only thing alive in the almost viscous dark.

Munnar said, "I think I will stay at Aunty's house tonight. My dormitory will be locked by now." A pause. "Megan, can I ask you something?"

"What?"

"Do you love Ajai?"

"Oh, I don't know," I muttered.

Letty and my uncle had long since gone to bed, but there was a letter from Mama on my dressing table, propped against the old picture, obscuring a corner of Letty's fragile smile and one of her partially closed eyes. Too tired to open the letter, I lay fully dressed on the bed and sank into deep, dreamless sleep.

I awoke at my usual early hour, bathed, dressed and took Mama's letter to my library. As always upon entering, I felt peace steal over me like a drug. I thought of my uncle and Nila in here the night of the dinner for the Minister, but no alien shadows lurked in the room, no hostile vapors. It embraced me, held me safe. Outside, in the dusty dark-green depths of the banyan tree, birds clucked and sang. A monkey swung down a twisted dangling root, cocked its head at me, then swung back up again. Sighing with contentment, I stretched out on my stomach on the window seat and ran a fingernail under the flap of the letter.

"I thought I'd find you here." Letty stood in the open doorway clad in her magenta robe. "Good heavens, Megan! You look as if you've seen a ghost."

I scrambled to my feet and stood there staring at her, filled with guilt and confusion.

"Child, what is the matter? Did I frighten you?"

I could only shake my head.

"What is it?"

"I thought you'd be angry," I said in a low voice.

"Why should I be angry?"

"Because I didn't ask your permission to use the library. I discovered it one day when I was helping Maharaj weed the kitchen garden."

"I know. I've known for some time this was where you spent your mornings. Why did you think you needed my permission? You have the freedom of the house. I've always told you that."

"But this . . . this room is different, somehow," I stammered. "It seemed abandoned and . . . and I thought maybe you wanted it kept that way."

She looked around. "Where did all this come from?" she asked, indicating the new furnishings.

"From Uncle. He came in here one day looking for a book of poetry, and he said that the old furniture should have been thrown away long ago. The next day all this was here, and the room had been cleaned. He told me I could use the room since—" I stopped abruptly.

"Since what?"

"Since . . ." I licked my lips. "Well, since no one else used it," I finished miserably. I couldn't bear to look at her. I felt as if I'd been caught prying among her things, or stealing from her purse.

"Quite right," she said, briskly. "Now, have you read your mother's letter?"

"Not yet. I was going to when . . . when . . ."

"Yes, yes. When I came in and frightened you out of your wits," she finished for me impatiently. "Well, read it. I got one too."

My hands shook so I almost dropped the letter trying to open it; then the single sheet of paper trembled in my grasp. I could barely read Mama's precise sloping handwriting. Somehow I managed to decipher the contents. Mama and Aunt Margaret were planning to visit Nerbudapur for my eighteenth birthday, which would take place in three weeks, so the three of us could celebrate together at Mass as we had always done on all my other birthdays. They had collected on one of Grandpa's bonds. They couldn't wait to see me again. Mama hoped Aunt Margaret's knee would travel well, and she trusted that Letty would see to it that Aunt M. received the best of medical care should she need it.

"Well, shall we put them in the green wing?"

I nodded.

Suddenly, the briskness vanished. Looking anguished, she cried out, "Megan, I'm scared."

Startled, I said, "Of Mama and Aunt Margaret? But why?"

She stood there twisting her hands. "It's been so long since I've seen them. What if they haven't forgiven me for Pa?"

"What is there to forgive? Grandpa was wrong. I've thought that for a long time."

"You have?"

"Yes."

"Why didn't you ever tell me? I thought all along that you too held it against me."

"I didn't think you wanted to talk about it. You never mention Grandpa."

"Oh, Megan," she said, her eyes soft with gratitude. Hesitantly, she entered the room and sat on the window seat. It was only then I realized that all this time she had been speaking to me from the doorway.

"Megan, please sit down. I want to tell you something. I started to tell you in the garden that evening Munnar came with the news of Ajai's arrest."

I sat beside her and waited.

She took a deep breath and began to speak, eyes on her folded hands in her lap. "I used to love this room, I thought of it as my haven, my cocoon. I'd sit here for hours reading, or sewing, or writing letters. Sometimes I just sat still in the big chintz chair. It relaxed me after seeing patients all day. I even napped in the chair if your uncle was later than usual. He would come in and wake me and we'd go to bed.

"At first I enjoyed my work, then it became increasingly difficult to see my patients grow big with the children I would deliver." She cupped one hand and slowly drew it towards her. "So many slippery little bodies. The tiny bottoms I slapped, then held my breath waiting for that first feeble squall. The mothers tired but transported, holding their babies. Oh Megan, I can't describe how some of them literally blazed with triumph. I wanted to feel that, at least once." She gave a short laugh. "There was a certain irony, really, about my doing this day after day, month after month, when more than anything in the world I wanted a child of my own. I wanted a girl, Megan—a girl exactly like you." She glanced briefly at me, and away. "Not a boy to help me cross the river to the life beyond, and all the rest. A girl." She sighed. "But I would have been grateful for any child.

"One day a woman came to see me. She was my age at the time, thirty-seven. A broad peasant face. Grossly overweight, and fairly advanced in pregnancy. She said, 'My belly is swelling with tumor.' 'When was your last blood flow?' I asked her. 'Some seven months now,' she replied. Can you imagine the stupidity? I examined her, told her she was pregnant. 'How can it be?' she said, her face taking on that peculiar radiance I'd seen so many times before, and then she began babbling about being married for twenty-two years without blessing . . . " Her voice trailed. She sighed again, her shoulders sagged. "The child was stillborn. Perfect in every way—only dead. The mother was uncomprehending. Finally her husband had to tear the child from her arms." She paused, then continued softly. "I can still see her cuddling that dead infant against her massive breast, trying to stuff her teat into its mouth." She paused again. "The awful thing was I felt a terrible elation when the baby died. I thought—God help me—it's not fair that this fat ignorant woman should have a child . . . I knew then it was time to stop. I never went back to the office."

She stopped talking. I sat very still beside her, hardly daring to breathe.

"I began to spend all day in this room," she haltingly continued. "One day after another, each like the one before." Her voice dropped, became a monotone; I could barely hear her. "About a fortnight later the wire came about Pa's death, followed by Lavinia's letter. I don't know if it was grief, anger, guilt—that stroke he had after I left. Your uncle came home early that evening; he'd been worried when I abruptly stopped going to work—poor man, he simply didn't understand; medicine is his life . . . He found me here . . . I had slit my veins."

She sat slumped forward, head bent, hands on her knees. That chair! That stained chair and carpet! Blood stains! *Letty's* blood. In a convulsive movement I slid to my knees. Wrapping my arms around her, I buried my face in her lap.

My dear Mama:

I'll be so happy to see you and Aunt Margaret again. You can't know how much I've missed you. I'm so excited! Aunt Letty is, too.

The only thing, Mama, is that she is so frightened at seeing you both again after such a long time. She thinks you have not forgiven her for Grandpa, which is silly, I know, but

Dear Mama:

Aunt Letty and I will be at the station to welcome you. I have missed you and will be happy to see you again. I want to prepare you for the change in Aunt Letty. Please don't act surprised or upset because it will only upset her

Dear Mama:

Aunt Letty and I will meet you at the station. We are very much looking forward to seeing you again. You will find the weather here much warmer than Madras. We stay indoors during the day because of the heat, and often sleep outdoors at night.

I hope Aunt Margaret's knee is better. I can't believe that I'll see you again in only a few days!

Love and kisses,

> Your daughter,
> Megan

CHAPTER FOURTEEN

But she *had* lived, I told myself repeatedly since that morning in the library; fragile as she was, she had survived. Not just in escaping death by my uncle's fortunate intervention, but by her choosing life, no matter how tentatively: in the tending of her roses, in her benevolence (as she saw it) to the servants' families, in her impulsive suggestion that we go to the club, in her graceful presence during the dinner for the Minister, and in all the preparation and forays to the bazaar *that* had entailed. Small things, perhaps, but even *I* saw them now as landmarks along her slow hard trek to recovery.

I felt grateful to Letty for entrusting me with her confidence. She was the only adult to treat me as an equal, as someone capable of understanding and compassion. My heart flooded now as it had that other time she had poured out her pain to me: the night I'd found her in my room after the picnic at Marble Rocks. I'd felt quite differently then, both during the telling and in the days that followed. What accounted for the difference in my reaction? One reason, maybe, was Letty herself. That night she'd been incoherent, frightening. Later, her refusal to acknowledge the incident confused and burdened me. But the morning in the library she had been fully in control of what she was saying. And once said, she had continued to speak freely of her feelings, her fears. It was as if the flow of words, once started, could not be stanched. Another reason, perhaps of more significance, was that I discovered *I* had changed. Toward Letty. Inch by inch. My early resentment had given way to a grudging pity, to a feeling of protectiveness, and, finally, to love. Not the love of a child for an adored aunt, nor the love I felt for Mama, which was tinged with a sense of duty, but something very different that sprang from deep inside my heart and spirit.

All of which is not to discount the fact that the night before, as sleep crept over me, my eyes heavy, my heart slow, I was suddenly jolted awake by a vision of Letty sitting in the old chintz chair, scalpel in hand, delicately opening a vein. Had she clenched her fist to make the vein more prominent? Had she clenched her teeth as the blood spurted? What had she been thinking of as oblivion spread through her and about her in ever-widening circles?

In the garden now, I watched her move among the rose bushes in the powdery yellow light that precedes sunset, pinching, snipping, cupping a rare bloom gently in her hand. "This was the start of the rose garden," she said. "This very bush." She bent to sniff the rose and her orange chiffon sari slid from her shoulder. It struck me that she chose these brilliant saris to brighten her life. She straightened. "At first, after my accident," she always referred to it as her accident, "I stayed in my room all day. Then one morning I looked out the window, that one, there." She pointed with the clippers at her bedroom window overlooking the garden. "I saw a gardener planting this bush. I called to him. He told me that my husband had ordered him to plant it in full view of my window, that there were two more bushes to come. Each day I watched the buds form, unfold and fall apart. Over and over. I asked my husband to bring me a book about the care of roses, and I learned how they should be pruned, about pesticides and fertilizers. The gardeners were not doing the job properly, you see. They were cutting the stems too long, were not careful about removing the dead blooms. So, well . . ." She gave a short laugh. "It got me out of the house."

The sun slid behind the mango grove and the sky was suffused with color that warmed our skin and bronzed Letty's crimped hair.

"The reason I'm telling you all this, Megan, is because I want you to know how much you've helped me. Since you came to stay, I've begun to think . . . maybe, just maybe . . ."

I waited, but she didn't complete the sentence. I said, "But I've done nothing, really."

"Oh yes, you have. You see, I draw energy from you. Like a vampire." She laughed gaily, waving the clippers. "Feeding off your freshness and honesty. There. What do you think of that?"

My face and neck burned at the word, honesty, and I turned away, stooping quickly to pick up a black-spotted yellowed leaf. I was not honest about my uncle and Nila! But, I quickly told myself: How could I possibly tell Letty, and risk the consequences? I spread a scoop of fertilizer into the damp earth at the roots of each bush, then worked it in with a trowel.

"Did I tell you that Uncle has talked about Ajai to the Minister who came to dinner?"

"No."

"He told me that this morning before he left for work. Perhaps Ajai's sentence will be reduced."

"Good."

"Oh, come. I thought you'd be delighted."

"I don't know, Aunt Letty." I sat back on my heels and brushed the hair from my forehead with the back of my wrist.

"I shouldn't have gone to Nagpur. He wasn't pleased to see me."

"Perhaps he was embarrassed to be seen in jail."

"He wasn't embarrassed with Munnar."

"Munnar is different. They've grown up together, like brothers almost. You'd better get up from there. I'm going to dust the bushes." I rose, trowel in hand. Letty lay the clippers in the basket on top of the dead blooms and diseased leaves, and began to dust pesticide over foliage. "The black spot is really bad this year." Almost casually, she said, "You're in love with him." It was a statement.

I didn't answer.

"Megan, no one promised that love marches bravely to trumpet blasts. Love falters and fails and starts up again on shaky feet. Not moonlight and roses and madly throbbing hearts. That was invented for frustrated spinsters."

"Aunt Margaret is a spinster," I reminded her.

"I know that," she said testily, and continued to dust the leaves until they looked as if they were covered with a fine ash. The harsh odor of pesticide smothered the lingering scent of roses. "Does Aunt Margaret still read penny romances? I can still remember some of the titles: *Lover Claim My Heart,* and *Unto Us Beloved.*"

"What about, *Love Rides a Frantic Horse?*"

We laughed together.

"Megan, what do they look like?"

"To me, Mama looks a great deal like Grandpa. Aunt Margaret never changes . . . Aunt Letty," I said, "please don't worry."

"I'm trying not to. Really."

At the station, Letty and I fought our way through the crush of passengers arriving and departing, coolies staggering bent-legged under piles of luggage balanced on their heads,

and vendors of hot tea, hair clips and film magazines. We
stood side by side, Letty in a burgundy sari with a gold border
and I in my lilac Punjabi costume. We were surrounded by the
unrelenting beggars and enveloped in the smells of burning
coal, engine smoke, cooking food, hair oil, urine and musk.
Letty looked pale and made no attempt at conversation which,
in any case, would have been difficult in the pandemonium. I
made up my mind I would ask Mama the truth about Papa,
make her explain his absence.

The train arrived and disgorged crowds of travel-stained
people who mingled with those already on the platform.
Dodging vendors and others, I ran up and down the length of
the train looking for Mama and Aunt Margaret, without
success. I returned to stand by Letty, craning my neck to look
in every direction. Had they missed their connection?
Changed their minds? The congestion thinned a little. In a
clearing I saw two elderly English women, sallowed by the
Indian sun, in shapeless crumpled frocks of some indetermi-
nate color, chosen no doubt as appropriate for the journey
because of their ability to hide soil. How sensible, and how
like Mama.

My uncle did not make a hit with Mama. I could tell. When
he finally came home at nine o'clock he hugged her exuber-
antly and bellowed his welcome, while Letty hung back. Not
one for embraces, Mama stood stiffly in the fleshy circle of his
arms. By this time, she was swaying with exhaustion; Aunt
Margaret had already gone to bed with a cup of Ovaltine and
two digestive biscuits.

We sat down to a festive dinner of potato *bhaji* and *paratas,*
followed by chicken *pilav*. There was a bowl of zinnias on the
table and Letty's best linen serviettes and runners. Mama
hardly glanced at Letty, hardly spoke to her, just made general

144

comments, addressing no one in particular. If Letty noticed the tension vibrating like a flung knife whose point had lodged in the table's gleaming surface, she gave no sign.

"Well, dear sister-in-law," my uncle boomed. *He,* I was quite sure, had sensed nothing. "At last we are meeting. And how are you finding our lovely young lady?"

Lines radiated from Mama's tight lips, which she parted, but did not relax, to say, "She looks . . . different."

Earlier, in the back seat of the car, riding home from the station, Mama had fingered my sleeve, giving it a little tug. "Why aren't you wearing a frock?" she asked. I told her I'd outgrown them.

"And so very beautiful," my uncle went on. "You must see her in a sari." He bunched his fingertips to his lips then spread them apart in the air. "Like an actress. Like Nargis."

"An Indian actress?"

"Yes, Mama," I cut in quickly. "A very famous Indian actress."

Letty picked delicately at a piece of potato.

I leaned forward gazing at Mama, my eyes pleading with her to relax. Then, remembering my own reaction when I first arrived, how bitterly disappointed I had been to find Letty so changed, I sat back in my chair with a sigh. Now, Mama faced not only the new Letty, but the new me as well, sitting opposite her in my lilac Punjabi dress. Time, I thought, in time she'll get used to things.

"By the way, Megan," my uncle said. "Ajai will be home in a week. His sentence has been reduced on humanitarian grounds. I told the Minister that Mrs. Pande is suffering from TB." He winked. "Of course, you and I know that the lady is fully recovered now—"

"Who is Ajai? What sentence?" Mama looked sharply at me and I felt the wretched color rush to my face.

"He is a young friend of Megan's," my uncle said. "You

know these young college students. How hotheaded they are. Something about a strike."

"Megan, what is this all about?"

"They were striking for supplementary exams," I muttered into my plate, "so they could make up deficit grades."

Letty came to my rescue. "Oh, Megan knows very little about it," she said. "Ajai is Munnar's friend, actually. A brilliant student. Should make a splendid lawyer. Munnar is studying engineering. It's amazing to see these young people grow up, choose professions . . ."

She'd managed to divert the subject, for the time being, anyway. After a few moments, during which I struggled for control and continued to look down at my plate, I heard Mama's chair scrape against the floor. I looked up to see her rise, unsteadily. "I'm afraid I must excuse myself," she said. "Do forgive me."

"Shall I come to your room to say goodnight, Mama?"

"Better not. You'll only disturb Aunt Margaret."

CHAPTER FIFTEEN

Aunt Margaret tried to make up for Mama's chilly mood, but the truth was they seemed hopelessly out of place in Letty's house, inhabiting their shapeless frocks with the indifference of travellers taking temporary shelter in a *dak* bungalow. Beauty and youth past and done with, it seemed they'd shed, with some relief, vanity as well. They were two dun-colored sparrows beside Letty, who was a bright tropical bird in her splendid saris.

From time to time, Mama would glance at my neatly combed hair and my new tunics and scarves and I would see her bafflement. Possibly she was looking for the disheveled girl with mosquito-bitten legs. Once she removed her glasses and examined the lenses as if she questioned their accuracy, and I noticed how the skin under her eyes sagged in half-moon folds. Then I felt a rush of love for her, and also a remorse. For what? I was not sure. Perhaps, for changing from the girl she remembered, and missed. I knew how awful it was when people changed—like building a house brick by brick only to have it all come tumbling down in a heap. Yet, there were times when I flaunted my new self, flicking my scarf jauntily over my shoulder, conscious of the way my tunic tightened over my breasts, lifting my hair languidly from the back of my neck and, once, even blowing into my damp armpits, knowing full well that Mama did not acknowledge either breasts or armpits—all the while some part of me, an inner eye, say, coolly noted her reaction . . . Maybe, after all, I did understand the remorse.

The morning after they arrived, Letty and I took them on a house tour. We went from room to room, Mama surreptitiously feeling curtain material, checking surfaces for dust with a forefinger. We admired the views from the verandahs that had different creepers growing on each trellis, tasted preserves and pickles in the storeroom surrounded by the dusty scent from bags of grain, stopped to speak to Maharaj in the kitchen.

Letty linked arms with Aunt Margaret, saying, "Come. I want to show you the outside before it gets too hot."

We stepped into the sunshine-filled courtyard where the flagstones felt pleasantly warm underfoot. In an hour they would be shimmering with heat, but by then we would have retreated into the darkened, shuttered house.

"This is the rose garden," Letty said, when we reached it. "Megan is becoming quite a gardener. I wish you could have seen it last month. Every bush heavy with blooms. This heat makes them go dormant."

The sloping shadow of the house lay aslant the garden, dividing it into light and shade: crotons flamed in the sun while bougainvillea, blood-dark, hung sensuously in shadow. In the middle were the rose bushes.

"Ah," Aunt Margaret sighed. "We used to have roses when we lived on Brock Road. Remember, girls? We'd sit outside in the evening. That heavenly scent." She bent to sniff a yellow bloom whose petals were traced with the palest pink.

"I remember," Letty said, "that's why I enjoy these so much, I think."

"They were such a nuisance," Mama said. "I always swore if we shifted from that house, I'd never bother with a garden again."

Letty led us to the library. "And this," she said, throwing open the door, "is Megan's favorite haunt."

"What a delightful room," Aunt Margaret exclaimed. "Old *Tatlers,* and *Illustrated Weeklies.* I know where I'll spend *my* mornings."

"Before breakfast, Aunt Margaret," I said, a little unsteadily. It was the first time I'd been in the room since the morning of Letty's confession. "It's lovely, early in the morning, to watch the monkeys play in the banyan tree out there, and to listen to the birds." Despite my unease, I still loved the room. Aunt Margaret's presence in it would be a comfort, help dispel the ghosts, the way she had done when I was small. Afraid of the dark then, I would clutch her hand as together we marched into an unlit room singing "Alexander's Ragtime Band."

Mama moved slowly past the shelved books, scanning titles.

"No Bible, Letty?"

The question hung in the air. It was the first time since Mama arrived that she'd addressed Letty directly.

"I don't know," Letty said, distantly, a hand to her cheek. "There used to be one. Somewhere."

"It's sad about Letty," Mama stated, as she sat beside me on my bed. Letty had retired to her room after lunch. Aunt Margaret, too, was resting. "She has a terrible life. Oh my, this is a hard bed." She tested the mattress with her palm. She leaned forward, her hair escaping from her bob-pin in a grey twist, to earnestly ask of me, "Are you sure you're comfortable here?"

149

"Oh, yes," I said, deliberately misunderstanding. "I like hard beds."

She shook her head ever so slightly. It could have been a tremor, or even a random play of light. She exhaled audibly. "I'm quite sure, Megan," she said, after a small pause, "you've noticed her unhappiness."

I recoiled at the complicity in her voice. Also, I was beginning to sense that this was more than a discussion about Letty.

"She manages."

"But one doesn't manage life. Don't you see? One lives it." She peered at me; there was a cloudiness around her blue eyes. "This is what comes from marrying outside one's community, race and religion . . ."

Ah, here it comes, I thought. I braced myself for the lecture. My uncle's comment at dinner about Ajai must have sat all night long on Mama's muslin-clad chest like an accusing, taunting demon. Then it hit me that Mama's own marriage had failed even though she and Papa had shared the same background. In a stab of cold rage, I decided that she had driven Papa away. What man could live with her self-righteousness, her pious platitudes?

". . . lacks sharing, I always say. Remember Poppy Dawson? She married that Church of England curate. What was his name? Oh, you know, the one with the chopped-off chin."

"No. I don't."

"And he was one of us. English as you and me. But, of course, the marriage foundered. And all on account of religion. How could it not have?"

I thought of Poppy Dawson, a doughy girl with massive raw-looking ankles, and her poor curate whom I did, indeed, remember simply because of his strange chin. Or the lack of it. I snickered.

Mama looked stricken. She rose abruptly and went to stand by the window, arms folded, the curve of her upper back plain above the square-cut neckline of her brown cotton dress.

Suddenly contrite, I said, "I'm sorry, Mama. It's just . . . I was only thinking of what you said about Poppy Dawson's husband. About his chin."

She looked out of the window, rubbing her arms as if they were cold. "He couldn't help his chin. You shouldn't make fun." An automatic rebuke. Then she faced me and said, "His religion, however, was quite another matter!"

She moved about the room and when she caught sight of the old picture on the dressing table, she picked it up and examined it. Watching her reflection in the mirror, I saw a wistfulness come over her face. And as I watched, I felt as if I were dissolving into her skin and bones, settling into her flesh, peering out from behind her steel-framed glasses; for just a second I saw myself old, while Mama gazed at her young self.

"My hair was so long then," she murmured. "I could sit on it. And thick. When I washed it, it was like laundering a blanket . . . I wonder how the glass broke?" She traced the path of the crack with a fingertip. "I think I'll have it replaced for her. Or, maybe," she turned to me suddenly, holding the picture to her chest, her expression accusing, "since it's tucked away here, she doesn't even see it."

"Aunt Letty told me she put the picture in my room so I'd have something familiar to look at. I think she usually kept it on her own dressing table."

"Oh, did she?" Mama replaced the picture amid the clutter of pencils and books, brush and comb, a teacup, a shoebox filled with Mama's and Aunt Margaret's letters; she moved to the open wardrobe. "Where are your frocks?" she asked, "I'll let them out for you. Piece them at the sides. You look so . . . native in those clothes."

"I gave them away to the servants."

151

"Megan! They were pure Liberty cotton."

"They didn't fit, Mama."

"They could have been made to fit. Waste not, want not, I always say. Well, if they're gone, they're gone."

In shutting the wardrobe door, she spotted Shiva's picture on the wall. "My goodness, this nasty thing!" The door did not catch and swung slowly open with a drawn-out creak, blocking the picture from view again. She slammed it shut. "Why in heaven's name do you put up with it?"

"Because I like it."

"My God! It's a heathen thing, child."

I stood quickly. "No different from the picture of Pan and the Minotaur in your bedroom in Madras. Mama, this picture comforts me. When I'm lonely I talk to it."

"Pray to it, you mean."

"No." I shook my head, considering. "Just . . . talk to it."

"But don't you see?" She said in a low, desperate voice. "That's praying. I'm going to have this out with Letty. I'll not have her corrupting you." She moved toward the door. "She promised me she would see that you fulfilled your religious . . ."

"No, Mama. No!" I ran to block her way.

". . . duty. Only on that condition did I agree—" She stopped, stared at me blankly. "What do you mean, No?" We faced each other.

"Don't upset her."

"Upset her? She deserves to be upset. It's unthinkable putting that picture in your room, as if . . . as if she intended all along to wean you away—an impressionable young girl— from me, our ways, our God. Just look at your clothes! And hers, too. Those hideous saris. And that Ajai, whoever he is. I suppose she wants you to follow her example, to prove a point. Well, we'll see about that."

"I won't let you hurt her," I said, planting myself stubbornly in the doorway.

Mama's head jerked back as if I'd struck her. She groped her way backward to sit on the bed.

"So, it's come to that. Has it?" Her voice was thick with emotion. She sat, hands on knees, staring straight ahead.

"She's been through a lot, Mama," I said pleadingly.

She did not respond at first, and I thought she'd not heard. Then she said in a flat voice, "Well, she's not alone. And in her case, she only brought it upon herself. Do you know that your grandfather went down on his knees to her to plead with her not to leave? Poor old man. He never recovered from that stroke." She turned to look at me; her eyes brimmed with tears. "She's been through a lot, you say. She's caused a lot, too. And now she's taken you away from me."

Grandpa on his knees to Letty? Oh God, that would be like Papa kneeling before me. The thought made my stomach turn over. I approached the bed slowly. So Letty had been right: Mama had not forgiven her for Grandpa. But how was I going to keep Letty from seeing that? And how was I going to convince Mama that Letty had not deliberately set out to lure me away?

"Mama," I put out a hand and touched her shoulder. "She has not taken me from you. Please, Mama, you must believe me. If you only knew how I've missed you and Papa and Aunt Margaret. We have each other. Aunt Letty has no one." I came round to sit beside her. She smelled of starch and talcum powder. "Did you know that her baby was born dead?" I took her hand in mine. "And she could never have another one."

Mama gave a little gasp. Her eyes widened as she turned to me. "Oh my. She never wrote about that. Poor Letty. But," she added gravely, after a pause, "God has His ways. If the child had lived, it would have been a Hindu." Abruptly she changed the subject. "Tell me about this Ajai."

"He's . . . ah . . . he's a friend of Munnar's. They grew up together. He's studying law, and . . . ah . . . is interested in politics—"

"Never mind about all that." She gestured impatiently. "You never give a direct answer. I want to know what he is to you."

I forced myself to look her in the eye. "A friend."

We gazed at each other in silence. I thought that surely she would hear the hammering of my guilty heart. Finally, she turned away with a sigh. "Well, you've always been truthful. I'll say that for you. But you can't be too careful with your everlasting soul."

Mama thawed a little after I had told her about Letty's dead baby, though she still remained wary, especially with me: eternally vigilant. Why had I pictured it all so differently? I'd thought that we'd all live together as we had done during those early years in Madras, singing boisterous songs around a piano even though I knew perfectly well there was no piano in Letty's house, or crowding round the wireless for news of the war when the war had been over for more than three years.

Through it all Letty remained serene, which was something I discovered one morning to my astonishment. Preoccupied as I was with Mama, I had lately been less observant of Letty. We had driven to Gangaram's Book Shop with Aunt Margaret, who had run through her stock of romance novels. Mama had elected to stay behind and write letters. To whom? I'd asked nonchalantly, thinking of Papa. She assured me that the scope of her correspondence was varied and voluminous.

Gangaram's was located halfway down Mahatma Gandhi Road, a main thoroughfare of the city with six lanes of frenzied traffic. Letty and I sat on a bench next to the open front door while Aunt Margaret stood some distance away examining one thin paper-covered book after another. Outside, crowds streamed by on the pavement, sidestepping the legless beggar who propelled himself along on his hands.

Letty lit a cigarette. I recalled Mama's reaction the first time she saw that happen. Shocked, she had thrown it up to Letty that smoking was both unladylike and unhealthy, not to mention smelly. Letty had replied that what Mama said was true, but since life was a series of bargains and balances, she would continue to smoke, smelly or not.

"Aunt Letty," I ventured, "does Mama upset you?"

"In what way?" She turned to me, her brows drawn together in a perplexed frown. The hand holding the cigarette between two square-tipped fingers was bent at the wrist, the cigarette tilted away from me.

"Well, she's so . . . so . . ."

"Cantankerous?"

"No, not cantankerous," I said sharply; after all this was my mother we were discussing. "Just a little . . ."

"Argumentative?"

"Maybe a little," I conceded, chin on hands, elbows on knees. "I don't know."

"But we've always argued, Megan." She patted my back. "It's the nature of things. We're sisters, after all."

"I don't remember you arguing before." I faced her accusingly.

Letty smiled. "You were very young then." She drew on her cigarette, squinting against the smoke. "How we used to squabble as girls. Aunt Margaret was always the mediator. Pa would simply put on his hat and stamp out of the house. 'Vacating the war zone,' he called it. Actually, Megan," she said, gazing at Aunt Margaret in her grey cotton dress and sensible oxfords, who was leaning forward to examine yet another book, "I'm enjoying them, very much."

The tension, then. Had I been blowing it up out of all proportion? Had it been another of my wild imaginings? Letty did seem very much at ease, calmer than I'd ever seen her before. As her self-appointed champion, I felt curiously let down, dispensed with. I sat listening to the street noises:

horns, bells, sputtering scooters, jumbled voices that swelled and faded past the open doorway. A man passing by spat a wide arc of bright red betel juice into the gutter without breaking stride.

"But," I blurted finally, "you were so anxious when you got Mama's letter saying they were coming."

"I was nervous, of course, at first," she said thoughtfully, as she leaned forward to stub out her cigarette in a bucket of sand by the door. "After all, I hadn't seen them in years." She placed a hand on mine. "But it's comforting how quickly one can slip back into a family even after all this time. It's the most reassuring thing in the world. It's what I've missed all these years." She squeezed my hand. "You were right. I had nothing to fear from them."

I was not so sure.

It was coziest with Aunt Margaret. In the library, she and I leafed through dusty old magazines that worms had tunneled through microscopically. In an *Illustrated London News,* I found a spider, flattened but intact, legs brittle, fine as hairs. Prone on the reed mat with its pattern of elephants, I read of how the English were going about restoring war-scarred London, how signboards were appearing in parts of the city to remind Londoners of various landmarks that no longer existed: "Site of the Black Boar" or "Stone's Chop House (soon to be rebuilt)." Prefabricated houses were springing up in the heart of London next to bombed-out buildings. I looked at all the pictures of the royal procession on the occasion of the silver wedding anniversary of the King and Queen, which followed a route from Buckingham Palace to St. Paul's; cheering spectators lined the streets. Had Papa been among them? I wondered, waving a small Union Jack, perhaps?

Beside me, Aunt Margaret chuckled. She lay an open *Tatler*

across her lap and removed her glasses, massaging with a finger and thumb the red indentations on either side of the bridge of her nose. "Have you ever noticed how some people resemble their pets? Just look." She held out the magazine to me, pointing at the picture of a man with a long narrow face and large ears who stood at the head of his horse. "I'd swear they were related. I wonder," she said, sitting back and flipping the pages, "if there is a mutual recognition of sorts that takes place between animal and owner. Maybe that's why they become so attached."

"Like Mr. Brambleby and his basset hound. Papa used to say they were truly kindred souls and it was enough to make him a believer in reincarnation." I turned back to peer intently at the pictures of the royal procession, concentrating on the crowds along the road that were smiling, waving flags; some held small children on their shoulders. I willed Papa's face to float to the front of the picture.

"What is it?" she asked. "You've been staring at those pictures forever."

I glanced up into her dear face with its translucent bones, so close to the skin. "Oh, I only wondered if I could spot Papa in the crowd. Here," I handed the magazine to her. "I was looking at these pictures of the Silver Jubilee and wondered if Papa might not have been there, too. Cheering. You know."

She looked briefly at the pictures; her mouth tightened. "Megan, child," she said, laying the magazine aside. "Those pictures are minuscule, absolute blurs."

"I know. Maybe if we had a magnifying glass."

"No dear. Your father was not at that parade."

"How do you know?"

"It's useless looking for him in pictures."

Sitting up, I turned slightly away from her. I promised myself that soon I would confront Mama, *demand* the truth from her, harsh though it may be—but not yet. Not just yet.

I felt the focus of Aunt Margaret's gaze, but I could not face the dreadful compassion I knew it held.

"She's going dotty looking for him in pictures," I overheard Aunt Margaret tell Mama. In the hallway outside their room, I stood frozen, staring blindly at a green wall—the color that had so offended Letty's mother-in-law. I had come to tell them lunch was served. "She must be told."

"She's my child," Mama answered heatedly. "Not yours, and not Letty's. I'll decide what she should be told."

CHAPTER SIXTEEN

The night before I had dreamed of Ajai. A strange dream. Earlier that day, Letty had told me, discreetly—unlike my uncle who had brought up the subject in front of Mama—that Ajai had been released. She went on to apologize for my uncle's tactlessness. It was all right, I told her, because certain things needed to be settled between Mama and me.

I said I dreamed of Ajai. But I did not see him or hear him, only felt him. In the dream I was standing by a neem tree, the same tree we'd stood under that evening at the club, only now it was part of a vast whispery forest. Invisible hands were on my belly, stroking my thighs, tracing the hollow places. I knew they were his, could only be his. I pressed myself against the tree, stretching my arms around its trunk as far as they would go, the bark rough against my skin. I moved my body against it, gently. And as I did, I felt its life enter me, along with a mounting ecstasy. I woke to the sound of my own moaning. My thighs were damp and slippery.

When Letty suggested we go to the club the next evening,

159

I took it as an omen: good, or bad, I was not sure, but I wanted to see that tree again, feel the imprint of its bark against my skin.

At the club, we sat sipping our drinks under the soaring canopy of rain trees, surrounded by the cacophony of crickets and an occasional frog. My uncle had left us there and gone off to his bridge game. Lit by a dying sun to the pearly sheen of whipped egg whites tinted pink, fluffy clouds wafted above the fretwork of foliage. Bursts of laughter came to us through the open door of the bar.

"Remember Cleo, girls?" Aunt Margaret asked, balancing a double sherry on the arm of her chair. She was looking very smart in a navy silk with white polka dots. "Wasn't she gorgeous? Queen of the Night, if you please. Black as the Ace of Spades—"

"She was dark grey," Mama interrupted, and sipped her port. *Her* only concession to the occasion was a pink celluloid clip in her iron-grey hair instead of the usual bob-pin. Since she was clad in her basic brown, I think I would have preferred the bob-pin. The effect of the clip was as jarring as if she held a rose in her teeth.

"She was black," Letty said. She held her glass in both hands under her chin.

"I should know," Mama argued. "She was my cat."

"Then you've forgotten. I distinctly remember the color of her fur because it stuck to the scalpel when I did the postmortem."

"You cut up Cleo!"

"Only in the interest of science, Lavinia."

"Well, she certainly was a lovely cat," Aunt Margaret said peaceably, a hand twisting the pearls at her throat. "Whose dog was it that killed her?"

I excused myself and walked away to the sound of Letty and Mama wrangling over the color of Cleo's fur; their constant bickering made me uneasy. Besides, I wanted to be by myself to think of Ajai and my dream. As I passed the deserted tennis courts, I felt the clenching pain of his absence in my throat. It was now two days since Letty had told me he was back, yet he hadn't contacted me. I realized now he wasn't going to contact me. I would never again see the way a smile lit his eyes first before his lips, nor would I ever caress the place where his hair curled above the neck of his *kurta,* as I so longed to do.

I approached the tree cautiously, half-listening to the throaty cluckings of birds that roosted above. I hesitated before I put out my hand and touched the trunk, afraid I might invoke something uncontrollable. I waited. Nothing happened. I pressed my palm against it, then the tender inside of my wrist, then my entire arm. Nothing at all. It was an ordinary neem tree near the tennis courts of the Nerbudapur Club, not part of the magic forest of my dream. Though still so vivid, that's all it was: only a dream. I asked myself now why I'd been so certain the hands belonged to Ajai. Maybe they weren't hands at all; maybe it was only the wind. I turned away and went back to join the others.

They were still sitting there: three aging women who resembled each other not so much in the slope of forehead and the speckled hands, but rather in the gestures and mannerisms that bore the imprint of shared heritage. Would a stranger seeing us there together connect me with them? See the stamp of them on my face?

Mama looked up at me. "Where did you go?" she asked.

"Down by the tennis courts."

"How did you scratch your arm like that?"

I looked at the long, red weal on my inner arm with some surprise. "I don't remember," I mumbled. "Maybe when I leaned against a tree, or something."

161

"Coo-ee, everybody." Nila floated toward us in a sea-green sari the exact shade of her eyeshadow. Her hair was artlessly piled on her head with little tendrils at her temples, the front of her ears, the nape of her long golden neck. "I have not seen little Megan for so long." She drew out the last two words: so-o-o lo-o-ng. "Ah, I see your relatives have arrived."

My uncle must have told her they were expected. Instantly, I knew Letty thought the same thing; she made the introductions. "This is my Aunt, Margaret Curtis. My sister—Megan's mother—Lavinia Manning. Nila Bhatt, a neighbor."

"And family friend," Nila added.

She dragged a chair over the straw-dry grass and sat down. Letty signaled to a passing waiter. "What will you have, Nila?"

Settling herself in the chair, Nila said to Letty, "Oh, please do not bother about me." Then she turned to the hovering waiter and said crisply, "Bring me a pineapple juice with only one ice cube." She lifted a gently curved hand to pat the air around her unswept curls.

Mama was charmed with Nila as of course I had been, at first. Soon she and Nila were chattering away, Nila telling Mama how she'd dressed me in a sari the day of the parade. "She was a hit, let me tell you. Everyone said how well a sari suits her." She darted a sidelong glance at Letty, which seemed to take in Letty's stiff, heavy sari of fuschia silk and to confirm Nila's impression of her own innate elegance. I don't know if Letty caught the look, but I saw her take a long swallow of her drink.

Nila said to me, "There is a dance here next Saturday. Why don't you come?"

Dances. That's all she thought about. What was it Letty once said of her? "She's as fluttery as an insect, with a brain to match."

"But that's your birthday, Megan," Mama said.

162

Nila clapped her hands. "Then we must celebrate. Leave it to me. I will arrange everything. Never mind the dance. We will have a party at the old palace. My husband can get a special pass. Megan, I will dress you. Oh, it will be so much fun."

I looked quickly at Letty and found she was smiling, with relief, almost. "Why, Nila," she said, "that's very kind of you, indeed. I'm sure Lavinia will be happy to help with the preparations. Won't you, Lavinia? What a lovely opportunity for you to get out of the house and meet people."

"We'll see the palace very soon now," Colonel Bhatt said in his precise way. "This is the best time of day to approach it, at sunset. The Maharaja modeled it after the famous Floating Palace of Jaipur. Notice, if you will, how the willow fronds meet their reflection on the water as if they actually grow out of it."

It was the first he'd spoken since we left the outskirts of Nerbudapur. Mama and I were riding with the Bhatts, while Aunt Margaret was to come later with Letty and my uncle. I sat beside Colonel Bhatt, who drove, with Mama and Nila in the back. The road was unpaved and winding, lined with banyan trees and dotted with roadside stalls selling sugarcane juice and green coconuts. Perhaps it was the heat and the billowing dust, but no one seemed inclined to make conversation. I couldn't help thinking of the last time I'd seen Colonel Bhatt, at the dinner for the Minister. Facing straight ahead at the dusty road, I stole a sideways glance at him. There was a military set to his head, but the dark glasses he wore made it difficult to read his mood. Maybe behind the glasses he'd been stealing glances at me, thinking the same thing.

"After the Maharaja's favorite wife died in childbirth," he

continued, his moustache dark against his upper lip, "he couldn't stand the place any longer, or so the story goes, and he cleared off to Darjeeling." He held the steering wheel lightly, and I saw again the position of Ajai's long-fingered hands as he drove. I shut my eyes, but the image stayed with me.

Soon we crested an incline, and there was the palace. Surrounded by willows that licked at their own reflection, it rose from the lake shimmering with restless, watery light while the setting sun made rubies of small pointed windows. Repeating itself on the water, it seemed partially submerged. A jeweled iceberg.

"It's lovely, Nila." I turned to thank her.

"My pleasure." She sounded restrained. Was it the black sari she wore instead of the usual pastels, unaccented but for the jet and diamond earrings? Or was there something else in the car? A tension, like a pot of some thick, bubbling liquid.

Mama, also in black—a rusty-looking silk—said, "Yes, you should be grateful to Nila. She went to a lot of trouble for this party. My, I hope that lazy *chowkidar* got those chandeliers dusted and remembered the toilet paper." Mama had enjoyed all the preparations for the party. In the preceding week, she'd gone happily off to Nila's every morning after breakfast.

Nila said, "Not too many people accepted. If only we had more time. Then what fun it would have been."

"My dear," her husband said, "I doubt if Miss Manning has met half the people you invited. After all, the party is for her. Or am I mistaken?"

Nila huddled against the car door. She did not answer.

Pristine rolls of toilet paper graced every bathroom. Mama was relieved. Chandeliers sparkled: great branches of crystal with dangling teardrop prisms. In the marble durbar hall

164

where the Maharaja used to meet with his subjects and where the party was to take place, life-size paintings tilted forward from walls. They depicted solemn, moustached maharajas with tufted turbans and curly-toed shoes. Tapestries hung in the dining hall. In one corner, perched on a stool, was a stuffed monkey holding cymbals that clanged at the press of a button. It was an evil-looking thing. Long tables held platters of small iced cakes, curry puffs, gold-foiled confectionery, little clay saucers of sweet curds. The hot food, Nila said, would be brought out later. Letty had paid for everything, although Nila and Mama had made all the arrangements.

French doors opened onto a sweeping courtyard gone to seed. A dancing stone cupid, headless, teetered on one toe in the center of a crumbling fountain. Other statuary, also missing limbs, faces, dotted the landscape where trees were being suffocated by vines. Long-dead trees, completely overgrown, raised truncated branches sleeved in bright green.

The place was full of ghosts. I could almost feel them brush past me on the broad curving staircase as Mama, Nila and I climbed the steps to the women's quarters on the third floor, the *zenana*. I fancied the rustle of silk, the scent of musk, the faint tinkle of ankle bells. In one of the small square rooms, Nila tied my sari, a present from Letty. It was a white and gold brocade, far too grand. Perhaps Letty felt that if she were not going to tie my sari, then she would at least choose it. Orange light filtered through a window with its wooden fretwork screen and made an intricate pattern on the low bed in the corner. Was this where the Maharaja's favorite wife had died in childbirth? I imagined her lying there: a pale, frightened girl who knew she was going to die. Had the child lived? I made a mental note to ask Colonel Bhatt.

"This sari is too heavy," Nila said disgustedly. "Chiffon. Voile. *These* are the things to wear in hot weather, not bro*cade*. I will have to pin this so it does not fall down. Where

I'll find a pin in this place, I do not know." She left to hunt down the *chowkidar* to see if *he* knew.

Mama handed me a long flat box. "Happy birthday, child."

"What is it?" I shook the box and heard a muffled rattle.

"Don't *do* that." She flapped her hands at me. "Can't you just open something without shaking it to pieces?"

Inside lay a pearl necklace, creamy and lustrous against dark blue velvet.

"Oh Mama!"

"They were my mother's. I saved them for you. Here, let me fasten them." She lifted the beads from their case. I felt her dry fingertips behind my neck. She was wearing eau de cologne. "There. Go and look in the mirror."

I moved to a spotted cheval mirror that stood against a wall. The pearls had the same muted gleam as the folds of my sari. I liked the way they felt smooth and cool against my skin. Nila had pulled my hair back into a chignon. I looked older than my eighteen years. And thinking that, I felt most keenly the absence of my father; this was my birthday, the first he'd missed. There had been no word from him, not even a card; although that morning, before we left for Mass, Mama had given me a new missal that she said was a present from him. *Papa,* I thought, *do you look for me in unexpected places the way I search for you in pictures? Do you see my face on other eighteen-year-old girls you pass in the street?*

I turned from the mirror. The sari was lead weight, the room stifling.

"No, Miss Manning," Colonel Bhatt said in his clipped accent. "The baby died also. If I'm not mistaken, it was a male child, too. The Maharaja's only son. No doubt that had something to do with his massive grief. I believe the cord was wrapped around its neck. It strangled."

I shivered. One more small ghost. We stood off to one side in the dining hall, watching Mama and Nila order the servants around. Mama wanted the monkey removed, but the *chow-kidar* refused.

"What happened to all the Maharaja's subjects when he left?" I asked, chewing on a fingernail. "Did he just . . . abandon them?"

He did not reply at once. His gaze was fixed on his wife as she leaned over a table to straighten a flower arrangement. Her sari was tied low on her hips exposing a wide expanse of skin between it and her brief, black *choli*-blouse. The bones of her bent neck glistened, each as finely articulated as the pearls in my necklace. "The eldest daughter's husband ruled for a short time," he went on, his eyes following Nila's movements, "but, as you know, after Independence, our government appropriated the principalities." Suddenly, briefly, he closed his eyes as though the slope of Nila's hips and buttocks were too exquisite to behold, too painful, and turned to face me, his back to the room. He cleared his throat and continued purposefully, "This left the princes with little more than the palaces they lived in. But without the income, most of them could not afford the upkeep."

By now Letty, Aunt Margaret and my uncle had arrived: Letty resplendent in gold tissue, Aunt Margaret in her polka-dot silk, and my uncle in a white sharkskin dinner jacket that puckered across his shoulder blades. They duly commented on how nice I looked. Aunt Margaret insisted I have some sherry; it was my due, she said. Soon groups of others came too, none of whom I knew. The rooms began to fill with chattering, festively garbed guests. Nila need not have worried for their lack. I was surprised the young Sikh was not among them.

Under the haughty eyes of painted maharajas, we danced to music from the radiogram brought over from the Officers'

Club. Aunt Margaret was spinning around in the arms of one of the young officers, her cheeks scarlet, her troublesome knee forgotten, it seemed. Earlier, Mama had waltzed with the same dutiful young man. But it was Nila who claimed attention. She danced as though lost in some sweet reverie, as though she danced alone, chin lifted, lashes lowered, wearing a dreamy half-smile.

My sari was hot and heavy; I was out of breath from dancing and had drunk more sherry at Aunt Margaret's instigation. "After all, you are eighteen now, love," she'd said. I slipped outside into the courtyard; its decay was softened by moonlight as well as by the wine I'd consumed. I sat on a stone bench beside a headless griffin. In the silvery light it was possible to believe that the griffin's head was simply tucked under a wing, like a roosting bird. With light, laughter and music streaming from the french doors and the windows, it seemed the ghosts had departed, or gone to bed. But if one were to happen by, I knew I would greet it politely, even shake its hand. I would tell it, "I know I'm trespassing; I know I do not belong, but it's my eighteenth birthday, you see."

"Megan."

I drew my breath in sharply. My heart knocking, I turned to watch Ajai approach in his familiar garb of *pyjama* and *kurta*. "I thought I'd never see you again," I said in a cracked voice.

"Good God, why?" He sat beside me. His clothes were very white in the moonlight, his face shadowed. He seemed thinner.

"I thought you were angry with me for coming to the jail with Munnar. I didn't mean to offend—"

"Please." He took my hand. "I am the one to apologize. To you. For my behavior that day. The thing is, I was embarrassed. I want to appear always at my best before you."

"But you were your best," I declared passionately.

He released my hand and turned away with an impatient sound. "How innocent you are! Don't romanticize prison." He rose and walked to the fountain and stood there awhile, his back to me, then returned to stand above me. "You know, worse than the beating and facing a light all night long, was the loss of my own clothes. It was as if they had taken away my individuality, my . . . my*self*. . . along with my things. I couldn't face you without the protection of those things . . . There you were, completely unexpected, rosy, filled with some vague concern—"

"Vague concern!" I leaped up in anger. "Don't you talk to me about vague concern, rosiness. I couldn't bear it, I tell you. I had to see you."

Ajai grabbed me by the upper arms, shook me gently—maybe he thought I was getting hysterical. He touched my cheek with a fingertip. With a small gasp, I reached up and held his hand against my face. It's the wine, I thought, it's the wine that's making me so bold, even as I felt something inside me unfold like a flower.

Moving very close, he wrapped the other arm around me. "Sweet . . . my sweet," he whispered in my hair.

I lifted my head and his lips traced a path down my face to my chin. I felt his arm slide down my back, tighten around my bare midriff. His fingers were warm in the hollow of my waist. I wanted to feel them on my belly, my thighs. My veins sang with wine. He removed the hand I held trapped against my cheek and holding the nape of my neck, kissed me softly. I stood very still; I was a vessel brimming with precious liquid.

He pressed his lips to my neck, his breathing uneven. "Little girl," he said in a choked voice, and releasing me, stepped away.

Acutely annoyed at this development, I snapped, "I'm not little. I'm eighteen today."

He laughed shakily. "Yes, I know. I have something for

169

you." He reached in his pocket and withdrew a small object that he placed on my palm, closing my fingers over it, my hand in both of his. It was a three-inch cross, carved from soapstone. "For a conscientious little Christian," he said.

I looked at him to see if he were making fun of me, but I couldn't tell.

"Thank you," I said, and breathed deeply in an effort to control the thrumming inside. "Have you had something to eat? Drink?"

"It doesn't matter. I came out only to see you. I went to the house. Maharaj told me you were all here."

"You drove out all this way only to see me?"

"Megan," Mama called. "Megan, are you out there?"

"Oh God! Yes, Mama. We're here."

"We? Who's with you?"

"Come," I whispered to Ajai. "You have to meet my mother."

Mama reacted to Ajai as I had known she would. She was standing by the bronze front door rigid as a battering ram. As we stepped inside the vestibule, I made rapid introductions. She took one look at my face and I knew she knew that Ajai was more than just a friend, that what I'd told her that afternoon in my room was simply not true. ("You've always been truthful. I'll say that for you," she'd said).

"Look, Mama, Ajai brought me a gift," I said in a voice that sounded high and artificial.

I opened my hand. She stared at the cross as if it were a dead mouse that lay on my palm. In the light, it looked very oriental—even pagan, seen through Mama's eyes—elaborately carved with puffy mango-shaped leaves twining around it. In the place where on a crucifix Christ's head might droop, bulged a thick-petaled lotus, disproportionately large.

Ajai said, "A worker at the mine likes to carve things. It took him two days to make that. He got a bit carried away, I think."

I was afraid to look at him.

Letty called, "Ajai, dear boy." I glanced up as she hurried towards us in her gold sari and took Ajai's hand in both of hers. "What a lovely surprise! Ah, I see you've met Lavinia. Now you must come with me and meet Aunt Margaret, as well." She took him away.

I felt Mama's intense gaze, but turned back to the cross pretending to still be absorbed with it. Finally she said, "And what will you do with *that?* It's too large to hang around your neck. Maybe you can mount it on a board. Put it up in the place of that heathen picture in your room; it might be an improvement. Though that's arguable."

Then she marched off, spine stiff in her rusty black dress, and left me standing there.

CHAPTER SEVENTEEN

It was Mama's way to smolder in silence for days before things came to a head, usually over a lesser offense than the one that had displeased her in the first place. As a child I had dreaded these lengthy fits of pique that hovered over us like a false ceiling, and sometimes, when I could bear it no longer, I would invite the explosion of her anger by breaking a vase or an ashtray as if by accident, or by spilling tea on a freshly laundered tablecloth. Anything was preferable to her tight-lipped silence.

But, not this time. Now, all Mama's ire could not dull the sheen of my happiness. *I am loved* was a refrain in my heart and my mind. I heard it through the day: when I lay in my bath, or brushed my teeth; half-awake, as I turned over in bed, it whispered inside me. When Mama caught my eye at lunch, as I spooned up my soup, it swelled triumphant: an anthem, a marching song, a war cry. I ignored all her reproachful glances, steeled myself against her reddened eyes. She was not going to turn me into a passionless woman like herself, reeking of starch and self-mortification. Why was I an only child? I asked myself; had my parents not enjoyed the act of love enough to create another one? It was Mama, I decided; she had *denied* Papa, and so had deprived me of my father. No, I would not be like her. I would love as fiercely, as passionately, as Letty. Letty should have been my mother. I girded my anger around me like armor.

Yet when I was finally summoned to the room Mama shared with Aunt Margaret, I found myself wilting despite my brave resolve. As I walked down the corridor I felt fear crystallizing around my heart—not of Mama, but of my own mounting resentment towards her. Within that diamond-hard shell I found nothing. Suddenly, I thought that with my father already lost to me, I would be absolutely alone if I lost Mama. Like Letty. Orphaned.

The room was a sickly green, the color of the mildew that coated my shoes during the monsoon season. It was furnished just like mine, except there were two beds instead of one. In addition, a large crucifix hung on the wall facing the beds. I recognized it as the one from Grandpa's bedroom at home. On Mama's side of the night table was a rosary and a bible with curling flags of yellow paper marking favorite passages. Aunt Margaret's side held an open novel, face down, and an empty sherry glass. But I was not interested in the room or its furnishings. I sat glowering in a wicker armchair. Aunt Margaret sat on her bed. Mama paced the floor, her arms folded across her chest.

"You are coming home with us," she said, marching back and forth in her beige cotton dress tht rustled like dried leaves. "This has gone on long enough."

"I can't leave now."

"Why?" She stood before me. "Because of that Hindu you've fallen in love with? Don't deny it. I can always read your face."

"Yes," I said in a low voice. "I am in love with Ajai. But that's not why I'm staying . . . Aunt Letty needs me."

"Bosh!" She resumed her pacing. "All Letty needs is a bottle of whiskey. This is all her fault. I hold her directly responsible."

"Lavinia," Aunt Margaret chided, "you're being terribly unfair." She coughed once; the hand at her mouth shook slightly.

"She had nothing to do with it," I said coldly. "She didn't make me fall in love. These things just happen."

"All of a sudden now you're an authority on falling in love," Mama said. "You were an innocent girl when you left Madras."

"Lavinia, please." Aunt Margaret extended an arm. "Leave it alone. It will pass."

Mama turned on her aunt so swiftly she staggered a little. "And if it doesn't? What then?"

"For heaven's sake! It's not as if the child said she was going to marry him. A little reason—"

"Be quiet, Aunt Margaret," Mama snapped.

"No," Aunt Margaret replied as she massaged her forehead with two fingertips. "I won't be quiet this time. I let your father silence me when this sort of thing happened with Letty, but I will not let you silence me now. I'm not sure whose was the greater sin: John's, or Letty's. Or mine, for that matter. I should have given my brother a good tongue-lashing at the time. Fanaticism in God's name is a sin." She coughed some more behind a cupped hand; her face seemed flushed.

Mama went to sit on her bed. We formed a triangle, we three generations of women, with Mama and Aunt Margaret opposite each other, and me forming the peak. "I should have known this would happen," Mama said bitterly.

"Then why did you send me here?"

174

She looked away. "Because . . . because I wanted you to have the things I couldn't afford to give you."

Aunt Margaret cleared her throat, but said nothing.

"I'm eighteen. I want to stay here, for now."

"I can't let you," Mama cried, leaping to her feet. "For *your* soul's sake, as well as mine. You know she won't watch you as I would. I'll keep you safe."

I brought my hands down on the arms of my chair. "I don't want to be kept safe, Mama. I want to be responsible for my own safety. Don't worry. I don't plan to marry, anyone."

"What then? You say you love him, yet you don't want to marry him."

"I don't know. No, I don't want to marry."

"Does he love you?"

"I . . . think so," I said, not looking at her, fiddling with the folds of the blue chiffon scarf draped across my shoulders. "I hope so."

Mama made a strangled sound, then said, "You lied to me. You told me before he was only a friend."

I sat straight up in my chair. "As you lied to me. Why have you not told me the truth about Papa?"

She sank back down on the bed, shook her head slowly, staring fixedly at the floor. "I can't do it. I can't do what Pa did. I don't have the moral strength." She took a deep breath. "All right. Come home when you can, then. Only, come home."

She had avoided my question. Had she backed down because of it? And why hadn't I pressed her further? Was I afraid she'd reverse herself about letting me stay? Was I staying *only* on Letty's account? Questions flitted through my mind, questions I couldn't answer. Maybe, I didn't care to.

Aunt Margaret sighed deeply. "You know, I think I'll lie down for a bit," she said. "I'm a little tired." She tilted carefully down and lifted her feet, in their black oxfords, onto the green-striped counterpane.

As if grateful for the distraction, Mama was instantly full of solicitude. I left feeling dissatisfied. Mama had still not told me about Papa. And my victory, if it could be called that, was a hollow one, even anticlimactic. What was it all for? I reminded myself morosely that I knew nothing of Ajai's emotions toward me, only the fervor of my own. Perhaps I presumed too much. I felt all my brave sentiments of the past week start to trickle away.

By evening Aunt Margaret had a temperature of 102 degrees and a dry harsh cough. Letty started her on sulfa and we kept a saucepan of water simmering on a portable stove in a corner of the room. Mama, Letty and I began a vigil. For the next two weeks we sat in turns with Aunt Margaret round the clock. Most of the time she dozed against the pillows piled behind her except when the coughing spells would seize and shake her about like a dog with a kitten. These seemed to last forever, but were probably no more than a few minutes, after which she fell back on the pillows, sweaty and trembling. We mopped her face with flannels dipped in a mixture of water and eau de cologne. Her skin took on the pale blue transparency of the milk glass vase Letty had placed on her night table, which held whatever blooms the rose bushes were able to provide in the continuing heat. Occasionally she sipped orange juice reinforced with glucose, or a little broth. My uncle checked her regularly, listening to her chest and heart, his broad face grave.

"Shouldn't she be in hospital?" Mama asked, fingering her rosary. I had just come in to relieve her.

"She is better off at home," my uncle said gently. "You are doing everything that could be done for her in hospital. If she should need special equipment or oxygen, then we will bring it in. Believe me, she will be more comfortable here."

Mama nodded. Of course, now there was no question but that she and Aunt Margaret would have to delay their departure for Madras for several weeks. Mama blamed herself. "She was too frail to travel," she said to me, "but she just insisted that she wanted to be with you on your birthday and . . . to see Letty again before she . . . before she—" Mama broke off and pressed her fingers to her trembling lips.

"Don't worry, Mama," I said, coming to stand beside her, sounding more confident than I actually felt. "Aunt Margaret will be all right. I simply *know* she will."

"But pneumonia at her age? The other day, after her bath, she had the fan going full blast to dry her hair. Do you suppose that caused it?"

I had never known Mama so quavery, not with me, at any rate. It was unsettling.

"I don't know. Mama, why don't you go and rest in my room?"

"I should have scolded her at the time, I suppose, but I don't like to carp." She flashed me a look. "At least, not all the time." She hesitated, and it looked as if she wanted to say something more, but she only said, "Yes, all right. I'll go. But you call me if there's any change."

I promised I would.

I sat in the wicker chair that Mama had just vacated and watched Aunt Margaret sleep, her chest lifting with each wheezing breath. Her waxy eyelids fluttered occasionally. What did she dream about? I wondered. Did she dream? Or was her sleep dark and deep as a hole? All my life she'd been there, a buffer between Mama and me, Grandpa and me, Letty and Mama, Grandpa and Mama. What had *she* gained from it all? She'd reared Mama and Letty after their mother died giving birth to Letty, and then she'd helped rear me, offering me unconditional but not stifling love. Dear, dear Aunt Margaret! Had she ever loved a man and been loved in return?

177

All the romance novels she read. Had she coveted the touch of a man's eager, caressing hand? Or was the fiction enough?

I rose and went to pour water from a kettle into the pan simmering on the stove. Damp heat rose about my face. I felt in my pocket for the letter Ajai had sent to me that morning through Munnar. I carried it about with me, a talisman, a scapular. I took it from my pocket and read it yet again, although I knew the words by heart.

Megan, my dear:

I know about your aunt's illness and so will not intrude. Besides, I have the feeling your mother would be much happier if I stayed away. Am I right? For this reason, I am sending this to you through Munnar instead of by post. I hope you will reply—when it is convenient. I know this must be a deeply anxious time for you and your family, and I have much concern on your behalf. I wish your aunt a speedy recovery.

There are things I want to tell you, need to tell you, about my feelings, but I find they are difficult to write down. On the other hand, telling them to your face is even more terrifying. I can see your face now—so earnest, so sweet, so very young. I know you don't like me saying you are young, but it is the truth. I am your senior by six years, and I must be very careful in what I say, how I say it.

Since that night in the palace garden, the night of your eighteenth birthday, you have filled my thoughts. I fear I am becoming obsessed. A delicious obsession, I hasten to add. Can I hope that you too think of that night, Megan? And of me?

I await your answer.

Ajai

Ajai—

I long to see you. Never mind Mama. Please come.

—Megan

I wrote the note in my library with the sun streaming through the window and Munnar trying to read over my shoulder.

"Stop it!" I covered the square of lavender paper with my hand. "That's bad manners."

"I was not trying to read your silly letter," he said in an injured voice. "I was only trying to see the title of the book you are using to write on."

"Liar!"

He went to flop down on the window seat. "Such a short letter. How could I help reading it? Why are you so secretive? I have never been involved in an active romance. Ajai also did not want me to read his letter." He ran his hand through his hair. He was wearing a blue striped shirt, open at the collar, and navy slacks.

"But that did not stop you."

"Only because it was not in a sealed envelope. I never read sealed letters, but an open note is different. It is like reading a postcard. Postmen read postcards. Ajai tried to find an envelope; he went from room to room in the dorm. Kuppuswami tried to sell him one for eight annas."

"That's outrageous! You can buy a whole packet for only four annas at the corner shop."

"Kuppuswami is like that only, a crafty Madrasi, always trying to make a profit on something. He won't lend a bit of toothpaste even. Anyway, your correspondence would not be possible without me. If I were Kuppuswami, you would have to pay at least twelve annas per letter."

"Does Ajai know you read his letter?"

He shrugged. "Maybe." Adding virtuously, "I had to check if there was anything improper."

"Munnar, you are impossible! Well, you're not going to read this one." I folded the note in two and slipped it inside the matching envelope. I sealed it firmly. "You won't open it, now. Will you?"

"Of course not," he said indignantly. "What do you think I am?"

179

IN THE FOREST AT MIDNIGHT

*   *   *

The following day, late afternoon, I found Letty and Mama changing Aunt Margaret's nightdress, the process being conducted discreetly beneath a draping sheet.

"She's turned the corner," Letty announced. "Her temperature is down." Letty was wearing a long, flowered housecoat. Her hair was rumpled and curly from the steamy room, making her look younger, prettier.

"Thank God," Mama said fervently. Relief showed plainly on her face despite its greyish pallor of the past several days.

"I'm going to send Gopi in with a cup of nice warm Horlicks for you," Letty told Aunt Margaret. "Then for supper you can have toast with your Marmite. We have to strengthen you up."

Mama brushed Aunt Margaret's hair and made two skinny white plaits, one on each side of her pale, pinched face with its blue-shadowed eyes.

"I'll stay with Aunt Margaret," I said. "You two look as if you can stand a cup of tea, or some sherry."

They left.

I went to stand by the bed. "Aunt Margaret, do you feel like looking at the latest *Illustrated London News?*"

She shook her head, but patted the bed for me to sit down. Her eyes were closed; she groped for my hand. Her fingers felt cool and dry.

"I want to talk to you," she whispered. "I've been lying here thinking these past days, and there is something I must do. Should have done before now. But first I have to tell you about something that happened a long time ago."

"Are you sure you're up to it?"

She nodded. "It has to be done. When I was a young girl, my father left us. I'm sure you didn't know that; we never talk of such things."

180

"No. But, please don't tell me if it will upset you."

She opened her eyes and smiled at me, squeezing my fingers reassuringly. "John was fifteen and went to work in the Mills. I was thirteen and stayed in school. Our mother, your great grandmother, taught music and took in mending, great piles of clothing she never caught up with. It was hard for John. The church sodality brought us bundles of second-hand clothes every few months. John was too proud to accept charity. Our mother said false pride is a sin and wouldn't let John take the clothes back. Of course, he never wore anything but what he could buy for himself. John never forgave our father, I think. But my feelings were not so clear. I felt as if some essential part of me had been cut out—nothing that showed, but I felt diminished, different, as if I were missing a kidney, or my spleen. I felt people's pity and would cross the street to avoid speaking to someone.

"Then, years later, my father returned. On a social call, mind you. He said he just wanted to see if we were all right. John wouldn't come out of his room. He was furious at Mama for letting him in the house."

"And your mother? What did she do?"

"She was the soul of what is proper in such a situation, I suppose. Although, God knows, it wasn't your everyday social call. She served him tea and biscuits and made polite conversation. I went to sit on the sofa beside my father. I wanted him to put his arm around me just to see if it would be the same. He gave me a bag of toffee, instead. Of course it wasn't the same. Too much time had gone by. I had *forgotten* how to love him. He even looked different. This man had a moustache and a keychain that looped across his paunch. He looked prosperous. You know what my mother said when he left? She said, 'Good riddance to bad rubbish.' "

"Oh, Aunt Margaret."

181

"Now, Megan, what happened to your father is quite different. I know your mother will be very upset with me for telling you, but I am too weak for her to attack, thank God. Child, your father is in a leper sanitorium near Madras."

He's going for treatment, Mama had said. The words pinged in my head.

"Does he have leprosy?"

"Yes, love."

"My father is a leper?" I was testing the word on my tongue, my mind.

"He's afflicted with the disease."

"Where is he, Aunt Margaret?"

"At that American Hospital in Vellore. I thought you should know, my dear, because, you see, when my father came to visit us, that's when I started to hate him, not so much for leaving us, as for making me forget him. I sat beside him that day and felt nothing. He could have been anyone off the street. Distance and time take the keenness off everything, even love." She squeezed my hand again. "I don't want that to happen to you. I don't know why Lavinia won't admit to herself that your father has leprosy. We are as susceptible as anyone to the diseases of this country. After all, we chose to live here knowing that."

I was light-headed with rage and revulsion at my mother. I managed to bend down and kiss Aunt Margaret's cheek.

"Thank you for telling me," I whispered. "I'm so very, very glad you're better."

Mama and Letty were drinking tea at the dining table, bathed in the orange glow of the setting sun streaming in the open french doors. Mama glanced at my face and started from her chair. "Is she all right? Who's with her?"

"Gopi." I stared at my mother without speaking. I thought

182

if I were to open my mouth again, I would vomit. Finally, I said, "I know about my father."

Mama sank back in her chair, her lips ashen. She said, in a dull voice, "Who told you?"

"*You* should have told me. You and Papa. Instead you let me imagine all kinds of things. That Papa had deserted us and gone back to England. That he had someone else. That he was tired of us." I tried to keep my voice steady and strong, although I trembled with rage. "All these months he's been sick, and you kept me from him. I didn't even know where to write to him."

"I did it for you," she said in the same flat voice.

"You did it for *yourself*. You cannot admit to *yourself* that he has leprosy. Have you ever gone to see him? Do you even care about him?"

Mama appealed to Letty. "Explain to her. Tell her that it's a contagious disease."

"You must do this yourself, Lavinia," Letty said gently. "She had a right to know."

"I'm going back to Madras," I said. "I'm going to be with Papa. He's been alone too long."

"You said you were staying. I can't leave now. Aunt Margaret—"

"I said, *I* am going. Alone. I want to see Papa alone. I don't want to be with you, or see you. I'm leaving this minute."

Mama gasped. "Letty, I beg of you. Make her see."

Letty said, "This is something she must do, Lavinia. Try to accept it." To me she said, "The next train for Madras leaves at five in the morning." She looked at her watch. "Twelve hours from now. Stay till then. Someone will take you to the station."

"I can't be in the same house." I went to my room and grabbed my purse, then I ran out the front door, down the steps and the long driveway. Dimly I thought of that other

183

time, in Madras, when I'd run from my mother to Pushpa's sweetshop. A car swerved to avoid me as I rushed through the gates.

"Megan," someone called. I didn't stop. I felt a hand grasp my arm and turn me around. It was Ajai. "My dear, what is it?" He bent to peer in my face. "Is it an emergency? Your aunt?"

I shook my head, conscious of the tears that welled up in my eyes and rolled down my face. He led me to the car and helped me in, then got in himself. "Can I take you somewhere quiet?"

I nodded.

"Good. I saw Munnar today, he gave me your note. I came at once. I brought a picnic basket. I was hoping I could persuade you to go with me down to the river, if only for an hour. My mother has packed us all kinds of wonderful things." He spoke softly, soothingly. "*Samosas* and *pakoras* and her own special blend of coffee. That's what you need—a cup of strong, hot coffee." Once he touched my hair, stroking it away from my face.

I sat staring straight ahead, not seeing anything, unable to focus. Why was I crying? I wondered, in a detached way. I would go to see my father. I had broken with my mother, true, but in some recess of my brain, I recognized that this would have happened sooner or later, even without Papa. Each time we clashed, my anger toward her increased. Now, it burned with a strong, bright flame, which I would feed, and would nourish, but would not allow to consume me. Then why the tears? Was I grieving for something I did not even understand? Maybe it was not grief, maybe it was relief. A washing away of something as with rain, after which there would be renewal.

*   *   *

We stopped at a point higher up the river from the soapstone mine that belonged to Ajai's family. The trees were more dense here, forest-like. Ajai spread a striped *dhurrie* and went back to the car for the picnic basket. He poured a cup of coffee from the thermos and came to hold me against him, the cup to my lips. The coffee was hot and sweet; it burnt my tongue. His gentleness made the tears flow even faster. He put the cup aside and drew me down on the carpet where he cradled me in his arms like a baby.

"I have never seen anyone weep like you," he murmured in my hair. "You do not utter a sound; your face is so still. Only the tears. It is very moving."

Holding onto his shoulders, I pulled myself up to press my lips against his. I took his lower lip lightly in my teeth and swept my tongue across it, continuing to kiss him, until with a small groan he opened his mouth and our tongues met and clung. I placed his hand on my breast. He let it rest there, but he drew slightly away.

"You are defenseless tonight. Just let me comfort you."

"Then comfort me," I whispered, covering his hand with mine and moving it against me.

"Are you sure?"

I nodded.

He slipped his hand under my tunic and fumbled with my brassiere. I sat up and unfastened it, then lay back on the carpet. He lay beside me and lifted my tunic, his fingers caressing my skin in slow circles. I gasped when I felt his mouth warm and wet on my breast, his fingers and tongue caressing, seeking. I was sick with longing for him. "Oh please," I moaned, "I want you."

He entered me, then stopped. "I didn't know," he said, his breath swift against my throat.

"What is it?"

"You're a virgin."

185

Alarmed, I said, "Does that matter?"

"I'll stop if you want me to."

"No, no!"

I was not prepared for the pain; it raced through me, but I lay very still and absorbed it. You are a woman now, I told myself. You are lying with your lover.

What would Mama say if she knew?

We were slippery with sweat. Ajai moved off me. After a while, he traced my mouth with a fingertip. "I hurt you. I'm so sorry."

"It didn't hurt very much," I lied.

He laughed softly. "This is the first time I've made love to a woman who wept through it all."

"I'm not crying now." It was true; the minute I felt the searing pain, my tears dried up. "Have you made love many times?"

"No."

"Who were they?"

"They were not very nice women."

"Prostitutes?"

"And what do you know about prostitutes?" Ajai kissed the end of my nose, then sat up. "You're bleeding!" He bent to kiss my thighs, and reached for his handkerchief to gently clean my blood and his semen from me. "Megan, I want to marry you. We must not do this again without getting married first. I don't want to get you pregnant."

I was silent.

"Did you hear what I said?" He was straightening my clothes.

"Yes."

"Will you?"

"Ajai, every single marriage I've seen has been miserable.

My parents, my aunt and uncle, the Bhatts. Even my great-grandfather left his family. I found that out today."

He leaned over me, hands braced on my shoulders, and looked into my eyes. "But, that's absurd. There are as many happy marriages for the unhappy ones. My parents, for instance. My sister and her husband. I too thought that there was no place in my life for marriage, that I would be too busy with my career, my work, my various causes. But, Megan, I don't think I can do any of that without you."

I reached up and held his face in my hands. "I'm leaving in the morning. I'm going back to Madras to see my father."

"Your father! I've never heard you mention him."

"No." I lifted up on my elbows. "Ajai, listen to me. My mother sent me to stay with Aunty because she didn't want me to be there in Madras when my father left. These past four months he's been in a . . . leper sanitorium. He has . . . leprosy. My mother didn't talk to me about this. She just . . . sent me away and let me imagine whatever I wanted. I just found out the truth, and I . . . I want to make it up to my father."

"But it's not your fault that your father has leprosy, or that your mother kept it from you."

"Ah, but it is—I mean, not the fact that he has the disease, but I should have stood up to my mother. I've let her run my life. She would like nothing better than to wrap me in cotton and seal me away like a mummy. She wants my *soul,* not for the God she preaches about, but for *herself.*"

"Parents make mistakes, Megan. Even good intentions sometimes have the opposite effect. I understand that you must go to your father. I'll wait for you. No matter how long it takes."

"I can't promise you anything. I don't know what I will find. If my father will have only half a face. But I'm glad you do see. It's terrible enough to have such a disease, without your family abandoning you." I was stroking his face, tracing the arch of his eyebrows, his nose, remembering the cleft in his chin.

He pressed his lips painfully to mine; I felt my teeth cut into the back of my lip, and tasted blood. When he moved away, I lay back on the carpet, and said, "But I'll spend tonight with you—"

"I don't want one night from you like a whore," he shouted, slamming his fist on the ground. "I love you. I want to spend *every* night of my life with you."

"Then will you take me to the station now? I'll sit in the waiting room."

"What about your mother, your aunt?" he said in the same desperate voice. "Don't you owe them any explanations?"

"I owe my mother nothing. Aunt Letty will understand. My train leaves at five in the morning."

He buried his face in my belly; I felt his tears warm on my skin. "Oh, my love, my love." My fingers were in his hair, caressing at last that sweet place at the back of his neck I'd always longed to touch.

CHAPTER EIGHTEEN

The woman was young—less than thirty years old—a widow, judging from the white sari and clean-shaven head that made her dark eyes seem enormous, whenever she raised them. Most of the time, however, her eyes were downcast as she sat swaying to the motion of the train, ringless hands folded in white cotton lap, wrists, ears and neck bare of adornment for such things were forbidden her now. I knew all this from Letty, who had once explained to me the customs that bound Hindu widowhood. I imagined the woman as she might have been at an earlier time, in a scarlet sari with tinkling bangles at her wrists and a jewel in one delicate nostril; saw her laughing face raised to her young husband, who smiled down at her, strong white teeth flashing. Now she seemed only the hull of some exotic moth, long flown. She had barricaded herself behind suitcases, piles of bundles on each side of her. Was she being sent back to her father's house?

I sat on the berth that spanned the width of the compartment, hemmed in by her bundles, unable to escape the blazing sun that streamed in the open window. The motion and rhythm of a train were second nature to me now, since I had arrived back at the house in Madras only the night before after the long journey from Nerbudapur. The servants had been surprised to see me instead of Mama and Aunt Margaret. I had eggs on toast and Ovaltine for supper, washed the clothes I was wearing, the only clothing I had brought with me, and went straight to bed. In the morning, I ironed the clothes I'd washed and then bathed, dressed and made my way back to the station where I caught this train for the journey to Vellore, and my father.

If only the woman would move her bundles onto the suitcases in front of her, I might be able to inch out of the sun and feel the feeble sweep of air from the single fan wheezing overhead. But her impassivity and the gravity of her shoulders prevented me from suggesting that. I could only think that a woman so young was newly widowed. How had her husband died? Had it been swift? An abrupt cessation of life—both his as well as her own—for I knew that from now on she would cease to exist in a society that would blame her for her husband's death and would deem it retribution for some sin she had committed in a previous life. Even her own people would hold it against her.

I thought about all this to distract me from my own physical and mental discomfort, as sweat plastered me to the imitation-leather upholstery and apprehension about Papa's condition intensified with each diminishing mile. I thought of beggars without noses holding out clawed hands, and I tried to tell myself that my situation was not as dreadful as that of the young widow. At least my father was alive, and I was grateful for that. No matter what, I would try to accept his physical condition. I turned to look out the window at the mustard fields fanning by in rows, brilliant in sunshine.

The other passengers in the Ladies' Second Class compartment included two Americans, probably missionaries, who sat on the far side of the widow, and, on the opposite berth, an elderly Muslem chaperone and her four young charges. As soon as the train left the station, they threw off their black, tent-like *bourkas* with relief, emitting a powerful odor of perspiration. All traveled with mountains of luggage, shoved under seats, stored overhed, and clogging the aisle, making it difficult to reach the toilet. I escaped there as often as possible to get away from the scorching sun and to rinse my flaming face. I stayed in the toilet as long as seemed civil, sitting on the pot and mopping my face with a wet hanky.

Once, I thought of my mother. I wondered if she had tried to locate me on the night I left Letty's house. But Ajai and I had spent that night on the river bank, under the stars, listening to the courthouse clock chime away the hours, marking off our time together. When it struck four, he drove me to the station; no one was waiting there to accost me. Perhaps Letty had convinced my mother it was best not to interfere; perhaps my mother had arrived at that conclusion herself—that it was time to let go.

At Vellore station coolies clustered around the compartment, while the Muslim women struggled back inside their voluminous wraps. Seeing that I had no luggage, the coolies concentrated on the Americans, who were generally known to tip handsomely. I emerged into white, noon heat and was instantly surrounded by beggar children who slapped their bellies and cried, "*baksheesh baksheesh.*" Older beggars huddled in dejected piles in the sloping eaves of buildings. I took a *jutka* to the hospital, sitting with my legs extended on the straw-spread floor of the covered cart while the cart man flayed his skinny horse into a half-hearted trot, its hooves churning up thick yellow dust. I drew the edge of my scarf over my face; I saw everything through a mauve mist. There was an unreality about it all. Trees, traffic, the surrounding hills, shimmered dream-like in the heat, although the straw poking the backs of my legs through my trousers was convincing enough. Yet I felt this was safe, this jouncing, prickly ride—I didn't want it to end—I was afraid to leave the shelter of the cart, afraid of what lay ahead.

Before long, we passed through a gateway between high walls. " 'ospitaal," the cart man announced. I climbed down and paid him. My stomach was emitting sounds of hunger, but I knew it was only simple terror. I looked around me, seeing a cluster of red-brick buildings with broad verandahs, shady trees and flower beds, with people strolling about and reading on benches, some with bandaged hands, others on crutches. A blind man tapped his way past me. Encountering an enormous bougainvillea, he prodded it with his cane, trying without success to get around it.

"Can I help?" I asked, springing forward.

"What devilish thing is this?" he said, flaying at the bush the way the cart man had his nag.

"Let me take your arm." I said, and did so.

"You may have my arm," he replied. "Both arms if you wish. If I could only see again."

I steered him around the plant. He thanked me.

"I came to see my father," I said, more to reassure myself. "Mr. Manning."

"The English gentleman. Yes, he is expecting you."

I was weak with joy and relief to see Papa again, to see him whole. Thinner and very pale, he walked towards me as I stood on the verandah of the Visitors' Building. His skin had lost the healthy ruddiness from the Bellary days when we had hiked on the rock and explored the old fort, but he had suffered none of the gross defects, the missing features I had so dreaded. He did not embrace me, did not so much as touch me, just gazed. But the love and admiration in his face reached

192

out like hands to stroke my cheek, cup my chin. I held away, too. Though I knew as I gazed back that I had not forgotten how to love him, as Aunt Margaret had feared.

"You are taller than I remembered," he said at last, the familiar lock of his thin, fair hair falling across his forehead. "So very . . . womanly. Maybe it's your clothes. They are most becoming.

"It's Punjabi dress. Very comfortable. Outgrew all my frocks," I said gruffly, trying to control the wobble in my chin, my voice. I looked down at my clothes, pretending to adjust them. I was not going to dissolve into tears; I would not embarrass my father that way.

He suggested that we walk outdoors. "It's pleasanter in the fresh air," he said, leading me through the landscaped grounds, past carefully tended plots of cannas and zinnias, shrubs of hibiscus and bougainvillea, to a grove of tamarind trees beyond. He was wearing grey trousers and a long-sleeved, white cotton shirt. From time to time, he reached up to pull the collar close around his neck.

We sat on a slatted bench; all the while he told me about the wonderful things that were being done at the Medical Center, and how lucky he was to have been diagnosed early. Hansen's disease, he called it—not leprosy. I had the feeling he kept talking in an effort to span the awkwardness and reach surer footing, like a swimmer feeling for solid ground, a climber seeking a toehold. It dawned on me then that despite his obvious pleasure at seeing me again, he felt at a disadvantage— just as Ajai had in that jail in Nagpur. Would I *ever* learn? Reflexively, I reached out to him. He recoiled.

"Safer not to touch," he said in a brisk voice, patting the air between us, his eyes on my outstretched hand. I dropped it.

Tugging at his collar again, his cuff slid back on his arm and I saw a pale round patch on his wrist. Almost simultaneously, I saw two more on the side of his neck that he'd obviously been at pains to keep hidden. I looked away quickly, staring at the distant hills. My heart dragged in my chest like a rock, while Papa continued to tell me about the Medical College that was to be built in the valley near the leprosarium, about the Nurses' Training School, about the original hospital four miles away, that had been expanded many times over.

By now, I was less concerned with Papa's outer manifestations of illness. I began to notice his manner, the way he sat, the patient slope of his shoulders, the forbearance of his hands. There was a stillness about him, a folding in on himself, that reminded me of something I couldn't quite place. I saw that the signet ring was missing from his left hand—and then I remembered. The image of the young widow on the train was suddenly vivid in my mind. My father had the same air of stoic acceptance! Chilled to the core, I shut my eyes. Oh Papa, I cried silently, what have we done to you?

"Tired?" He was smiling at me.

I shook my head. "Where's your ring?"

"Left it in Madras. No need of it here, certainly." He cleared his throat, said softly. "I see no trace of the child in you. I've missed all that, seeing you change into a woman."

"I didn't want you to miss all that," I said, my voice clumsy with jarring emotions, "as I didn't want to miss *you* for four months. Papa, why?"

"The initial stages of the disease are contagious—"

"I'm not talking about that. I'm talking about why I was never told the truth."

"I suppose we wanted to spare you," he said carefully, leaning forward to rest elbows on knees, hands clasped as in prayer beneath his chin. Breeze stirred his hair, blew it in his eyes; he smoothed it back. In this light the grey in his hair paled the gold. "You can't imagine what your mother and I went through." He paused, cleared his throat again. "At the time, it seemed the best thing to do." He glanced at me over his shoulder. "I had a wire from your mother. She sounded quite frantic."

I said nothing.

He straightened. "I won't press you to write to her; that must be your decision. You are a woman now. I can only hope you try to remember we love you very much."

There seemed nothing more to say. We sat in silence under a tamarind tree on a garden bench and struggled to think of something to talk about. Was this what Aunt Margaret had meant? This forgetting—not of how to love, but of loving-ness?

"Papa, are there any places in Vellore where I can stay?" I asked. "I'm willing to work."

"Oh, no! No, you must go back to Madras."

"Isn't there a place here for relatives?"

"Not for people of our class." He took out his handkerchief and wiped his face, then pulled his collar closer around his neck. "You can come here on Saturdays, if you wish. Actually, there's no need to come at all."

"But that's why I came back. To be with you."

"To make it up to me." He nodded, smiling. "Yes, I know. That's what your mother said in the telegram. All the same, I'd feel better if you were in Madras."

It was a relief to get back to Madras from Vellore. I had a sense of consolation I had not known the previous night after the tense journey from Nerbudapur. Now as I walked home from the station through the twilight, I savored familiar landmarks. I passed the school, the church, Scott Shop, the small pink temple with peeling paint. I knew it all. I was home.

The aloe in the front yard seemed smaller, more contained. I went among the rooms in the house, remembering. In the parlor, I ran my fingers across the piano keys; some of them stuck. One key had lost its ivory. I saw the wireless, the picture of the Sacred Heart. Grandpa's body had been laid out in this room. The table in the adjoining dining room was covered with the same flower-sprigged oilcloth as before. The picture of The Holy Family in its chipped-gilt frame hung behind the chair where Grandpa had sat at the head of the table. On the opposite wall was the school clock that only Papa kept wound. I climbed the stairs to Grandpa's room. Cobwebs hung in corners, dangled from the ceiling. Dusty vials of pills and holy water still stood on the table along with a stack of out dated *St. Anthony's Messengers*. There was the chair where Grandpa had sat in a half-crouch following his stroke, when we gathered in his room each evening to say the rosary.

Back in the parlor, I found express letters from Mama, Letty and Ajai had been piled on the desk blotter. I read Letty's first.

Saturday, 6th of May.

Megan, dear,

I hope the journey was not too awful. Ajai came to tell me he had seen you off. How lucky for you he was there to help you board the train. It was not too difficult to prevent Lavinia from running after you when you left the house; I think she recognized—and respected—your anger. Someday I hope you will understand her motives; she genuinely believes she was protecting you.

I packed up your clothes and sent them on to you. They should arrive within a week, I should think.

Aunt Margaret grows stronger by the day, but it will be some time before she can travel.

Uncle sends his love. And so do I!

Aunt Letty

My first impulse was to destroy Mama's letter without opening it. I sat at the desk and stared at the long, sloping handwriting on the envelope. Finally, I picked it up and, sliding a forefinger under the flap, opened it. I scanned the contents. True to form, Mama chose to pretend there had been no confrontation, that I had not fled the house in anger. My mother, the ostrich! The letter was full of chatty details about Aunt Margaret, Letty, Mama herself. Disgusted, I tore it in half and flung it in the dustbin.

I carried Ajai's unopened letter around in my pocket, touching it from time to time as I ate dinner and afterwards while I sat in the parlor listening to the news on the wireless. Finally, back in my room and unable to prolong anticipation a second more, I opened it.

My dearest,

I went to see your aunt to reassure her that all was well with you, that I saw you safely on the train. The very fact that she asked no questions about where you spent the night, makes me suspect she knows we were together. If so, she did not seem surprised—or displeased.

I carry the *dhurrie* from that night in my car. Today I came to the river bank to sit on the carpet like a Mussulman on his prayer rug. In a sense, this has become almost a hallowed spot for me. I sat with the handkerchief in my hands—the one I wiped you with—and thought of that night, and of us. And I sit here now, writing to you.

I long for you. If you do not wish to marry, then let us go away together. I will take you on any terms; there is nothing I would not do for you. Trust me, beloved.

Ajai

It was unjust that he had both the handkerchief and the carpet, I thought; if only I too had something from that night besides the memory. He had said he would wait for me. How long could he wait? The right thing for me to do, I told myself, would be to release him so he could go on with his life, maybe marry a girl from his background who would devote herself to his happiness, like Prethima did with Vijay. I should not have coerced him into making love with me. It was not fair to him. And yet I knew I would always remember that night on the riverbank. It would live inside me, essential as my soul.

Tentatively, I touched my breasts and imagined his long fingers, delicate with love, his tongue, my tongue, as we tasted each other, tasted ourselves on each other, the agony of our wanting. I moaned, curling around the slow, deep ache of my lust.

The next morning I awoke to crows cawing loudly in the casuarina tree outside my bedroom window. I heard the neighborhood servants argue as they stood around the stand-pipe across the street collecting the day's water supply that sloshed in their pots and pails. I rose, dressed, ate breakfast and set about cleaning the house. The servants thought I'd gone mad. They stared at me open-mouthed, giggling behind their hands when they thought I wasn't looking.

Grimly, I washed curtains, walls and floors. I snagged cobwebs in tall corners on the end of a broom as small lizards scuttled away in panic. I threw away dusty tangles of paper flowers, drippy candle ends, and brittle palm crosses from long-ago Palm Sundays, cleaned out drawers and cupboards, made piles of clothes for the poor. Under a stack of Grandpa's shirts, wrapped in a handkerchief yellow with age, I found a velvet-covered box. Inside was a gold medal with the profile of the Pope on one side and the following inscription on the other:

Presented to
Letitia Anne Curtis
May 1923

Also in the box was a small scrap of paper with the words, "Letty's Catechism medal," in Grandpa's spidery writing. I replaced the medal in its case, wrapped it in the handkerchief, and put it back in the drawer where it had lain for twenty-five years.

RITA PRATT SMITH

*   *   *

"Where is your room, Papa?"

"Behind that brick building," Papa said, pointing. We were sitting on the same bench under the tamarind tree. I wondered if this was his special retreat like my library at Letty's house. "There are small separate units for each patient. There's reason to believe that isolation at night prevents the disease from spreading."

"Is it very contagious?"

"No. Only mildly so. Less contagious than TB, for instance. Caught in time, it can be cured. The trouble is, many are afraid to be identified. Heat, humidity, overcrowding, poverty. These are the major causes of the spread of Hansen's disease."

"Then how did you get it?" The words startled me. How *could* I have asked him that? I thought.

But Papa answered calmly, running a palm over his silvery hair. "Don't know, Megan. No one knows why one person and not another is susceptible. It may have happened when I was traveling to all those villages, sleeping in station waiting rooms. Who knows? Anyway, in a few months, I should be back home, and at work."

"But, if you go back to all those villages—"

"I won't. They've been very good to me at work. Gave me a six-month leave of absence, with pay. No, when I go back, it will be to the Head Office in Madras."

I gazed at the serration of rocky hills that surrounded Vellore. "Once you told me that we would return to England if India ever became independent."

"I know. But now all this has happened. You see, I'll have to return for checkups periodically. And . . . there's the security of staying in India for the moment. Here I have a job; we have a home. Someday, maybe."

A woodpecker hammered away noisily in a nearby tree. Ragged village children hunted for fallen tamarind pods, cracking them open to suck the tart flesh, then spitting out the seed. Papa seemed more relaxed today. This was my second visit. Perhaps he had finally found his footing with me. His clothes were always the same: grey trousers and a long-sleeved white shirt. Was it a uniform he had adopted, like prison garb, perhaps? I bent to pick up a tamarind. "I must look for work, Papa. I've only sixteen rupees left."

He turned to face me, concern in his pale blue eyes. "Why didn't you say something, you little goose?" he said with affection. "I have plenty of money. Most of my salary goes to your mother, except for a stipend that is sent to me. Haven't spent an anna. Nothing to spend it on. Let me give you some. I'd like to think I can still help you."

"It's not just that." I threw the pod to the children; they rushed to pick it up. "I need something to do."

"Oh yes," he said, nodding. "You have to decide what you want to do. Either college, or some kind of training. But wait till I come home first, and we can talk about it; our lives all came to a halt when I got sick, and you were sent away. Soon everything will be back to normal."

I returned to find the parcel of my clothes had arrived, at last. Letty had added vitamins and sticking plasters, a thermometer, analgesic powders, a jar of Marmite and a packet of safety pins. There were two other items in the box—the picture of Shiva that had hung in my room in Nerbudapur and the cross Ajai had given me on my birthday. I was astonished at my delight at seeing both again.

I hung Shiva's picture facing my bed. Ajai's cross I slipped under my pillow. I had something of him now.

A week later when I saw my father again, he was in a marvelous mood.

"Of course love changes," he said, munching on a cucumber sandwich. I had packed a picnic lunch of cucumber, and bacon and tomato sandwiches, hard-boiled eggs, and a thermos of tea. We spread it all out on a tablecloth, under Papa's favorite tree, surrounded by the faint, acidic odor of tamarind. "It would be frightening if it didn't. Good Lord, imagine going on and on frenzied that way." He took another bite. "Thank God, sanity eventually returns. Wonderful idea, this picnic. Best grub in ages."

"But it changes for the worse," I said. "People become habits. Bad habits."

"Or, good habits. There's no denying some marriages flop like a *chappati,* and nothing in the world can revive them. But, there's a lot to be said for the average marriage. Your mother and I have been married some twenty years. One of our greatest disappointments was not being able to have another child. But what we have is sufficient, I think—respect, love. You." He smiled at me and stretched out alongside the tablecloth, propped up on an elbow.

So they *had* tried to have another child, I thought, as I bit into a bacon and tomato sandwich. The tomato was squishy. "What are you trying to tell me, Papa? That I should marry Ajai. On the one hand Mama screams eternal damnation, and then you turn around and say—"

"I say nothing of the sort, so don't put words in my mouth. This is a discussion on marriage, not whether, when, or whom you should marry. I know nothing about this young man except what your mother has written. Tell me about him." He sat up to peel an egg.

"He's studying law and he's interested in politics."

"Splendid! That tells me everything. Come on, tell me some more."

"He's Hindu—I'm sure Mama has made *that* point very clear—by birth only, not by belief. His family is very progressive about the caste system."

"They may be progressive, but what concerns me is the huge difference in your backgrounds. Do you love each other?"

"Yes. He wants us to marry. Though I don't know. Whatever for?"

"Love, I suppose."

"The kind of love you mean is like brushing one's teeth."

He sat muching on the egg, an arm resting on a bent knee, the other leg extended. "Rubbish!" he said between mouthfuls. "What foolish romantic notions do *you* have of love? Riding off into the sunset? Climbing the stairs to bed? Living happily ever after? Those are fairy tales. Love is loyalty, commitment, taking a chance. If you don't take chances, you stagnate. It's like saying you won't go to college because you might fail.

"Let me tell you about the first time I saw your mother, but first pour me some tea, Megan, please. Best damn egg," he said, brandishing it. "All we ever get here is scrambled. Ta, ever so much," he said, as I handed him the thermos cap filled with warm, milky liquid. "She wore a yellow dress and held a bunch of purple flowers she was supposed to present to the Governor. All that gorgeous chestnut hair piled on her head. Her skin seemed to reflect light and color." He sipped his tea. "She was the loveliest thing I'd ever seen."

"It's obvious you approve of marriage."

He looked astounded. "Of course," he said. "What else is there?" He sipped his tea, eyeing me over the rim of the cup. "It's shocking that someone so young should have so jaded an outlook. I can only think that your mother and I had something to do with it."

I didn't answer.

"Did we?"

"When you left I thought you'd deserted us," I said dispassionately, "because I'd never seen you and Mama

202

affectionate; you don't even sleep in the same bed. I thought that you were separating because you didn't love each other. Aunt Letty's marriage is different, but seems just as bad. Papa," I cried out, "I've never seen two loving married adults."

"Ah," he said, staring into the cup of tea as if he were reading leaves. "I can see how that might have discouraged you. But . . . as I said . . . love changes." He smiled ruefully. "My father used to say, 'Marrying is easy. Housekeeping is hard.' "

"For instance," I persisted, "why hasn't Mama come to visit you?"

"Because I asked her not to."

"If I'd asked you first, would you have let me come?"

"Probably not," he said chuckling, as he brushed his hands together to rid them of egg crumbs. "But I'm very glad you did."

CHAPTER NINETEEN

I wish I could have explained—to myself, at least—my aversion to marrying. I struggled to understand. It seemed as if I had tumbled into a pit without any knowledge of having fallen, but found myself there, nonetheless, floundering in a welter of doubt. Was it Aunt Margaret's tale of my great-gandfather's faithlessness that had been the hand at my spine? The final shove? But, on consideration, I knew this was not so. It had contributed, certainly, firming my convicion that I came from a long line of marital misfits, but I think I had decided, long before Aunt Margaret's story, that happy marriage was a myth.

It was not that I loved Ajai too little, but that I loved him too much. I knew I could not bear it if, like my uncle, he were to caress another woman's wrist with a fingertip. Or if, like Letty, I were to become a lonely, frustrated woman, a tippler. And what had brought about the transformation in Mama? The picture Papa had painted of her as a girl in a yellow dress holding a bunch of flowers with a face that reflected light and

color—the loveliest thing Papa had ever seen—haunted me. It
was impossible to reconcile that image with Mama as she was
now, plain and tough as a shoelace.

Papa had said, "If you don't take chances, you stagnate."
He had not convinced me. If I had only heard that from
someone credible who spoke from the shelter of enthusiasm,
I might have believed. As it was, I felt my parents *had*
stagnated.

How I wished I did not feel this way. It would be infinitely
simpler all the way round if I were to marry Ajai. Our night
together was permanently fixed in my consciousness—I saw
everything with new eyes. However, in the past two weeks,
I had begun to reflect on it in much different terms, for I began
to suspect I was pregnant.

At first, I did not believe it. I convinced myself that the
confusion of the past weeks—my quarrel with Mama, my
concern over Papa, the journey back to Madras, all the visits
to Vellore—had been too much of a strain. My system must
be upset. My period would return when I settled down and
relaxed. I checked my knickers several times a day and even
woke once in the middle of the night convinced that my blood
had soaked through the mattress and puddled the floor.
Another time, rejoicing at the familiar stickiness between my
legs, I rushed to the bathroom only to find my pants perfectly
dry, perfectly white. I probed myself with a hanky around my
finger, wondering as I did it whether it would damage me.
And the instant answering thought: *Anything* was better than
being pregnant. How was it possible? I wondered. How was
it that Letty and Mama were never able to conceive again,
despite years of trying, and that Prethima had to make
offerings before the Shiva *lingam* in order to conceive? It
simply could not happen this way, in one night, after one
painful act of love.

I got my bicycle from the godown and rode for miles, but

the exertion only made my backside sore and my legs ache for days. If only I would forget about it, I told myself, busy myself with other things. With renewed frenzy I cleaned the house again, concentrating on Mama's room, which I had been reluctant to enter before, and on Aunt Margaret's. Spartan, neither room shed light on its occupant; each could have belonged to a cloistered nun, except for the frivolous picture of Pan and the Minotaur in Mama's room. Where had she come by that? I wondered; it was a ridiculous thing. Imagine her objecting to my Shiva! Of course, there on the dressing table, where it had always stood, was the snapshot of Letty and Mama. I picked it up and gazed at Mama's hair all piled on her head. Chestnut hair. Was that when Papa had first seen her?

And, standing there in my mother's room, gazing at the two young faces framed behind the glass, I finally knew with absolute certainty that I was pregnant. The knowledge did not come to me in a blinding flash or a thunderclap, but reached me first through my fingertips as I held the old picture. It seeped into me by degrees, moving slowly up my arms, into my heart, and then my brain.

I spent every Saturday with Papa. As for the rest of the week, I had taken to spending a large portion of each day at the club library. I missed my books at Letty's house. Here, in the house in Madras, there was little to read beside religious tracts, encyclopedias, Aunt Margaret's romances and some of my old textbooks from high school. I relished the silence in the library, the dry scent of bookpaste and paper, the books themselves that lined the walls in neat, reassuring rows. It was also a refuge from the unforgiving house crowded with memories and echoes of happier times in which the eyes of the Sacred Heart followed me, liquid with reproach. There at the club library I read *Illustrated Weeklies,* some of the English papers, Nehru's *Discovery of India,* novels by R. K. Narayan, and Mulk Raj Anand.

One day, as I walked past the school and Patterson field on my way to the library, I thought of Grandpa and our evening walks to the club, to Pushpa's sweetshop in the bazaar. Pushpa! I remembered the potions she had mixed up for Grandpa. Maybe there was something she could give me to bring on my period. By now I was almost four weeks late. I had stopped writing to Ajai when I realized I was pregnant; there seemed no point. Though I still loved him, the intensity of my feelings had undergone a change. It was as if my love had lost its center and its heart, become a cloud and an abstraction, something like contemplating hunger after seeing a beggar forage for food. For when the knowledge of my situation finally took hold in my mind and I grasped that inside me was a clot of tissue and cells that continued to grow and change shape, physical desire simply vanished. I was hollow as a sleeve, a recoveree from a long illness that had left me weak, disinterested.

When I was younger I sometimes thought of marrying in a cloud of white satin and tulle, and then, suitably later, of announcing to a faceless, adoring husband the glorious news of my pregnancy. Naturally he would be overjoyed, wrap his arms around me, pamper me, bring me strange foods to satisfy my strange cravings.

Not once had I imagined it would be like this.

Pushpa was quarreling with the prostitutes across the street when I got there. It seemed the brothel cat had been doing his daily business in the dirt beside Pushpa's lower step.

"Mix the shit in with your *jamuns,*" a wiry woman in an orange sari screeched in Hindi from behind a barred window.

"No one would taste the difference. They even look the same." The others laughed. One woman, who sat in the doorway, was oiling her hair with long slow strokes, hands glistening. Another, wearing no *choli*-blouse, lounged beside her; her top teeth stuck out like a shelf.

"I will explain for your shrunken intelligence that my sweets are prepared fresh daily," Pushpa yelled back, also in Hindi, shaking her fist. "Highest quality ingredients. You whores will never again taste a single one. Not one *jellabi*, not a single *jamun*. No more credit. And when I catch that filthy beast you harbor for God knows what disgusting purposes, I will sing hymns as I pound its head with a brick." Dignified as a duchess, though breathing hard, she turned away from the jeers and the flatulent noises the women made with their tongues. Settling herself cross-legged behind her wares, she tranferred her displeasure to me.

"Why are you wearing such clothes?" she demanded irritably.

"This is Punjabi dress."

"You are not Punjabi," she said, wiping her perspiring face with a corner of her red sari. "You are not even Indian."

"But I am Indian. I was born in this country. I love it."

"The flower should know the root," she said firmly, as she sat there, compact, round as a hassock, waving a piece of rope over her sweets.

"Is that all you have to say to me, Pushpa? I haven't seen you for five months."

"What kept you away?"

"I've been visiting my aunt in the north."

"*Accha.*" She wagged her head, accepting this information. "And you have returned Punjabi."

"I was told I look like a Kashmiri girl in these clothes."

She shrugged, spreading her palms. "How would I know? I have not even seen a Kashmiri—Look, look! There is that wicked cat." She snatched off her slipper and flung it at a large black cat with no tail, missing it. The animal scampered across the street to safety; the whores cheered.

"Misbegotten offspring of pigs!" Pushpa cursed them, then muttered to me against her hand, "Pretend they are not there. Dirty things."

I retrieved her slipper; she thanked me graciously. "You have eaten? Shall I send for tea?"

"No, thank you."

We sat there in the twilight amid the aroma jof Pushpa's sweets and her own sandalwood scent. I absorbed the bustle, color and curious intimacy of the bazaar at this hour when people, with an air of communal festivity, went about the daily business of buying or selling. Film music blared from the tea stall a few doors down. Two young girls walked down the street swinging their joined hands. Cows and dogs wandered freely. A man ducked into the open door of the brothel. Had Grandpa entered it in the same furtive way?

"Pushpa," I said in a low voice. "I need help."

"What kind of help?" she said guardedly.

"I'm . . . my period—I'm pregnant."

She continued to wave her rope. Not looking at me, she said, "You have lain with a man, then?"

Hysteria bubbled inside me. "No, an antelope," I said, and let out a high-pitched, nervous giggle.

"*Chup!*" she commanded, her eyes fierce. "Be quiet! It is not funny what you have done."

I began to cry quietly, my head bent. Presently, I felt her hand stroke my hair.

"How many weeks?" she asked, her voice gentle. I knew she meant how many weeks was I late.

"Four," I said. My voice shook.

She sighed. "It is a sad thing, but you are not the first or the last. I will give you a powder. You take it tonight. It may bring your flow. I will talk to someone also. If you do not start, come back in two days. I will tell what she said."

"What will she do?"

"A pointed stick. It is nothing. I will be with you."

I took the powder before dinner, mixing it with a tumbler of warm water as Pushpa had instructed. It looked and smelled like urine; I felt my stomach rise. What does it matter if it *is* urine? I told myself sternly, if it only works. Why, some orthodox Hindus drink their own elimination every day. It can't be much worse than drinking castor oil, which I'd had to do often enough as a child while Aunt Margaret stood over me to make sure I swallowed it. Surely I was past that stage of having to be coaxed to take medicine. I was not a baby. The word, "baby," settled me. I pinched my nose and gulped the stuff, but my traitorous stomach rebelled. Spewing from mouth and nose, I rushed to the bathroom and stood there retching in the basin as though my stomach would turn itself inside out.

I cleaned up the mess in the hallway, then sat shivering in the front room as Frank Sinatra sang "Oh What a Beautiful Morning" on the wireless. I would go back to Pushpa in two days, to that woman Pushpa knew and her stick. What else could I do? There was no one I could talk to. I couldn't tell Papa. I couldn't pray—I was never able to talk to God as if he were in the same room, like Grandpa had done or like Mama, with a faith honed to a razor sharpness—and now that I was about to commit sin, it was best I did not consult God first. Loneliness spread around me, wide and dark as the night sky. I knew now what Mama and Aunt Margaret had felt after I'd left for Nerbudapur and Papa went to Vellore, but at least they'd had each other then. If only I could talk to Letty; she alone would understand. I sat there, my stomach still raw

210

from Pushpa's powder, thinking about my aunt, longing for the reassuring tinkle of ice cubes in a glass, for her husky, smoke-filled laugh. And then I remembered: She had a phone! I *could* talk to her.

But, what if Mama answered? Why then, I would just hang up. I ran to the telephone box at the end of the road. O please God, let Letty be there. Please. I will make a novena—

She answered.

"Aunt Letty—" I was panting.

"Megan! What's the matter?"

"I'm . . . oh please help me . . . I'm pregnant. I vomited up something Pushpa gave me . . . she said this woman would use a . . . a pointed stick."

There was a brief silence, then she said urgently, "Now, listen to me. You are to come here, immediately. I'll help you, if that's what you want. Don't you dare go to a bazaar woman! That's very, *very* dangerous. Promise me you'll come here."

I nodded.

"For God's sake! Did you hear what I said? Say something."

"I promise."

There was an audible expulsion of breath. "Good girl." She spoke rapidly as though afraid that someone might enter the room and find her on the phone. "Now, try not to worry. I won't say anything to your mother. She and Aunt Margaret are leaving shortly for Madras. I'll see you soon." She hung up.

Stupidly, I nodded again at the phone. What a marvel it was! How clear Letty's voice had sounded! The receiver started to hum in my hand; I replaced it. For an instant, standing there in the lighted cubicle surrounded by darkness, I felt that I was on a bright planet, stalled in some galaxy, lost in time and space. Then I opened the door and stepped into the warm night, thinking as I did so: But I'm not lost now. For

211

now I would go to Letty. She would know what to do. She would help me.

The following day I went to Vellore to see Papa, to tell him I was leaving. As usual, I waited for him on the verandah of the Visitors' Building. I watched small, dark birds at play in freshly watered grass. The air smelled of damp earth and the fragrance of cork blossoms. Doctors in white coats and blue-saried nurses passed by. *Jutkas* and other vehicles brought visitors and the sick, while the very poor entered the gates on foot with the patience born of hoping for everything and expecting nothing. Then I saw Papa hurrying towards me, buttoning his cuffs as if he'd got into his shirt on the run. I watched as he reached up to smooth his hair.

"What a surprise!" he called out. "I wasn't expecting you till Saturday. Today's only Tuesday."

"Yes."

"Come along, let's go outside. What a coincidence! Got a letter from your mother just today. They'll be home tomorrow night. You can bring them down on Saturday."

We walked toward our tamarind grove. "I won't be here. I came to say goodbye."

"Won't be here?" he echoed. "Why? Where will you be, then?"

I watched a kite-hawk glide in lazy circles against a vivid blue sky. "I'm going back to Nerbudapur."

He stopped and faced me. "Now, see here, Megan," he said, his face reddening. He took out his handkerchief and wiped the back of his neck. "If you're doing this to spite your mother, I simply won't have it. This ridiculous attitude of yours has got to stop."

"It's not that—"

"To keep blaming your mother for something she and I decided together is unjust, and unlike you—"

212

"Papa, please—"

"If we did the wrong thing by you, we did it together. Parents have a responsibility. One day you will know what it is—"

"For God's sake, Papa," I said harshly, wanting to strike at him, to wound. "I'm pregnant!"

He continued to glare at me, holding his handkerchief behind his neck. Then the pupils of his light blue eyes dilated, and the flush disappeared from his face, leaving behind a pallor that was intensified by the faint glaze that sprang to his skin. Without a word, he replaced his handkerchief in his pocket and walked on, leaning forward as if heading into a strong wind. Filled with self-loathing, I followed more slowly.

We reached the bench in silence, and I sat staring down at my hands, which I squeezed between my knees to keep them from shaking. My eyes felt hot and dry as though I had a fever; my throat closed with anguish. *Oh, Papa. Papa.* "Letty said she'd help me," I said dully. "I'm sorry."

I heard a sharp intake of breath and looked up to see his lips pressed together, tears running down his face. It was the first time I'd seen my father weep. I did not believe it possible. In that instant, I knew that things had changed forever between us.

Terrified of this altering of roles, I cried out. "Papa, forgive me!" I was not sure if I asked his forgiveness for my condition, or for having told him of it.

Blindly, he placed a hand on my shoulder. "Who is—?"

"Ajai," I whispered.

I waited till Papa composed himself. After a while, he said quietly, "Did he seduce you?"

"No."

"Does he know?"

I shook my head.

"We did a terrible thing to you. Sending you away like that. I understand that now."

"I can blame no one for this," I said wearily, "not even Ajai. I think *I* seduced *him*."

"What will you do?"

"I don't know."

"Marry him, my girl," Papa urged, leaning an elbow on a knee and turning to look into my face. "For the sake of the child, at least."

I turned away. "I can't do that. I need to be sure, and now I . . . I'm so awfully muddled. I must sort this all out."

"Good Christ!" He took his hand from my shoulder. "You're not shopping for a hat!"

I realized only when he'd removed his hand that we'd experienced the first physical contact since I'd begun to visit him here. My heart swelled with love for him.

"I know, Papa," I said, my voice breaking. "Please don't make it any harder."

"Well, I suppose you have to decide about this for yourself," he muttered, "but don't wait too long." Then, he said, "Thank you for telling me. It took courage."

Don't thank me, Papa; it was not courage, at all. "I'll write to you. You decide if you want to tell Mama."

"I won't tell her. It's not my place. God be with you, my daughter. I am not a religious man, but I place you in God's hands."

CHAPTER TWENTY

I saw Letty as the train was steaming into Nerbudapur station. She stood near the bookstall in a bright yellow sari tied unfashionably high so that her shoes showed, and she clutched the strap of a black leather purse in both hands as she anxiously scanned the train. As usual, her hair was set in tight waves, each hair firmly in place—and she was the most comforting sight in the world. When she finally caught sight of me, she raised her arm.

We embraced without speaking. Although I was perfectly capable of carrying my own suitcase, she insisted on hiring a coolie. "Mustn't strain yourself," she said, and led me through the crowds to the parked car, an arm around my waist as if I were ill.

Outside, there was no sign of the chauffeur. I wondered if he'd gone for a cup of tea. Letty opened the boot of the car as the coolie swung my suitcase down from his turbaned head. Then she paid him, slid into the driver's seat, and started the car. The afternoon sun reflected blindingly off the car's bonnet.

"I didn't know you could drive," I said, putting up a hand to shield my eyes.

"Oh yes," came her brisk response as she backed the car into the street amidst the clamor of bells, horns and flatulent scooters. "At one time I used to drive everywhere. I started again when Aunt Margaret was recovering because I found it so much simpler to run errands myself than to have the driver take his own sweet time. No, that's not true. It wasn't simple at all," she said slowly. "I had to force myself to do it. Lord! That first time I drove to the chemist and back, I thought I'd conquered the world." She laughed shakily. "Anyway, I knew we'd want to talk and he'd only be in the way, an extra pair of ears." She gave me a sidelong glance. "How are you?"

"I'm all right," I said. Inertia made my tongue heavy. "Sorry I'm in this fix."

"I was in 'this fix' as you call it when I married your uncle," she said matter-of-factly.

I glanced at her in surprise. "Was that when you left the house in Madras?" My condition, having elevated me to adulthood, now gave me license to ask that of her.

"Yes."

It was generous of her to tell me. I touched her shoulder in gratitude. Nevertheless, I could not bring myself to ask: What was it like for you? How did you cope? The truth was I was paralyzed with a lethargy that went beyond ordinary tiredness. I could do no more than sit there and stare out of the window, through the shimmering heat and dust, at the shops, roadside stalls and overflowing garbage containers. Meanwhile, Letty expertly steered the car through the helter-skelter traffic, dodging between a tonga and a bullock cart, swearing at the drivers of both.

"By the way," Letty said. "Nila seems to have done a bunk. She's been gone for weeks. The servants' gossip is she left with one of her husband's young officers."

This news was no surprise. "And Colonel Bhatt?" I asked listlessly. "How is he?"

"I don't know. He sounded quite cheerful when he rang up to ask about Aunt Margaret. Definitely not the stricken husband. He's probably relieved to be rid of her."

"He was very kind to me," I said, and lay my cheek in the angle of my elbow resting on the open window.

She darted another glance at me. "You must be very tired. You can nap when we get home."

Maybe I was tired; I couldn't tell.

"It's Ajai's?" Letty said, her eyes on the road.

"Yes."

"Does he—?"

"No."

"Are you going to tell him?"

"I don't know."

"You don't have to decide anything just yet," she said quickly. "I'm going to take you to Kashmir for a short holiday. When Uncle goes to Delhi on Saturday for the new Session, we'll go with him, spend a few days there, then fly on to Kashmir. It will do you a world of good."

Presently Letty slowed the car to turn in at the gates, where carved in the stone posts was the word NIRVANA. *The state of bliss when one merges with the Absolute,* Letty had once explained. Absolute happiness. I thought of the first time I had passed through those gates with Munnar. How full of apprehension I had been then and, in the weeks that followed, how very resistant to Letty with her strange saris, her crimped hair. How bitterly I'd resented her for having changed. Yet, like it or not, everything eventually altered, shifted, switched around, metamorphosed—the weather, the country, the world itself—nothing remained the same; I saw that now. Here, for instance, was yet another aspect of Letty: driving a car and talking of flying to Kashmir when only a few months earlier she'd been terrified of leaving the compound, had confined her movement outside the house to the servants' quarters and the rose garden. As for myself—

"How are the roses?" I asked, all in a rush.

"What? Oh, they are loaded with blackspot. A proper mess, poor things. I haven't had much time lately, what with Aunt Margaret being ill and coping with Lavinia—"

"Was it awful?"

"Grim, but not awful. Although, come to think of it, I should be grateful to them for forcing me to take charge. I regained my—well, my self-confidence, actually, through them. Here were these two dependent women . . . Anyway, they left only two days ago. Your trains must have crossed. Here we are." She brought the car to a stop at the front steps, under the colonnaded porch with its tubs of ficus and banks of potted ferns leading up the front steps. "Off to bed with you. Don't worry about your suitcase. Someone will bring it in. We'll talk later. Try to get some rest."

I woke to a mindless panic of displacement, of being no one, belonging nowhere. I thought I was still on the train. Then I saw the setting sun outline the drawn shade at the window—an oblong of orange light—and, as the thumping of my heart calmed, my eyes lit on the familiar wicker chair by the wardrobe. As my head cleared, I heard the faint singing from the servants' quarters and the ticking of the clock on the dressing table beside the old picture of Mama and Letty. With relief, I realized I was back in my room at Nerbudapur.

I rose and unpacked my suitcase, which someone had placed on the small bench at the foot of my bed. I hung my tunics and scarves in the wardrobe and made neat piles of my underwear and trousers on shelves, as if the care spent on such activity could bring some order back to my life. I hung Shiva's picture on the wall and slipped Ajai's cross under my pillow. Then I bathed, put on fresh clothes, and feeling more rested, went to join Letty in the garden. Wicker chairs and a table had been placed on the lawn. Letty was reading the newspaper, her half-glasses riding low on her nose. At my approach, she raised her head, turned to me and smiled. Over the tops of the spectacles her blue eyes were ringed faintly with brown, like Mama's.

"Ah, there you are. Feeling better?"

"Yes, thank you." I sat in the other chair. "Cleaner, too. All that coal dust."

"Good. Gopi is bringing tea." She put aside the paper and removed her glasses. "Tell me about your father. How is he?"

I folded my hands in my lap and thought briefly before I answered, "Well, it seems to me he is ever so resigned . . . as if it were somehow his own fault. There's no other way to describe it. I saw him on Saturdays. I wanted to stay in Vellore, but he wouldn't hear of it. He said there were no accommodations for people of our class. On his neck and arms are these white patches," I pointed to the corresponding places on my own body, "which he tries to keep covered with long sleeves and high collars." I paused, remembering Papa's habit of tugging at his collar. "Physically, at least, there's been no startling change. I was relieved for that."

"Yes," she said, nodding. "Fortunately it was caught in time. It was plucky of you to go to him."

"Not really. I couldn't *not* go."

Gopi arrived smiling her welcome at me over a tray that held a cup of tea, a glass of whiskey and ice and a plate of sliced madeira cake. She placed the tray on the table and withdrew.

"No, thank you. No cake." I picked up my cup. "How was Mama?"

Letty put the cake plate back on the tray. "Well, of course, she was dreadfully upset when you left. But, you knew that, I'm sure. She cried for days. The slightest thing would set her off. Thank goodness Aunt Margaret was weak as a kitten, or fur would have flown between them to be sure. But the fact is, you should have been told about your father. There's just no getting around that and Lavinia knew it."

I said, "Mama has always treated me like a baby, as if I am incapable of understanding." Not pleased with the shrillness of my tone, I finished weakly, "It was finally too much."

"Yes, I know." She sipped her drink, holding the glass in both hands under her chin, elbows resting on the arms of her chair. "But I think some truths are beginning to sink in. Lavinia is coming round to the fact that you are developing into a strong woman, that you are not just her baby girl. I think she sees that, unless she lets go, she'll lose you. Hah! A contradiction if there ever was one."

We sat in silence, feeling the weight of what we did not speak about, and listened to the *muezzin* calling from the mosque, a faint sweet wail weaving in with the music from the servants' quarters to create eerie, hypnotic sounds like the notes from a snake charmer's flute.

I wished desperately that Letty would reintroduce the topic of her having once been in my predicament so I could then talk to her about myself, but since she only sat there sipping her drink, I was suddenly tongue-tied.

"Where did Nila go?" I blurted finally. I wondered what my uncle thought of this state of affairs, and if the young officer Nila was said to have left with was the handsome Sikh.

"I don't know," Letty answered, resting her glass on the arm of her chair. "I doubt if anyone does. Colonel Bhatt, perhaps, and he isn't saying. Odd, but as I said, he didn't strike me as a distressed man."

I thought of the afternoon Nila had showed me her poems, when at one point it seemed she was on the verge of sharing

220

a confidence, but then had abruptly changed her mind. I saw again the light in her green eyes, the glow on her face. I wondered now if that had been her secret: that she was contemplting leaving. Then I forgot all about the Bhatts, for Ajai's car had just entered the gates. Panic-stricken, I watched its rusted, dented, rattling approach up the curved drive, and glanced questioningly at Letty.

"I've said nothing to him," she said soothingly. "He's taken to coming here two or three times a week. I think it's his way of touching you through me. Shall I ask him to leave?"

I shook my head.

He parked the car where he always did, under a rain tree, and raised a hand in greeting before he opened the door and got out. He started toward us, then stopped suddenly when he saw me. I thought he might turn back to the car and, perversely, I felt a wrenching disappointment even though seeing him again made me want to weep. Had I made myself forget the force of his beauty, that combination of grace and symmetry of form that always made me tighten up inside like a fist?

"I need to see Maharaj about the chicken *tanduri* for dinner," Letty murmured, and excused herself.

He approached slowly, his eyes on mine, and came to stand before me in his habitual muslin *kurta* and cotton *pyjama*. His face could have been carved from stone. Only his brown eyes under their straight black brows moved restlessly, searching my face.

At last he spoke. "When did you return?"

"This afternoon." I forced myself to sit still, to return his gaze.

"Why did you stop writing?" he asked in the same flat tone.

I looked away. Seeing him again made me forget. Now I remembered, and a sick feeling rose inside me. "If I told you, you would not like it."

221

"Tell me anyway," he said grimly.

"I can't."

He grabbed my wrist; I held back. "You are going to walk with me even if I have to drag you," he said, pulling me from the chair. "And you are going to explain this nonsense."

Still holding my wrist, he led me away from the house, past the kitchen garden and the library, to the untended area of the compound where the gravel path gave way to weeds that grew tall and dark around dying teaks. Startled grasshoppers shot away at our approach. My head began to ache; the sick feeling grew worse.

"Yes," I said, fighting the urge to massage my temples. "I suppose you deserve an explan—"

"You *suppose?*" he said harshly, releasing me so suddenly that I staggered.

" . . . only, I don't know how to explain it," I finished hopelessly, rubbing my wrist.

He stopped and turned to face me. "Oh, you don't know how to explain it," he mocked, emphasizing each word. "So, finished! The end. I must accept that and leave quietly." He caught me by the shoulders and bent to look into my face. "Tell me one thing. Do you still love me?"

"Oh, yes!"

"Don't you feel a responsibility to that love?" He shook me. "Have you forgotten that night on the riverbank? Was that only a distraction for you because you had quarreled with your mother?"

I gasped. My head felt tight as though my brain had suddenly swelled. "I have not forgotten." The words came from somewhere deep in my throat. "My God, why do you think I am here?" Be careful, an inner voice cautioned, don't hurt him like you did Papa. I took a deep breath, filling my lungs. "I've thought of nothing else in the past four weeks, but not in the way you think. I wasn't sure if I should tell you—"

He stared at me. "Tell me what?"

I simply stood there, looking down at my feet. I felt his hands tighten on my shoulders. Then he released me.

"*Hari Ram!*" he said softly. "Are you pregnant?"

I covered my face with my hands.

"It's true, then. Is it?"

I continued to remain silent.

I felt his arms come around me. I wriggled free, still covering my face. "Please don't," I mumbled into my hands. "It would only make it harder."

"Marry me, please! You must, now."

I dropped my hands. "How would we manage?"

"We'll *find* a way."

"No! I can't let you do that!" I cried out, clenching my fists at my sides in an effort to keep my voice steady. "If you have to give up your studies, your ambitions, you will grow to hate me before the baby's first birthday. I could not bear it if you were to hate me for spoiling your life."

He made a brushing-away gesture and an impatient sound. "I told you before, my life is nothing without you. Now you are carrying my child. What else is there but to marry?"

I turned away from him. "I don't know. I just don't know. I am going away with Aunt Letty."

There was a brief silence, then he said very quietly behind me. "Are you considering an abortion?"

I didn't answer.

"Don't I have anything to say about this? It's my child, too."

"It's not a child," I said wearily. "It's an embryo. I'm tired. Will you please go now?"

"Megan, I beg of you. Don't send me away. It is also my problem."

At that, I whirled around. The taut misery in his face gave me a rush of pure pleasure, like a surge of lust. I thought, this is how love can turn to hate in an instant, how murders are committed.

"How can it be your problem?" I lashed out. "You're not pregnant."

He flinched. I knew I was being cruelly unfair. I had wanted him to make love to me that night more than I'd ever wanted anything in my life; I had been the aggressor. Now I was punishing him for it. But I could not help myself, any more than I could have helped what happened that night. My heart was a lump of steel, cold as ice, chilling me to my toes and the tips of my fingers, freezing my mouth shut.

Ajai turned and walked rapidly away. I watched him leave, his back straight and proud. I *had* hurt him, after all, even more than I hurt Papa. I sank to my knees among tangled weeds, thinking distantly of Grandpa's death and how I had felt nothing then until days later when I found the dead dog in the ditch and ran home weeping hysterically.

I could not grasp my loss, but I was certain the pain would come.

CHAPTER TWENTY-ONE

My uncle's manservant in New Delhi went by the unlikely name of Singaram, or Lion. He was a bony old Tamilian with the vermillion trident of Vishnu painted on his dark-skinned forehead, and tufts of wiry grey hair sprouting from his ears. He cared for my uncle with single-minded devotion: drawing his bath, removing his shoes and massaging his feet at the end of the day, mending his clothes and sewing on popped-off buttons with fingers nimble as a girl's. All this should have endeared Singaram to Letty. Instead, there was an ongoing battle between them. She said his cooking was inedible, that he couldn't cook even under threat of torture. In retaliation Singaram produced the same breakfast everyday—rubbery scrambled eggs on burned toast.

"You mean to tell me," Letty fumed to my uncle, as she poured tea, "that he can't even make *toast?* I'm beginning to think he's doing it deliberately."

"There are such high prices for everything in this city," my uncle said mildly, using his knife to scrape the black from his toast onto the grey tile floor. "I am lucky to have the rascal."

"And, if you ask me, he wants you and the flat to himself," she retorted, handing him a cup of tea. "With me anywhere else, but here."

My uncle patted her hand. "What does it matter, Lettoo? I am glad you are here. And Megan also," he added as an afterthought. "So," he said heartily, "where are you off to today? Some more sightseeing?"

He looked unfamiliar in the white homespun Indian clothing, so different from the tailored suits he'd worn in Nerbudapur. Perhaps he found it necessary, here in the nation's capital as a representative of the people, to declare his Indianness.

"No," Letty said, "today we are going shopping."

"Well, do not buy up all of Delhi."

Watching him munch contentedly on toast spread thickly with marmalade, I saw no sign of bitterness or even regret over Nila. In fact, the night before at dinner he'd made a reference to "poor old Bhatt," and added, "He is better off." I wondered if Letty had told him about my condition. If so, his manner toward me had not changed. He was as amiably indifferent to my presence as ever. He'd greeted me on my return to Nerbudapur as if he were unaware I'd ever left.

The New Delhi flat was a modestly furnished one-bedroom place which, according to Letty, cost a prince's ransom. It was on the top floor of a complex of similar dwellings stacked twelve floors deep. Letty said that at least we didn't have to listen to footsteps, and God knew what else, above us. Offices and shops occupied the ground level along with the New Savoy Bar & Grill, to whose kebabs my uncle was addicted; he ate them from a greasy newspaper cone, popping them into his mouth like peanuts. Letty blamed Singaram's miserable cooking for this addiction and said it would be on the servant's head if her husband dropped dead of a heart attack. Singaram replied in a staccato burst of Tamil that it was the *wife's* sacred duty to cook for the master of the house.

Letty and my uncle used the bedroom; Singaram stretched out on the kitchen floor every night as though clubbed; I slept on the fold-out sofa in the front room. When I couldn't sleep, I would go out onto the tiny balcony that opened off the front room and sit there for hours in the dark, with the stars above and the city spread out below like spangled velvet. To pass the time, I would try to identify the moving lights far beneath me. Cars were the easiest because they moved smoothly and did not lurch like lorries. Bicycle lights were dimmer than those on cars or lorries; they danced like glowworms, casting no beams. My favorite lights were the feeble kerosene lamps of the oxcarts that seemed not to move at all, so stately was their progress. Off in the distance, the lights of Connaught Circus, the central busines district, seemed to me to form a queen's necklace or a diamond crown.

I wondered what would happen if the balcony were to suddenly detach and crash to the pavement. I pictured myself lying there in the rubble, broken but graceful, my hair spread out in a halo around my head. Chestnut hair. There'd be a simple though elegant funeral. How Mama would weep that we had not reconciled before my untimely death. I would lie there in a snow white coffin, smiling faintly among puffs of satin, holding a single lily. The thought was enough to bring tears to my eyes. Sniffling, I wiped my nose on the hem of my nightdress. And Papa—but the memory of Papa struggling for control that afternoon in Vellore abruptly ended my self-indulgent fantasies.

I would not allow myself to think of Ajai. I forced him from my mind, pushed him out, biting hard on a knuckle while concentrating on the pain—and the awful tedium of these days in Delhi. Since our arrival two days before, Letty

227

and I had seen Red Fort, India Gate, Jumna Masjid, Qutab Minar (where I vomited climbing the stairs), and various temples. I had placed flowers at Gandhi's tomb. All part of my education, she told me, to bring me in touch with the history of our country. But hot, drowsy from lack of sleep at night and needing to urinate frequently, I found it difficult to muster enthusiasm. In two more days we would fly to Srinagar on a ramshackle plane to spend a week on a houseboat on some Kashmiri lake that Letty had picked out. It would do me a world of good, she said. As far as I was concerned, all this was only postponing the inevitable.

Connaught Circus was laid out in a vast ring of restaurants and shops. As Letty and I strolled along the arcade that circled the inside, I thought that I had never seen such glamorous women, nor so many beggars. The women, both Indian and European, were dressed in delicate saris or smart frocks and wore shoes with high narrow heels. They flitted in and out of shops filled with lustrous silks, embroidered slippers and vests, jeweled necklaces displayed on dark velvet, tiny enameled birds with sapphire eyes, jade carvings, filigreed silver. "Come! Come!" merchants beckoned from doorways. As we passed a carpet shop, the man unrolled a prayer rug at our feet and squatted beside it to stroke the silky nap with a lover's palm, first one way and then the other. The beggars hovered around us.

Letty waved the man aside.

"What is it we're shopping for?" I asked, stepping around the carpet seller, who deftly rolled his rug back up only to fling it open at the feet of someone else. The beggars attached themselves to the people behind us.

"A sari for you, of course. For tonight."

"Can't I wear the one you gave me for my birthday? I wore it only once." I brushed shoulders with a burly Punjabi woman carrying several bundles. Three young girls darted around us, their hair swinging in long plaits.

"Oh no," Letty said firmly. "This is the event of the season. You need something with more color. You are so pale these days." Adding hastily, "Not your fault, of course."

"No more lambent skin, eh?"

"What?"

"Nila. She used to say I had lambent skin."

"Please come, ladies! Look, only look! No need to buy!"

"I remember the bit about rusty hair—"

"Russet, not rusty."

"Your uncle was infatuated with her, you know." Letty said this as she might have told me about a corn on her husband's big toe. "But I think it's run its course. Oh do look at that awful thing!"

We stopped in front of a furrier's window where, nestled among the fur caps and scarves, was the stuffed, grotesquely grinning head of a civet cat with green glass eyes and long narrow teeth.

Reeling from Letty's revelation, I could only gaze back, repelled, into those flat glassy eyes. Green as Nila's. *Letty knew*. All this time she *knew*.

"Why on earth would they put something like that in a window," Letty complained. "It's so off-putting—Megan! Are you all right? Come away! Don't look at that ghastly thing." She led me away with an arm around my waist. "Oh dear," she lamented. "I *have* been thoughtless. Making you do too much. I only wanted to distract you."

The spell passed, leaving me drenched in perspiration. "I'm all right," I said. "Yes, it did give me a bit of a turn, but I'm all right now." It wasn't the head, it was what she'd just told me.

"Please take a look, missus! Very fine sari," a merchant called from a stool positioned in a doorway. "From all over India in one shop only!"

"I'll take you straight home," Letty said.

"No, I'm all right, really."

"Are you sure?" She searched my face. "Are you up to looking at a few saris in here? You can sit down."

"Yes, yes!" the shopkeeper urged. He'd climbed off his stool and bowed, waving us in. "Only come, missus. Very fine chair for sitting."

"You won't have to move a muscle. I promise you."

Trailing scent as she passed, a pale-skinned Parsi lady said airily, "They do have the best selection in Delhi, you know."

It was cool inside. The air smelled of perfume, hair oil, and the dry, woody odor of new cloth. Fans spun from a high ceiling among suspended tube lights. We sat in armchairs in front of a low, carpeted platform, and sipped deliciously tart frosty lime juice that the shopkeeper had sent out for. Folded saris of every hue and fabric were stacked behind glass-fronted cases.

"What you want? Tell me." The merchant stood there in his white muslin clothing, counting off on his fingers. "We are having Mysore silk, Benares silk, Kanjivaram silk, chiffon, georgette, lace. All kinds we are having."

"What do you think, Megan? Something soft?"

"Hah! Soft, soft." The man slid open a glass door and pulled out a pile of chiffon saris in rainbow colors. He spread them out before us. Sliding his hands into the folds of one, he lifted it like an offering. The sari settled on either side of him in pale pink drifts. "Look, missus, how soft."

"Do you like that, Megan?"

"It's lovely."

"I want to see the border on that blue one," Letty said, bending forward to pick it up. She ran a palm under the sheer fabric. "This is quite nice."

I placed my empty glass under my chair. "That mauve one, there." I pointed.

The sari was without the usual gold or silver trim, but the

pallu, the end that draped over the shoulder, had a lacy design, fine as a cobweb. It was the most elegant thing I'd ever seen.

Letty looked doubtful. "It's so plain."

"That's why I like it," I insisted.

"Take one with *jurri,* missy," the man urged, pointing to a sari with a wide gold border. "That cheap sari," he said of the mauve one I admired, "no gold *jurri.*"

"But I like it."

Letty sighed. "Well, if that's what you want . . . " She finished her lime juice.

We picked out a matching *choli*-blouse and underskirt. Letty paid for everything. I thanked her, and we left.

We lunched on the verandah of the Imperial Hotel, overlooking its lawn that had remained miraculously green despite the continuing, intense heat. Except for an ancient red-faced Englishman in khaki shorts and shirt who was enjoying his plate of curry and rice, the place was deserted. Letty ordered chicken cutlets and mint-flavored Kashmiri tea, to put us in the mood for our trip, she said, though she hardly tasted anything.

She sat there tearing apart a cutlet with her fork. She seemed intent on separating the crust from the filling. "I don't want you to think less of my husband," she said. "He is a good man and I know he loves me, but sometimes I'm not enough—or, maybe, I'm too much. I'm not a relaxed person; I'm too intense. And, God knows, he works very hard." She sighed. "I suspect he does it for recreation. Like other people take up badminton or polo."

I didn't know what to say, so I said nothing.

"I knew he was taken with Nila. I've known with every one of his flings, but I've never faced him. I . . . I just couldn't. I don't even know if he knows I know."

Unable to remain silent any longer, I said in a low voice, "How do you stand it?"

231

"I love him," she said simply.

My heart expanded. I had stopped eating and was staring off at a tree whose foliage rippled and swelled with breeze, a small green sea, high up and hypnotic. I wanted to tell Letty about myself, to give something back to her for allowing me into her confidence. Up to now, for some reason I did not understand, I had not been able to confide in her, and she seemed to respect my reserve. Even now, I didn't quite know how to begin.

I felt her hand cover mine where it rested on the tablecloth.

"Tell me," she said gently.

"Oh, Aunt Letty," the words tumbled out. "It would kill Mama to know I'm pregnant. I don't get along with her, but I don't want to be responsible for—" I stopped suddenly, clenching my lips between my teeth.

"Her death?" Letty said quietly. "Like I was responsible for Pa's?"

"I didn't say that!" I cried out as I turned my hand over to clutch hers.

"Did he die by inches?"

"He . . . never recovered."

She moved her plate to one side. "I'm sorry, I didn't mean to interrupt. Go on. You were telling me how you felt."

I almost groaned. There was so much I wanted to say, but I couldn't say any more for fear of hurting her.

"You are not liking food, madam?" A white-uniformed, red-sashed waiter was at our table bending over Letty's plate.

"No, no." Letty waved her hands at him. "Everything is simply delicious."

"Yes, madam," he murmured, and withdrew.

"Sorry, again, Meg love. You were saying."

Relieved by the interruption that enabled me to collect myself, I said as firmly as I could, "I'm thinking of an abortion. It would be best for everyone."

"I see." She patted my hand then withdrew hers. "You've talked to Ajai?"

"I told him I was pregnant. I didn't say I was considering an abortion. At least, not in so many words. I think he guessed. He . . . well, he wants us to marry."

"Is that such a bad idea?"

"I don't know. It's the wrong reason to marry."

"But you love him, I think," she said. Adding wryly, "What other reason do you need?"

I didn't answer.

"Megan," she began, "there is something I really must say. Then, if you still feel the way you do, I'll do everything I can to help you. I know this is terribly difficult for you and I don't want to complicate the situation, but have you considered this may be your only pregnancy? I was never able to conceive again. And, for that matter, neither was Lavinia. No, wait." She held up a hand. "Let me finish. I'm only saying this because I don't want you to do something you might regret later."

Desperate, I said, "But what about Mama?"

"Lavinia will be all right," Letty said, soothingly. "She's more resilient than you think. And make no mistake, she absolutely dotes on you. I saw how much she suffered when she thought she'd lost you, when you ran out of the house that day, and then didn't respond to her letters. She'll come around."

"What if she doesn't?" My head began to pound. "I can't take that chance."

She took my hand in both of hers. "I know you've considered all this carefully. And I also know this is the loneliest decision you've ever had to make. My heart aches to see you like this, so pale and anxious. I wish I could help you more, but only you can decide."

"I feel I'm being pulled into pieces. There's Mama, and

Ajai, and my own conscience . . . " I drew in my breath sharply.

"I know. It was like that for me, too." She squeezed my hand. "Even so, knowing all that I now know, while I wish some things were different in my life, I would still marry my husband all over again."

"Can I ask you something?"

"Of course."

"About Nila. If you'd . . . known . . . Why were you always trying to get me to go over to her house?"

Letty looked surprised. "Because you were so lonely. God knows I was no company for you then, trapped in my phobias. Nila's young and lively—the brain of an ant, of course, but I thought she'd be good for you, take you about, introduce you to people."

Again, I felt my heart swell.

That evening Singaram helped my uncle dress in the front room, leaving the bedroom free for Letty and me. It was a nondescript room with a brown, black and white chevron-patterned counterpane on the double bed and matching curtains at the window. A picture of Shiva dallying with Parvati was bolted to the whitewashed wall. Letty was daubing scent in her armpits and behind her ears. The room reeked of Evening in Paris.

"I was going to help you with that," Letty said, watching me tie my sari in front of the wardrobe mirror.

"I think I can manage. I've had two lessons. The pleats are hard to get even," I muttered grimly, as I struggled with the slippery chiffon, thinking of the first time Nila had draped me in a sari. It has been a mauve one, too. *It makes your eyes look like violets,* she'd said then. Had that influenced my selection of this one?

"You're doing splendidly." Letty was wearing an emerald silk, elaborately fringed, with a wide gold border. She sat down at the dressing table to brush her hair, eyeing me critically in the mirror. "A little rouge might be in order. Nothing garish," she added hastily, noting my reaction. "Just a touch. I'll do it for you."

"If it's just a touch, I'll do it myself. I don't like paint."

"Really Megan, how Victorian you are," she said, as she outlined her mouth with lipstick. "It's not paint, it's makeup."

"Victorian?" I snorted. "In my condition?"

"Now, now. We're going to a party."

For a finishing touch Letty loaned me carved amethyst earrings. She wore a collar of emeralds set in gold.

"Lettoo," my uncle called. "Please to making it snappy. Car is here." He had hired one for the evening.

"Yes, dear. Only a minute," she called back, as she rummaged in a trunk without the least haste, and finally drew out a beaded evening bag. "I only brought one," she told me apologetically. "We can share it. You can put your hanky and things in here."

"Yes. All right."

"Madam." Singaram poked his head around the door. "Car is waiting long time now." His sharp nose fairly twitched with rectitude. "Wasting Master's money."

"That wretched little Madrasi!" Letty swore aloud. "That miserable scrap of horse manure!"

The party was being hosted by one of my uncle's colleagues who lived in a mansion in a fashionable area of Delhi. A very wealthy man, my uncle told us as we rode in the car, who had made his money in the black market during the war. "A time of opportunity," he continued gloomily. "Opportunity some were smart enough to seize in both hands."

235

"Also a time," Letty snapped, "when others fighting for *swaraj* were rotting away in jail."

"True, true," my uncle replied, and wisely let the matter drop. His ears were probably still ringing from the tirade over Singaram's officiousness that Letty had delivered as we rode down in the lift.

The car let us out in front of a huge, handsome house with a wide verandah whose pillars formed sweeping archways. We entered the marble reception room through carved teak doors. Our host and hostess greeted us, bowing over joined palms, murmuring their delight at our gracing their humble establishment with our presence.

"Humble establishment, my eye," Letty muttered. "What's this supposed to be? A re-creation of Versailles?" We joined the other guests, both European and Indian, grandly dressed, who milled around. "Now circulate," she commanded. "Don't just stand in a corner. Introduce yourself to people. Have a good time." Then she moved away, presumably to do all those things, while I seethed at this latest irritating attempt on her part to transform me into a person of polish. I'd rather have stayed behind in the flat with Singaram, watching the lights from my blacony.

I accepted a cucumber sandwich from a passing waiter and nibbled it while I inspected the Moghul miniatures and the bronzes. In the crush of people the room was stifling. Adjoining rooms were equally congested. I thought of going to sit on the front steps, but I knew that would surely invite Letty's wrath. The next best thing would be to sit by an open window or a fan. I was suddenly very thirsty and, looking around, hid the rest of the sandwich in an urn of trailing fern, half-expecting Letty to swoop down on me. But she was nowhere to be seen.

"I am telling you that is the downfall of this country," said a small man with protruding teeth and a huge turban who was holding forth to a group. "Gandhiji, himself, preached that . . ."

I drifted over to a clutch of women who were discussing the servant problem. "Your ayah is a jewel. But she's a vanishing breed." "Yes, yes. Days of servants are over." They ignored me. I left them and wandered through the dining room with its tables and sideboards laden with food. People stood around in clumps sipping drinks, talking and smiling under bright chandeliers, faces shiny with perspiration. I picked an orange squash from a tub of ice, and crossing a dark hallway, almost dropped the slippery bottle. Lurking in the shadows was a crouching tiger. A second of heart-crashing panic before I realized it was stuffed. It was so realistic I could almost see its tail move.

Just then a door off the hallway opened, and I felt a blessed rush of cool air. A waiter came out carrying a tray, shut the door behind him, and hurried past me. I made straight for that door, opened it and stood there facing the darkened room, enjoying the drafts of delicious coolness that enveloped me. Lifting the hair off my neck, I took a swig from the bottle.

"The room is air-conditioned. Come in and shut the door," a man's voice, vaguely familiar, called.

"I'm sorry," I said, as I peered into the gloom. "I didn't know. I've never been in an air-conditioned room before. Do you know where the lights are?"

"Miss Manning? Is that you?" A lamp was turned on, illuminating a library, or a study. I saw a man with a drink in his hand half-rise from where he'd been sitting behind a desk. Other chairs were scattered around the paneled room.

"Colonel Bhatt!"

We stared at each other in silence, then he came round the desk to take my hand. He was wearing grey slacks and a white short-sleeved shirt. It was the first time I'd seen him out of uniform. He looked younger, more relaxed.

"Come in and sit," he said. "Shall I ring for refreshments?"

"No, thank you." I held up my bottle. "I've got this. I was thirsty."

I sat in one of the black leather armchairs while he brought me a low table upon which to set my drink. He sat on the edge of the desk. I was surprised that under the circumstances—what with Nila and all—I felt no awkwardness.

"I saw a tiger outside the door," I said. "Beautifully stuffed, of course. The art of taxidermy."

"That awful thing? Raj swears it was in that exact position when he shot it. I rather think he bought it from some down-at-the-heels maharaja. But, tell me about yourself. You left Nerbudapur in a bit of a hurry."

"Yes," I said, smoothing the folds of my sari. "You remember I once told you my father had gone to England without us. Well, I discovered that he's still in India . . . He's in a leper sanitorium, in Vellore. I went to see him."

"Oh, I *am* sorry. How is he?"

"He's getting better. In a few months he'll be home. Why were you sitting in the dark?" Even before the words left my lips, I realized that the question was impertinent. I began to mumble apologies.

"Please do not upset yourself." He took a cigarette from a box on the desk, hesitated, then held the box out to me. "Care for one?"

"No, thank you."

He lit the cigarette, drawing deeply on it, and exhaled slowly. "I'm taking refuge from that mob out there. Raj and Veena go in for circuses like this. I happen to prefer the dark, and the quiet. Besides, this is the coolest room in the house. What are you doing in Delhi?"

"I'm here with my aunt and uncle. And you?"

"Ah, yes," he said, tapping the end of his cigarette into an ashtray. "Your uncle, the Representative. A man of importance." He picked up his glass, swirling the liquid around, but did not drink from it. I thought of the time we'd seen my uncle and Nila in Letty's library, and understood his cynicism. "Well, I'm here because Raj, who is the owner of all this," he waved his cigarette at the bookcases filled with matched leatherbound editions, "is a distant cousin. I usually stay here when I'm in Delhi. I had to meet with Nila to work out a settlement. No doubt you've heard that she has gone away." It was a statement, flatly delivered, not a question.

"Aunt Letty mentioned it."

"A matter of mutual consent," he said quietly, stroking his moustache with the knuckle of an index finger, a gesture I remembered well. "We are, both of us, happier now."

There was nothing in his manner to convey heartbreak or betrayal. He did not elicit pity; rather he was a man strong in himself, sure of what he wanted.

"Is she here in Delhi?" I asked.

"No." He ground out the cigarette. "I'm only passing through." He finished his drink and set the glass down firmly on the desk. "You know, some people are not suited for marriage. It's not a flaw on their part." He shrugged. "Merely a fact of nature."

I took a sip of my orange squash and met his dark eyes. "I've come to that conclusion myself."

He laughed at that, flinging back his head and slapping the desk. "You are truly a most unusual young woman."

When I finally emerged from the study, I found Letty standing by the dining room door, looking around anxiously. "Where were you?" she demanded, as I joined her. "I've been hunting around for you."

"Oh," I said breezily, "I was circulating, conversing, having a good time."

She looked at me suspiciously. "I wanted to introduce you to the Prime Minister. He popped in for about fifteen minutes; now that he's gone, your uncle's ready to leave. And so am I. The drinks here are ghastly. Local whiskey! That's carrying nationalism a little *too* far for my taste."

CHAPTER TWENTY-TWO

From the window of the plane I could see the naked tips of mountains—raw-looking as though freshly scraped—thrusting upward through clouds that made the plane bounce and my stomach lurch. Presently the sound of the engines changed and we were instructed to bring our seats upright and fasten our seatbelts to prepare for landing. As the plane began its descent, I saw pine-clad lower slopes cradling a lush green bowl of valley enameled with iridescent lakes, burnished metal rooftops and the silver loops of the river Jhelum.

"Now, try to enjoy it," Letty said coaxingly. "We're on holiday. It will help take your mind off things, give you time to think."

She meant well, but diversion was not what I needed.

"I've thought enough," I told her.

"Well," she said briskly, "I, for one, plan to have a rollicking time. The first holiday I've had in years."

At the Srinagar airport, we walked down a metal stairway and across the macadam to the terminal where we were immediately surrounded by houseboat owners shouting the merits of their crafts. Others held up signs: "Mr. Asquith & family," "Mr. & Mrs. McDermott," "New Delhi Rambling Club."

"Oh dear, I wonder what the man looks like?" Letty said, peering at the signs. "He said he'd meet the plane."

Finally, as the crowd thinned, we saw a tall emaciated man holding a sign waist high: "Dr. L. Dube & niece." It was Mr. Rahman, the owner of the houseboat Letty had rented. He wore a dark grey vest over white cotton tunic and trousers, and stood to one side out of the airport bustle, shoulders hunched, looking desolate.

"But I am thinking Dr. Dube is a man," he said, gazing down at us with moist mournful eyes as though he might burst into tears. "I was not expecting a lady."

"There is also a male Dr. Dube," Letty said. "My husband, but he is not with us. Is there a problem?"

The pained expression intensified. "No, no madam! No problem." He raised his joined palms, the sign flat between them. "It is only that I was having this picture in my mind of an Indian gentleman, but here you are two English ladies in Indian clothes. Is it not puzzling?"

"I'm sorry if we confused you." Letty glanced around. "Where do we collect our luggage?"

"This way, madam. Please." He rubbed the tip of his beaked nose with a knuckle, then proceeded to walk sideways slightly ahead of us, wringing his hands. "We are having very fine season," he said in funereal tones. I decided he was one of those people who is happiest only when miserable. "Sahibs are flocking to Kashmir. Last time before going off to England. Full occupancy in all seven houseboats I am owning. You will occupy *Lady Luck*. First class boat."

After picking up our luggage, Mr. Rahman ushered us into a taxi, got in himself, and we were off. He turned around from the front seat to tell Letty, "You are having an honest face. Like that I can always tell character. It is a gift from God. In fact, you are resembling exactly my mother."

"I'd like to verify that," Letty said, offended. It was obvious Mr. Rahman was older than she.

"Alas, dear lady." He spread his hands, then brought them together with a soft clap. A spark of animation lit his eyes. "That is not possible. My female relatives have departed this earth. All dead—but my wife, and she is strong as an oxcart, praise God."

We drove along dusty winding streets hemmed in by tongas, bicycles, cars; past green fields dotted with patches of wild flowers and grazing sheep. Mr. Rahman pointed out mosques, historic buildings, old bridges, a fort at the top of a hill. He never stopped talking. By the time we turned into a narrow lane and the taxi came to a stop in the middle of what seemed like a field, we'd learned that he neither imbibed nor smoked, but had instead a weakness for fishing and women, and had married only to please his dying father who later recovered and lived for fifteen more years.

"Jolly fellow," Letty whispered to me while Mr. Rahman, who had let himself out of the car, haggled with the taxi driver. "Can you picture him with a woman? I wonder what he looks like naked."

"There is my house." He held his arm straight out to indicate a low, spreading structure that resembled a chicken coop. Several children rushed out to greet us, then fell back to stare. "Some are my children; some are not," he said cryptically, hefting a suitcase in each hand. As we turned to follow him, Letty carrying the case of toiletries, he explained, "This is Lake Nagim. Most lovely. You will see. Lake Dal is too crowded. Many, many boats."

The *Lady Luck* was shaded by chenar trees and willows, while lily pads floated on the water's surface like pale green platters. The exterior was of unfinished wood, with white canvas awnings over the windows. We crossed the creaking gangplank and entered the side of the boat. The inside was lavish with carvings of stars, birds, animals and spread lotus blossoms all over the ceilings, walls and furniture. It made me think of brass lamps and geniis.

From the dining room window, I could see reflected on the broad smooth surface of water the scene from across the lake—houseboats and willows against a backdrop of tall deodars and lavender mountains. Occasionally a passing *shikara,* one of the narrow, canopied boats known as the water taxis of Kashmir, set this reflection wobbling off in all directions; then the reflection knit back together again. There was a tranquility, a sense of timelessness about the swiftly moving punts, the still water, the towering mountains.

"So, Missy," Mr. Rahman stood beside me, hands clasped before him, rolling his thumbs. "You are liking it, I think?"

"Oh yes," I said, turning away from the window. "It's . . . very nice."

Letty stood to one side still holding the toiletry case. "Well, that's a relief," she said. I thought I heard a barely suppressed sigh and was instantly remorseful I had not sounded more enthusiastic.

"My brother will be your guide," Mr. Rahman said. "He will take you to see carpet factories, floating gardens, Moghul gardens, like that. We have a watchman for every boat we are owning. So you need not worry. You will be safe."

The next morning I woke to the piercingly sweet song of a bulbul in the chenar tree. Then I heard the *muezzin's* call to prayer, faint but clear like a distant bell, and the soft splash of oars from passing *shikaras.* I rose and looked out of my bedroom window. The mountains, in purple shadow, were swirled in mist. Wrapping myself in a blanket, I stepped into the hallway. Letty's door was closed. I wandered past the galley and into the dining room, then across the parlor with its fat, cretonne-covered chairs and carved tables, to the front of the boat that was open like a small porch. I curled up on one of the built-in cushioned seats, feeling the cool dampness of early morning on my face.

As the sky brightened, the translucent grey of the water gave way to amber and then to salmon. Sharp as a coin, the sun edged over the mountains, spilling warmth over the slopes, and then slid into the water where it settled like a live coal. I had the sudden urge to sink into that warmth, to let it unfold the shell of apathy that gripped me; then I could emerge cleansed, lustrous, iridescent as a pearl. Throwing off the blanket, I went to the wooden steps that led to the water, and climbed down.

"Stop! The water is polluted."

I was so startled at hearing a man's voice behind me that I tripped on a loose board and tumbled into the water. It was like ice. Gasping and choking, my nightdress wrapping round my legs like a shroud, I grabbed at the bottom step as a brawny young man hurried down to offer me his hand.

"Look what you made me do," I sputtered wrathfully. "Are you the watchman?"

"I am Ali Akbar Rahman. I came to see if you ladies are awake and wanting hot water for your baths. Here, please take my hand."

"Go away. I can't come out with you standing there."

"I will turn around. You better come out quickly or you will get sick. That water is full of sewage. It is not for swimming."

"I wasn't going to swim," I said crossly, crawling up the steps, "I only wanted to feel the water." Shivering, teeth rattling, I wraped myself in the blanket and stalked past him, leaving a watery trail.

"I will send your bathwater right away," he called after me.

Letty was standing in the open doorway of her room dressed in a long flowered housecoat.

"Who were you talk—? What in the world happened to you?"

"What do you think? I fell in the lake."

"How?" She followed me into my room.

"I just fell in, that's all. I was going to test the water and this fool came up behind me and yelled, 'Stop!' "

"Who? Mr. Rahman?"

"Some other Rahman. Ali somebody or other. Only a perfect *idiot* would do something like that," I stormed as I dropped the blanket in a soggy heap.

I heard a muffled snort and turned to find Letty struggling not to laugh, face pink with the effort, fist jammed against her mouth.

"It's not a laughing matter! That water is full of sewage—"

At that, Letty collapsed on my bed clutching her stomach, tears rolling down her cheeks. "Oh dear," she gasped. "There's something hanging from your ear."

I flew to the wardrobe mirror. A lily stalk clung to the side of my neck like a fat green worm. Runnels of water from my sopping hair ran down my face and off the end of my nose. My nightdress, no longer white, stuck to my skin in patches.

"Ugh!" I stamped my foot. "Disgusting!"

When I heard the sound of water being poured into the galvanized metal tub in the adjacent bathroom, and the outer door slam shut after the departing servant, I swept from the room with all the dignity I could muster.

"Well, look at it this way," Letty said at breakfast over an excellent cheese omelet. "It's reassuring you can still work up a respectable rage. I was beginning to wonder if your nerve fibers were damaged; you've been going around like a sleepwalker. *Nothing* engaged you. I think Ali did you a favor by pushing you in the lake."

"He didn't push me. I said he startled me and I lost my footing." I buttered a piece of toast, then put it down uneaten. "Why does he have to be our guide? Why can't Mr. Rahman show us around?"

"That death's head! He's like a cadaver. Worse than one. At least they don't talk. If you don't mind earth-breaking boredom listening to stories about his women and fishing lures—"

"It's . . . well, Ali stares."

Letty finished her tea and wiped her mouth on her serviette. "You must look at him too. Or how would you know?"

"I just feel his eyes on me all the time."

"You should be flattered."

"Why?"

Wavelets of light undulated across the carved-cedar stars on the ceiling.

She laughed. "Because it's nice to be admired, Megan. Good heavens!"

So Ali escorted us to a carpet factory, wood carvers, *papier-mâché* merchants, and Letty bought tables, bowls and trays. "For your uncle's New Delhi flat," she told me. "These things will make it more cosy. I've been thinking it might be wise for me to go with him to Delhi for the sessions of parliament. Who knows in what state of health that creature, Singaram, will have him otherwise? All those greasy kebabs."

It is difficult to be prim in a *shikara*. Under the canopy, the deep seat and plump cushions are made for reclining. Nevertheless, conscious of Ali, who sat facing us in the prow of the boat, I began each excusion sitting bolt upright, but soon found myself curled against the pillows until I sensed his scrutiny and straightened up again. The boatmen sat in the back, rowing with heart-shaped paddles. We passed under ancient bridges, alongside vast expanses of lotus and by villages with balconied, peak-topped houses on stilts.

Letty and Ali were always in animated conversation. While the stooped older brother resembled nothing so much as an elongated walking stick, Ali was thickset with muscular arms and neck. He lifted weights, he said, played rugby in summer, skied in winter. One thing he shared with his brother was volubility; only the subject matter was different. Where Mr. Rahman could hold forth on the charms of foreign women wearing shorts, Ali harangued us at length about why Kashmir should be part of Pakistan, not India. "This is a Moslem state," he said, black eyes flashing. "If a plebiscite is held today, the majority of people would choose Pakistan."

"Kashmir was a princely state," Letty countered, "with a Hindu ruler. After Independence those states were absorbed into India, so Kashmir belongs to India. Why should we give it up?"

"But the people should decide. Why are we not allowed to vote? That would be the democratic way." He had a pencil-thin moustache and thick black hair that fell across his forehead.

Letty laughed. "Governments don't always work along those lines. Oh, do look at all the lotus. Aren't they magnificent? Quite the most spectacular flower—although I'm still partial to roses."

Neon kingfishers and dragonflies darted among the waxy pink and white cups the size of my spread hand, which swayed on long slender stems above a carpet of lily pads. And behind, always in sight, were the mountains, golden at noon, rose-colored at dusk.

Ali leaned over the side of the boat and plucked a flower, which he gravely presented to me.

Beads of milky moisture dripped into my palm from the stiff, thick stalk. "Thank you," I said, and felt the color flood my face.

RITA PRATT SMITH

*   *   *

The next day I wrote letters to Papa and Aunt Margaret and, on impulse, asked the watchman if he knew where I could find a bicycle. I thought it would be fun to ride to the post office. He pointed to Mr. Rahman's house. Hesitantly I walked towards it, hoping I would see the older man, but Ali was in front working on an old green scooter. He wore loose cotton pants and an undershirt that revealed the swelling muscles of his arms and chest. He stood immediately when he saw me, wiping his hands on a rag.

"Yes?" As usual his eyes fastened on my face. "You need something?"

Unnerved by that steady unsmiling gaze, I stammered, "I . . . can I . . . uh . . . borrow a bicycle?"

"My nephew has one, but he rode it to market."

"I have some letters to post and . . . well, I thought I'd enjoy the exercise." I turned to leave.

"Wait. I have to pick up a parcel. I can take you on the scooter." Then, at my obvious reluctance, he offered stiffly, "If you wish, I can post your letters."

Ashamed that I'd hurt his feelings, I said quickly, "Oh. No, actually I'd like to ride on the scooter. I'll just run in and tell Aunt Letty."

"As you wish." He bowed.

I walked back to the *Lady Luck,* wondering why I found his stares so unsettling. But for that, he was unfailingly polite. In fact, he hardly addressed me unless absolutely necessary. It was always Letty he spoke to when we went out. Giving myself a mental shake, I thought, Letty is probably right, it's nice to be admired. Anyway, I could put up with it for a few more days.

Letty insisted on coming to see us off. "Here, let me tie your scarf around you so it doesn't tangle in the spokes." She took the length of grey chiffon from my shoulders, looped it behind my neck, crossed it in front and tied it behind at my waist. Ali now wore a short-sleeved blue and white checked shirt, and white drill slacks.

"You can sit to the side, but astride is safer," he instructed. "Hold my shoulder, if you like."

"Yes, all right."

And away we went. Conversation was difficult. The few shouted comments I attempted were lost in the rushing wind that whipped my hair around my face and ballooned the back of Ali's shirt. I lapsed into an uneasy silence. His shoulders were hard beneath my hands; his hair grew into a tiny vee at the back of his head. Suddenly I thought of Ajai, of that special place at his nape, so smooth to the touch under the curling black hair. The memory, alive on my fingertips, was like a blow. I caught my breath.

The post office was a single-story yellow building set back from the street. Bougainvillea grew in the fenced compound. Inside, I bought stamps, affixed them and slid my letters through the slot. While Ali went to find out about his parcel, I decided to wait outside. Idly, I watched a rotund though attractive woman carefully descend from a tonga that had stopped at the gate. She wore a pale pink sari. A matching parasol and purse dangled from a wrist. There was something familiar about her—the languid walk, the set of her head, the long golden neck. My God, it was Nila! But a very fat Nila. How she'd changed! Then she saw me, and stopped.

"Megan! My dear, dear friend," she called out in her clear, high voice. "I do not believe it." Beaming, she rushed up and embraced me. "But what are you doing here?"

"I was about to ask you the same thing."

"Srinagar is my home. I am Kashmiri." She paused, and continued in a subdued voice. "So much has changed since I last saw you. Prem and I made divorce." Then the green eyes lit up again. She hugged her burgeoning abdomen. "But now

I am married again and going to have a baby. Is it not wonderful?"

Pregnant? Flabbergasted, I muttered, "Why, yes. If that's what you want."

"What do you mean? 'If that's what you want?' It's what every woman wants. I've longed for a child. It is, my goodness, why I am a female."

"I'm sorry, Nila. I didn't mean—I . . . I'm very happy for you."

"I have missed you," she said, taking my hand in both of hers. "There is so much I have to tell. You must come to tea. I will tell everything then. Everything. But not now. Tonga is waiting. Come Tuesday, three o'clock. Five hundred sixty-eight Jasmine Avenue." She hurried away into the building.

Typical of Nila, she left me there without bothering to find out the circumstances of my being in Srinagar, or even if I could come on Tuesday. I could have called out or gone after her. But what did it matter? I wouldn't go, anyway.

On the way home, I held Ali's parcel between us. It felt soft like fabric; a sari, perhaps. I wondered whom it was for. When we arrived, he pulled the scooter onto its kickstand, turned to me and bowed. I could almost hear his heels click. "Thank you for riding with me," he said.

"Thank you for letting me ride with you," I replied, sounding almost flippant in an attempt at being casual.

"Did she say who the father is?"

"No. It must be the man she's married to now."

Letty shut her book with a snap, tossing it aside on the parlor sofa where she sat. "And who is that? Did you ask her?"

"No. Of course not."

"Oh," she said, clasping her hands, "I do wish you had."

"She was in a hurry," I said, sitting on the arm of an overstuffed chair. Elbows at my sides, I spread my hands. "All she said was, come to tea. It's so like her: Come here. Come there. Come to a tea dance."

"Then you must go." She stood abruptly and went to stand by the window, looking out.

"Why do you always make me go over to see her?" I complained, sliding into the chair. "I don't much like her, you know. She's so—"

"Never mind what she is," Letty cut in sharply, turning to face me. Her face was pale, pinched; her reading glasses had slipped down her nose. "You don't have to like her. If she promised to tell you everything, I want you to find out—for my sake."

Puzzled at first by her increasing agitation, it finally dawned on me that Letty was frightened her husband might have fathered Nila's child.

My heart tight with pity and love, I slowly nodded. "Yes," I said, staring at a swirled design in the crimson oriental carpet, "yes. Of course I'll go."

CHAPTER TWENTY-THREE

I took a tonga to Nila's house. Facing backwards in the carriage, I saw plumes of dust fly from the large, spoked wheels, while my mind leaped ahead to Nila who would prattle away over curry puffs or cheese straws. I was uneasy about the afternoon. I didn't know if I could bring myself to ask Nila the questions Letty wanted me to do. And in the event Nila told me my uncle was the father of her baby, I did not know what story I'd concoct for Letty, but concoct one I would, for her peace of mind. She deserved that much. Although she tried hard not to show it and continued to take part in daily outings to gardens and old mosques, Letty seemed removed and highstrung ever since my encounter with Nila two days earlier. There were all the old signs of tension: the deepening of the furrow between her brows, the taut mouth and jaw, the unsteady hands. The night before, after several drinks, she had retired early without her dinner. I ate alone.

The afternoon was warm, but the motion of the tonga

created a breeze. Buildings three and four stories high rose straight up on both sides of the narrow road, which was relatively deserted. Since this was the hottest time of day, shops were closed till five.

Presently we turned down a tree-lined street. "Jasmine Avenue," the tonga driver said, pointing straight ahead with his whip. The scent of frangipani reached me, and I knew where the street got its name. Low walls surrounded modest houses with small front yards, some abloom with flowers, some bare, a few paved with concrete. The tonga came to a stop before one of these. I paid the driver.

As I was opening the gate, I saw a movement behind the muslin curtain at the front window. Nila must have been watching. Even before I reached the door, she threw it open. Vastly pregnant, she wore the pink sari I'd seen her in at the post office. Her brown hair was piled on her head, wispy curls brushing the long golden neck.

"You came!" she cried. Still holding the doorknob, she flung the other arm around my neck. "I was not sure, so I did not prepare anything."

"It doesn't matter."

"No, no. I will send the servant to the cafe for kebabs."

"Don't trouble yourself, Nila."

"No trouble. I feel hungry this time every day. Must be the baby. Come in. Come in." She led me to the front room which opened off the small, dark entry hall and left me there while she went through the house calling out, "*Chokra, chokra,*" to the servant.

It was a room that lacked definition, with its white walls and curtains, its unpainted wicker furniture. There was a sense of impermanence in its total blandness. I thought of her airy front room in Nerbudapur with its chintz cushions and its baskets of phlox and daisies. While I sat there, I reflected on the coincidence of my meeting Colonel Bhatt and then Nila, all in the space of a week. I wondered if I should mention this to Nila. But that would only prolong the afternoon, I decided; she would want to know details, what he said, what I said. No, best to keep it simple.

Nila returned to lie on the settee with her feet elevated on pillows, her head resting on her bent arm. It was a position reminiscent of that afternoon in Nerbudapur, when she had stretched out on the sofa surveying me from under the fans of her lashes, then had leaped up to suggest I wear a sari to the parade. How much had happened since then!

"I must lie like this," she explained, "because my feet are swelling, three days now. So, tell me what you are doing in Srinagar?"

"I'm here on holiday with Aunt Letty. We're staying on a houseboat on Lake Nagim, but only for two days more."

"Your aunt must be feeling better. There was a time when she never left the house for months."

"She is."

I thought her next comment would be about my uncle; instead she said, thoughtfully, "Is it not strange? Who would have thought some months back that you and I would meet again like this, with everything changed? . . . Changed for me, anyway. You are just the same . . ."

Oh no, I'm not.

" . . . as pretty as ever."

I had dressed with care, brushing my hair to a shiny bronze and tying it back with a ribbon. I don't know why I had gone to the trouble; except, now it pleased me that she still thought of me as pretty.

"Yes," I said. "It's strange how things change."

"Do you remember Ranjit? You have met him. He was at the parade and also at the picnic at Marble Rocks." She turned her face to me, her eyes searching. "We are married now."

"Yes. I remember him." As I suspected, it was the young Sikh.

"He has loved me for a long time. When I became

255

pregnant, I asked Prem for divorce." Her green eyes, with their fringe of smokey lashes, were anxious. "So. Are you going to say anything?"

I shook my head.

She gazed at me in silence, her expression slowly hardening into defiance. "You think it is bad that I left my husband, don't you? That I am wicked because I lay with another man."

"If the child is Ranjit's," I began cautiously, "then . . . it is best that you left your husband."

"What do you mean, 'If the child is Ranjit's?' " she said heatedly. "Whose would it be otherwise?"

Relief flooded me. I could tell Letty the truth now. I was useless at making up stories. After a deep breath, I said, "I'm sorry if I offended you. What I meant to say is: It is better for everyone that the child is Ranjit's and not your hus—I mean, Colonel Bhatt's, that's all."

With some difficulty, she pulled herself into a sitting position. Nibbling on a cuticle, she stared at the stone floor. Finally, she said, "Megan, I am going to tell you something I have never told anyone, not even Ranjit . . . Prem will never make a child. He is a fine man, but he could not love me as . . . you know, a man loves a woman. Do you understand what I am saying?"

"I think so," I said slowly. He's homosexual, Letty once told me, a man whose sexual preference is other men.

"He tried two or three times, for my sake." She shook her head sadly. "It is against his nature—"

"Nila," I cut in quickly. "You don't have to tell me any more."

"But I must tell you, Megan. Please." She extended an arm, then dropped it, her eyes grave and pleading. "There is no one else I can talk to . . . On our wedding night he cried and told me he had done injustice to me. Like that he said it, injustice. He was afraid to tell his family his true feelings because—I do not know if you know this—in the Hindu religion the married state is everything. They would have been very upset." She laced her fingers under her belly, cradling it. "When our families made our marriage preparations, Prem simply kept quiet.

"It was hard for both of us, living together. I do not know what Prem did; I did not want to know." She raised her chin challengingly. "I slept with other men. Some promised to marry me. None did, of course, till Ranjit."

"My uncle?"

She met my eyes calmly. "Yes. He did not speak of marriage though, and I knew he would never leave your aunt. In his own way, he loves her very much. Then when I fell in love with Ranjit, I broke off with your uncle. He tried to get me back, but I said no."

"I saw you talking at the club, the day of the parade."

She nodded. "Yes, I know. I had only just met Ranjit. We fell in love later."

"There was another time too that I saw you together, in my aunt's library, during the reception for the Minister."

"You did?" she asked, surprised. "Funny, in such an out-of-the-way place. Prem also said he saw us. I wonder who else did. Ah yes, that time he was pressing me to go back. He asked me to meet him in the library. He said there was something important he had to tell me. But it was only the same old thing. 'It is finished,' I told him. He caught my arm. Then I told him I was pregnant. It worked like magic." She leaned her head back and laughed. I saw the pure line of her throat. She was still so lovely despite the heavy breasts, the swollen belly. "He did not even ask the name of the father, only rushed straight out of there—and he never came to me again. That night when Prem and I went home . . . I told him too."

"Why did you have the birthday party for me? If you

wanted my uncle to leave you alone, why didn't you just ignore us?"

"What does he have to do with you? I had the party for you because you are my friend. I was polite with your uncle whenever I saw him at the club. After all we were neighbors. What would people think if we suddenly stopped talking? But he never bothered me again."

A sturdy young mountain boy came in carrying a tray with two cups of brimming tea and a plate of kebabs. He placed them on the table and Nila dismissed him. I accepted a cup of tea, but declined the dry-looking kebabs. Nila ate several. I was reminded of my uncle's fondness for the same spicy meat, and thought it ironic that all that remained of their affair was a mutual craving for kebabs.

"One day I almost told you about my baby," Nila said, lying down again. "I was so excited and wanted to tell you because you are my good friend, but I promised Prem I would keep it quiet until we made the divorce. Everyone thinks I deserted him. My parents cursed me." She sighed. "That is the price I must pay."

The diagonal drape of her sari slid to one side, exposing her bare midriff. Golden skin began the tight slope of her abdomen that crested impressively beneath pink chiffon folds; and as I watched, I saw it move. I blinked. Nila seemed unconcerned, went on talking about how generous Prem had been, even to arranging a transfer for Ranjit, while I kept staring at her belly. There it was again! This time a knot appeared above where her sari was tied.

"Nila," I whispered. "Your stomach is moving."

"Where is it moving to? You better run after it." She clapped her hands, laughing aloud at her own joke. "My dear, it's only the baby. He moves about whenever I eat. Maybe it is a sign he will have a good appetite."

Awestruck, I said, "Does it hurt?"

"No. Sometimes it's uncomfortable, but never hurts. That will come later, I am told."

Impulsively, I said, "May I touch your stomach?"

"Of course. Ranjit touches and kisses and sings songs to it. You would think we were the only people in the world to make a baby."

If you only knew, I thought. Suddenly afraid, I hesitated briefly, then yielded to my compelling curiosity. I knelt beside her and placed my hands on her abdomen. It was firm, like a well-inflated soccer ball. For a while there was nothing; then I felt the stirring. An instant slight nudge against my palm. I pictured it curled around its thumb, a small translucent prawn with staring guppy eyes, fluid-borne—and a warm moistness filled my chest, slid down my belly and into my pelvis. Something was loosening inside me, an inner thaw, flowing earthward. I felt the sting of tears, tasted them in my throat, realizing only then that the image I had invoked was of the embryo within me, not the fully-formed baby inside Nila.

I stood abruptly.

"Ah," she said, sitting up again and patting her hair, "I hear Ranjit's motorcycle coming down the road. You know, Megan," she added softly, "we do not have as much as Prem and I did, but in a way we have so much more."

I stood by the window remembering that small push against my palm.

"*Piara,*" he called from the back of the house. I heard the sound of brisk footsteps on stone.

"I am here," Nila called back. To me she said, "He always calls like that, '*Piara.*' It means darling."

He stood in the doorway, tall in his khaki uniform and turban, his beard neatly rolled. Then he crossed the floor in two strides to stand beside Nila. There was something vaguely menacing about the way he looked at me, and suddenly I was reminded of a family of monkeys I'd encountered once. The father had faced me with bared teeth, positioning himself in front of his mate and infant, growling, until I backed away. In the same way, Ranjit stood ready to defend his wife, and I marveled at the fierce protective instinct that existed in both primate and man. The thought flashed: They've been treated cruelly for flouting the rules, and now it's hard for them to tell friend from foe. As Nila had said, "It's the price I must pay." I felt a grudging admiration.

"You remember Megan, Ranjit," Nila said, reaching for his hand. "She is my very dear friend. She and her aunt are staying on a houseboat."

His face relaxed then. "It's good of you to come and see Nila. She's been lonely." Seeing the plate with only three kebabs left, he said, "*Piara,* you know you are not supposed to have salt. The doctor said it is bad for you and the baby."

"Now, Ranj, don't scold." Nila pouted, rubbing her cheek against his hand. "I will be good for the next month, I promise. Then, thank God, I can eat tasty food again, after the baby comes."

"Let me see your ankles." He sat beside her and lifted her bare foot. Holding the heel in his hand, his thumb caressed the pearly skin of her instep. "Still some swelling. Come, you must lie with your feet up." His hands on her shoulders, he gently urged her down, then propped up her feet.

"I must see to your tea," she protested.

"I will see to it myself. You rest."

An aura of gentle intimacy surrounded them like perfumed space, rays of light. I looked away, feeling again the prickle of tears.

"Megan," Nila said, after her husband had left the room, "what is the word for when your heart and body is . . . is . . . ?"

260

"Satisfied? Fulfilled?"

"Yes, ful-filled." She separated the syllables, as though tasting the sounds. "A good word. Filled full." She paused, her eyes far away. "For me love is like nourishment, food for the soul. One day you will find it so, too."

Still your tears, my lovely, Pushpa had crooned to me that long-ago evening in the bazaar. *Your day will dawn.*

Ranjit took me back on his motorcycle, but politely declined to come in.

Mr. Rahman was talking to Letty in the parlor. He sat hunched in a flowery chair, bony hands between knees, " . . . then after the couple has finished the consummating, then comes the woman, who inspects the sheet. Sheet *must* be bloody. Nowadays, though . . . "

Letty sat on the couch, arms across her middle, a frozen expression on her face. How long had she been subjected to that mournful monologue? I sat beside her.

"That's very interesting, Mr. Rahman," she said, standing abruptly. "Thank you for your company, but I really shouldn't keep you any longer."

"Yes, ladies. I must be wending on my way."

"Lord God!" Letty moaned, after Mr. Rahman left. "I wish he'd wended sooner. He was here for a solid hour. I've a crashing headache. What did you find out? You've been gone for hours."

"She's married to Ranjit Singh, a Sikh. I don't think you know him. I met him twice. At that parade and then at the picnic at Marble Rocks. He's a captain—"

"Yes. All right." She turned and reached for the silver cigarette case that lay on a carved walnut table. "Get to the point." The lighter in one hand, an unlit cigarette in the other, she stood there waiting.

"I'm getting there." Powerful with truth, I managed to sound injured and pompous at the same time. "The child is his. I told you so. Otherwise why would she have left with him?"

"Because he was the only one who would have her, that's why," she said, and lit the cigarette. Eyes blinking rapidly, she drew deeply on it. With a small groan, she blew smoke at the ceiling, then turned to me. "Did she—?" Puffs of smoke escaped as she spoke. She toyed with the lighter, her eyes on her hands. "What did she say about my husband?"

"That he loves you very much."

Her face grew pink with pleasure. "She said that? Really?" She sank into a chair. "What else?"

"Well—uh—she said that she and Ranjit are very happy. They live in this small house—"

" 'A little nest where roses bloom?' " She picked a flake of tobacco off her tongue.

"No. No roses." I knew I would not be able to describe the luminous contentment of Nila and Ranjit without sounding foolish. Besides, in view of Letty's frame of mind, it was better to let the subject drop. "What time are we going to the Floating Gardens?"

"Oh no." She suddenly went limp, put a hand to her forehead. "I'd forgotten all about it. Would you mind very much if I didn't go? I've had an awful day—"

Alarmed, I said, "I don't want to go alone."

"Why not? You'd better see everything you can. We'll be leaving soon. Anyway, Ali's already arranged for the *shikara* at six. Mr. Rahman said so."

I sighed. "Very well, but I'm going to suffer through it all."

Ali always helped us into *shikaras* by first stepping in himself, then offering us his hand. I had always been careful of the loose board on the bottom stair leading to the water, but this time I forgot. His other hand slid up my arm to steady me. I felt his fingers against my breast. For the second time that day, a spreading warmth slid through me.

"I'm sorry. I could have capsized the boat. Thank you for keeping me upright," I babbled, as I carefully lowered myself onto the cushions.

"It is not easy getting into a *shikara* if you are not used to it," he said solemnly.

Conversation was laborious. Never adept at chatter, I struggled to think of something to say, but my mind did not respond. Finally, I ventured, "Do you think there'll be a plebiscite?"

"No."

"Oh." Then, "Why not?"

"Because no one in India cares how Moslems feel."

"Oh."

Ali and I had never exchanged more than a few words; there was always that awkwardness. Letty was the one who had no difficulty keeping up an animated discussion. I began to feel resentful. She'd had a hard day, she said. Well, *I'd* had a hard day too. And now to have to put up with this. Who asked to come to Kashmir?

I had no heart for the vivid sky, the birdsong in willows, the sweet wail of *muezzins* from various mosques along the canals. All I wanted was for the evening to be over.

Ali began to sing. Softly at first, then as his voice grew full and rich, he began to relax. He drew up his feet and rested his arms on his knees, wrists loosely crossed. His white shirt glimmered in the violet dusk. He sang about love, and longing, and lost dreams. Freed from having to make conversation, and under the spell of Ali's voice, I found myself relaxing too. I thought of the picnic at Marble Rocks, the boat ride by moonlight, the boatmen's chants, and of how Ranjit had looked down at Nila with such longing as she sat beside him. Now they were together. *Love is food for the soul,* Nila said today. Without it then, would the soul starve to death? Just shrivel up like a leaf and fall to earth, become dust? Was the soul like a sheet of white paper, or did it have color and form? Was it the size of a fist, a heart, a womb? Lulled by the rhythmic splash of oars, I let myself think of Ajai, let the images of him flow over me: his hands with their long, elegant fingers, the way his mouth shaped words, and the sensations those hands and that mouth could evoke in me . . .

The boat rocked. Ali was beside me, embracing me.

Stunned, I demanded, "What are you doing?"

"You were looking at me with love. You are always looking at me."

"I like that!" I said indignantly. "*You* are the one who stares." I tried to push him way; I might as easily have moved a tank.

He laughed. Grabbing my hands, he held them above my head in one of his, while with the other, he pushed me against the cushions, pressing against me, pressing his mouth against mine. No! My mind cried out. *It is Ajai I want.* I tried to calm myself, to think. I knew Ali wouldn't hurt me, not with the boatmen just beyond the curtain, but I didn't want this either. When he raised his head and drew slightly away, I said calmly, "I am pregnant."

In an instant, he regained his seat, and sat there breathing hard. "I am very sorry," he said in a low voice. "I did not know. I thought you wanted me. You rode on my scooter. You came out alone with me this evening."

"It's all right," I said, suddenly exhausted. "I'm sorry, too, if I gave you the wrong impression."

"Will you tell my brother?"

"No."

*　　*　　*

In bed I spread my hands over my flat abdomen; I recalled the feel of Nila's firm distended one, and that brief small push against my palm.

I saw again the image of the embryo inside me as it had flashed in my mind that afternoon as I knelt beside Nila. With a start, I realized I was stroking my stomach as though my hands obeyed some mysterious signal of their own.

CHAPTER TWENTY-FOUR

Soaking wet, with algae in my hair, I spoke eloquently, lucidly, in favor of plebiscites to an unseen applauding audience, while nearby a woodpecker hammered away in a chenar tree. Clapping merged with hammering . . . I awoke to the sound.

Someone was knocking on Letty's door.

Instantly alert, I struggled into a robe.

"Who is it?" I heard Letty ask.

"Your pardon, memsahib," the watchman replied in singsong Hindi, "but there is a Sikh gentleman here who is saying it is most urgent he speak with you. His wife is gravely ill. I told him the hour is late . . . "

I opened my door. Letty stood in the hallway talking to the watchman, whose head and shoulders were covered in an old brown shawl. Further down the hall stood Ranjit. In the dim overhead light that created more shadows than illumination, his face was gaunt, his eyes cavernous.

He came forward in a state of great agitation. When he

266

spoke, his voice was frantic, ragged. "Please help me. I cannot locate the doctor. It is my wife. She has gone into labor."

"She can't be, Ranjit!" I cried. "Her time's not till next month."

"She should be in hospital," Letty said.

"I have tried to tell her," he said distractedly, "but she keeps asking for you. Insists only you can save our baby. I am desperate. She goes on saying that it is God's punishment on us, that our baby is doomed." Tears rolled into his beard.

"Who's with her now?" I asked.

"The *chokra*. She made me leave and come for you. Please. I have a taxi waiting."

"We'll come," Letty said, adding in a brisk aside to me, "there's no time to dress."

Nila lay very still under a sheet, eyes shut, hair spread in tangles on the pillow. Her skin looked thickened and waxy, and was glazed with sweat. The frightened servant boy stood beside her holding a soggy flannel to her forehead as though it were cemented in place.

Ranjit fell to his knees beside the bed. "We are here, *piara*," he said softly. "They came." He picked up her hand and pressed his face to her palm.

Nila smiled wanly. Opening her eyes with effort, she closed them again as though the lids were weighted and had fallen shut by themselves. Her lips moved, but she made no sound.

Letty told Ranjit to go to a phone box and ring for an ambulance. She asked the servant for hot water and gave him instructions on how to sterilize string and a sharp knife. To me she said, "Find clean sheets and towels."

Nila's sari was wet, the mattress damp. I thought at first she'd urinated in bed. "She's lost her water," Letty said, as we undressed Nila and placed dry towels under her. Her belly was a pearly globe, rivered with blue veins. We covered her with a fresh sheet. All at once her eyes and mouth flew open. Veins bulged in her forehead as she began to pant, the sound rattling deep in her throat. Leaning over her, Letty placed a palm on Nila's abdomen, while she looked at the second hand on her watch.

"That was a long, hard one," she muttered. "If this keeps up, the ambulance won't get here in time." As Nila's eyes closed again, Letty said soothingly, "That's it. Just rest . . . Rest for now." To me, she said, "Where is that bloody *chokra?* Get that hot water here. Make sure he sterilizes that knife and string."

I ran to the dark, smokey kitchen behind the house. The servant had followed Letty's instructions correctly and was just taking the kettle off the fire. He had boiled the knife and string in a separate pan. "I'll take this," I said in Hindi, lifting the hot pan with a kitchen towel. "You bring the kettle."

Even before we reached the bedroom, I knew Nila was having another, stronger pain. I heard the guttural panting rise to a shriek.

I rushed in, my heart hammering. "Here it is. Everything's here." I looked around for a place to put the pan, finally placing it on the stone floor. I took the kettle from the servant, told him to boil more water and bring it to us.

Letty washed Nila's haunches with soap and warm water, washed her own hands in a basin, and had me pour hot water over them in a final rinse. The room grew steamy. A thick, sticky odor hung in the air.

Distraught, Ranjit burst in. "Ambulance is on its way," he said, out of breath. "How is she?" He knelt beside the bed and smoothed the damp hair from his wife's forehead.

Letty was examining Nila, her fingers deep inside. "She is fully dilated. It won't be long now. Get behind her," she told Ranjit. "Let her pull on your hands."

Half-lying, half-sitting on the bed, Ranjit took Nila's hands in his. He bent his head to whisper in her ear, brush his lips to her forehead that glistened with sweat. Nila's legs were bent at the knees; Letty spread them apart, folded back the sheet, and turned to wash her hands again, with me providing the final rinse.

"Now hang onto your husband's hands, and start pushing . . . Come on, Nila. *Push* . . . A big one this time . . . Come, mother," she crooned, "push your baby out. *Push* . . . Ahhh . . . here's the head . . . "

I saw the dark crown of hair appear, slip back, appear again while Nila's opening dilated and contracted like the pupil of an eye.

"Push!" Letty urged. "Push!"

Nila gripped Ranjit's wrists until the tendons leaped in the angles of her elbows, and ridged the sides of her neck. Her breath came in great gasps through ash-colored lips.

With an immense grunt from Nila, the baby's head emerged, face down. One shoulder slid through, then the other. Its body was covered with a whitish substance like curds. Watching the child slide into Letty's hands, I thought, *this* is love.

"Ahhh! Beautiful . . . That's it . . . mother, that's it . . . A boy!"

Face glowing, a high priestess, Letty lifted the infant by its heels and smacked its bottom. It let out a thin, sharp cry. She lay him, still linked to his mother, on Nila's belly.

Once more Letty washed her hands and I rinsed them. "Knife and string, Megan."

"Right here." I took the pan to her and watched as Letty milked the umbilical cord into the baby, square-tipped fingers strong and sure. Then she tied the cord off at each end and cut it with the knife. A few drops of blood oozed from the cut ends like sap from a severed lotus stem.

Letty bathed the baby in the basin, holding onto his far arm, with his head and neck supported by her wrist. She dried him, wrapped him in a fresh towel, and handed him to his mother. The two women gazed at each other as the baby was passed from one to the other. Finally Nila whispered, "God bless you." Letty said nothing.

Nila unwrapped her son and examined the small body, each finger and toe, the tiny bud-like penis. She sniffed his mouth, ears, minuscule palms. She tasted his skin with the tip of her tongue in the place behind his ear, then licked his forehead as though she were both annointing him and taking something back into herself. The baby butted blindly against her arm, her breast. Nila placed her nipple in his open, seeking mouth and lay back with a sigh.

Ranjit enfolded them in his arms. It was as if a circle had completed itself around them, binding them together, male and female, husband and wife, father and mother, parent and child. This too is love, I thought, the natural order of things.

So absorbed was I in the drama of the moment, I forgot about Letty. She sat in a wicker chair, hands on her knees, beside a table that held the basin and damp, crumpled towels. Her hair was wet; sweat ran down her face like tears, stood in the hollows of her throat, and darkened the shoulders of her flowered housecoat. Her eyes glistened. Perhaps she *was* weeping; I couldn't tell. If so, they were tears of triumph; that much I knew. There was an invincibility to her, a tenacity, a fortitude. Watching her sit there, shoulders sagging with weariness, I thought she'd never looked more happy.

I became aware of a nearby cricket scraping away, its sound hovering on the edge of consciousness. The room was sparsely furnished. Besides the double bed, there was only a chest of drawers, the chair and table. The walls were bare. It was any room, anywhere, anonymous as the night; I was surprised that its walls had not absorbed and reflected back all the pain and passion of its occupants. When the walls suddenly began to pulse with red light, I was not at all startled; then I realized the ambulance had arrived.

Nila and her son were carried out on a stretcher. Ranjit offered to escort Letty and me back to the houseboat, but Letty declined.

"Your place is with them," she said. "Don't worry about us."

"I cannot thank you enough," Ranjit said, stooping to touch Letty's feet. "I am your servant forever."

Letty stepped back. She touched his shoulders. "No," she said gently. "I am the indebted one."

He did not reply. Perhaps he had not heard. His eyes were already straying to the ambulance with its spinning red light.

But I heard. And understood.

The *Lady Luck* was bathed in the silver light of dawn as we crossed the gangplank. A mist lay over the lake, and the eastern sky was brushed with palest rose. Birds were chirruping softly in the chenar tree. A rooster crowed in the distance. From a faraway minaret a *muezzin* called the faithful to prayer.

"Will the baby be all right?" I asked as we entered the boat and walked down the hallway to our rooms.

Letty stretched hugely; her mouth gaped in a yawn. "I think so," she said. "His color was good, and he was breathing well. He'll be all right, I'm sure."

"You must be exhausted."

"Just my shoulders and upper back. All that stooping." She paused in the doorway of her room, and turned around. "They really are happy, aren't they? Who would've believed it of her? Wonders never cease. Well, good night—Good morning, actually. I'm off to bed."

271

Wide awake, I sat by my bedroom window and looked out across the lake, watching the mountains change from mauve to pink to amber. I thought of Nila and Ranjit, and their baby—the living proof of their love. That love like theirs was possible, could endure, no matter what the obstacles, was a wonderment to me. How were they able to survive, forsaken by family and society? Yet survive they had, so far. True, the future was uncertain—for them, for anyone. Who knew what lay ahead: a broken heart, illness, death? There were no assurances, I understood that now. Love would change—must change—evolve like the seasons, the phases of the moon, yet maintain its essential steadfastness. It was also clear that there were peaks and valleys in love, in life. Letty's performance tonight was a peak; my mood of the past several weeks was an abyss. I wanted to climb to a peak like Letty, like Nila, grapple myself to the top. If I didn't cling there for even an instant, I would never know that heightened joy.

When, bathed and changed, I left my room at mid-morning, I found Letty reading the newspaper at the dining room table. She looked rested and fresh in a crisp voile sari with a sprigged design of blue flowers.

"Sleep well?"

"No," I said, as I sat facing her. "I was too excited. But I'm not really tired. Did you sleep?"

"Like a top, An eventful week, would you say?"

"Yes."

"Sorry you came?"

"No."

"Neither am I."

As before, when I came to her pregnant in Nerbudapur, I wanted her to ask me leading questions, steer me into a discussion. Surely she'd guessed how the events of the past night had affected me. I longed for her reassurance, but I didn't know how to seek it, especially since I was unclear myself of what I wanted to do. So I said nothing, and she continued to read her paper.

"Well, I see the Mountbattens are getting ready to leave India. No doubt there'll be oodles of pomp and pageantry in Delhi. A huge waste of money." She folded the paper back on itself, and folded it in half again. "Speaking of leaving," she said, without glancing up. "Are you all packed? We catch the afternoon flight."

"Yes."

Outside I heard a bulbul singing, the splash of water from passing *shikaras*. With my fingertip, I traced the outline of a chenar leaf carved into the border of the table top. "Aunt Letty," I said hesitantly. "I've been thinking—"

She lowered the newspaper and peered at me over the tops of her glasses. "About what?"

"Well." I licked my lips, watching the play of watery light on the carved wall above her head. "I don't know how—"

She waited.

"It's . . . It's about the baby."

"Nila's?"

I shook my head.

"Yours, then."

"Yes, mine." I took a deep breath. "I'm not sure what to do."

She sighed and put the paper down. Did I imagine a trace of reluctance on her part at my reopening the subject? "Do nothing. Have the child."

"But it's not that simple—"

"It's very simple, Megan," she said, as though I were a child and she was telling me to tie my shoelaces. "Marry Ajai and live with us until he gets established. He's finishing his final year, I believe."

273

"Oh no. That wouldn't be right," I said, embarrassed. "It's not what I—"

"Why not? The house is large enough to accommodate us all. It will be lovely to have a child in the house."

"That's very generous, but—"

"You will be doing us a favor, actually."

"No. Thank you, anyway." I tried again, "I've been think—"

"Why not?" she repeated testily, as she sat back in her chair and removed her spectacles. Sighing again, she said, "All right, then. Go and live with his people. It's the Indian way. There're nice enough. You'll probably like them."

"Not that, either."

"You're being unreasonable. What then? You're surely not going to live with *your* parents, for heaven's sake!"

Damn her! She was being deliberately obtuse. At the end of my endurance, I snapped, "Stop harping on where I'll live and what I'll do. I'm trying to talk to you about something *important*—I want to keep my baby!"

Letty gazed at me in silence, then she flung her arms in the air. "Good girl! I knew you'd come through."

There, I'd said it! I'd made the decision on my own. Though relieved, I glared at Letty. An infuriating woman, if there ever was one.

"You will please tell your friends how excellent service we are providing on our boats." Mr. Rahman hung around the taxi in the noon sun, bending his long body to peer in the window at us sitting inside, as the watchman loaded our suitcases in the boot. "And you yourselves must return many times. I will give you still better houseboat. The *Mascot*. I would have given this time to you, but I did not know if you could appreciate so fine a boat. You know how it is, some ignorant peoples. But that is water flowing over the bridge—"

"The *Lady Luck* was more than adequate, Mr. Rahman," Letty reassured him from the window. The watchman came to the side of the car and salaamed deeply. Letty gave him a tip.

"Maybe you are knowing some European ladies who are wanting suntan," Mr. Rahman said wistfully. "They may lie on upper deck in utter privacy."

"Ah yes. We will spread the news about you, Mr. Rahman. Never doubt it. Goodbye. Good fishing!"

"Godmost speed, dear ladies."

My eyes swept over the *Lady Luck* and the Rahmans' chicken-coop house, the chenars, willows and mountains, the darting kingfishers and flat lily pads—a world different from mine, a fantasy world reminiscent of harems and veiled women weaving intricate tales in musk-scented evenings. Yet it was here, in this storybook world, that I had faced my reality.

Points of light lay across the surface of the lake like scattered diamonds. It was the crystalline brightness one blinks at upon emerging from a dark place. I gazed entranced, the sight filling my eyes, and when I finally looked away the brilliance stayed with me.

As the taxi began to move, Ali stepped from the shadow of a chenar tree and raised his arm.

I hesitated only briefly before I raised mine in return.

CHAPTER TWENTY-FIVE

Once I'd made the decision, Letty was in a frenzy to get back to Nerbudapur. We didn't even break journey in Delhi to see my uncle; Letty called his office from the New Delhi airport where the plane had landed to say that we were going directly to the railway station. As our taxi hurtled along congested streets, with only forty-five minutes to spare before the six P.M. express left for Nerbudapur, Letty kept urging the Sikh driver on to even greater speed.

Finally, in desperation, he snapped, "Madam! I am already driving five miles above speed limit! You are wanting me to lose my license, I am thinking."

"Heavens, man, it's the last direct train tonight."

"Then, heavens, take an indirect one," he shot back.

"Cheeky blighter," she muttered, but sat back on the seat.

I patted her hand. "If we miss it, we'll take the morning train, Aunt Letty." I felt strong and confident. "What does one night matter?"

Our luck held out. Although we were late, the train was

even later. Letty went to buy our tickets, leaving me with the suitcases and the additional odds and ends she had acquired in Kashmir—rolled-up carpets, bulky parcels of *papier-mâché* bowls, and carved walnut tables dismantled and wrapped in gunny sacking. She had intended everything for my uncle's New Delhi flat, but we were, instead, carting the lot back with us to Nerbudapur. Ten minutes after our mad dash from taxi to teeming platform, the train arrived. There was the usual frantic pushing of passengers trying to get on the train while those still on it were trying to get off. This situation was further complicated by the crush of coolies, beggars and vendors. Nothing remarkable for an Indian railway station; what was remarkable was that now I saw and heard with heightened clarity—the brilliance of a diamond on the side of a young girl's nose, the curve of a child's downy cheek, the lilting cadence of the tea vendor's chants, the practiced whine of some beggars and the abject despair of others, the smooth rich brown of a man's bare back—as if, blind and deaf, sight and sound had been restored to me miraculously.

"Whew! That's as fast as I've moved in ages." Letty dabbed at her forehead and upper lip with a hanky as she settled herself against the seat. "Are you all right?"

"I feel quite—uh—healthy, actually," I offered.

"You'll talk to Ajai soon?"

"Yes." For all my new-found confidence, I felt a great unease about facing Ajai with my decision. My rejection of him not ten days earlier had been too overwhelming. How would I explain my change of heart and the circumstances that had brought about the change? One by one, each in turn had penetrated the shell of my inertia: the sight of Nila and Ranjit's shining happiness, my hands on Nila's swollen abdomen and the miraculous movement of the infant within, the drama of birth, Letty's triumph, and even Ali's embrace which, ironically, had made my senses leap from lethargy into longing—for Ajai.

"When?" Letty persisted.

"Tomorrow." I curled up into a corner of the berth and pretended to doze. Suddenly I was reluctant to talk, especially about Ajai.

Letty struck up a conversation with one of the other passengers in the compartment, a woman who taught economics in some Nagpur college. Soon they were arguing about the dowry system. Listening to them, I found my pretense becoming reality and before long I had drifted off to sleep.

Letty woke me as we approached Nerbudapur; it was close to midnight. Groggy with sleep, I went to the lavatory to wash my hands and splash water on my face. Somewhat refreshed, I smoothed my hair with my hands and then went to help Letty collect all the ample assorted pieces of our luggage. She looked exhausted; I didn't think she had slept.

At the station we took two tongas, one for our belongings and one for ourselves. Letty seemed disinclined to make conversation, so we rode without speaking through deserted streets under a high, golden moon. The only sounds that punctuated the silence were the echoing hoofbeats of the horses and their harness bells that jingled rhythmically, indecently loud.

Letty went straight to bed. I lay awake in my room listening to my heart pound in my ears and throat. Don't get into a state, I told myself, it's not good for you or the baby. What happens with Ajai, happens. But I knew I wouldn't sleep anymore that night.

I'd considered sending a note to Ajai's college, or ringing him there. In the end, I decided I would go to see him; I would not give him any advance warning, no opportunity for him to refuse to see me. If he sent me away as I had sent him, then it was no more than I deserved. I knew he often spent evenings at the soapstone mine, supervising the work or studying on the riverbank. I would look for him there, as many evenings as it might take, until I saw him and spoke to him.

Letty offered to drive me, but I had to do this on my own. I rented a bicycle and pedaled the five or so miles, while breezes pushed my hair back and cooled my flushed face.

When I saw Ajai's car I was filled with relief that gave way to a growing sense of dread. I braked and slid from the seat none too gracefully. Then I saw him and the familiar longing took hold of me. My hands began to shake and I tightened my hold on the rubber grips until my knuckles showed white. He was talking with another man as they stood in front of the shack surrounding the mine shaft—or, rather, it was the other who spoke and Ajai who listened and nodded occasionally, arms folded, head bent.

I knew the moment he saw me, although I was still too far away to see the direction of his gaze. Was it the force of my own that made him look up? I felt his shocked awareness, felt the quivering tension seize him like the instant freeze of an endangered forest creature before flight. I walked slowly toward him, pushing my bicycle, my eyes never leaving his. I was close enough now to see his face grow cold and aloof. The man had stopped talking and was watching us with avid curiosity, glancing from Ajai to me and back again.

"Yes, I understand, Balu Ram," Ajai said, as he dismissed the man. "I will let my father know. Tomorrow evening we will talk again."

With obvious reluctance and many backward glances, Balu Ram left. Ajai turned his back on me, but did not walk away. I leaned my bicycle against a tree and wiped my sweating palms down the sides of my tunic. My lips were dry; I licked them. There was an unreality about my doing these things, as if I were standing some distance away, a spectator, watching myself.

"I must talk to you," I said finally, in a low voice.

Still he said nothing. I waited.

"You have every right to be angry," I ventured. "I came to—"

"This has something to do with rights, has it? Who gave *you* the right to assign or take mine away?"

"I was going to say that I'll understand if you refuse to talk to me. You don't have to speak—"

He whirled around, his handsome face contorted. "Now you are telling me when to speak. This is *my* damn property. Get on your bloody bike and hop it."

"You are twisting my words. I didn't tell you *when* to speak. I only said—"

"I know what you said." He hurled the words at me. "I'll give you two seconds to get the hell off my land."

"And then what will you do?" I shouted back. "You'll knock me down? Fling me off your stupid *property* into the road? I'm carrying your child. And I intend to *have* your child. *That's* all I came to tell you, you bloody bully. You think all of this has been easy for me? You and your theatrics! Our hero in the throes of suffering."

Blindly I grabbed my bike and mounted it, but in doing so the cuff of my trousers caught in the chain. I pressed down on the pedal thinking the forward motion would free my cuff, instead the wheels locked and the cycle wobbled. I whimpered, afraid I'd fall and hurt my baby. Ajai sprang forward grabbing the handlebar and seat.

"Back pedal, back pedal," he yelled.

While Ajai held the bike and me upright, I did as he instructed and the wretched cuff, steaked with chain oil, pulled clear. Then everything grew dark.

When I awoke, I was lying in Ajai's arms while he sat on the patchy grass. *This is how it all started,* I thought, remembering that other evening I'd lain in his arms on the riverbank. Now I tasted the salt of his tears on my lips, felt them drip on my face.

"*He Ram!* Oh God!" he cried. "Megan, sweet love! What have I done?"

I lay still a little longer, savoring the pressure of his arms around me, his scent of soap and freshly laundered clothes and the slight tang of sweat. "Sweet love," he had called me.

"What you have done," I whispered, "is get me pregnant."

His arms tightened around me and he hid his face in my hair. "Oh God, you gave me such a fright."

"Ajai, you asked before. Now it's my turn. Will you marry me?"

He laughed softly. "What? And make an honest woman of you?"

"Let me see your face," I begged, as I caressed his shoulders, the back of his neck.

"In a little while." I felt his spread hand moving on my stomach. "The baby is all right, then?"

"Yes."

"I was very angry when you were considering—"

"I know, my love, I know." I kissed his neck and the place on his chest where the dark hair curled at the deep neckline of his *kurta.* "Ajai," I whispered. "Do you remember the other time you held me like this?"

"Did we do this before? Let me think. Ah yes, I dimly remember a very tearful young lady seducing me."

"Is the carpet in your car?"

He let me see his face then. His eyes were shining, his smile very bright. "Why, Miss Manning, how very forward of you."

*　　*　　*

Much later that night, Ajai drove me and the bicycle home.

"Will you tell your parents?" I asked anxiously.

He reached for my hand. "Of course. Tonight. They'll want to meet you."

"I met your father—I'm nervous, Ajai."

"There's no need." He placed my hand on his thigh and returned his to the steering wheel. "They've been after me to marry for years."

I laughed shakily. "But not in such a rush. Will you tell them why?"

"No. What about your parents? How will they take it?"

"My father will be relieved. He knows I'm pregnant. My mother doesn't need to know. I don't owe her anything."

"Even so, I think you should tell her, Megan." He squeezed my hand. "She won't be overjoyed, but she has a right to know. Will I see you tomorrow?"

"Of course. Come to tea."

He unloaded the bicycle and leaned it against one of the columns of the front porch, then pulled me close. "Try to rest, beloved," he whispered, "I can tell you're under terrible strain. Things will work out."

I held his face between my hands and kissed him softly on the lips.

I found Letty waiting for me in my room, sitting on my bed. One look at my face and she leaped up to hug me, laughing with delight.

"Come along." She took me by the hand and led me to the front room. "This calls for a drink. You can have a small glass of sherry."

We sat down with our drinks and I told her about my conversation with Ajai in the car. I was astonished at her reaction.

"But, of course, you must tell your mother," she insisted. "She has a right to know."

"Those were Ajai's words. I will tell Papa and Aunt Margaret," I said. "I owe Mama nothing."

"Oh, yes, you do," came the swift, emphatic reply. "She gave you life, and all her love. You owe her your respect, at the very least."

"Why? For four months she let me imagine the worst of Papa, that he had deserted us, that he didn't care about me, and all the time he was stuck in that sanitorium."

"True, but part of the responsibility for that belongs with your father. Why don't you blame him?"

"Because he was the one who was ill and abandoned. She didn't even go to see him. She kept *me* from him."

"Of course she kept you from him. You are her child. She would do anything to protect you. Lavinia was wrong not to tell you. *That* was her mistake, and she's paid dearly for it. If you don't recognize that your father's illness was anything less than devastating to her then, frankly, I'd be very disappointed in you."

I stared mutinously into my glass of sherry.

Letty sighed loudly.

In the end, I decided to write to my mother. Not because Letty had convinced me, but simply because if I didn't assume full responsibility for my decision to marry, Mama would blame Letty for the whole business. I wrote long letters to Papa and Aunt Margaret, and a brief note to Mama that Ajai and I were marrying a week from Saturday.

Her reply was even briefer. Two days later I received a telegram that read, "Arriving Nerbudapur Tuesday P.M.— Mama."

Oh, God! I had that to look forward to. In two days she would be here.

Letty and Ajai were sympathetic.

"It might not be too bad," Letty said.

"Do you really believe that?" I asked, bitterly.

She didn't reply.

"What can she do?" Ajai asked. "You've made your decision. She can either accept it or reject it. If she rejects it, the loss is hers."

Letty remained silent. Was she thinking perhaps of Grandpa, and *his* reaction all those years ago?

CHAPTER TWENTY-SIX

I thought of the last time Letty and I had stood beside each other on the station platform awaiting the arrival of Aunt Margaret and Mama. Then Letty had been nervous and I protective; now our roles were reversed. Unlike that other time when I had run up and down the length of the platform looking for Aunt Margaret and Mama, I spotted Mama straight away this time.

I was unprepared for the rush of pity I felt for her. She seemed to have aged in the six weeks since I'd last seen her. Her eyes had dark circles under them and her skin was a sickly grey color. *Did I do this to her?* I asked myself, and felt guilt wash over me.

She offered her cheek to be kissed, first to Letty and then, after a slight hesitation, to me.

"Hello, Mama."

She nodded, tightening her lips.

Her manner was distant. Yes, Aunt Margaret was well. No, Papa would not be home for at least another month. The journey had been tiring; she preferred to go straight to bed; she would see us in the morning.

"Not even a cup of tea, Lavinia?" Letty was solicitous.

"No thank you."

Letty and I ate the special dinner of chicken *korma* and kedgeree.

"She looks ill," Letty said, her eyes full of concern. "I'd like to examine her, if she'd let me. Will she be all right without dinner?"

"I don't know. Maybe she just needs the rest. I had no idea she looked so bad. No one told me. Aunt Margaret said nothing about it in her letters."

"Now, don't get yourself so upset you lose sight of why she's here."

Mama cornered me after breakfast the following morning. Letty excused herself, saying she had a million errands to run, that she would be gone until lunch.

"Will you come to my room, or shall we talk in yours?" Mama said, her tone chilly.

"The house is empty. Why don't we sit in the front room?"

"The servants will hear."

"All right, then. Let's go to your room."

We walked down the corridor together. Her body in the starched cotton dress was very frail; her shoulder blades looked brittle. "Are you well, Mama?" I blurted.

"Perfectly well, thank you," she said with asperity.

In the room I waited till she sat on the side of her bed, then I sat in the wicker chair. I decided to take the offensive. "Mama," I began, "if you are here to try to alter my decision, I'll tell you straight out, it's quite useless."

"I see." She sat with her hands folded in her lap, her head bowed. "Once you told me you wouldn't marry. May I ask what changed your mind?"

I exhaled deeply. "Mama," I said gently. "To answer that I would have to tell you first why I *didn't* want to marry. I don't want to hurt your feelings."

She raised her head, but did not look at me. "Hurt my feelings?" she murmured. "You've broken my heart."

"Do you mean in the physical sense? Are you having problems with your heart?"

"No."

"I'm relieved to hear that. I wonder how such expressions come about? Why not a broken lung, or a shattered spleen?" I was babbling.

"Stop it! This isn't a joke."

I sagged in the chair. "I don't know what it is you want. Please, just let me get on with my life."

"It's the next life you need to be worried about, child," she said earnestly, looking at me now, leaning forward, her hands on her knees. "Not this one. It never was this one. You were taught that. You took prizes for catechism. I was so proud of you."

"And now you are not. Is that it?"

Her expression changed to one of such sorrow; tears sprang to my eyes.

"I know you think I came here to try to change your mind," she said, hesitantly. "And yes, I must admit, I had hoped I could." She shut her eyes briefly. When she opened them again, they were very bright. "You've changed, child— I must remember to stop calling you that." Her lips were dry-looking, ashen. "If I can get a special dispensation from the Archbishop of Madras—he's a distant relative. You see," she went on to explain, "a non-Christian can't participate in a sacrament. But with a dispensation you can be properly married in the church. Would you consider delaying your marriage till we can work something out?"

"You mean he would give us a dispensation on the strength of family ties?"

She ignored my sarcasm. "It might help. We have to try everything." She looked desperate.

I went to sit beside her on the bed; she leaned away from me, and in that moment I realized this was how it would always be between us—she would love me from a safe distance and on her own terms. I felt a vague regret at what we both had missed.

"Well?" she prompted.

"No, Mama. I can't."

"Why not?" she said sharply. "What is the rush? Are you pregnant?"

I could have evaded the question, for her sake, but I would not deny the child curled beneath my heart. "Yes," I answered her clearly. "Yes, I am."

"My God!" She rose jerkily and moved away to stand by the window, clasping her upper arms, her back to me. "As bold as brass, if you please. No apologies. Nothing. I suppose you are proud of yourself."

"I wouldn't have told you if you hadn't asked, but now you know why we can't delay the marriage."

"Have you thought what this will do to your father? Do you even care?"

"Papa knows."

She gasped and spun around, a hand at her cheek. "I suppose Aunt Margaret knows too," she said bitterly. "I'm the only one shut out, punished. I am your mother. I have done my best for you, whatever you may think. You'll see soon enough what it's like to be a parent."

I stood, too. "This isn't getting us anywhere. There really isn't anything left to say."

"Are you becoming Hindu?"

I looked at her in amazement. "Why would I do that?"

"You will continue to practice your faith, then?"

"Why not?"

She sighed and rubbed her arms. "Well, at least that's something. And the child? Will it be baptized?"

"I will have to discuss that with Ajai. I'm going to get a cup of tea. Would you like one?"

"Might as well."

End of round one, I thought, as I left the room. I knew my mother would not give up as long as she drew breath, but I'd made one discovery that morning. In my mother's physical and emotional distancing of herself from me, she had unwittingly set me free, cut the cord herself.

"How will you manage?" Mama asked at lunch. "I understand your . . . ah . . . young man is still a student."

"I'll get a job," I said, as I spooned potato *bhaji* onto my plate. "It's time I did something."

"Doing what?" Mama persisted. I noticed she ate very little. "You have no skills."

"I don't know. I'll find something. Ajai said he could do tutoring in the evenings, and his family has given him the soapstone mine. I could tutor too, maybe start a nursery school; I like children. I'll find something. We'll manage."

Letty wiped her lips on her serviette. "We'll help, Lavinia," she said. "We'll make sure they're all right."

"Oh? That hardly sets my mind at ease. Where were you when she got pregnant, Letty?"

"Comforting you. Don't you remember how you carried on when she ran from you and spent the night away? Surely you can't have forgotten."

Mama pressed her knuckles to her trembling lips.

"She's about six weeks pregnant, Lavinia," Letty continued. "It's time you know she's had a very thin time of it—"

"And came running to you, not to me."

"She *couldn't* come to you. Doesn't that say something? You are a foolish woman, Lavinia. The years have not brought you wisdom, it seems. If you alienate your daughter you will lose your grandchild as well. How can you risk so much?"

"She's *my* daughter."

"She came to *me* for help."

"You have taken her away from me. You've always coveted her."

"Oh, for God's sake," I protested. I had listened to them go at each other and realized that although they quarreled about me, it went much deeper than that: the battle lines had been drawn a long time ago. The eruption was long overdue.

Mama put down her serviette and pushed back her chair. She stood there, her starched frock encasing her like a shell. Her face was very pale, the bones in sharp relief. "Do *not* take the Lord's name in vain," she said, looking straight ahead, her yellow fingertips resting on the polished tabletop. "I live by my beliefs, the beliefs that were instilled in me, and the two of you, I might remind you. I think I will go to my room to rest now." She swayed.

Alarmed, I stood, too. "Are you all right, Mama?"

"Stupid, I'm told. Wisdom, it seems, went straight past me, but I'm quite hale. Thickheaded people often are. Now, if you will excuse me."

She left, back straight as a flagpole.

"Whew!" Letty said. "It's worse than I thought. Was it awful this morning?"

"No, not as bad as this."

"She has to blame someone, I suppose."

"But not you."

"Yes, me. Truths were revealed this afternoon. I've known

290

since you were a little girl that she resented our attachment. She always took you from me whenever I cuddled you. If it were not for your father's illness, she never would have sent you to me. I know that now. Poor Lavinia. She's like a wounded animal. Give her time. She'll come round."

"I'm not so sure."

Mama came to my room before tea. She stood in the open doorway, hands at her sides. "I believe it's time I met your young man," she said stoically.

"You have met him."

"You know what I mean."

"Yes. Will this evening be soon enough?"

"It will have to be. I'm taking the afternoon train tomorrow."

"But that's Thursday! Two days before my wedding! Won't you stay?"

"When and if you marry in a church of God, I will be there to witness it and give you my blessing."

"I see. There's one thing—uh—when you—uh—meet—"

"I think I know what you are struggling to say in that tongue-tied fashion. Don't worry. I remember my manners, even if you don't."

"I'm sorry. Won't you come in and sit down."

"No thank you. I've said everything I came to say."

Letty suggested we go to the club, and to my surprise Mama agreed. I wore the mauve sari Letty had bought for me in Delhi and the pearl necklace Mama had given me on my eighteenth birthday. Wearing a turquoise sari, Letty drove the car, with Mama beside her in her old black silk. Ajai and I rode in the back.

"You look very lovely," he whispered.

"I prefer you in *kurta* and *pyjama,*" I whispered back. "You look strange in a suit."

"I know, but I felt the occasion called for something dressier. By the way, it's not considered good form to tell your future husband he looks strange."

I laughed.

"Share the joke, you two," Letty tossed over her shoulder.

"I told him he looked strange," I said.

"I think he looks distinguished," Letty offered. "Very barristerial."

"There you have it," Ajai said, and squeezed my hand.

Mama said nothing at all.

At the club, sitting under the magnificent old rain trees, Mama seemed to almost relax as she sipped her port, as if having spoken her mind, she had done her duty and the rest was in God's hands.

"How is that charming Mrs. Bhatt?" she asked. "What a lovely party she organized for Megan's birthday."

"That charming Mrs. Bhatt, now Mrs. Ranjit Singh, is living in Kashmir, and has a baby son," Letty said, holding her glass in both hands under her chin.

"Aunt Letty delivered him," I announced generally, "and I helped."

"Dear me," murmured Mama. "When did all this happen?"

"The baby was born about a week ago," Letty said. "When she remarried is anyone's guess."

"What happened to her former husband?" Mama asked, studying Ajai covertly.

"Colonel Bhatt still lives next door, to the best of my knowledge," Letty answered.

"And how is . . . *your* husband, Letty?"

"Quite well, thank you. He's terribly disappointed he can't

get away for the wedding, but afterwards I plan to join him in Delhi for the rest of the session. That way Megan and Ajai can have the house till we get back."

"My, how convenient." Mama took another sip of her port.

"Yes," Letty agreed. "It will save me shutting up the house."

"And when will you get on your feet?" Mama asked Ajai point blank.

"I'm sorry," he said smoothly. "I'm afraid I don't understand your question."

"Very simple, actually. How soon till you earn a living?"

"I've a year still to go before my degree," Ajai answered in the same unruffled tone. "Not too long after that, I hope."

Letty made quite a show of signaling the waiter, sticking her arm in the air and waving to get his attention. "Refills, anyone? Another port, Lavinia?"

"Might as well," Mama said, staring into her empty glass.

"Ajai? Another beer?"

"Please."

"Nothing for me, thanks," I said, furious with Mama. *Remembered her manners, indeed.* I should have known it was too much to expect that she could harness her tongue.

At a table nearby someone's birthday was being celebrated. Candles on a cake were extinguished to applause and loud compliments. Then everyone sang "Happy Birthday."

Ajai said, "Megan tells me you are leaving tomorrow, Mrs. Manning. I am sorry you won't stay for the wedding."

"Yes, well," Mama said absently, as she watched the party at the other table, "to our way of thinking it will not be a *real* wedding, you see. That can only take place in a church."

"I assure you being married by a judge makes it very legal and binding—"

"Ah, but not in the eyes of God."

293

Letty groaned. "Oh Lord! Lavinia do shut up."

"No, Aunty." Ajai held up a palm. "I want to know what it would take for Mrs. Manning to give her daughter her blessing."

"Ajai," I begged. "Let it alone. I don't care if she gives us her blessing. We have Papa's, and your parents', Aunt Margaret's, Aunt Letty's. It's enough."

"The thing is, Megan," he said, his voice grave, "I'm afraid one day you'll find you *do* care. Mrs. Manning, what if we agree to be later married by a priest of your church?"

"Oh my, no priest will marry you. You've not been baptized. Only Christians can participate in our sacrament of marriage."

Letty lowered her face to her hand. I wanted to throttle my mother, very slowly, till the breath whistled in her narrowing gullet.

"Short of becoming a Catholic," Ajai very calmly insisted, "is there no other way?"

I stood and faced my mother, fists clenched at my sides. "Mama," I said in a low bitter voice. "It's not your place. This is for Ajai and me to decide."

Unfazed, she said, "He asked me a question, and I intend to answer. The Archbishop is distantly related, I could talk to him about a special dispensation."

Ajai came to stand beside me. He held me firmly to his side, his arm around my waist. "It's all right, my dearest," he said softly. "If it can be done, then why not do it. In the long run, you'll be happier, I think. I want that more than anything." He addressed Mama challengingly, "So, Mrs. Manning, will you give your daughter your blessing?"

"Provisionally," was her cool response.

Letty snorted.

*   *   *

Mama's mood improved dramatically after that. The color returned to her face; she stood up straighter, her shoulders squared. Her eyes regained their sharp, inquisitive gleam. Briskly she informed me that, technically, I'd be living in sin until I married in the church. She advised me not to partake of the sacraments. "Go to Mass, by all means," she said, "but best not to add insult to injury by taking holy communion in a state of sin. Once you are properly married, of course, you can confess everything; then you can receive the Host."

"Lavinia," Letty said, pouring tea. "You have the soul of a bazaar money lender. More toast?"

"No, thank you," Mama said tartly. "I pride myself on being a pragmatist. One takes what one can get. Of course, if Ajai converted—"

"Mama," I warned. "*No more.*"

"I shall simply tell the Archbishop he has to grant the dispensation, that you are going to have a baby. It will mean another soul for Jesus."

"Suffer little children to come unto me," Letty said under her breath as she savagely buttered her toast.

"Wear your pearls on your wedding day," Mama ordered. "I wore them on mine."

"*Which* wedding day," I asked with heavy sarcasm. "The civil or the religious."

"Both."

Ajai, Letty and I took Mama to the train. We helped her settle her belongings in the ladies' first class compartment, and in the ten minutes before departure, we stood talking on the platform. She was in fine fettle. Looking Ajai over appraisingly, she said, "I agree with my daughter, native dress suits you very well."

That was as close to a compliment as she could manage.

295

Ajai was amused. "Why, thank you, Mrs. Manning."

"Since we are about to be related, I suggest you call me Lavinia. I don't think you want to call me Mama."

"Why not?" he teased.

"No, best not to try—"

"At least not until after the *real* wedding, shall we say?"

She smiled thinly. "Take care of my daughter, young man."

Ajai circled my shoulders with his arm. "That will be my pleasure," he said gravely.

"Things turned out as well as could be expected," Mama said. "Fortunately you are not a practicing Hindu—oh, sorry, Letty."

"Perfectly all right, Lavinia," Letty retorted. "Subtlety has never been your strong point."

"Atheists have more leeway to negotiate," Ajai murmured.

The whistle sounded.

"Well, I'm off." Mama kissed the air beside my ear, presented her cheek to Letty, shook Ajai's hand. From the window she called to me, "Don't forget your pearls, and Papa wants lots of pictures."

I smiled and nodded.

She waved once, then shut the window.

CHAPTER TWENTY-SEVEN

I was surprised and delighted when a very pregnant Prethima, along with Vijay, Ashok and their grandmother, arrived the following day. I had written Prethima to tell her of our plans; their presence, however, was entirely unexpected. Letty was somewhat less than enchanted.

"You'd think they'd know to pick up the phone, or to drop me a note, at least," she complained. "But no, they simply walk in. That battle-ax better stay out of my way. With everything else that needs to be done, I don't need her interference."

"I'll try to keep her occupied," I promised. "I rather like the old lady."

"I'd like her too—stuffed." Then she hurried away to call the caterers on some detail about the banquet the following day.

"Your aunt has made a very good match for you," Letty's mother-in-law said to me that night as we sat on the back steps and watched the darting fireflies. "He is from the princely caste, she tells me. Not as good as Brahmin, but quite respectable. So when is the priest coming tomorrow?"

"A judge is performing the ceremony."

"What? No priest to recite the *mantras*. No sacred fire to walk around. How can blessings come from a judge? He is an ordinary man, not the gods' representative. What is your aunt thinking? I am going to talk to her now. Terrible business."

"Oh no," I said hastily. "Aunt Letty had nothing to do with it. That decision was made by Ajai's family. The judge is an old friend."

"*Accha,* that is how they are doing it." She wagged her head, and added magnanimously, "It is their choice. All peoples are different. Some believe, some do not. I have not seen a godless wedding before. I am very interested."

A godless wedding. Though poles apart, I thought it ironic that Mama and Letty's mother-in-law were kindred souls, agreeing in essence, if not in dogma.

Early the following morning my uncle called from Delhi. Letty came to wake me. Sleepily I stumbled to the telephone.

"My dear young lady," came the familiar hearty voice. "I called to wish you happy wedding day. I would like to be there with all of you, but I have an important vote I must stay for. When will the priest be arriving?"

Apologetically, I said, "We are being married by a judge, Uncle."

He made a disgusted sound. "Those Pandes are notoriously irreligious. Traditions mean nothing to them." He paused, and added hastily, "Though I must say Ajai is a very good boy. So you will soon be a married woman. I hope you will be very happy."

"Thank you, Uncle, and thank you for calling."

"Now let me speak to my Letty."

I handed the phone to her and went back to my room, the last I would spend in it. Since Letty was leaving for Delhi in two days and Ajai and I would be staying in the house in her absence, she suggested that she and I exchange rooms for my wedding night. Ajai would be more comfortable in a double bed, she said, and we'd have more privacy in her wing of the house.

I sat at my dressing table and picked up the old picture of Letty and Mama. I remembered holding it in my hands some six months earlier when I had first come to Letty, awkward and angry at being sent away from home, bitter at my parents for keeping the truth of my father's absence from me, and disturbed by my inability to give voice to that bitterness. Who would have predicted that I would fall in love, conceive and marry in such a short span of time. Not the traditional order of such events, perhaps, but the order in which they happened to me.

Telegrams arrived from Papa and Aunt Margaret addressed to Mrs. & Mrs. Pande. Papa's said: "Congratulations and all the best. Stop. Take pictures. Stop. Love, Papa." Aunt Margaret's: "All my love always. Aunty M."

Later in the day a basket of oranges was delivered from Colonel Bhatt along with a note expressing regret that he was unable to attend and wishing us much happiness.

Ashok, Munnar and Vijay ran innumerable errands, rented chairs and tables, set up tables in the rose garden, rearranged the front room to accommodate the additional chairs. Prethima and her grandmother constructed elaborate, splashy displays of flowers, and made intricate *colum* designs on the front steps and the courtyard, sifting rice powder from their fists: snakes for fertility, birds and flowers for long life and happiness.

At three in the afternoon Letty, Prethima and her grand-mother led me into Letty's dressing room for the ritual dressing of the bride. Prethima deftly draped me in the heavy crimson sari, while Letty crouched at my bare, hennaed feet to fasten silver, bell-adorned chains around my ankles. Prethima rouged my lips and cheeks and outlined my eyes with kohl. Letty pinned the bride's *tikka* in my hair so that the short strand of seed pearls lay along my center parting and the pearl-encrusted pendant rested on my forehead. Pearl *jhumkas* were clipped to my earlobes. Then with great ceremony the grandmother painted a small red dot between my eyebrows.

At last I was ready. My ankle bells tinkling with each step, I walked between Letty and Prethima, with the grandmother leading the way. My heart pounded so loudly in my ears; I thought surely the sound was audible to the others.

"Oh, wait!" I stopped. "Mama's pearls."

Letty said, "I'll get them."

She returned with the necklace, fastened it around my throat, and we proceeded to the front room.

As we entered, the various groups who stood around conversing fell silent. Ajai, tall and handsome in his dark, high-collared *achkan* and crimped, close-fitting trousers, stood beside Munnar, his eyes fixed on the doorway. When he saw me his face brightened with admiration and love. We smiled at each other across the room.

The ceremony itself was over in minutes. The judge said something, we said something, and we were married. Everyone crowded around congratulating us, wishing us joy— Ajai's parents, his sister and her husband, Ashok, Munnar and Vijay. Prethima hugged me and shyly shook Ajai's hand. Her grandmother made us bow down so she could place her hands on our heads to bless us. "This is a very good girl. Modest and respectful. Treat her well," she told Ajai sternly. Letty embraced us, an arm around each. "I know you'll be very happy."

"Thank you, Aunt Letty. Thank you for everything."

She blinked very rapidly, touched my cheek, then turned away, saying briskly, "Ashok, Munnar, make yourselves useful. There's champagne to be poured for the toast." The Pandes had provided a case of champagne.

There were others whom I didn't know: the Pandes' friends and relatives, Ajai's professors, Munnar's professors. They all bowed over joined hands. Someone hung scratchy garlands around our necks.

Letty's mother-in-law was tight-lipped with disapproval about the champagne, especially the elder Pandes' consumption of it. My normally reserved father-in-law gaily insisted she try some, saying that prohibition would come soon enough with the new puritanical government, and that she should enjoy it while it was still legal. She jerked her sari around her and marched off, her sharp chin in the air. My mother-in-law recited Urdu love poems to anyone who would listen and a few who wouldn't, shouting the flowery phrases at their backs.

Ajai and I circulated among the guests, thanking everyone for coming to our wedding. Occasionally separated when others engaged us in conversation, we were inevitably drawn to each other again as if by magnets. In one such moment together, Ajai leaned down to whisper, "Tell me, my modest and respectful bride, whom I've been commanded to treat well, when are all these people going home? My parents seem bent on polishing off their champagne."

"I think dinner comes next," I said, wanting to touch him.

Ashok came to refill our glasses. "Only two more bottles," he reported.

Ajai uttered fervent thanks.

Vegetarian food was served in the dining room, non-vegetarian in the rose garden, far from the house and any possible contamination of Letty's mother-in-law. She joined us for the wedding cake, but pronounced it inedible and rushed from the room to spit out what she had taken in her mouth.

Finally, at ten o'clock, Letty suggested we retire. "Who knows how long this will continue," she told me. "Why not just slip away. You've been up since early morning. You must be exhausted."

A tray on the bedside table held a decanter of wine and two glasses. In addition, flowers had been placed on windowsills and a bowl of fruit on the chest of drawers. Ajai poured wine and handed me a glass.

"To us," he said, touching my glass with his.

"To us," I echoed, suddenly unsure.

I sat on the side of the bed; he came to sit beside me. "Ajai," I said, not looking at him. "Does it matter to you I am not a virgin?"

He laughed. "Megan, my foolish love, I very much doubt we'd be here like this if your virginity were still intact."

"I know. But . . . isn't that the tradition of the wedding night? The excitement of discovery. Do you feel . . . cheated?"

Ajai finished the rest of his wine and placed his glass on the tray. "Do you, Megan?" he said very quietly. "Is that what you're trying to say?"

"No," I said, my eyes still averted. "But . . . it's just . . . "

He took my glass from me though I hadn't quite finished, and put it aside. "Then what is all this, bridal jitters?" His hand beneath my chin, he turned my face to his. "What is it?"

I looked into his clear brown eyes so full of love. "Maybe . . . I am a little nervous," I admitted. "I . . . I don't want to disappoint—"

"The logic of all this escapes me." Gently Ajai removed my earrings. "My love, you offered your virginity to me. I took it." He spoke very softly. I felt his hands take the pins and *tikka* from my hair. "You are carrying my child. Do you know you are even more desirable to me now than when we first met?" He knelt, unfastened the bell-adorned ankle chains, and kissed each hennaed instep. Looking up at me, an expresssion almost of pain on his face, he said, "How can you possibly think you will disappoint me?" He took my hands in his. "Will you stand now so I can undress you?"

"You desired me when we first met?" I asked, as he drew me to my feet.

"I was a goner the first time I saw you blush." Ajai unwound the six yards of silk and let it slither around me to the carpet where it settled in whispery crimson folds. One by one, the rest of my garments collected at my feet. He brushed his lips against my bare shoulder and I shivered.

"Should I undress you now?" I whispered, my eyes sliding shut as he took me in his arms. I felt his long-fingered hands move slowly over my bare skin, pausing to cup and stroke, moving, pausing again, and my body's warm, wet response.

"Only if you want to," he murmured against my open mouth.

With clumsy, urgent fingers I unbuttoned his *achkan,* then struggled with his tight trousers.

Ajai laughed softly. "Here, let me. You have to unbutton them first."

We stood fully unclothed before each other for the first time. I gazed in wonder at his beauty and saw his arousal. I raised my eyes to his then and found he was watching my face intently. Ajai smiled and held out his hand; I placed mine in his.

Convinced at last of my own appeal, my head high, my heart full, I walked to the bed with my husband.

EPILOGUE

Papa once said, " 'Marrying is easy. Housekeeping is hard.' "
It was *his* father's saying. In reflecting on the past year, I
realize there is much truth to it. Caring for a baby and having
to work at the same time is certainly difficult. It becomes
increasingly hard each morning to leave Preminda with the
ayah and go to work. Since we live above the offices of the
Nerbudapur Times, where I write about how to lay a formal
table, shine a toaster with baking soda, disjoint a chicken—
that sort of thing—I can race upstairs during the day and nurse
Preminda. It is a time of pure peace and happiness for me
when I hold her sweet weight in my arms and feel the tug on
my breast, which invokes feelings in me both sensual and
maternal. Then I dash back downstairs to matters of how to
repair cigarette burns on furniture and remove tea stains from
carpets, while I yearn to stroke the satin skin of my daughter's
shoulders and inhale the scent of her mouth. She has just
begun to laugh out loud, a rich, throaty chuckle whenever
Ajai hoists her in the air.

She has his clear brown eyes and curly dark hair, but her skin is the color of mine. Sometimes when I catch her steady, brown-eyed gaze, my heart clenches with self-recognition, and sadness. I do not want my daughter to be like me. I want her life to be filled with laughter and light-heartedness, not the weighty introspection with which I have always been burdened. And, if I can help it, she will not be an only child.

After Letty and my uncle had returned from Delhi, Ajai and I came to live here in the heart of Nerbudapur, high above the street that never sleeps. Film music and drums fill the night, while during the day the rhythmic clatter of the printing press is a background for vendors' cries and traffic sounds.

It was not easy to get this job: I was too young, the chief editor had said at first, too inexperienced. To prove myself, I offered to work for a month for nothing. I've often wondered if Letty had my uncle intercede on my behalf; though, of course, that might not have been the case at all, and she herself has never so much as dropped a hint. It's just a feeling I have—knowing my aunt as I do.

I take pride in my work. I enjoy putting words together on a page, choosing exactly the right word. The test of my skill as a writer comes when I can salivate over my own description of, say, braised cabbage seasoned with coconut and a touch of mace. And I find much satisfaction in seeing a completed piece in print, with the words: "By Megan Pande" appearing at the top of the column. It's what I do best. Someday I would like to go to college, get a degree. Someday.

I began writing about all this shortly after Ajai and I were married, during the evenings when he was at the mine or out tutoring students in their homes. It was something to do those times we spent apart. After the birth of our daughter, however, and after our household had settled once more into its routine, I found my purpose in writing had undergone a change. I have come to see it now as a means to help me look at the past as honestly as I can, as a means to give some shape to what went before. Perhaps if I can understand the past, the future may be easier to cope with.

Ajai does not know about the ledgers in which I write, nor about the completed ones that lie in the bottom drawer of the wardrobe under my clothes. Am I being deceitful? I do not know. I tell myself that what I write belongs to me, and is therefore separate from our love and our life together.

Financially, it's a precarious balance, but we manage on my salary, the money Ajai earns tutoring, and the income from the mine—our mine, our special place. Papa helps. In a few weeks Ajai will have passed the bar, but I suspect that even then things will not change substantially for us because of the causes he espouses. He will continue to devote himself to the poor and the oppressed, and, like them, we too will always remain poor. Perhaps we will always live in upstairs flats. Munnar disapproves of our living conditions. When *he* marries, he tells us, he will live in a fine house with fruit trees in the garden.

In bed, I love to feel Ajai's hands and mouth on me, and I love to pleasure him in the same way. I know the mole on his left hip. I've circled it with my tongue many times. He tells me my breasts are exactly the right shape and size. His hands convince me.

Letty, of course, delivered our daughter—in a hospital— under less dramatic circumstances than Nila's baby. But for me, as I held my daughter for the first time, I knew I'd scaled Mount Everest. It did not matter that I might never again feel such transcendent joy or swelling triumph. For that moment, I clung to my peak.

After Preminda's birth Letty began to work again on a part-time basis. She stops in to see Preminda every day, playing "pattycake" with her and allowing her to chew on the stethoscope. But it is my uncle who is Preminda's delight.

"Where is my tadpole, my teddy bear?" he booms as he thumps up the stairs. Preminda, sitting on the front room floor, flaps her chubby arms, gurgling. Spouting nonsense, he enters and scoops her up. "My angel, my buttercup." He nuzzles her belly, kisses her under the chin. She squeals and clutches his double chin in her fists.

He brings her presents. A toy kangaroo two feet high, squeaky rubber toys. His most recent present is a pair of tiny, finely wrought gold earrings. He insists her ears be pierced at the age of two in a special ceremony, just like other small Indian girls. I can't bear for my child to be mutilated.

Ajai's mother is a vague woman whose interests extend only a little beyond writing poetry and combating the dowry system. She dresses with a grand indifference to detail. Once she wore her *choli*-blouse inside out to a garden party for Women Poets of North India. Unsure of what I should do, I finally reached around her in an embrace and drew the end of her sari over her shoulders. Ajai's father continues to suffer from insomnia. He comes over to make sure Ajai studies hard enough. Gravely, he dandles Preminda. As though sensing his mood, she sits on his knee, composed; her infant dignity is heartbreaking.

"You should apply coconut oil to her hair," he advises. "It is cooling for the brain."

"We like her hair soft, Papa," Ajai says. He reaches out to run his long fingers through his daughter's curls. "Isn't she the most gorgeous baby in the whole world?"

"Possibly. Although I have read in *National Geographic* that the most beautiful children are in Scandinavia."

In a huff, I pick my daughter off my father-in-law's lap.

How well I remember my in-laws at our wedding and the quantities of champagne they'd consumed.

Aunt Margaret continues to grow more frail. She has not seen Preminda, and it grieves me that she may never see my child. I would like them to touch hands—my great-aunt who nurtured me, and my daughter whom I love above all others—to exchange grace for grace. Papa is back home and working again, but he must have weekly injections. Mama was jubilant when she managed to get the special dispensation from the Archbishop for Ajai and me to marry in the Catholic church. We took the train to Madras where we were to be married in the parish church our family had always attended. My uncle was unable to get away. Letty asked if we wanted her to accompany us. "I can get someone to cover for me," she offered.

"There's no need," I told her. "We're doing this only to humor Mama."

Dutifully we went through the bare-bones ceremony. It resembled rites for the dead, stripped as it was of the usual trappings of ordinary Catholic marriages—wedding bells, organ music, candles and flowers. Our marriage being quite out of the ordinary, we were denied all that, but Mama, unfamiliar, almost startling, in rose-colored silk and pill-box hat heavy with cherries, stood triumphant.

Besides my family and ourselves, there was no one else.

"After all," Mama pointed out, "you're six months with child. Hardly a blushing bride. Best to keep it quiet."

Unused as I'd become to western clothing, my legs felt very bare beneath the white maternity frock Mama had ordered made for me. Ajai wore a suit. No handsome, high-collared *achkan,* no tight trousers so difficult to take off. No red sari for me, no pearls in my hair, or tinkling ankle bells. No champagne; for by now prohibition had been enacted into law in Madras. Instead we drank orange juice at the Connemara Hotel where Papa took us to lunch.

"I was polite but firm with His Grace," Mama said, holding

a precariously balanced forkload of chicken salad at chest level. "I pointed out it was in the Church's best interest since you are—as they say—*enceinte*. Think of the child, I told him, a lamb of God. He said the strangest thing. Now let me think—Oh yes! That he was inordinately fond of lamb, but all we get here in India is mutton."

"Was this audience before or after lunch?" Papa joked.

"Arthur! It was an allegorical statement, I am quite sure. He looked off into the distance when he said it." Mama gestured.

"Probably only looking ahead to his next meal," Papa said. "Is the old boy still overweight?"

Aunt Margaret laughed. "Arthur, you are irrepressible." She patted Ajai's hand. "Welcome to the family, my dear."

And so went our second wedding.

Mama came to Nerbudapur at the time of Preminda's birth. Shortly thereafter she had the hospital chaplain baptize our infant daughter Mary Philomena; no wasted time, no chances taken. It was done more for Mama's benefit, I feel sure, than Preminda's. That way if Mama were to expire suddenly, her everlasting soul would not be in jeopardy for having an unbaptized granddaughter. As usual, her officiousness had caught me off guard. Now, however, when I hold my daughter close to my heart, I think: what do such things matter? To Ajai and me she is our plump and fragrant Preminda, child of our flesh.

Mary Philomena. Why hadn't Mama named me that? It's funny about names. I've never understood why I was not given a saint's name. Was it some capriciousness on Mama's part? Or was it her way of avoiding offense by not choosing one saint's name over another? *Philomena.* What a name!

My old rage at Mama has burned away at last. What remains is difficult to assess. She still has the capacity to annoy, even anger me, but it doesn't linger like a live ember, and her approval is no longer necessary to me. She came again to Nerbudapur when Preminda was two months old. All the physical displays of love—hugs, caresses, kisses—that she always withheld from me, she now lavishes on my daughter. I think the turning point in Mama's attitude toward Ajai came about when she decided that, unlike my uncle, he had no objections to me practicing my faith.

My faith. I'm uncertain what that is anymore. I picture faith as thick and dark as an umbilical cord, rich with nourishment, lore and fantasy. These elements sometimes blur in my mind and my heart with the grandeur of legend about Shiva and Parvati and their fat little Ganesh. I'm still connected, I think. When I've lost something, I pray to St. Anthony, and when I want something very badly, I still say, "Please God."